The Last Cato

The Last Cato

A NOVEL

Matilde Asensi

TRANSLATED BY PAMELA CARMELL

rayo

An Imprint of HarperCollinsPublishers

HarperCollins books may be purchased for educational, business,
or sales promotional use. For information, please write:
Special Markets Department, HarperCollins Publishers,
10 East 53rd Street, New York, NY 10022.

Grateful acknowledgment is made to Indiana University Press
for permission to reprint excerpts from Dante Alighieri's
Divine Comedy, translated by Mark Musa.

FIRST EDITION

Designed by Jennifer Ann Daddio

Printed on acid-free paper

Library of Congress Cataloging-in-Publication Data
Asensi, Matilde, 1962–
[Ultimo catón. English]
The last cato: a novel/Matilde Asensi; translated by Pamela Carmell.
p.   cm.
ISBN-13: 978-0-06-082857-8
ISBN-10:   0-06-082857-9
I. Carmell, Pamela.   II. Title.

PQ6651.S386U5813   2006
863'.64—dc22   2005051654

06   07   08   09   10   DIX/RRD   10   9   8   7   6   5   4   3   2   I

For

PASCUAL, ANDRÉS, PABLO, AND JAVIER

CHAPTER

1

All things of great beauty—from works of art to sacred objects—suffer the unstoppable effects of the passage of time, just as we do. Their life begins the moment their human creator, aware or not of being in harmony with the infinite, puts the finishing touches on them and surrenders them to the world. Over the centuries, life also brings them closer to old age and death. While Time withers and destroys us, it bestows upon them a new type of beauty that human aging could never dream of. Not for anything in the world would I want to see the Colosseum rebuilt, its walls and terraced seats in perfect condition, or coat the Parthenon with a gaudy paint job, or give the Victory of Samothrace a head.

Deeply absorbed in my work, I gave those thoughts free rein as my fingertips caressed one of the rough corners of the parchment manuscript in front of me. I was so wrapped up in what I was doing that I didn't hear Dr. William Baker, secretary of the archives, knock at my door, nor did I hear him turn the handle or open the door and look in. When I finally noticed him, he seemed as though he had been standing in the doorway to my office for eternity.

"Dr. Salina," Baker whispered, not daring to cross the threshold, "Reverend Father Ramondino has entreated me to request that you proceed to his office immediately."

I looked up from the manuscript and took off my glasses to get a better look at the secretary. He had the same perplexed look on his oval face as I had. Baker was a small, compact American. His features reflected his family heritage, and he could have easily passed for southern European. He had thick tortoiseshell glasses and thin hair, part blond, part gray, which he meticulously combed to cover as much of his shiny scalp as possible.

"Forgive me, Doctor," I replied sharply, my eyes wide. "Can you please repeat what you just said?"

"His Most Reverend Father Ramondino wants to see you in his office right away."

"The prefect wants to see me? Me?" I couldn't believe what I had just heard. Guglielmo Ramondino was the executive director of the Vatican's Classified Archives, second only to His Excellency Monsignor Oliveira. I could count on one hand the number of times he had summoned me or one of my colleagues to his office.

Baker let a slight smile come to his lips and nodded.

"Do you happen to know why he wants to see me?" I asked, backing down.

"No, Dr. Salina, but I'm certain it's very important."

Still smiling, he closed the door softly and disappeared. By then I was in the throes of an anxiety attack: sweaty palms, dry mouth, racing heart, and trembling legs.

When I had a better hold of myself, I got down off my stool, turned off the light, and cast a pained glance at the two exquisite Byzantine codices that rested open on my desk. With the help of those manuscripts, I had dedicated the last six months to reconstructing the famous lost text of the *Panegyrikon* written by Saint Nicephorus, patriarch of Constantinople in the ninth century, and I was on the verge of completing my work. I sighed, resigned, a deep silence surrounding me. My small lab was furnished with an old wooden desk, a pair of tall stools, a crucifix on the wall, and several shelves crammed with books. It was located four floors belowground and formed part of the Hypogeum, the section of the Classified Archives very few people had access to. To the rest of the world and to history, this part of the Vatican was invisible, nonexistent even. Many historians and researchers would have given half their lives to consult the documents that had passed through my hands over the last eight years. But the mere suggestion that someone outside the church could get permission to come here was pure entelechy: A lay person never had access to the Hypogeum—and never would.

On my desk, in addition to my books, rested piles of notebooks and a low-wattage lamp (to avoid overheating the manuscripts), scalpels, latex gloves, and folders full of high-resolution photographs of the codices' most damaged pages. The long, swiveled arm of a magnifying glass rose, twisted like a worm, from the far end of my wooden workbench. Hanging from that swayed a large red cardboard hand with stars glued all over it. That hand was a memento from five-year-old Isabella's last birthday party. Of the twenty-five offspring contributed to the Lord's flock by six of my eight brothers and sisters, she was my favorite. My lips drew up a smile as I remembered charming Isabella: "Aunt Ottavia, Aunt Ottavia, let me spank you with this red hand!"

The prefect! My God! The prefect was waiting for me, and there I stood, frozen like a statue, thinking about Isabella! I tore off my lab coat and hung it on a hook on the wall. I grabbed my ID (a big C was stamped next to a terrible picture of me), went out into the hallway, and locked the door to the lab. My staff worked at a row of desks that extended all the way to the elevator doors, some fifty meters. On the other side of the reinforced concrete wall, office workers filed and refiled hundreds and thousands of records pertaining to the church, its history, its diplomatic negotiations, and its activities from the second century to the present. More than twenty-five kilometers of bookshelves hinted at the massive amount of preserved documents belonging to the Vatican's Classified Archives. Officially, the archives contained only documents from the last eight centuries; however, documents from a thousand years before were also under its protection and were kept in high-security files found only on the third and fourth underground floors. Originally housed in parishes, monasteries, cathedrals, or archeological excavations, such as the Saint Angelus Castle or the Apostolic Camera, these valuable documents did not see the light of day once they reached the Classified Archives; the same light, along with other equally dangerous elements, could destroy them forever.

I quickly walked to the elevator, but paused for a moment to watch a member of my staff, Guido Buzzonetti, as he labored over a letter from Güyük, the great khan of the Mongols, sent to Pope Innocent IV in 1246. A small, open bottle of an alkaline solution sat a few millimeters from his right elbow, immediately next to some fragments of the letter.

"Guido!" I exclaimed, horrified. "Don't move!"

Guido looked at me terrified, not even daring to breathe. The blood rushed out of his face and spread to his ears; they looked like two red cloths framing a white shroud. If his arm moved even slightly, the solution would spill on the manuscripts, causing irreparable damage to a rare historical document. All activity around us stopped. You could have cut the silence with a knife. . . . I grabbed the bottle, capped it, and set it on the far side of the table.

"Buzzonetti," I whispered, my eyes boring into him. "Collect your things and report to the vice prefect at once."

I had never allowed that kind of slipup in my lab. Buzzonetti was a young Dominican who had studied at the Vatican School of Diplomatic and Archival Paleography, with a specialty in Eastern codification. I myself taught his class in Greek and Byzantine paleography for two years before asking the Reverend Father Pietro Ponzio, vice prefect of the Archives, to offer him a job on my team. But no matter how highly I esteemed Brother Buzzonetti nor how valuable I knew him to be, I couldn't allow him to continue working at the Hypogeum. Our material was unique, one-of-a-kind, irreplaceable. If, in a thousand or two thousand years, someone wanted to consult the letter from Güyük to Pope Innocent IV, he could. Pure and simple. What would happen to an employee of the Louvre who set an open can of paint on the *Mona Lisa*'s frame? Ever since I was put in charge of the Vatican's restoration and paleography lab, I had never allowed this type of carelessness from my team. Everyone knew that. And I wasn't going to start now.

As I pressed the elevator button, I was fully conscious of how much my staff disliked me. More than once, I'd felt their reproachful glares boring into my back and had thus learned never to count on their affection. I wasn't made director of the lab eight years ago to win the love of my subordinates or my superiors. Firing Brother Buzzonetti pained me deeply; only I knew how bad I would feel over the next few months. But making that kind of decision was exactly how I'd gotten where I was.

The elevator came to a silent stop at my floor and opened its doors, inviting me to step in. I stuck my security key into the control panel, swiped my ID through the electric sensor, and pressed the button that would take me to the ground floor. Seconds later I was standing before huge glass doors. The sunlight streaming in from the San Damaso patio penetrated my brain, blinding and dazing me. In the artificial environment on the lower floors, my senses got so turned around that I couldn't tell night from day, and on more than one occasion, the first light of the next day had taken me by surprise as I left the archives after long hours engrossed in my work. Still blinking, I glanced distractedly at my watch. It was exactly one o'clock in the afternoon.

To my surprise, the Reverend Father Guglielmo Ramondino wasn't waiting for me in his comfortable office. Instead, I found him pacing back and forth in a huge vestibule, a grave look of impatience wrought deeply on his face.

"Dr. Salina," he muttered, offering me one hand while gesturing toward the door with his other. "Come with me, please. We have very little time."

It was hot in the Belvedere Garden that early March afternoon. Tourists scrambled to peer through the windows of the grand corridors as if we were part of some exotic animal exhibit in a zoo. I've always felt strange when I walk through Vatican City's public areas. Nothing bothers me more than for my gaze to be met by the lens of a camera no matter which way I look. Sadly, some prelates enjoyed flaunting their status as residents of the world's smallest state, and Father Ramondino was one of them. Dressed like a clergyman and with his jacket open at the breast, his enormous figure was visible for miles around. The path he led me on, toward the Apostolic Palace and the secretary of state's offices there on the first floor, closely mirrored the route taken by tourists making their rounds. He told me we would be personally received by His Eminence the Most Reverend Cardinal Angelo Sodano (with whom, it seemed, Father Ramondino had a long and close friendship) while he flashed broad smiles right and left as if he were part of an Easter Sunday parade out in the provinces.

The Swiss Guards posted at the entrance to the diplomatic offices of the Holy See didn't blink an eye as we passed on through. Nor did the secretary priest who kept track of the office's comings and goings and who carefully wrote our names, ranks, and occupations in his record book. Rising from his seat, he then led us down a long corridor whose windows looked out over Saint Peter's Square. The secretary of state was already waiting for us.

Although I tried to hide it, I was heading toward the prefect with the distinct sensation of having a sharp pain needling my heart. Surely my summons hadn't been precipitated by mistakes I'd made on my job; still, I mentally recalled everything I'd worked on and any act I might have committed that would have merited a reprimand from the church's highest authorities.

The secretary priest finally stopped in a room that was identical to all the rest, the same decorative motifs and frescoes adorning the walls. He asked us to wait a moment, then disappeared behind a door that seemed as light and delicate as a veil of golden leaf.

"Do you know where we are, Doctor?" The prefect gestured nervously, a smile of deep satisfaction on the lips.

"More or less, Reverend Father," I replied, looking around attentively. I detected an unusual fragrance, like still-warm, freshly ironed clothes, combined with varnish and wax.

"These are the offices of the secretary of state's Second Section," he pointed with his chin. "The section that's in charge of diplomatic relations between the Holy See and the rest of the world. It's headed up by the archbishop secretary, Monsignor François Tournier."

"Ah yes, Monsignor Tournier!" I nodded with great conviction. I didn't have the slightest idea who he was personally, but the name was certainly familiar.

"Here, Dr. Salina, is the best place to see the spiritual power that the church has over governments and borders."

"Why are we here, Reverend Father? Our work has nothing to do with this sort of thing."

He looked at me and lowered his voice. "I don't know why," he said, clearly agitated. "In any case, I can assure you it has something to do with a matter of the highest importance."

"But Holy Father," I insisted, obstinate, "I work in the Classified Archives. Any matter of highest importance should be dealt with by you, as prefect, or by His Eminence Monsignor Oliveira. What am I doing here?"

The prefect looked at me as if he didn't know how to respond, patted me cheerfully on the shoulder, then left me and walked over to a circle of prelates basking in the warm rays of the sun that streamed through the large windows. It was then that I realized that the scent of freshly ironed clothes was coming from them.

It was nearly time for lunch, but nobody seemed concerned. Feverish activity was clear along the corridors and offices; a steady stream of ecclesiastic and civil traffic stretched from wall to wall and into every corner. Never having been there before, I entertained myself by observing the sumptuous room, the elegant furniture, the paintings, and the priceless value of the decor. Half an hour before, I'd been working alone, in complete silence, wearing my white lab coat and glasses. Now, here I was surrounded by the highest levels of international diplomatic service of one of the greatest centers of power on earth.

Suddenly, I heard the creak of a door opening and a tumult of voices which then made everyone's head turn. Immediately, a boisterous throng of journalists, some with TV cameras and others with handheld tape recorders, appeared in the main hall, bursting out in guffaws and exclamations. Most were foreign, mainly European and African, but there were many Italians, too. Altogether, I'd guess forty or fifty reporters flooded the room in a matter of seconds. Some stopped to greet the priests, bishops, and cardinals who, like me, were ambling around; others hurried toward the exit. Almost all stole glances at me, surprised to find a woman where there usually wasn't any.

"Lehmann was dealt quite a blow with one stroke of the pen!" exclaimed a bald journalist wearing thick glasses, standing next to me.

"Looks like Wojtyla doesn't plan to resign," said another, scratching his sideburns.

"Or they won't let him resign!" a third boldly suggested.

The rest of their words were lost as they moved down the corridor. The president of the German Episcopal Conference, Karl Lehmann, had made some dangerous statements weeks before, saying that if the pope were not in any shape to guide the church responsibly, he should retire. The bishop of Mainz had not been the only one to express such a suggestion in light of the Extreme Pontiff's bad health. His statement had fallen like boiling oil on the pope's inner circle. Apparently the secretary of state, Cardinal Sodano, had just addressed such ideas in a stormy press conference. The waters were churning, I thought to myself apprehensively, and they wouldn't stop until the Holy Father rested in the ground and a new, firm-handed shepherd assumed the universal government of the church.

Of all the business at the Vatican, the election of a new pope interested people most. It was without a doubt the most fascinating, the most politically charged of the church's worldly events. It demonstrated not only the basest ambitions of the Curia Romana, but also the least pious aspects of God's representatives. Unfortunately, we were on the threshold of such a spectacular event. Vatican City was teeming with maneuvers and machinations on the part of the different factions interested in placing their candidate on Saint Peter's throne. One thing was certain: It had been a long time since we in the Vatican had felt that the end was near for the pontificate. As a daughter of the church and a nun, I was hardly affected by all such problems, but as an investigator with several projects pending for approval and financing, I could be deeply affected. During the current pontificate, with his marked conservative leaning, it had been impossible to carry out certain types of investigation. In my heart, I yearned for a Holy Father who was more open-minded, less worried about entrenching the official version of the church's history. (So much material was labeled *Classified* and *Confidential*.) However, I didn't hold out much hope for such an unlikely revamping. The cardinals named by the pope had accumulated great power, and after more than twenty years, it looked like the election of a pope from the progressive wing was virtually impossible. Unless the Holy Spirit itself was determined to exert its powerful influence in such an unspiritual appointment, the conservative group would surely be the one to designate the new pontiff.

Just then, a priest dressed in a black soutane approached Father Ramondino and whispered something in his ear. The reverend father raised his eyebrows, signaling for me to get ready. They were waiting for us. We were free to enter.

The exquisite doors opened silently. I waited for the prefect to enter first, as protocol mandated. A sitting room three times the size of our waiting room and completely decorated with mirrors, gilded moldings, and frescoes—which I recognized as Raphaels—held the smallest office in its corner that I had ever seen in my life. It was barely visible at the opposite end of the large room, and consisted of nothing more than a classical writing desk situated on top of a rug and paired with a high-backed chair. To one side of the sitting room and under the slender, elegant windows that let the outside light filter in, a group of ecclesiastics seemed to be in the midst of an animated discussion. They were seated on small stools almost completely hidden under their cassocks. Behind one of them, standing at the fringes of the discussion, was a strange, taciturn, secular man. His bearing was so obviously military that I had no doubt he was a soldier or a policeman. He was very tall (over six feet), stocky, and compact, as if he lifted weights all day and chewed glass during meals. His blond hair was cropped so close that the nape of his neck and his forehead gleamed.

Seeing us walk in, one of the cardinals, whom I recognized immediately as the secretary of state, Angelo Sodano, got to his feet and came to greet us. He was a man of medium height, about seventy years old. He had a broad forehead due to partial baldness, and his white hair was slicked back under his purple silk zucchetto. He was wearing old-fashioned tortoiseshell glasses with large square lenses, a black soutane with purple trim and buttons, and an iridescent sash with matching socks. A discreet gold pectoral cross glittered on his chest. His Eminence beamed a wide, friendly smile as he approached the prefect to exchange the customary kiss on each cheek.

"Guglielmo!" he exclaimed. "I'm so glad to see you again!"

"Eminence!"

Their mutual delight was clear. So, the prefect had not dreamed up his old friendship with the most important executive in the Vatican (after the pope, of course). I found myself more and more disoriented and perplexed, as if this were all a dream and not a tangible reality. What had I done to be here?

The other people in the room watched the scene with the same attention and curiosity as I. They were His Eminence Cardinal Carlo Colli, the vicar of Rome and president of the Italian Episcopal Conference, a calm man who seemed good-natured; the archbishop secretary of the Second Division, Monsignor François Tournier (whom I recognized by his violet zucchetto, worn only by the cardinals); and the quiet, blond soldier, who deeply knitted his transparent eyebrows as if the entire display was displeasing to him.

Suddenly, the prefect turned and ushered me forward by the shoulder until I stood even with him.

"This is Dr. Ottavia Salina, Eminence," he said. Sodano examined me from head to toe in a matter of seconds. Fortunately, that day I had worn a pretty gray skirt and a salmon-colored sweater set.

"Eminence…," I whispered, curtsying and bowing my head in respect; I kissed the ring the secretary of state placed before my lips.

"Are you religious, Doctor?" he asked.

"It's *Sister* Ottavia, Eminence," the prefect hurried to clarify. "She's a member of the Order of the Blessed Virgin Mary."

"Then why are you dressed in secular clothes?" the Archbishop Monsignor François Tournier inquired suddenly without even rising from his seat. "Can it be that your order does not favor habits, Sister?"

His tone deeply offended me, and I decided right then that I wasn't going to be intimidated. At this point in my life in Vatican City, I had been in this situation a zillion times, and I was hardened by a thousand battles on behalf of my gender. I looked him in the eye and answered, "No, Monsignor. My order gave up our habits after the Second Vatican Council."

"Ah, the Council...," he muttered with clear disgust. Monsignor Tournier was a very good-looking man, a viable candidate for prince of the church, one of those dandies who always take a great photograph. "Is it proper for a woman to pray to God with a bare head?" he asked himself aloud, citing Saint Paul's First Epistle to the Corinthians.

"Monsignor," the prefect emphasized, in my defense, "Sister Ottavia has a doctorate in paleography and art history and holds numerous other academic titles. She has directed the Restoration and Paleography Laboratory of the Vatican's Classified Archives for eight years, is the educational director of the Vatican School of Diplomatic and Archivist Paleography, and has won numerous international prizes for her investigative work, among them the prestigious Getty Prize. Twice, in 1992 and 1995."

"Aha!" exclaimed the secretary of state, Cardinal Sodano, as he took the vacant seat next to Tournier. "Good! That's why we have requested your presence, Sister." Everyone looked at me with evident curiosity; but I remained silent, expectant, so that Sodano wouldn't even think of reciting—for my benefit—the passage from Saint Paul that reads "The women shall fall silent at the assemblies/ That they are not permitted to take the word." I supposed that the monsignor—like the rest of those in attendance—would prefer his own sister-servants (they each must have at least three or four) to someone like me. Or perhaps even those little Polish nuns from the Order of Infant Mary who, dressed in their habits and with a veil covering their heads, occupied their time by preparing the meals for His Holiness, cleaning his living quarters, and making sure that his clothing was always spotless; or like the sisters belonging to the Congregation of the Pious Disciples of the Divine Master, who are the Vatican's telephone operators.

"Now," continued His Eminence Angelo Sodano, "the archbishop secretary, Monsignor Tournier, will explain why you've been summoned, Sister. Guglielmo, sit here, next to me. Monsignor, I yield the floor to you."

Monsignor Tournier, with the confidence of those who know that their good looks smooth all of life's difficulties, serenely rose from his chair. Without looking, he extended his hand toward the stern soldier, who then handed him a bulky dossier in a black file. My stomach turned, and for a moment I thought that whatever I'd done, it must have been terrible. I was convinced I'd be dismissed from my position that very day.

"Sister Ottavia." His voice was grave and nasal, and he didn't look at me as he spoke. "In this folder you will find photographs that are . . . how should we describe them . . . unusual? Yes, without a doubt, unusual. Before you examine them, we must warn you they show the body of a recently deceased man, an Ethiopian whose identity we're not sure of yet. You will observe that these are enlargements of certain sections of the cadaver."

"Perhaps it would be advisable to ask Sister Ottavia if she will be able to work with such disagreeable material." His Eminence Carlo Colli, the vicar of Rome, interjected for the first time. He looked at me with paternal concern and continued. "That poor, unfortunate man, Sister, died in a painful accident and was completely disfigured. It's quite unsettling to look upon those images. Do you think you can tolerate it? If not, just tell us."

I was paralyzed. Deep down, I had the feeling I was the wrong person for the task.

"Excuse me, Eminences," I stammered. "Wouldn't it be more appropriate to consult a forensic pathologist? I don't understand how I can be of use."

"You will see, Sister," Tournier cut me short, taking back the floor. He began a slow stroll within the circle of listeners. "The man in the photographs was implicated in a serious crime against the Catholic Church, as well as against all other Christian churches. We are very sorry, but we cannot give you any more details. What we want is for you, with the greatest discretion possible, to study certain symbols, strange scars that were discovered on his body when his clothes were removed for the autopsy. *Scarifications*, I believe, is the correct word for this type of, how should we put it, tattoo ritual or tribal marks. It seems that certain ancient cultures had a custom of decorating the body with ceremonial wounds." He opened the folder and glanced at the photographs, "Those on this poor, unfortunate man are quite odd. They depict Greek letters, crosses, and other images that are equally…artistic? Yes, without a doubt, *artistic*."

"What Monsignor is trying to say," His Eminence the secretary of state interrupted with a warm smile, "is that you must analyze all those symbols, study them, and give us the most complete, exact interpretation possible. Of course, you can use all the resources of Classified Archives and any other services the Vatican has at its disposal."

"In any case, Dr. Salina can count on my complete support," declared the prefect of the archive, watching for the approval of those present.

"We thank you for the offer, Guglielmo," emphasized His Eminence. "But although Sister Ottavia usually reports to you, this time it will be different. Please do not take offense, but as of right now, and until the report is finished, she will report directly to the secretary of state."

"Don't worry, Reverend Father," Monsignor Tournier added smoothly, with an elegant wave of unconcern. "Sister Ottavia will have at her disposal the inestimable cooperation of Captain Kaspar Glauser-Röist, here present. He is a member of the Swiss Guard and one of His Holiness's most valuable agents in the service of the Court of the Sacred Roman Rota. He is the one who took these photographs and is in charge of the investigation in progress."

"Eminences…" It was my trembling voice. The four prelates and the soldier turned to look at me. "Eminences," I repeated with all the humility I was capable of. "I am infinitely grateful that you have thought of me for such an important matter, but I'm afraid I cannot carry it out." I softened my words even more before continuing. "Not just because it is impossible for me to leave the work I'm in the middle of right now, which takes up all my time, but because I lack the basic knowledge to handle the databases in the Classified Archives. Also, I'd need the help of an anthropologist to be able to focus on the more prominent aspects of the investigation. What I mean, Eminences, is I don't think I can do what you ask."

Monsignor Tournier was the only one who showed any signs of life when I finished. While the rest were in shock, Tournier's sarcastic grin made me suspect he had opposed my assignment to the case from the very beginning. I could hear him saying contemptuously, "A *woman....*" His sly, mordant attitude made me do a one-eighty.

"However, after more thought, perhaps I could take a look, as long as you gave me enough time."

Monsignor Tournier's mocking expression vanished as if by magic while the tense expressions of the rest relaxed, sighing with great relief and satisfaction. One of my biggest sins is pride, I admit—pride in all its variations of arrogance, vanity, haughtiness. I will never repent enough nor do enough penance, and I am incapable of rejecting a challenge or getting cold feet when any doubt is cast on my intelligence or my knowledge.

"Splendid!" exclaimed His Eminence, the secretary of state, slapping his knee. "Then there's nothing more to talk about. Problem solved, thanks be to God! Very well, Sister Ottavia. From this moment on, Captain Glauser-Röist will be at your side to collaborate on anything you might need. Each morning, when you begin your work, he will give you the photographs. You will return them to him when you're finished at the end of each day. Any questions before you get started?"

"Yes," I replied, puzzled. "Will the captain be allowed to enter the restricted area of the Classified Archives? It's not a secular area, and..."

"Of course he will, Doctor!" Prefect Ramondino affirmed. "I will see to it myself. I'll have his pass ready by this very afternoon."

A little toy soldier (for what else is a Swiss Guard?) was about to put an end to a venerable and secular tradition.

I had lunch at the cafeteria in the Archives and spent the rest of the afternoon packing up everything on the desk in my lab. Postponing my study of the *Panegyrikon* irritated me more than I could admit, but I'd fallen into my own trap. I couldn't get out of a direct order from Cardinal Sodano. Besides, I was intrigued and felt a tickle of perverse curiosity.

When everything was in perfect order and my office was ready for the new task that began the next morning, I gathered my belongings and left. Crossing the Bernini Colonnade, I left by way of the Via di Porta Angelica and walked distractedly by numerous souvenir stores filled with the crowds of tourists that had flooded Rome for the great jubilee. I clutched my purse and picked up my pace. Although the pickpockets of the Borgo more or less recognized those of us who worked in the Vatican, since the Holy Year had begun—the first ten days of January, when three million visitors flood the city—pickpockets from all over Italy had swelled their numbers, the result of which made me as alert as ever. The afternoon light streamed slowly in from the west, and I— who'd always had a certain aversion to such light—couldn't wait to curl up at home. I was almost there. Luckily, the head of my order had decided that having one of its nuns in such an outstanding position as mine merited the purchase of a furnished apartment near the Vatican. So, three sisters and I had been the first to live in a tiny apartment located in the Piazza delle Vaschette. It overlooked the baroque fountain, which long ago flowed with the angelic water known for its great curative powers for gastric troubles.

Sisters Ferma, Margherita, and Valeria, who worked together in a public school nearby, had just gotten home. They were in the kitchen, fixing dinner and chatting happily. Ferma, fifty-five and the oldest, still stubbornly wore a uniform. After habits were retired, she'd donned a white shirt, a navy blue cardigan, a skirt that reached below her knees, and thick black stockings. Margherita, the mother superior of our community and director of the school, was only a few years older than I. Our relationship over the years had gone from distant to warm, then from warm to friendly, but not any further. Lastly, young Valeria from Milan taught four- and five-year-olds, among whom increasingly numbered the children of immigrant Arabs and Asians, with all the problems of communication this brought to a classroom. I had recently seen her reading a big book on the customs and religions of other continents.

The three respected my work at the Vatican, but they didn't know the details of what I did. All that they knew was that they shouldn't ask too many questions; I assume they must have been warned firmly by our superiors, for in my contract with the Vatican, one clause was explicitly clear: Under penalty of excommunication, I was forbidden to discuss my work. However, once in a while they liked to hear what I'd recently discovered about the first Christian communities or the beginnings of the church. I only talked about good things, the things I could divulge without undermining the official history or the props of their faith. How would I explain to them that in a zealously guarded writing, Ireneo, one of the fathers of the church in the year 183, was cited as the first pope—not Peter, who wasn't even mentioned? Or that the official list of the first popes, collected in the *Catalogus Liberianus* from the year 354, was completely false, and that the alleged pontiffs who appeared on that list (Anacleto, Clement I, Evaristo, Alexander) hadn't even existed? Or that the four Gospels had been written after the Epistles of Paul, the true forger of our church, following his doctrine and teachings, and not the other way around as everyone believed? Why tell them any of that? My doubts and fears, my internal struggles and great suffering, which Ferma, Margherita, and Valeria clearly sensed, were a secret only my confessor could be a witness to. All of us who worked in the third and fourth subterranean floors of the Classified Archives had the same confessor, the Franciscan father Egilberto Pintonello.

After putting supper in the oven and setting the table, my three sisters and I went to our small chapel and sat on floor cushions around a shrine where a tiny candle permanently burned. Together, we prayed the painful mysteries of the Rosary, and soon we grew quiet, gathered in prayer. It was Lent. On Father Pintonello's recommendation, I reflected on Jesus's forty days of fasting in the desert and the devil's temptations. It was not exactly my taste, but I've always been tremendously disciplined. It would never have occurred to me to go against my confessor's suggestions.

As I prayed, the meeting with the prelates came back to me again and again, blocking my prayers. I asked myself how I could possibly succeed at my work if they were going to keep information from me. Besides, the subject was very strange. "The man in the photographs," Monsignor Tournier had said, "was implicated in a serious crime against the Catholic Church, as well as against all other Christian churches. We are very sorry, but we cannot give you any more details."

That night I had horrible nightmares. A beaten, headless man who was the reincarnation of the devil appeared to me around every corner and down a long street. I stumbled down that street, like a drunk. He tempted me with power and the glory of all the kingdoms of the world.

*A*t exactly eight o'clock the next morning, the doorbell rang insistently. Margherita answered the door and came to the kitchen right away with a concerned look on her face. "Ottavia, a Kaspar Glauser is waiting for you downstairs."

I was petrified. "Captain Glauser-Röist?" I mumbled through a mouth full of bread.

"He didn't say anything about being a captain," Margherita said, "but the name sounds right."

I hurried to finish the rest of my breakfast without chewing and gulped my coffee.

"A problem at work." I excused myself and rushed out of the kitchen under my sister's surprised gaze. The apartment in the Piazza delle Vaschette was so small that in a second I had time to straighten up my room and pass through the chapel to say good-bye to the Lord. I grabbed my coat and purse from the hanger at the front door and ran out, closing the door behind me, totally confused. Why was Captain Glauser-Röist waiting for me downstairs? Was something wrong?

Hidden behind impenetrable black glasses, the robust toy soldier leaned, expressionless, against the door of a flashy, dark-blue Alfa Romeo. It is a Roman custom to park right in front of the door, even if you're blocking traffic. Any good Roman will explain to you that this saves time for everyone involved. Despite being Swiss—all the members of the small Vatican army had to be—Captain Glauser-Röist must have lived in Rome for many years to have seamlessly adopted its worst cus-

toms. Oblivious to my neighbors' ogling, the captain didn't move a muscle when I finally opened the door to my building and came out to the
street. In the strong sunlight, I was very happy to see that the hulking
Swiss soldier looked a bit older than at first glance. Time had left some
wrinkles around his eyes and on his deceptively youthful face.

"Good morning," I said, buttoning my coat. "Is something wrong,
Captain?"

"Good morning, Doctor." His very proper Italian didn't hide a
slight German inflection in the way he pronounced his *r*'s. "I've been
waiting outside the Archives since six this morning."

"Why so early, Captain?"

"I thought it was time to get to work."

"I start work at eight," I mumbled, irritated.

The captain cast an indifferent glance at his watch.

"It's eight ten," he announced, cold as a stone yet just as pleasant.

"Is that so? Well then, let's get going."

What an irritating man! Didn't he know that the boss always arrives
late? It's one of the perks of being in charge.

The Alfa Romeo crossed the alleys in the Borgo at top speed. The
captain had also adopted the suicidal Roman way of driving. Before you
could say amen, we were crossing the Porta Santa Anna, leaving the
Swiss Guard's barracks behind. If I didn't scream—or open the door
and throw myself from the speeding death trap—it was only thanks to
my Sicilian roots and the fact that I'd gotten my driver's license in Palermo, where the traffic lights are for decorative purposes only and the
rules of the road are based on the laws of physics, the use of the horn,
and general common sense. The captain stopped the car abruptly in a
parking space that had a plaque emblazoned with his name. He turned
off the motor, a satisfied look on his face. That was the first trace of
human emotion I'd observed in him, and it really got my attention.
Clearly he loved to drive. We walked toward the Archives through parts
of the Vatican I didn't know existed, passing a modern gym full of machines as well as a shooting range. All the guards came sharply to attention and saluted Glauser-Röist as we passed.

One thing that had really piqued my curiosity over the years was the origin of the Swiss Guard's gaudy, multicolor uniforms. In the Classified Archives, there was nothing that confirmed or debunked the rumor that Michelangelo had designed them. However, I was sure that one day we'd find some proof when we least expected among the vast quantity of documents still left to study. Unlike his fellow soldiers, Glauser-Röist didn't wear the uniform. On the two occasions I'd met him, he was dressed in civilian clothes that were clearly very expensive, almost too expensive for the meager salary of a poor member of the Swiss Guard.

We crossed the vestibule of the Classified Archives in silence, passing in front of Reverend Father Ramondino's closed office, and entered the elevator simultaneously. Glauser-Röist stuck his brand new key into the control panel.

"Do you have the photographs on you, Captain?" I asked as we descended toward the Hypogeum.

"I do, Doctor." More and more he resembled a sharp rock on a steep mountainside. Where did they find this guy?

"Then I suppose we can start work right away, yes?"

"Right away."

My staff's jaws dropped when they saw Glauser-Röist come down the aisle toward the lab. Guido Buzzonetti's desk was painfully empty that morning.

"Good morning," I said in a loud voice.

"Good morning, Doctor," someone murmured so I didn't go unanswered.

If a thick silence followed us to my office, the shout that escaped me as I opened the lab door could be heard all the way to the Roman Forum.

"Jesus! What happened here?"

My old desk had been shoved heartlessly into a corner, and in the middle of the room was a metal desk and a huge computer. Other hulking devices had been set on small plastic tables that came from some empty office. Dozens of cables and plugs crisscrossed the floor and hung from my old bookcases.

Horrified, I clapped my hands over my mouth and cautiously stepped inside as if I were walking into a nest of snakes.

"We need this equipment for our work," answered the Rock, behind me.

"I hope you're right, Captain! Who gave you permission to enter my lab and assemble this mess?"

"Prefect Ramondino."

"Well, he should have consulted me!"

"We set up the equipment last night after you left," in his voice there was not even the slightest note of remorse. He was limited to informing me of the facts and that was that, as if everything he did was beyond discussion.

"Splendid! That's splendid!" I repeated, utterly furious.

"Do you wish to start work or not?"

I spun around as if he had slapped me and I looked at him with all the disdain I could muster.

"Let's get this over with as soon as possible."

"At your orders," he murmured, again dragging out his *r*'s. He unbuttoned his jacket and from some unfathomable place took out the same bulky dossier in a black file I'd seen the day before. "It's all yours," he said holding it out to me.

"What are you going to do while I work?"

"Use the computer."

"To do what?" I asked, astonished. My computer illiteracy was an unresolved issue I knew I'd have to confront someday. Up until then, like any good scholar, I found it very comforting to scorn those diabolical pieces of electronic junk.

"Solve any problem you may have and access all the information on any topic you wish."

And that's how we left it.

I started by examining the photographs. There were a lot of them— thirty, to be exact. They were in the chronological order of the autopsy, from start to finish. After a quick once-over, I chose the ones where I could see the entire body spread out on the metal table in the positions of dorsal and prone decubitus (face up and facedown). At first glance, what stood out was the fracture of the pelvic bones, the very unnatural arch of the legs, and a huge lesion in the right parietal area of the cranium that had left the gray gelatin of the brain exposed amid slivers of bone. I found the rest of the images useless. The body probably had a number of internal lesions that I had no way to evaluate; nor did I think they were relevant to my work. But I did notice that—most likely due to the accident—the man had bitten through his own tongue.

That man could never have passed for anything but what he was: Ethiopian. Like most Ethiopians, he was very thin and reedy, with gaunt, fibrous flesh. His extremely dark skin pigmentation was striking. The planes of his face were definitive proof of his Abyssinian origin: very pronounced high cheekbones, sunken cheeks, broad knobby forehead, thick lips, and narrow nose. His large black eyes were open in the photographs, and this really caught my attention. A nearly Greek profile. Before they had cleaned up the section of the head that remained intact, his hair had been matted down, tightly curled, rather dirty, and blood-stained. After he was shaved you could clearly see a fine scar in the shape of the uppercase Greek letter sigma (Σ) in the very center of his skull.

That morning I studied the terrible images over and over, reviewing any detail that seemed significant. The scarifications stood out like highways on a map, some disgustingly fleshy and thick and others nearly imperceptible, some fine as silk threads. Without exception, all were rose-colored, even reddish in spots, which gave them the repulsive look of grafts of white skin onto black. By midafternoon I had stomach cramps, I was light-headed, and the table was covered with notes and sketches of the deceased's scarifications.

I found another six Greek letters distributed over the body: a tau (T) on the biceps of the right arm; an upsilon (Y) on the left arm; an alpha (A) in the center of the chest over the heart; a rho (P) on the abdomen; an omicron (O) on the quadriceps of the right thigh; and another sigma (Σ) on the same spot on the left thigh. Right below the alpha and above the rho in the lung and stomach area could be seen a large chrismon, a very common monogram in the tympana and altars of medieval churches.

The two first Greek letters of Christ's name, *XP*—chi and rho—were superimposed onto it.

This chrismon, however, had a very peculiar variation: a horizontal bar had been added, giving the symbol the added appearance of a cross. The rest of the body, except the hands, feet, buttocks, neck, and face, was covered with the most original-looking crosses I'd ever seen in my life.

Captain Glauser-Röist sat for long stretches in front of the computer, typing mysterious instructions without taking a break. From time to time, he came up behind my chair and stood there in silence, studying the evolution of my analysis. I was startled when, out of the blue, he asked if it would help to have a life-size drawing of the human body so I could record the scars. Before answering I moved my head in exaggerated nods and shakes to relieve the pain in my neck.

"That's a good idea. Captain, how much are you authorized to tell me about this poor man? Monsignor Tournier mentioned that you took these photographs."

Glauser-Röist rose from his chair and turned toward the computer. "I can't tell you anything." He quickly struck several computer keys quickly and the printer began to chirp and expel paper.

"I need to know more," I protested, rubbing the bridge of my nose under my glasses. "Maybe you know some details that would facilitate my work."

The Rock wasn't moved by my pleading. He cut pieces of tape with his teeth and stuck those sheets of paper to the back of my door. The complete silhouette of a human being took shape.

"Can I help you in some other way?" he asked when he finished.

I glared at him. "Can you consult the databases of the Classified Archives from that computer?"

"From this computer I can consult any database in the world. What would you like to know?"

"Anything you can find on scarification."

Without missing a beat he got to work. I grabbed a fistful of markers from a box on my desk and planted myself in front of the life-size paper silhouette. A half hour later, I had managed to rather faithfully reconstruct the painful road map of the victim's injuries. I had to ask myself why a sane, strong man only thirty-some years old would let himself be tortured in this manner. It was quite strange indeed.

Besides the Greek letters, I found a total of seven beautiful crosses, each one completely different from the others: the first, a Latin cross on the inner part of the right forearm; the second, a Latin immmissa cross (with a short crossbar in the middle of the staff), on his left forearm; the third, a branched cross (with tree limbs) on his cervical vertebrae; the fourth, an Egyptian ansate cross on his dorsal spine; and the fifth, a bracketed cross on his lumbar vertebrae. The remaining two Greek crosses were called decussates (in an X) and were located on the back of his thighs. The variety was admirable; yet they did have certain elements in common: They were all enclosed or protected by circles, squares, or rectangles (like tiny medieval windows or arrow slits), and in each case the top edge of the enclosure was crowned with serrated teeth, always numbering seven.

At nine that night we were dead tired. Glauser-Röist summed up what few references to scarifications he had located. It was a religious practice limited to a strip of central Africa that unfortunately didn't include Ethiopia. In that region, apparently, the primitive tribes had the custom of rubbing a grass mixture into the incisions, usually made with small pieces of cane as sharp as knives. The decorative patterns could be very complex, but basically they corresponded to the geometric shapes of sacred symbols, often as part of some religious ritual.

"That's it?" I asked, disenchanted, after he had read his most obvious and meager report.

"Well, there is something more, but it's not significant. The *queloides*—that is, the thickest, enlarged scarification marks—are a genuine sexual lure for men when women exhibit them."

"Oh, go on...," I replied with a look of wonder. "Now, that's funny. It never would have occurred to me."

"In any case," he went on, nonplussed, "we still don't know why those scars are on that man's body." I believe that was the first time I noticed that his eyes were a washed-out gray. "Another peculiar piece of information, also irrelevant to our work, is that this practice is becoming fashionable among young men in many countries. They call it 'body art' or 'performance art,' and one of its most prominent followers is the singer and actor David Bowie."

"I can't believe it...," I sighed, with a slight smile. "Do you mean they let someone cut them like that just to be fashionable?"

Well...," he murmured, as disturbed as I. "It has something to do with eroticism and sensuality, but I wouldn't know how to explain it to you."

"Don't even try, thank you very much," I dismissed him. Tuckered out, I got to my feet and mentally put an end to that first exhausting session. "Let's get some rest, Captain. Tomorrow is going to be another very long day."

"Allow me to take you home. It's too late for you to walk alone through the Borgo."

I was too tired to refuse, so I once again risked my life in that spectacular little sports car of his. When we said good night, I thanked him, feeling guilty for the way I had treated him—although I must say, the remorse did pass quickly. I rejected his offer to come pick me up again the next morning, since I hadn't heard Mass for two days and I wasn't going to let another day go by without doing so. I'd get up early and go to Saint Michele and Magno Church before work.

Ferma, Margherita, and Valeria were watching an old movie on TV when I walked through the door. They warmed up some supper for me in the microwave, and I ate a little soup. I didn't have much of an appetite; I'd seen too many scars that day. I shut myself away in our chapel before going to bed, but I couldn't concentrate on my prayer—and not just because I was so tired (which I was), but because three of my eight siblings had called from Sicily to ask if I was planning to attend our annual celebration of Saint Giuseppe in honor of our father. I said yes to all three and went to bed, utterly exasperated.

*C*aptain Glauser-Röist and I spent several hectic weeks locked away in my office from eight in the morning till nine at night, Monday through Sunday. We reviewed what little information we received from the archives. The question of the Greek letters and the chrismon proved relatively simple to solve; it was a different matter entirely to decipher the enigma of the seven crosses.

On the second day, I was closing the door to the lab and studying the paper silhouette taped to my door out of the corner of my eye, when the solution to the Greek letters hit me as if I'd been slapped in the face with a glove. I couldn't believe I hadn't seen it the night before: reading from the head to the legs, from right to left, the seven letters formed the Greek word *STAUROS—ΣΤΑΥΡΟΣ*—which means, of course, "cross." At that point, it was unquestionable that everything on the Ethiopian's body was related to the subject of crosses.

Several days later, after poring over the story of old Abyssinia (Ethiopia) several times, with no luck; after consulting a variety of documents on the Greek influence on that country's culture and religion; after long hours of scouring dozens of books on all styles of art from all eras, extensive files on sects sent by various departments of the Classified Archives and exhaustive information on chrismons that the captain found on the Internet, we made another very significant discovery: a monogram of the Name of Christ on the Ethiopian man's chest and stomach corresponded to the well-known Monogram of Constantine, which had not been used in Christian art since around the sixth century.

Surprisingly the cross, as a religious symbol, was not the object of any kind of adoration in Christianity's early beginnings. The first Christians completely ignored the instrument of his martyrdom, preferring happier, decorative symbols and images. Also, the Roman persecutions were few, limited more or less to Nero's known acts after the burning of

Rome in 64 and to the two years incorrectly named the Great Persecution of Diocletian (from 303 to 305), according to Eusebio.* During
these Roman persecutions, public display and adoration of the cross
had undoubtedly become very dangerous, so symbols such as the lamb,
the fish, the anchor, or the dove appeared on the walls of the catacombs·
and houses, on headstones, personal objects, and altars. Without a
doubt, the most important drawing was the chrismon, the monogram
formed by the first Greek letters of the name of Christ (X and P, chi and
rho). It was widely used to decorate sacred places. There were multiple
variations of the chrismon, with any religious interpretation you may
want to assign them. For example, there were chrismons on martyrs'
tombs with a palm branch in place of the P, symbolizing Christ's victory.
Monograms with a triangle in the center expressed the Mystery of the
Trinity.

In 312 of our era, Emperor Constantine the Great, who worshipped
the sun, had a vision of his decisive battle against Maxentius, his main
rival for the throne of the empire. One night he dreamed that Christ appeared and told him to engrave those two letters, X and P, on the upper
corner of his army's banners. The next day, before the battle, legend has
it he saw that seal appear, along with a transverse bar to form the image
of a cross, over the dazzling sphere of the sun. Below it were the Greek
words *EN-TOYTΩI-NIKA*, better known in the Latin translation as *In
hoc signo vinces*, "With this sign you will vanquish." Constantine soundly
defeated Maxentius in the battle of the Milvian bridge. His banner with
the chrismon, later called "Labarum," became the empire's flag. This
symbol took on extraordinary importance in what was left of the Roman
Empire. After the western part of the territory, Europe, fell to barbarian
armies, the symbol was still used in Byzantium until at least the sixth
century, after which it completely disappeared from Christian art.

So, then, the monogram that our Ethiopian bore on his torso was
exactly the same as the one that the emperor saw upon the sun before his
fateful battle. It bore the telltale crosspiece, distinguishing it among the
many variations and making it a curious—indeed, downright strange—

---

*Eusebio (260–341), bishop of Cesarea, *Hist. Eccl.; De Mart. Palaestinae.*

detail. It hadn't been used in fourteen centuries, as the father of the church, Saint John Chrysostom, attested to the symbol in his writings, recording that by the end of the fifth century the symbol had largely been replaced by the one True Cross, the same one that to this day continues to be publicly displayed with exuberance and pride. It is true that during the Romance and Gothic periods, the monogram would re-emerge, but these symbols had evolved away from the simple, concrete monogram that Constantine used.

So, once the mystery of the chrismon was apparently solved (with that of the word *STAUROS* spread over the body), we were then mired down in a matter even more perplexing. Every day our desire grew to unravel that imbroglio, to understand what that strange cadaver was trying to tell us. Still, we stuck to our assignment, to explain the symbols, despite what all the other clues were trying to tell us. We had no choice but to continue down the path we were assigned and to clear up the meaning of the seven crosses.

Why seven, and not eight or five or fifteen? Why were all the crosses different? Why were they all framed by geometric forms like medieval windows? Why were they all dignified by a small radiate crown? We would never figure it out, I told myself. It was too complicated, too absurd, too random. I raised my eyes from the photos and the sketches and turned my attention to the paper silhouette, hoping the placement of the crosses would provide a clue, but I saw nothing that would help me figure out the hieroglyphic crosses. I lowered my eyes back to the table and focused wearily on studying the strange small crowned windows.

Glauser-Röist hardly said a word those days. He wasted hours typing away on the computer. I started to feel quite bitter toward him for foolishly wasting his time in front of that screen while my brain was slowly turning to mush.

Sunday, March 19—the day of San Giuseppe and the festival in honor of my father—was fast approaching, and I began preparing for my trip to Palermo. I didn't go home very often, maybe two or three times per year; but, like any good Sicilian family, the Salinas remained inextricably united, for better or for worse, and beyond the grave if need be. Being the next-to-last of nine siblings (that's where my name, Ottavia, comes from) has many disadvantages, especially where survival tactics are concerned: There was always an older brother or sister ready to torture you or crush you under the weight of their authority. (Your clothes are all hand-me-downs, "your" space actually belongs to the first person to get there, your triumphs and failures have already been experienced by those who came before you.) Nevertheless, the bond I shared with my eight brothers and sisters was an indestructible one: Despite my twenty-year absence, as well as that of Pierantonio (a Franciscan in the Holy Land) and Lucia (a Dominican stationed in England), we could be counted on to organize any family activity, buy any gift for our parents, or make any group decision that would affect the family.

The Thursday before my departure, Captain Glauser-Röist returned from lunch in the Swiss Guard's barracks with a strange metallic gleam in his gray eyes. I was slogging away reading a disjointed treatise dealing with Christian art of the seventh and eighth centuries. I hoped in vain to find some allusion to the design of one of the crosses.

"Dr. Salina," he whispered the minute he closed the door. "I've thought of something."

"I'm listening," I replied, pushing away the tedious abstract in front of me.

"We need software that fact-checks the crosses on the Ethiopian man with all the catalogues from the Archives and the library."

"Is that possible?" I asked.

"The Archives' information service can do it."

I thought it over for a few seconds.

"I don't know…" I mulled it over. "It'd be very complicated. It's one thing to type some words into the computer and search databases for them but it's a whole other thing altogether to take one image and compare it with others. They could be different sizes, incompatible formats, taken from different angles. The quality of the images might not even be good enough for a computer to recognize them."

Glauser-Röist looked at me with compassion. It was as if we were climbing the same staircase and he was always a few steps ahead of me, always having to turn back to look at me.

"The search for images doesn't use those factors." There was a hint of commiseration in his voice. "You know how in the movies the police use computers to compare the image of a murderer with digital photographs of criminals they have on file? They use parameters such as space between the eyes, width of the nose, coordinates of the forehead, nose, and jaw, and so forth. Those programs use numerical calculations to detect fugitives."

"I doubt very much," I said angrily, "that our information service has a program for locating wanted criminals. We're not the police, Captain. We're the heart of the Catholic world. In the library and the Archives, we only work with history and art."

Glauser-Röist turned and opened the door.

"Where're you going?" I asked incredulously, on seeing that he was about to leave without answering my question.

"To talk to Prefect Ramondino. I'm certain he can set it up with the IT department."

O n Friday after lunch, Sister Chiara picked me up and we left Rome behind on the highway headed south. She was spending the weekend in Naples with her family and was delighted to have company for the ride. Chiara and I weren't the only ones leaving Rome that weekend. To fulfill one of his more ardent wishes, His Holiness was making a supreme effort in the middle of jubilee to travel to sacred places in Jordan and Israel (Mount Nebo, Bethlehem, Nazareth). One had to admire how the approach of an exhausting trip revived a body in such sad shape. The pope was a true world traveler; contact with the multitudes invigorated him. The city I was leaving behind that Friday was boiling with activity and last-minute preparations.

In Naples I caught the night ferry, the *Tirrenia*, that would stop in Palermo very early Saturday morning. The weather was excellent that night, so I wrapped my coat tight around me and settled into an armchair on the second-floor deck, where I could enjoy a peaceful crossing. Any time I crossed that sea toward home, my mind was invaded by the hypnotic memories of the years I lived there. As a little girl, I had wanted to be a spy. At eight, I lamented there were no more world wars for me to take part in, like Mata Hari. At ten, I was making small flashlights out of little batteries and tiny bulbs—stolen from my older siblings' electronic games—which I then used to spend nights hiding out under my covers, reading adventure stories. Later, at the School of the Providential Virgin Mary (which I was forced to attend upon turning thirteen, after a fateful little romantic escapade I had with my friend Vito), I continued to read compulsively as a form of catharsis, transforming the world to my imagination's content and making it conform to the way I wanted it to be. Reality was neither pleasant nor happy for a little girl who viewed life through a magnifying glass.

In boarding school, I read the *Confessions* of Saint Augustine and the *Song of Songs* for the first time. I discovered a deep similarity between the feelings spilled across those pages and my turbulent, impressionable inner life. I suppose that those works helped to awaken the early concerns of my religious vocation, but I would still have to endure many years of schooling and experiences before I could profess it. Smiling, I recalled that one unforgettable afternoon in which my mother caught me with a smudged notebook in which I'd detailed the adventures of the American spy Ottavia Prescott... She couldn't have been more scandalized if she'd found a gun or a pornographic magazine under my bed. To her, my father, and the rest of the Salina family, literary pursuits were senseless ones, more suited to unemployed bohemians than to the young daughter of an affluent family.

The moon shone a luminous white in the dark sky. The pungent scent of the sea carried by the cold night air grew so intense I covered my mouth and nose with the lapels of my coat, then drew my blanket all the way to my neck. The Roman Ottavia, Vatican paleographer, now seemed as distant as the Italian coast, while the Sicilian Ottavia came surging from some remote place she had never really abandoned. Who was Captain Glauser-Röist?... What did I have to do with a dead Ethiopian?... In the midst of all these questions and my reverting to my roots, I fell into a deep sleep.

When I opened my eyes, the sky was growing brighter with the red glow of the eastern sun. The ferry entered the Gulf of Palermo at a good clip. Before we docked, as I folded my blanket and re-packed my travel bag, I could make out the thick arms of my oldest sister, Giacoma, and of my brother-in-law Domenico waving lovingly from the dock. I was home.

The sailors on the ferry, the other passengers, the soldiers on the pier, and the people waiting on the dock watched me with intense curiosity as I came down the gangway for it was impossible to miss Giacoma, the most famous of the *new* Salinas, and her very discreet convoy—two impressive armored cars with dark windows and kilometric proportions.

My sister squeezed me until I nearly broke in half, while my brother-in-law gave me loving pats on my shoulder. One of my father's men gathered my luggage and put it in the trunk.

"I told you not to come get me!" I protested into Giacoma's ear. She turned me loose and flashed a bright smile, as though what I said hadn't registered. My sister, who'd just turned fifty-three, had long hair as black as coal and wore makeup as bright as van Gogh's palette. She was still beautiful and would have been even more attractive if it weren't for those twenty or thirty extra pounds she carried.

"You're such a silly goose!" she exclaimed, pushing me into the arms of stout Domenico, who squeezed me again. "Do you think I'd let you arrive in Palermo alone and just take a bus home? Impossible!"

"Besides," added Domenico, looking at me with paternal reproach, "we're having some problems with the Sciarra family."

"What's going on with the Sciarra family?" I was worried. Concetta Sciarra and her little sister, Doria, were my childhood friends. Our families had always gotten along well and growing up we had played to-gether many Sunday afternoons. Concetta was a generous, caring person. After her father's death two years before, she had assumed control of the Sciarra's family business. From what I had heard, the relationship between our families was very good. Doria, however, was the other side of the same coin: devious, envious, egotistical, and always looking for ways to blame others for her evil actions, she had professed a blind envy of me since we were little. She stole my toys and books and often broke them without one bit of remorse.

"They're cutting into our markets with cheaper products," explained my sister, defiantly. "It's an unbelievably dirty war."

I didn't say a word. Such a serious action seemed despicable to me, since they were clearly taking advantage of my father's inevitable decline. He was nearly eighty-five. But Concetta should be smart enough to know that as debilitated as Giuseppe Salina was, his children were not going to allow such a thing.

We sped away from the dock, not breaking at the red light at the intersection of the Via Francesco Crispi, then turned right toward La Cala. We blew past the signals at the Via Vittorio Emanuele, too. Our three vehicles enjoyed complete right-of-way at any intersection and stop sign. We turned at the Normandos' palace and left the city on Calatafimi. A few miles from Monreale, in the middle of Conca d'Oro Valley (it was so beautiful and green, all covered with flowers in bloom), the first car made a quick right onto the private road to our house, the old, monumental Villa Salina built by my great-grandfather, Giuseppe, at the end of the nineteenth century.

"While you freshen up and unpack," my sister said, smoothing her black hair with both hands, "Domenico and I will pick Lucia up at the airport. She gets in at ten."

"What about Pierantonio?"

"He got in last night from the Holy Land!" squealed Giacoma, elated. I smiled wide, happy as a lizard in the sun. Pierantonio's presence, confirmed at the last minute, turned the gathering into a gala. I hadn't seen my brother for two years. He's the best, sweetest man in the world. Not only did he and I share an extraordinary physical resemblance, more than I did with the rest of the family, but we also had a similar temperament and character that had made us literally inseparable. After finishing his brilliant studies as an archeologist, Pierantonio entered the Franciscan order, at age twenty-five, when I was fifteen. A year later, he was sent first to Rhodes, in Greece, and then to Cyprus, Egypt, Jordan, and finally Jerusalem, where in 1998 he received the title of guardian of the Holy Land, which was a post first established by Pope Clement VI in 1342 to assure the continued Catholic presence in the sacred cities after the final defeat of the Crusades. In other words, my brother was a truly important figure in Christianity's Eastern reaches, and around him he projected that special aura known only to truly sacred, polemical people.

"Mama must be so happy he's here!" I exclaimed, delighted, glancing out the window.

Protected by iron doors and high concrete walls, the old four-story house had changed over the years. Numerous surveillance cameras around the villa's perimeter scanned every movement. In my childhood the guards' quarters had been just ramshackle wooden boxes which housed cane-backed chairs inside. They'd been transformed into genuine control posts on both sides of the sliding iron door, equipped with computerized remote control of every security device and alarm.

My father's men gave a slight nod as our car passed. I could not help a shout of joy when I recognized Vito among them, my old childhood friend.

"It's Vito!" I shouted as I waved frenetically out the back window. Vito smiled timidly, almost imperceptibly.

"He just got out of the *giudiziarie*,* smiled Domenico, pulling his jacket around his gut. "Your father is glad to have him back."

The car finally came to a stop in front of the house. My mother, dressed in black as always, waited for us at the top of the steps leaning on her ever-present silver cane. Seventy-five years of intense life had exhausted the noble Sicilian woman's back but the proud bearing of the youngest daughter of the Zafferano family hadn't diminished one bit.

I took the stairs two at a time and hugged my mother as if I hadn't seen her since the day I was born. I had missed her so much and felt a childish relief to find her in such good health. Her kisses were firm and

---

*The *giudiziarie* prison, located near the port of Palermo, is the most sophisticated and best-guarded prison in Italy. Members of the Mafia serve their time there.

her body was still as hard and energetic as always. With a knot in my throat, I thanked God that nothing had happened to her while I was away. Smiling, she took a step back to look me over carefully.

"My little Ottavia!" she exclaimed with a happy face. "You look wonderful! Do you know your Pierantonio has already arrived? He really wants to see you. I want you two to tell me everything." She put her hand on my shoulder and gently nudged me inside the house. "How is the Holy Father doing? How is his health?"

The rest of the day was one continuous parade of family members. Giuseppe, the eldest, lived in the villa with his wife, Rosalia, and their four children. Giacoma and Domenico, who also lived in the villa with our parents, had five children who were home from the University of Messina and boarding school. Cesare, the third child, was married to Letizia and had four fine kids who, fortunately, resided in Agrigento. Pierluigi, the fifth child, arrived midafternoon with his wife, Livia, and their five children. Salvatore, the brother immediately older than me, was the only one who was divorced. Even so, he showed up that evening with three of his four children. Finally, Agueda, the youngest (she was already thirty-eight!) came with Antonio, her husband, and their three offspring. Their youngest was my dear five-year-old Isabella.

Pierantonio, Lucia, and I were the priest and nuns of the family. I always had a sinking feeling when I compared my mother's expectations for her children with what we did with our lives. It's as if God granted mothers the clairvoyance to predict the future. Or, and this is most worrisome, God adapts his plans to that of our mothers.

Mysteriously, Pierantonio, Lucia, and I had taken our vows as my mother always yearned for. I still remember her saying to my brother when he was seventeen or eighteen, "You can't imagine how proud I'd be if you became a priest, a good priest. And you'll be a good priest because you have the perfect character to lead with a firm hand. A diocese, at least." Or combing Lucia's beautiful blonde hair while she whispered in her ear: "You're too smart and independent to submit to a husband. Marriage is not for you. I'm sure you'd be much happier living a life like one of the nuns at your school: travel, study, freedom, good friends…" And *then* there was what she said to me: "Of all my children, Ottavia, you are the most brilliant and the proudest... You have such a strong character only God could make you the person I'd like you to be." She repeated this with the conviction of a soothsayer. She did the same with all my brothers and sisters. Their occupations, studies, or marriages fit her predictions like a glove.

I spent the whole day with little Isabella in my arms, going from one end of the house to the other, talking to family members, greeting aunts and uncles, cousins and acquaintances who came by to wish my father well and to bring him gifts. I was reunited with so many people; no sooner had I hugged and kissed someone than I'd lose sight of him again. All I remember is that my father—in a gesture of infinite weariness—looked proudly at me and caressed my cheek with a wrinkled, weathered hand before being abducted by the surging crowd. More than a home, the whole thing seemed like a fair.

By midafternoon, I had terrible back pain from carrying Isabella all day. She took no pity on me, and refused to let go of my neck. Whenever I tried to set her down, she wrapped her legs around my waist like a monkey. When it was time to fix supper, we women headed for the kitchen to help the maids while the men gathered in the hall to discuss family matters and business. Moments later I wasn't surprised to see the tall figure of my brother Pierantonio among the baking dishes and frying pans. I couldn't help notice that the way he moved was similar to Monsignor Tournier's elegant mannerisms. The differences between the two were vast, of course. For starters, one of them was my favorite brother. Still, they shared that radiant self-assurance and charisma.

My mother was obviously captivated as she watched him approach.

"Mama," Pierantonio said, kissing her cheek, "will you lend me Ottavia? I'd like to take a walk with her in the garden and catch up before dinner."

"Does anyone care how I feel?" I called from the other side of the kitchen, deftly sautéing some vegetables. "Maybe I don't want to go."

My mother laughed. "Now, now! What are you even talking about?" She joked as if it were inconceivable I wouldn't go for a walk with my brother.

"And the rest of us—are we just invisible to the two of you?" protested Giacoma, Lucia, and Agueda.

Pierantonio, the flatterer, kissed each one, then snapped his fingers as if he were summoning a waiter. "Ottavia, let's go."

Without missing a beat, Maria, one of the cooks, took the skillet I held from my hands. It was one big conspiracy.

"In all my life," I said as I took off my apron and set it on a bench in the kitchen, "I've never seen a Franciscan priest less humble than Father Salina."

"Guardian, Sister," he replied. "Guardian of the Holy Land."

"And so modest!" guffawed Giacoma. Everyone broke out in a chorus of laughter.

If I could have been a spectator and watched my family from a distance, one thing would have stood out: The Salina women adored Pierantonio. No one ever enjoyed a more fervent, submissive flock of honey-tongued sweet talkers. Like a god, his most trivial wishes were carried out with the fanaticism of the Greek Bacchae. He knew it, enjoying like a child playing the part of a capricious Dionysus. My mother was completely to blame. She had infected us with her blind worship of her favorite son like a virus. Why wouldn't we indulge the little god in every whim when he bestowed his wit and kisses upon us? He was so easy to make happy!

Pierantonio put his arm around my waist and steered me out to the back patio toward the garden door. "Tell me how things are going!" he exclaimed bombastically the minute we set foot on the soft grass around the house.

"You tell me!" I replied, looking at him. His hairline had receded a bit; his wild eyebrows gave him a savage air. "How can the important guardian of the Holy Land abandon his post when His Holiness is set to arrive in Jerusalem?"

"Wow! You shoot to kill!" he laughed, putting an arm around my shoulders.

"I'm so happy you're here, you know that. But I'm puzzled. I know the pope leaves tomorrow for your jurisdiction."

He looked at the sky distractedly, acting as if the point weren't important. But I knew him too well. That gesture conveyed just the opposite.

"Well, as you know . . . Things aren't always what they seem."

"Look, Pierantonio, you can fool the priests, but not me."

He smiled, still looking at the sky.

"Okay, okay! Are you going to tell me why the illustrious guardian of the Holy Land leaves when the sovereign pontiff is about to arrive?" I persisted before he could start talking about how beautiful the stars were.

"I can't tell a nun employed by the Vatican the problems we Franciscans are having with the high prelates," he said, regaining his cocksure attitude.

"You know I spend my life locked up in my lab. Who am I going to tell?"

"The pope?"

"Yeah, sure!" I uttered, stopping in my tracks in the middle of the garden.

"Cardinal Ratzinger? . . ." he hummed. "Cardinal Sodano? . . ."

"Come on, Pierantonio!"

Something must have shown on my face when he mentioned the secretary of state, because he opened his eyes and arched his eyebrows maliciously. "Ottavia . . . Do you know Sodano?"

"I was introduced to him a few weeks ago," I admitted evasively.

He took me by the chin, lifted my face, and pressed his nose to mine. "Ottavia, little Ottavia . . . What are you doing hanging around with Angelo Sodano? What are you not telling me?"

It's awful for someone to know you so well. And it's awful to be the second youngest in a family of brothers and sisters so highly skilled at manipulating.

"Well, you haven't told me the problems you Franciscans are having with His Holiness, and look what you've asked me," I hedged.

"Let's make a deal," he proposed happily, taking hold of my arm, urging me to walk again. "I'll tell you why I'm here and you tell me what you know about the all-powerful secretary of state."

"I can't."

"Yes you can!" he fussed, cheerful as a child. You'd never guess that that exploiter of little sisters was fifty years old! "In secret confession. I've got the vestments in the chapel. Let's go."

"Listen, Pierantonio, this is very serious."

"Great! I love it when you're serious!"

What made me maddest was knowing that if I'd concealed just a little bit more I wouldn't have been in that situation. I was the one who let the cat out of the bag right in front of this insatiable gundog, and the more discomfort I showed, the hungrier he was going to get. I had to put an end to it.

"That's enough now, Pierantonio. Get serious. I can't say anything. Especially to you. You, more than anyone, ought to understand that."

My voice must have sounded really severe, because he backed off and drastically changed his attitude. "You're right," he conceded, a repentant look on his face. "There are things you can't tell. But I never imagined that my sister would get mixed up in Vatican intrigues!"

"I'm not. They just needed my skills for a strange investigation. Very strange. I don't know." I murmured pensively, pinching my lower lip. "I *do* find it disconcerting."

"Some strange document? Some mysterious code? Some shameful secret from the church's past?"

"I've seen all that. I wish I could tell you! No, it's something even more out of the ordinary. What's worse, they're keeping information from me."

My brother studied me, a determined look on his face. "So, go over their heads."

"I don't understand," I said, stopping to poke at the grass with my shoe. The night was cool. Soon the lights in the garden would go on.

"Go over their heads. Don't they want a miracle? Well, give them one. Look, I have a lot of problems in Jerusalem, more than you can imagine." He started to walk again, slowly, and I followed him. More than ever my brother seemed like an important head of state weighed down by responsibilities. "The Holy See has entrusted us Franciscans in the Holy Land with very diverse, very difficult tasks, everything from reestablishing Catholic worship in our area to protecting pilgrims, to getting biblical studies and archeological excavations up and running again. We run schools, hospitals, dispensaries, nursing homes, and above all the guardian is involved in a multitude of political conflicts with our neighbors of other religions. My biggest problem right now is the Holy Cenacle where Jesus instituted the Eucharist. These days it's a mosque run by Israeli authorities. The Vatican keeps pressuring me to negotiate a sale. But do they give me any money? No!" he exclaimed angrily. His forehead and cheeks turned bright red. "Right now, I have 320 religious people from thirty countries working in Palestine-Israel, Jordan, Syria, Lebanon, Egypt, Cyprus, and Rhodes. Don't forget that the Holy Land is a region in conflict, where they fight with all manner of guns, bombs, and disgusting political maneuvers. How do I hold up this house of cards built of religious, cultural, and social work? Do you think my order can help? They haven't got a lira! Do you think your rich Vatican has given me anything? Nothing! Not one cent! The Holy Father diverted money from the church: Millions and millions slipped under the table through figureheads, fake businesses, and bank transfers in fiscal paradises to prop up the Polish Solidarity Union and bring down Communism in his homeland. But how many liras do you think he's given for our projects? Nothing! Nada! Zip!"

"You can't be serious, Pierantonio," I whispered, pained. "The church takes up an annual collection all over the world for you."

His eyes flashed in anger. "Don't make me laugh!" he shot back. He turned and headed back to the house.

"Okay, but at least finish telling me how to get the information I need," I begged as he took giant steps, putting a lot of ground between us.

"Be smart, Ottavia!" he exclaimed, not turning around. "The world is full of ways to get what you want. You just have to prioritize, figure out what's important and what's not. Figure out at what point you're willing to disobey or act on your own, on the fringe, even..." He hesitated. "Even going against your own conscience."

My brother's voice had a distinctly bitter tinge to it, as if he had spent his entire life disregarding his own conscience. I asked myself if I would be able to do such a thing; if it would be worth it to go off the reservation to get the information I needed. But before I could articulate these thoughts, I already knew the answer: Yes, of course I would. The only question was how.

"I'm ready," I said, right there in the middle of the garden. It would have been a good time to recall the expression "be careful what you wish for, because you just might get it." But I didn't.

My brother turned around.

"What do you want?" he bellowed. "What is it that you're looking for?"

"Information."

"You can buy information. And if that doesn't work, you can get it yourself."

"How?" I asked, unsettled.

"Investigate, make inquiries, ask the people who are in possession of the information you need. Interrogate them wisely, search the archives, the boxes of files, the offices, computers, and even the wastebaskets... And if you find something valuable, take it."

I spent a restless, sleepless night, tossing and turning in my childhood bed. Lucia was sleeping next to me, her leg exposed by a tug of the sheet, and she was snoring softly. Pierantonio's words were still ricocheting around in my mind, and yet I still couldn't see how I could do the things he suggested: Was there any good way to get information out of that rocky cliff of a man, Glauser-Röist? How could I get into the offices of the secretary of state or Monsignor Tournier? How could I search the Vatican's computers if I didn't have the slightest idea of how those machines worked?

I fell asleep out of pure exhaustion as daylight seeped in through the blinds. I dreamed about Pierantonio. That I recall. But it wasn't a pleasant dream. I was so happy the next morning when he looked refreshed, his hair still wet from a shower, celebrating Mass in our chapel.

My father, the honoree that day, was seated in the first pew next to my mother. I looked at their backs; my father's was more curved and fragile. I was proud of them, of the wonderful family they had created, of the love they had given their nine children and now were giving to their numerous grandchildren. I thought about how they'd spent all their lives at each other's side. They'd had quarrels and problems, sure, but also an indestructible, inseparable union.

At the end of the Mass, the youngest children went to play in the garden, tired from sitting still during the ceremony. The rest of us went inside for breakfast. At one end of the large dining table, grouped away from the adults, sat my oldest nieces and nephews. When I got the chance, I grabbed Giacoma and Domenico's fourth child, Stefano, and drew him into a corner.

"Are you studying computers, Stefano?"

"Yes," the boy looked at me with concern, as if I were about to attack him. Why were teenagers so weird?

"Do you have a computer hooked up to the Internet in your room?"

"Yes, Aunt," he smiled with pride, relieved that his aunt wasn't going to hurt him.

"I need you to do me a favor."

Stefano and I spent the whole morning locked up in his room, drinking Coke, glued to the monitor. He was a bright boy who moved around the Internet and handled search engines with ease. By lunchtime, after giving my nephew a handsome sum of money for the terrific job he did (didn't Pierantonio tell me to buy information?), something inside me had suddenly clicked. All those hours of my poring over research, of searching for meaning in the scars on that poor dead Ethiopian's corpse, had finally paid off with the clarity I had suddenly been blessed with.

And just like that, as though a light had been turned on within me, I knew who my Ethiopian man was, how he had died, and why the various Christian churches were so interested in him. It was so serious a matter that my legs were beyond trembling as I descended the stairs for lunch.

CHAPTER

2

J got back to Rome Monday night,
plunged into a sea of confusion and
fear, for I would have never imagined I
was capable of disobeying. Against the
wishes of the church, I'd retrieved important data
by unorthodox means. It made me feel uncertain
and intimidated, as if at any moment a divine
bolt of lightning would strike me. Following the
rules is always simpler: by doing so, you avoid the
remorse and blame and uncertainty that comes
with disobeying them. Above all, you feel proud
of your work. In my case, I felt no satisfaction
with myself or with my wretched snooping
around. How was I going to face Glauser-Röist?
Blame was written all over my face; and he, of all
people, was sure to notice.

That night I prayed for consolation and forgiveness. I'd have given anything to forget what I
knew and get back to the moment when I'd said
to Pierantonio, "I'm ready." I wanted to simply
reverse that phrase and recover my inner peace.
But that was impossible. The next morning when
I closed the door to my office and saw the sad
silhouette taped up, so deliberately covered with

notes and scribbled labels, I recalled the Ethiopian man's name: Abi-Ruj Iyasus. Poor Abi-Ruj, I thought to myself as I slowly approached the table where the terrible photographs of his battered body lay. He'd died a horrible death you wouldn't wish on anybody, though surely in keeping with the magnitude of his sin.

My nephew Stefano, his index fingers poised at the keyboard and his brown hair falling into his eyes, had asked me what I'd been looking for when I forcefully asked him for help, and I responded, "Accidents... Any accident in which a young Ethiopian man died."

"When did it happen?"

"I don't know."

"Where did it happen?"

"I don't know that either."

"Sounds like you don't know anything."

"That's right." I had shrugged.

With only that to go on, he began scouring thousands of documents. He had several windows going at the same time, each one displaying a different browser: Virgil, Yahoo Italia, Google, Lycos, Dogpile, and others. We ran searches using words like *accident* and *Ethiopian*, taking advantage of the vast number of Web pages. We did so in English, too. Thousands of documents turned up on Stefano's computer. He rejected them as soon as he verified that the accident in question had nothing to do with the Ethiopian man mentioned several paragraphs into the article, when he found out that the Ethiopian was eighty years old, or when he read that the accident and the Ethiopian that popped up were actually from the days of Alexander the Great. None had anything to do with what I was looking for. In a virtual folder called "Aunt Ottavia," he saved only those pages that held some remote tie to what we felt may be useful in our search.

"I have some good news, Dr. Salina."

"Oh, yeah? Tell me...," I murmured, not the least bit interested.

Stefano logged off the Internet near lunchtime, and we started to review the material we had filed. After the first time through, we eliminated all Italian documents. After the second meticulous screening, we finally got what we were looking for: five press reports published between Wednesday, February 16, and Sunday the 20th of the same year. An English edition of the Greek newspaper *Kathimerini,* a bulletin from the Athens News Agency, and three Ethiopian publications called *Press Digest, Ethiopian News Headlines,* and *Addis Tribune.*

The story said that on Tuesday, February 15, a small rented Cessna 182 had crashed into Mount Helmos, on the Peloponnese peninsula in southern Greece, at 9:35 p.m. The dead included the pilot, a twenty-three-year-old Greek man who'd just gotten his pilot's license, and the passenger, Ethiopian Abi-Ruj Iyasus, age thirty-five. According to the flight plan given to airport authorities in Alexandroupoli, in northern Greece, the plane was headed for the Kalamata Airport, on the Peloponnesus, and was due to land at 9:45 p.m. Ten minutes before, without any SOS, the plane flew over the heavily wooded Mount Helmos at an altitude of 7,736 feet, abruptly descended 2,000 feet, then vanished from the radar. Firemen in nearby Kertezi were immediately alerted by airport authorities. They hurried to the site and found the wreck, still smoking, scattered over a radius of a kilometer. The dead pilot and passenger were hanging from nearby trees. The story was then picked up in Greek newspapers, the report was corroborated by correspondents they had in the area. In the *Kathimerini* there was also a very blurry snapshot of the accident where I was able to make out Abi-Ruj on a stretcher. It was hard to recognize him, but I had no doubt it was the same man I had so intensely studied. His face was etched in my memory after having looked at his autopsy photographs over a thousand times. The correspondent from the Athens News Agency described in detail both men's mortal wounds. Apparently, the scarification hidden under his clothes had gone unnoticed.

"Good morning, Doctor."

"Good morning, Captain," I answered without looking up at him. I couldn't take my eyes off poor Abi-Ruj.

An offhanded sentence in the Athens News Agency report grabbed my attention. The firemen found, lying on the ground at the feet of Iyasus's cadaver, as if it had slipped out of his hands after taking his last breath, an ornate silver box which, they surmised, had opened on impact, and strange pieces of wood had fallen out of it.

The Ethiopian newspapers gave very few details about the accident, mentioning it only in passing. They requested readers' help to locate the relatives of Abi-Ruj Iyasus, who was a member of the Oromo tribe, a community of shepherds and farmers in central Ethiopia. They sent their request to refugee camps (the country was going through a devastating famine), but additionally—and this was the strangest part—to the religious authorities of Ethiopia, since they found "very valuable holy relics" in the deceased's possession.

"You might want to turn around and take a look at what I have to show you," the captain insisted.

The door to the lab behind me opened and closed softly. It was Glauser-Röist.

I grudgingly turned around. The Swiss man's craggy face wore an enormous smile. In his hand was a very large photograph. I took it with all the indifference I was capable of mustering and cast a disdainful glance at him. My expression changed immediately once I realized what I was looking at. Within the image you could make out a wall of red granite, brightly lit by the sun. On the wall were two small crosses within rectangular frames topped off by small seven-pointed radiate crowns.

"Our crosses!" I uttered enthusiastically.

"Five of the most powerful computers in the Vatican have been working nonstop for four days to come up with what you have in your hand."

"Just exactly what do I have in my hand?" I would have jumped for joy, except at my age that might have been fatal. "Tell me, Captain, what do I have in my hand?"

"A photograph representing a portion of the southwestern wall of the Orthodox monastery of Saint Catherine of Sinai."

I could see that Glauser-Röist was as happy as I was. His grin was earnest and wide, although his body didn't move a millimeter. He was as steady as ever. His hands were shoved deep into his pants pockets, and his face expressed a joy I never would have expected from a man like him.

"Saint Catherine of Sinai?" I whispered. "The Monastery of Saint Catherine of Sinai?"

"You got it. Saint Catherine of Sinai. In Egypt."

I couldn't believe it. Saint Catherine of Sinai was a mythical place for any paleographer. Its library, while inaccessible, was the most valuable repository in the world of ancient codices, second only to the Vatican's. And like the Vatican Library, it too was shrouded in mystery.

"What does Saint Catherine of Sinai have to do with our Ethiopian man?" I asked, puzzled.

"I don't have the slightest idea. In fact, I'd hoped we'd work on that today."

"Well, then, let's get to it," I agreed, pushing my glasses up onto the bridge of my nose.

The bowels of the Vatican Library contained a large number of books, memoirs, compendiums, and treaties on the monastery. Yet most people didn't have the vaguest idea that such an important place existed: an Orthodox temple located right at the foot of Mount Sinai, in the heart of the Egyptian desert, surrounded by sacred summits and built around a site of outstanding religious importance. It was the place where Yahweh, in the form of the burning bush, gave Moses the Ten Commandments.

The history of the temple was legendary. Around the fourth century, in 337, Empress Ielen, the mother of Emperor Constantine, built a beautiful sanctuary in that valley. From that moment, numerous Christian pilgrims began to journey there. Among those first pilgrims was the famous Galician nun Egeria, who traveled through the Holy Land from the Passover of 381 until the Passover of 384. In her skillfully narrated *Itinerarium*, Egeria recounted that where the monastery of Saint Catherine of Sinai would later be erected, a group of hermits tended to a small temple whose apse protected the sacred bush, which was still alive back then. Because the temple was located on the road connecting Alexandria to Jerusalem, the hermits were constantly attacked by ferocious groups of desert nomads. Two centuries later, Emperor Justinian and his wife, Empress Theodora, ordered the Byzantine builder Stefano de Aila to construct a fort to protect the holy place from raids. According to the most recent investigations, the walls were reinforced over the centuries and to a large extent even rebuilt. Of the original building, only the southwest wall remained, and it was adorned with the same strange crosses that were scattered on our Ethiopian's skin. The primitive sanctuary was repaired and improved by Stefano de Aila in the fourth century; since then, it has drawn the admiration and amazement of scholars and pilgrims throughout the world.

In 1844 a German researcher was admitted to the monastery's library, where he discovered the extremely famous Codex Sinaiticus, the complete copy of the New Testament, the oldest copy ever found, which was dated to the fourth century. Of course, this German researcher, one Tischendorff, stole the codex and sold it to the British Museum, where it still remains and where I had the opportunity to eagerly observe it because, at the time, I was working on its twin, the Codex Vaticanus, which was from the same century and most likely of the same origin. The simultaneous study of both codices would have allowed me to carry out one of most important works of paleography ever. But it was never made possible.

By the end of the day, we had managed to gather a thick, very interesting stack of documents about the strange orthodox monastery, but we still hadn't clarified what the relationship was between the scarification on our Ethiopian man and the southwest wall of Saint Catherine's.

My mind was used to quickly synthesizing and extracting relevant data from a tangle of information, so I had already concocted a complex theory based on the elements that repeated themselves in the history in front of us. Since I was not supposed to know a good part of it, I could not share my ideas with Captain Glauser-Röist, but I was dying to know if he had reached similar conclusions. Deep down inside, I burned with the desire to squash him with my deductions and show him who was the cleverest and most intelligent of the two. In my next confession, Father Pintonello was going to have to impose a very stern penitence to expiate my pride.

"Very well, we're done," Glauser-Röist said casually as the afternoon waned. Satisfied, he slammed closed a heavy volume on architecture which he had been studying.

"What's done?"

"We are, Doctor—our work. We're done."

"Finished?" I mumbled. My eyes were wide with surprise. Of course I knew my role in the investigation would end sooner or later, but it hadn't crossed my mind that I would be eliminated with such matter-of-factness and at such an interesting point.

Glauser-Röist looked at me for a long time with what little sympathy and understanding his rocklike nature allowed. It was as if over our twenty days together, a mysterious bond of trust and camaraderie had been created between us which I hadn't noticed.

"We have completed the work they assigned us, Doctor. There is nothing more for you to do."

I was so disconcerted I couldn't speak. I felt the knot in my throat tightening till I could hardly breathe. Glauser-Röist observed me at length. I grew so pale he must have thought I was about to faint.

"Dr. Salina," murmured the embarrassed Swiss Guard, "are you ill?"

Physically, I felt perfectly fine, but my brain was ticking away like a machine. I concentrated, hoping that my dissatisfaction would contain itself to the confines of my mind and not extend to the rest of my body. "What do you mean, there's nothing more for me to do?"

"I'm sorry, Doctor," he whispered. "You received an assignment and now it's done."

I opened my eyes wide and looked at him. "Why are they shutting me out, Captain?"

"Monsignor Tournier told you why before we started, Doctor. Don't you remember? Your paleographic knowledge was essential to interpret the symbols on the Ethiopian man's body. This is just one small part of the ongoing investigation which far surpasses anything you can imagine. Unfortunately, I am not authorized to tell you a thing, Doctor. Regrettably you must step aside and resume your usual work. Try to forget what has happened over the past twenty days."

Well, well! It was all or nothing for me. Of course, when facing such a powerful and unalterable hierarchy as the Catholic Church you either save yourself or get thrown to the lions.

"Do you realize, Captain," I enunciated clearly so he didn't miss one syllable of what I was saying, "that Abi-Ruj Iyasus, our Ethiopian, is but a small cog in a large gear that has been set in motion? For some reason, someone is looking to steal sacred relics from the True Cross. Do you realize, Captain?"

My God, what desperation was pushing me to talk that way! I was like an old actor in a Greek play speaking to the Gods.

"Behind all this there must be a religious sect that considers itself the descendants of traditions that go back to origins of the eastern Roman Empire, Byzantium, Emperor Constantine, and his mother, Saint Helen, who not only ordered the construction of Saint Catherine of Sinai, but also discovered the True Cross of Christ in 326?"

With its gray eyes, Glauser-Röist's colorless face, framed by the blond and metallic reflections of his head and jaws, looked even more like one of those ferocious white marble heads of Hercules on display in the Capitolinos Museums of the Palazzo Nuovo in Rome. But I didn't give him time to take a breath.

"Have you given any thought to the fact that on Abi-Ruj Iyasus's body we found seven Greek letters, $\Sigma TA Y PO\Sigma$, that signify "cross," seven different crosses with seven different designs that reproduce those on the southwestern wall of the Monastery of Saint Catherine of Sinai—and that each one of these crosses is topped by small seven-pointed radiate crowns? Do you realize that Abi-Ruj Iyasus was in possession of important relics of the True Cross at the moment he died?"

"That's enough!"

If looks could kill, I'd have been dead in an instant. The sparks that leaped from his eyes sent charges like flaming arrows in my direction.

"How do you know all that?" he roared, storming over to where I stood. He tried to intimidate me, but he didn't scare me. I was a Salina.

It wasn't especially hard to connect the strange pieces of wood found by firemen at the feet of Iyasus's cadaver with those "very holy and valuable relics" mentioned by the Ethiopian newspapers. What wooden relics could mobilize the highest levels of the Vatican as well as the rest of the Christian churches? The scarifications on Iyasus confirmed it. According to a legend generally accepted by ecclesiastic students, Saint Helen went looking for the Holy Sepulchre and discovered the True

Cross of Christ in 326, during a trip to Jerusalem. According to the well-known Golden Legend of Santiago of the Whirlpool,* as soon as Helen, then eighty years old, arrived in Jerusalem, she tortured the wisest Jews in the country until they confessed whatever they knew about the place where Christ had been crucified. Helen was relentless in her search, and soon she succeeded in wrenching the information out of them. Thus, they led her to the supposed location of Golgotha, the mount of Calvary—whose location still remains a mystery—where about two hundred years before, Emperor Adriano had had a temple built dedicated to Venus. Saint Helen ordered the temple to be demolished, and during the excavation they found three crosses. Jesus's, of course, and those of the two thieves crucified next to him. To find out which was the Savior's cross, Saint Helen ordered a dead man brought to the site and as soon as they placed the corpse on the True Cross, the man's body came back to life. After the miracle, the empress and her son built a lavish basilica on that site called the Basilica of the Holy Sepulchre, where they kept the relic. Over the centuries, numerous fragments of it were distributed throughout the world.

"How do you know all that?" the captain roared again, very angered, coming to within inches of me.

"Perhaps you and Monsignor Tournier thought I was an idiot?" I protested energetically. "Did you really think that by denying me information or keeping me in the dark you could use just the part of me that interested you? Come on, now, Captain. I won the Getty Prize for Paleographic Investigation. Twice!"

The Swiss man stood still for several, never-ending seconds, his eyes boring into me. Many thoughts must have passed through his mind at that moment: rage, powerlessness, fury, and finally, a flash of prudence.

Abruptly, and in utter silence, he gathered up the photographs, ripped down the silhouette of the Ethiopian, and put all the sketches,

---

*The Golden Legend (*Legendi di sancti vulgari storiado*), written in Latin in 1264, by the Dominican archbishop of Genoa, Santiago—or Jacobo—of the Whirlpool. Famous collection of the lives of saints, very popular in its time and in the following centuries.

notebooks, and images into his leather portfolio. He shut down the computer, and without saying a word—not even good-bye, not even turning around to look at me—he left my lab, slamming the door so hard the walls shook. At that moment, I knew I'd dug my own grave.

*H*ow can I explain what I felt the next morning? When I ran my ID through the card scanner, a red light blinked on the small screen and a siren went off. Everyone in the foyer of the Classified Archives turned to look as if I were some criminal. It was one of the most humiliating moments of my life. Two security guards, dressed as civilians and wearing dark sunglasses, stood in front of me before I even had time to beg God to let the earth swallow me. Very politely, they asked me to accompany them. I closed my eyes so tight they hurt. No, this couldn't be happening; surely it was a terrible nightmare and I would wake up at any moment. But the pleasant voice of one of those men brought me back to reality: I was to go with them to the office of the prefect, Reverend Father Ramondino.

Already knowing what the Reverend Father was going to say, I was on the verge of refusing to follow them and just begging the guards to let me go back home. But I didn't say a word, and accompanied them docilely, more dead than alive, knowing that my years of work in the Vatican were over.

It's simply painful to record what happened in the prefect's office. In a very correct and amiable conversation, I was officially informed that my contract was terminated. (I would be paid, of course, to the last lira what the law specifies in these cases.) The Reverend Father reminded me that my vow of silence concerning anything surrounding the archives and the library remained in effect until my death. He also said that he had been very satisfied with my services and hoped, with all his heart, that I found another job in keeping with my many talents. Finally, slamming his hand against the table, he told me that I would be seriously sanctioned, even excommunicated, if I said one word about the subject of the Ethiopian man. With a firm handshake, he bid me farewell at the door of his office, where Dr. William Baker, the secretary of the archives, was patiently waiting for me with a medium-size box in his hands.

"Your things, Doctor," he said with a contemptuous look.

I knew I'd become a pariah, somebody the Vatican never wanted to see again. I would be ostracized and would have to leave Vatican City.

"Will you give me your ID and key, please?" concluded Dr. Baker, handing me the box that contained my meager personal possessions. The closed box was sealed with wide, gray industrial tape. For an instant I wondered if it also contained the red hand Isabella had made me.

But the worst was yet to come. Two days later, the general director of my order summoned me to the main office. Of course, she didn't receive me herself; she was always loaded down with a thousand responsibilities. The assistant director, Sister Giulia Sarolli, explained that I had to leave the Piazza delle Vaschette apartment—as well as the community. I was being sent with great haste to our house in County Connaught, Ireland, where I would be made charge of the archives and old libraries in various monasteries throughout the area. There, Sister Sarolli added, I would find the spiritual peace I so needed. I was to present myself in Connaught next week, between Monday, March 27, and Friday, the 31st. Sister Sarolli asked me when I'd like to arrive in Ireland. Perhaps I wished to spend some time in Sicily, saying good-bye to my family before I left? I turned down the offer with a simple nod. I was so demoralized I couldn't even speak.

I had no idea what I would say to my mother. I felt an immense pain for her, she had always been so proud of her daughter, Ottavia. My leaving the Vatican was going to hurt her so much, and I felt responsible. What would Pierantonio say? And Giacoma? One good thing about my exile was that I'd have my sister Lucia close by, in London. She would help me bear my failure. Any way you looked at it, I was a failure. I had failed my family completely. They would certainly not love me less for leaving the Vatican for a remote, lost part of Ireland, but I knew that all my brothers and sisters, and especially my mother, would no longer view me the same way. Poor Mama. She was always boasting about Pierantonio and me. Now she'd have to forget about me and speak only of Pierantonio.

That night, the Friday of Lent, Ferma, Margherita, Valeria, and I
went to the basilica of Saint John of Letran to pray the Via Crucis and
to take part in the penitential celebration. Inside those walls, so filled
with history, I felt diminished, shrunken. I told God that I accepted the
punishment for my enormous sin of pride. I got what I truly deserved.
I had felt superior for easily obtaining something that had been denied
to me. Invested with this power, I had obtained my goal. Now, bent and
beaten, I humbly asked for forgiveness, seeking penance for what I had
done. I knew full well it was a belated repentance, that it could no longer
change my punishment. I was afraid of God, and accepted the Via Crucis as a test of divine mercy that allowed me to share with Jesus Christ
the pain he suffered at Calvary.

And as if all that was happening weren't enough, as if echoing the
pain gnawing inside me, Etna, the volcano which we Sicilians know so
well, and always watch with anxiety and fear, erupted spectacularly. A sea
of lava descended its slopes throughout the night until dawn, its mouth
spitting fire and ashes 3,200 meters into the air. Fortunately, Palermo is
pretty far away from the volcano, but the city still suffered electricity
outages and water shortages. I called home, very worried, and found
everyone awake, waiting for news updates on the local radio and televi-
sion. They calmed me down; no one was in any danger, the situation was
under control. I should have told them right then that I was leaving
Rome and the Vatican, bound for Ireland, but I didn't dare. I was afraid
of their disappointment and comments. When I was settled in Connaught, I'd think of a way to convince them that the change was a positive one, and that I was delighted with my new post.

The following Thursday, at one in the afternoon, I got on the plane
headed for my exile. Only Margherita came to see me off. She gave me two
sad kisses and earnestly begged me not to resist God's will, to try to adapt
joyfully to this new situation and to fight my strong temperament. It was
the saddest, most agonizing flight of my life. I didn't watch the movie and
didn't taste a single bite of the plastic food they set in front of me. I labored over what I'd tell my sister Lucia when I called her and what I'd say
to my family when I found the strength in me to talk to them again.

Nearly two and a half hours later, at five in the afternoon, Ireland time, we landed at the Dublin airport. We passengers, tired and on edge, entered through the international terminal to claim our luggage from the conveyor belts. I clutched my enormous suitcase, sighed deeply, and walked toward the exit, looking around for the sisters who were supposed to meet me.

I would probably spend the next twenty or thirty years in that faraway country. With a little luck, I told myself without conviction, I would adapt and be happy. As I listened to my train of thoughts, I knew perfectly well that I was lying to myself. That country was my grave, the end of my professional ambitions, projects, and investigations. Why had I been so stupid? Why had I tried so hard over the years, getting one degree after another, one prize after another, one doctorate after another? All that wasn't worth anything in that miserable town in Connaught, where I was sure to live until buried in the ground. I looked around apprehensively, asking myself how long I could stand my shameful situation, when I recalled with dark sorrow that I shouldn't keep my Irish sisters waiting.

To my surprise, there was no one from the Order of the Blessed Virgin Mary there to meet me. Instead, two young priests dressed in old-fashioned high clerical collars, soutanes, and black gabardine rushed up to take my luggage as they asked me in English if I was Sister Ottavia Salina. When I answered yes, they seemed relieved. They put my bag in their cart. One of the priests charged at it with outstretched arms as if it were alive and in need of tackling, while the other priest explained I had to board a return flight to Rome that left within the hour.

I didn't understand what was going on; they knew even less. During the few minutes I spent with them, they explained that they were the bishop's secretaries, sent to escort me from one plane to another. The bishop himself had given them their orders. The diocese had found a return flight just in time, and the bishop had made the reservation on his cell phone.

That was all I saw of the Republic of Ireland: its international terminal. At eight in the evening, I was off again on my way back to Rome. I'd spent the entire day flying from one country to another, like a confused bird. To my surprise, once off the plane I was escorted to the airport's VIP area. In a private waiting room, seated in a plush seat, the cardinal vicar of Rome, His Eminence Carlo Colli, president of the Italian Episcopal Conference, was waiting for me. He got to his feet slowly and extended his hand with a certain degree of embarrassment.

"Eminence," I said startled, quickly kissing his ring.

"Sister Salina...," he stuttered. "Sister Salina... You don't know how much we regret what's happened."

"Eminence, as you can imagine, I don't have the slightest idea what you're talking about."

He was referring to the ill treatment I'd received from the Vatican and my order over the last eight days. I wasn't ready to cave in so easily, so I let him think I was afraid of some new disgrace for which they were having me return.

"Is it a member of my family?..." I suggested with a look of deep concern.

"No, no! Oh, no, no! Blessed Lord! Your family is in perfect health!"

"What is it then, Eminence?"

The vicar of Rome was sweating profusely despite the air-conditioning. "Accompany me to the city, please. Monsignor Tournier will explain."

We went directly to the street through a side door. Right outside waiting for us was one of those black limos with the license SCV (*Stato della Citta del Vaticano*) that all the cardinals use for their personal business, which many sly Romans joke about and have changed to *Se Cristo Videsse* (If Christ could see you). As I took a seat next to the cardinal, I told myself something very grave must have happened. Not just because they'd had me spend an entire day going from one end of Europe to the other and back, but also because they had sent the president of the Italian Episcopal Conference as my personal escort.

The limousine arrogantly crossed the streets of Rome, which were crowded with tourists even at that cold hour of the night. We entered Vatican City through the Piazza del Sant'Uffizio by way of the more discreet and lesser known Porta Petriano, just to the left of Saint

Peter's Square. The Swiss Guards acknowledged us and waved us through. On our left was the enormous Basilica of Saint Peter; as big as it is, it should certainly be considered as another basilica. We drove into the wide Piazza di Santa Marta, whose gardens and fountains we skirted till we came to the main door of the newly erected Domus Sanctae Martae.

The Domus Sanctae Martae (named for Saint Martha, Lazarus's sister, who gave Jesus lodging in her humble home in Betania) was a splendid palace whose recent construction had cost close to $20 million. It was built with the twofold plan to provide comfortable lodging to cardinals during the next conclave and to serve as a luxury hotel for illustrious visitors, prelates, or anyone willing to pay its extremely high room rates.

As we entered the brilliantly lit, sumptuously decorated foyer, His Eminence and I were received by an ancient porter who escorted us to the front desk. When the hotel manager recognized the cardinal, he rose from behind an elegant marble counter and very solicitously accompanied us through a wide vestibule toward an impressive stairway which descended toward a bar with several rooms. Through some open doors, I caught a glimpse of a library and the administrative offices of the Domus. On the other side, in the shadows, was a legislative room of gigantic proportions.

The manager, always one step in front of us, slightly contorted his body backward to signal the cardinal's preeminence. Leading us to an enclosure inside the bar where there were several private rooms, he knocked respectfully at the door to the first room and half opened it, indicating we could go in. As soon as he completed a dignified bow, he disappeared.

It was a meeting room with a small oval table surrounded by modern black high-backed chairs. Three people were waiting for us. Presiding over the meeting was Monsignor Tournier, seated at the far end, looking glum. To his right was Captain Glauser-Röist, stony as ever, although he looked slightly different from the last time I'd seen him. I observed him more carefully and, to my great surprise, discovered that he had a beautiful tan, like he'd been lying in the sun for a week at some beach resort on the Adriatic coast. Lastly, to Glauser-Röist's right was an individual I didn't know, who kept his head down and his hands tightly laced as if he were very nervous.

Monsignor Tournier and Glauser-Röist stood to greet us. I noticed the papal photographs that hung in a line on the cream-colored walls. All the pontiffs of this century, in their soutanes and white zucchettos, looked affable, with paternal smiles. I gracefully saluted Tournier, then came face-to-face with the toy soldier.

"We meet again, Captain. Do I have you to thank for my interesting round-trip flight to Dublin?"

Glauser-Röist smiled. For the first time since we'd known each other, he dared touch me, taking my elbow and guiding me to where the man I didn't recognize remained immobile. He looked startled to death as we walked directly toward him.

"Doctor, allow me to introduce Professor Farag Boswell. Professor…"

The man got to his feet so quickly that a pocket on his jacket hooked on the armrest of his chair and wrenched him to a halt. He wrestled a moment with his pocket until he managed to unhook himself and only after adjusting the tiny round glasses on his nose was he able to look directly into my eyes, smiling timidly. "Professor Boswell, allow me to introduce Dr. Ottavia Salina, of the Order of the Blessed Virgin Mary. She's the person I've been telling you about."

Professor Boswell shyly extended his hand to me. I shook it without much conviction. He was a very attractive man, around thirty-seven or thirty-eight, almost as tall as the Swiss Rock and dressed casually (blue polo shirt, sports jacket, loose and very wrinkled khaki pants, along with dirty, worn hiking boots). He blinked nervously as he tried to keep his glance from fleeing mine. He was an unusual man, this Professor Boswell: His skin was olive-toned, like that of an Arab, and his features were a perfect blend of Jewish morphology, but his surprisingly blond hair fell softly over his deep turquoise blue eyes. Strangely enough, I took to this surprising Professor Boswell from the first. Maybe it was his awkwardness (he kept his eyes vigilantly glued to the carpet) or his timidity (he completely lost his voice when he was forced to talk), but I was engulfed by a sudden wave of sympathy for him that surprised me.

We sat down around the table, although now the archbishop secretary ceded the head chair to Cardinal Colli. Across from me were Glauser-Röist and Professor Boswell, and at my side sat the always agreeable Monsignor Tournier. Although I was dying to know what was going on, I decided I should act indifferently to the preposterously dramatic situation. Clearly, I was there because they needed me again. They had hurt me too much over the past week for me to lower myself and beg for an explanation.

The captain was the first to take the floor. "As you see, Doctor," he started in his baritone German voice, "events have taken an unexpected turn."

Glauser-Röist leaned over, picked up a leather pouch, opened it parsimoniously, and took out a package the size of a birthday cake wrapped in cream-colored linen. If I was expecting some gesture of reconciliation, well, that was it. Everyone present looked at the carefully wrapped package as if it were the most precious jewel in the world and followed it with their eyes as the captain gently slid it across the table and placed it right in front of me. I didn't know what to do. Except for me, it seemed like no one else was breathing.

"You may open it," Glauser-Röist said tentatively.

Many incoherent thoughts passed through my head, all at a dizzying speed. One thing was for sure: If I opened that bundle, I would once again become a cheap tool; easily used and replaceable. They had brought me back to Rome because they needed me, but I decided right then that I no longer wanted to collaborate.

"No, thank you." I pushed the package back toward Glauser-Röist. "I'm not at all interested."

The Rock fell back into his chair and adjusted the collar of his jacket with a long look, a mixture of respect and anger flashed in his eyes. "Everything has changed, Doctor. Trust me."

"Would you kindly tell me why? If I recall correctly (and I have a very good memory), the last time I saw you, exactly eight days ago, you were slamming shut the door to my office as you left in a huff. And what a coincidence—the very next day, I was fired."

"Let me explain, Kaspar," Monsignor Tournier cut him off and raised an admonishing hand in the Rock's direction as he turned toward me. There was a melodramatic tone of false contrition in his voice. "What the captain couldn't reveal to you is that...I was responsible for your firing. Yes, I know it is hard to hear..." I thought to myself that the world wasn't ready to hear Monsignor Tournier admit he had done something wrong. "Captain Glauser-Röist received very strict orders from me, I should add. When you revealed that you knew all the details of the investigation, he was obliged to...how should I put it...inform me, yes. You should know he lobbied energetically against your...firing. Today I'm here to tell you how much I lament the Church's mistaken attitude toward you. It was, without a doubt...a mistake, a deplorable mistake."

"The fact is, Sister Salina," Cardinal Colli said, "Captain Glauser-Röist has taken over this investigation, appointed by the cardinal secretary of state, His Most Reverend Eminence Angelo Sodano himself. Monsignor Tournier is no longer at the helm."

"The first two things I asked for," added Glauser-Röist, arching his eyebrows impatiently, "are that you immediately be included in the investigation as a member of my team and that your contract with the Classified Archives and the Vatican Library be reinstated."

"And so it was done!" confirmed Cardinal Colli.

"So, Doctor," the Swiss Rock summed up, "if you are in agreement with all that has been done to rectify our mistake, open the damned package!"

He gave the bundle a shove that sent it skating back to my side of the table. An exclamation of horror escaped from the throat of Professor Boswell.

"I'm sorry, I'm a bit unnerved," the captain apologized.

I was so disconcerted I didn't know what to think. I put my hands on the white linen package, in suspense, indecisive. I had recovered my job at the Classified Archives, I was no longer banished from the Vatican, and I was a member in good standing of Glauser-Röist's investigation team on a mission I longed for from the start. It was far more than I could have hoped for that morning when I got out of bed. As I weighed this good news, something tickled my palms, causing me to rub them and brush off some irritating grains of sand that were stuck to my skin. Surprised, I looked at the tiny white grains that fell like snow over the dark burnished wood on the table.

Glauser-Röist pointed. "That's no way to treat holy sand from the Sinai."

I looked at him as if I'd never seen him before. My surprise had no limits. "From the Sinai?" I repeated automatically, stunned, but trying to keep my excitement closely guarded.

"More precisely, from the monastery of Saint Catherine of Sinai."

"Do you mean…you went to Saint Catherine of Sinai?" I reproached him, pointing my right index finger at him. Incredible. While I was having the worst week of my life, he had been in a place that, by rights as a paleographer, was my due to visit. The Swiss Rock ignored my anger completely.

"That's correct, Doctor," he replied, returning to his more neutral tone. "I'm sure you'll have many questions for me. I assure you that I—" he stopped short and turned to Professor Boswell, who started to shrink down in his seat—"that *we* will answer all your questions without holding back any information."

I was annoyed, of course; still, I couldn't help notice Glauser-Röist's new attitude toward Monsignor Tournier and Cardinal Colli. During our first meeting, the captain had stayed discreetly in the background, attentive to Tournier's orders. This time he seemed completely oblivious to them, as if they were shadows against a wall.

"Okay, okay…" I raised my arms and let them fall with a heavy gesture of resignation. "Let's start with Abi Ruj Iyasus and end with this sand-filled package from the Sinai."

Glauser-Röist raised his eyes to the ceiling and took a deep breath before beginning. "Well, let's see. The accident of Cessna 182 last February 15 in Greece was the real beginning of this story. At the feet of Abi-Ruj Iyasus's corpse, the firemen found a very old silver box, decorated with enamel and gems that contained strange pieces of wood with no apparent value. Since the old box did in fact look like a reliquary of some sort, the civilian authorities consulted the Greek Orthodox Church, to see if they could offer any helpful information. The Orthodox clergy were taken by an urgent surprise when they verified that one of those dry wooden fragments was nothing less than the famous *Lignum Crucis** from the Docheiariou Monastery on Mount Athos. They quickly alerted all the other Orthodox Eastern patriarchates. One after another they verified that all the reliquaries that housed fragments of the True Cross were empty, so they decided to contact us Catholic heretics, since we are in possession of the majority of *Ligna Crucis* in the world."

The captain stretched in his armchair. "All this was carried out very quickly. Barely twenty-four hours after the accident, His Most Reverend Eminence, the secretary of state, was contacted by the Holy Synod of the Greek Church. As discreetly as possible, all the Catholic churches around the globe possessing *Ligna Crucis* were ordered to check their reliquaries, and soon, we found out that sixty-five percent of the cases were empty, including those that contained the most important fragments: the *Lignum* of Verona, the *Ligna* of Santa Croce in Gerusalemme and Saint John of Letran in Rome; those from Santo Toribio de Liebana and Caravaca de la Cruz in Spain; the one at the Cistercian monastery of Boissiere; and the one from the Sainte-Chapelle in France. Latin America had also been plundered: The important fragments from the Metropolitan Cathedral of Mexico and the one from the Brotherhood of Jesus of Nazarus from the consulate of Guatemala, among others, were also missing."

I've never felt the least devotion to relics. Nobody in my family was in favor of adoring exotic pieces of bones, fabric, or wood, not even my mother, whose tastes are Tridentine in matters of religion. Pierantonio was even less devoted to relics, and he lived in the Holy Land, where through his administration of many archeological excavations he was responsible for finding more than one body or object with a saintly scent. Nonetheless, the story the captain narrated frightened me. Many

*From Latin, log or wood of the Cross. The name is given to all relics of the wood from the True Cross.

devout people place their faith in such sacred objects, and under no circumstance should there be a lack of respect for the beliefs of these individuals. Over the years the Church itself had abandoned such dubious practices, but there still existed a very strong movement toward the veneration of relics. The most surprising thing was that it wasn't the mummified arm of Saint So-and-So, nor of the rotting body of Saint What-You-May-Call-It. We're talking about Christ's Cross, the wood on which the body of the Savior supposedly suffered torture and death. Even if all the *Ligna Crucis* in the world were to be considered frauds, it was still strange that those pieces of wood would be the only focus of a gang of fanatics.

"The second part of this story, Doctor, is the discovery of the scarifications on Iyasus's body. While the Greek and Ethiopian authorities unsuccessfully investigated the man's life, His Holiness, through the secretary of state and petitions to the churches of the East, decided we ought to figure out who was stealing the *Ligna Crucis* and why. If I recall correctly, the pope's order was to stop the removals immediately, recover the stolen relics, find the thieves, and bring them to justice. As soon as the Greek police discovered the strange scars on the Ethiopian, they passed that information along to His Beatitude the archbishop of Athens, Christodoulos Paraskeviades. Even though relations with Rome are not very good, he requested that a special agent be present at the autopsy. I was that agent, and you already know firsthand what followed."

I hadn't eaten all day and I was beginning to feel the unpleasant effects of hypoglycemia. It must have been very late, but I didn't want to look at the clock. I'd gotten up at seven in the morning, taken a plane all the way to Ireland, and returned to Rome that very night. I was so exhausted even my breath ached.

There was still so much of the story left to tell, I thought, looking at the linen shroud in front of me. Despite my curiosity, I knew that if I didn't eat something soon, I was going to faint onto the table. So I took advantage of the captain's sudden silence to ask if we could take a moment to eat since I was suddenly feeling dizzy. There was a murmur of unanimous approval. Clearly no one else had had dinner. His Eminence Cardinal Colli nodded to the captain, who took the package out of my hands and put it back in its leather pouch. He left the room for a few seconds and returned with the restaurant manager.

Shortly thereafter, an army of white-jacketed waiters entered the room pushing carts piled high with food. Once His Eminence blessed the food with a simple prayer, everyone, even timid Professor Boswell, pounced on the dishes. I was so hungry that, no matter how much I ingested, I wasn't satiated. I didn't lose my composure enough to make a pig of myself, but I ate as if I hadn't eaten in a month. Lack of sleep and fatigue were also probably to blame. Finally, seeing Monsignor Tournier's judgmental smile, I decided to stop.

During supper and as we were having an exquisite, steaming espresso, His Eminence Cardinal Colli described His Holiness's great hopes that we would resolve the complex problem of the theft. Relations with the churches of the East were worse than I could possibly imagine after so many years of fighting over ecumenicalism. If we recovered their *Ligna Crucis* and managed to put an end to the looting, perhaps the patriarch of Moscow and All the Russias, Alexy II, and the ecumenical patriarch of Constantinople, Bartolomeos I—the two most prominent Orthodox leaders in a pleiad of leaders and Orthodox Churches—might be willing to engage in a dialogue of reconciliation. Apparently, these two Christian leaders were facing off over the territory of the Orthodox churches in countries that were once part of the former Soviet Union; but together they formed an unshakable coalition against the Church of Rome on the subject of reclaiming Catholic-owned goods once seized by the Communist regime and which now were in Orthodox hands. In the end, all this was about the vulgar subject of property and power. The hierarchic structure of the Orthodox Christian churches (which did not exist, in theory at least) was a dense network formed by historic scheming and economic plots. The patriarchate of Moscow and All the Russias, in the hands of His Holiness Alexy II, sheltered under its wing the independent Orthodox churches of countries in Eastern Europe (Serbia, Bulgaria, Romania). The Patriarchate of Constantinople, led by His Very Divine Holiness Bartolomeos, harbored all the rest (in Greece, Syria, Turkey, Palestine, Egypt, as well as the very important Greco-Orthodox Church of America). Nevertheless, the divisions were not as clear as it would seem at first glance. Both factions had monasteries and temples in each other's sphere of influence. In any case, the Ecumenical Patriarchate of Constantinople, despite not having any power over them, "proceeded honorably" to represent all the rest of the Orthodox patriarchates of the world, including Alejo II, who seemed to totally ignore the millennia-old tradition, and was primarily concerned with preventing the Russian authorities from drawing the Catholic Church into their feud. Up till now, he had been quite successful.

In short, chaos. By resolving the theft, we would be able to help smooth out the rocky road to uniting all Christians. This would fuel the rickety motor of ecumenicalism.

For hours in that meeting room, Professor Boswell had not unglued his lips, except to eat. Yet, I could see that he listened very carefully to all the discussion. Once in a while, he slightly nodded or shook his head. He was the quietest man I'd ever met. He gave the impression that the world overwhelmed him. He was not comfortable in the least.

"Well, well... Professor Boswell," Monsignor Tournier blurted out as if he were reading my thoughts. "I believe it's your turn. Do you speak my language? Do you understand what I am saying? Do you understand any of what has been said here tonight?"

Glauser-Röist half closed his eyes and fixed his stare at the monsignor. Professor Boswell blinked. He cleared his throat in a desperate attempt to gain control over his voice.

"I understand perfectly, Monsignor," stammered the professor with a noticeable Arabic accent. "My mother was Italian."

"Ah, wonderful!" exclaimed Tournier, flashing a wide smile.

"In addition to Arabic and Coptic," Glauser-Röist clarified sharply, leaving no room for doubt, "Professor Farag Boswell has perfect command of Greek, Turkish, Latin, Hebrew, Italian, French, and English."

"Really, it's nothing," the professor hurried to explain, stuttering. "My paternal grandparents were Jewish, my mother Italian, and the rest of my family, including myself of course, are Coptic Catholics."

"But your last name is English, Professor," I said, confused, until I recalled that Egypt had once been a colony for the English.

"You'll like this, Doctor," said Glauser-Röist with a strange smile.

"Professor Boswell is the great-grandson of Dr. Kenneth Boswell, one of the archeologists who discovered the Byzantine city of Oxirrinco."

Oxirrinco! That was extremely interesting, but the best part was seeing Glauser-Röist in his role as the Egyptian's friend and champion.

"Is that true, Professor?" I asked him.

"It is, Doctor," confirmed Boswell with a shy nod. "My great-grandfather discovered Oxirrinco."

Oxirrinco, one of the most important capitals of Byzantine Egypt, lost for centuries, swallowed up by desert sands, was revitalized in 1895, thanks to the English archeologists Bernard Grenfell, Arthur Hunt, and Kenneth Boswell. It's considered the most important repository of Byzantine papyruses and a true library of lost work by classic authors.

"So, naturally, you are also an archeologist," affirmed Monsignor Tournier.

"True. I work..." He paused, rubbed his forehead, and corrected himself..."*worked* in the Greco-Roman Museum of Alexandria."

"You no longer work there?" I wanted to know, surprised.

"It's time for a new story, Doctor." Glauser-Röist leaned over again to the leather portfolio resting on the floor and again took out the package wrapped in linen, covered with sand from the Sinai. This time he didn't give it to me. He laid it carefully on the table. Holding it with both hands, he contemplated it with an intense metallic sparkle in his eyes. "That day after I left your lab, as you already know, I met with Monsignor Tournier, and caught a plane to Cairo. Professor Boswell was waiting for me at the airport, commissioned by the Copto-Catholic Church to serve as my interpreter and guide."

"His Beatitude Stephanos II Ghattas," interrupted Boswell, nervously placing his glasses at his side, "the patriarch of our church, personally asked me to do everything in my power to help the captain."

"The professor's help has been inestimable," added the captain. "We wouldn't have... *this*"—he pointed to the package with his chin—"if it weren't for him. When he picked me up at the airport, Boswell already had a vague idea of what I needed to do, and he put all his knowledge, resources, and contacts at my disposal."

"I'd like another cup of coffee," Cardinal Colli interrupted. "What about the rest of you?"

Monsignor Tournier glanced at his watch and nodded. Glauser-Röist got to his feet again and left the room. He took several minutes more than I could bear in that company, but finally he returned with an enormous tray of cups and a large coffee urn. As we served ourselves, the captain continued speaking.

Entering Saint Catherine of Sinai turned out to be a difficult task, explained Glauser-Röist. For tourists there is a limited schedule of visits and an even more limited route around the monastic enclosure. Since Glauser-Röist and Boswell didn't know what they were looking for or how to look for it, they needed plenty of freedom of movement and time. So, the professor concocted a risky plan that worked like a dream.

Even though in 1782 the Orthodox monastery of Saint Catherine of Sinai was freed from the Patriarchate of Jerusalem for vague reasons (it became known as the Orthodox Church of Mount Sinai), the patriarchate continued to have certain control over the monastery and its head, the abbot and archbishop. His Beatitude Stephanos II Ghattas used his influence to ask the patriarch of Jerusalem, Diodoros I, to send letters of introduction for Captain Glauser-Röist and Professor Boswell so that the monastery would willingly open its doors to them. Why should Saint Catherine accept the request from the Patriarchate of Jerusalem? Very simple—one of the visitors was an important German philanthropist interested in donating several million marks to the monastery. In fact, in 1997, desperately needing money, the monks had agreed for the first and only time in the history of the monastery to lend some of its most valuable treasures for a magnificent exhibition at the Metropolitan Museum in New York. The idea was not only to obtain the money the museum had paid handsomely for, but to attract investors to finance the restoration of their ancient library as well as their extraordinary, yet dilapidated, collection of icons.

Thus trying to find a way to get the investigation off the ground, Captain Glauser-Röist and Professor Boswell went to the offices of the

Orthodox Church of Mount Sinai in Cairo and told their barefaced lies. That same night they rented an all-terrain vehicle and set off across the desert to the monastery. The abbot, His Beatitude Archbishop Damianos, a kind, extremely intelligent man, received them in person and offered them his hospitality for as long as they wanted. That same afternoon, they began to inspect the abbey.

"I saw the crosses, Doctor," murmured Glauser-Röist, clearly moved. "I saw them. Just like those on the body of our Ethiopian. Seven altogether. The same ones in the scarifications. There they were, on the wall, waiting for me."

And I didn't get to see them, I thought. I didn't get to see them because you all left me on the sidelines. I didn't get to go to the Egyptian desert and jump over dunes in an all-terrain vehicle because Monsignor Tournier decided to fire me for knowing more than I should. I was sick with anger.

"I know I shouldn't be saying this out loud, but I really envy you, Captain," I heard myself say, gulping down my coffee. "I would've liked to see those crosses. They're as much mine as yours."

"You're right. I would have liked for you to see them, too."

"Sister," added Professor Boswell, "it may not be of any consolation…" He blinked and pushed his glasses as high as he could up on his nose. "But you would not have been able to do much in Saint Catherine. The monks don't readily admit women into the enclosure. They're not as radical as the community of the Mount Athos, in Greece, where not even female animals are permitted, but I don't believe they would have let you spend the night in the abbey or stroll around the place, as we were fortunate enough to have done. The Orthodox monks are similar to Muslims in their regard for women."

"That's true," echoed Glauser-Röist. "The professor is telling the truth."

I wasn't surprised. In general, all religions of the world discriminate against women, either relegating them to a puzzling second class or legitimizing their abuse and mistreatment. It's really a shame that nobody seems to want to find a solution to it.

The Orthodox monastery of Saint Catherine was located in the heart of the Wadi ed-Deir Valley, at the foot of a spur of Mount Sinai. It was one of the most beautiful places on earth, a rare harmonious collaboration between nature and mankind. A rectangular perimeter, walled in by Justinian in the fourth century, it sheltered unimaginable treasures and an endless beauty that struck dumb those astonished few who were admitted into its interior. The dryness of the desert and the barren, red granite mountains protected it but didn't prepare pilgrims for what they were to find inside the monastery: an impressive Byzantine basilica, numerous chapels, an immense refectory, the second most important library in the world, the number one collection of beautiful religious icons, all decorated with carved wood, marble inlay, silver with gold leaf, precious stones... A feast for the senses and an unequaled exaltation of faith that couldn't be found anywhere else in the world.

"For a couple of days, the professor and I roamed all over the monastery in search of anything that had anything to do with the Ethiopian man. The presence of the seven crosses in the southwestern wall was beginning to lose its meaning. I asked myself if this was simply a ridiculous coincidence and if we were headed in the wrong direction. But the third day..." His mouth widened with a huge smile. He turned to the professor, seeking his agreement. "The third day they finally introduced us to Father Sergio, the head of the library and the museum of icons."

"The monks are very cautious," explained the professor almost in a whisper. "That's why they made us wait two days before showing us their most precious objects. They don't trust a soul."

At that point, I finally looked at my watch: It was exactly three a.m. I couldn't hold out any longer, not even after two cups of coffee. But the Swiss Rock acted as if he hadn't seen my gesture or my spent face and continued unperturbed.

"Father Sergio came for us around seven in the evening after dinner, and guided us through the narrow alleys of the monastery, lighting our way with an old oil lamp. He was a heavy-set, taciturn monk who wore a pointed wool cap instead of the black cap like the rest."

"And he was constantly tugging at his beard," added the professor, as if the gesture had struck him as very amusing.

"When we arrived at the library, the father took from the pleats of his habit an iron ring loaded down with keys. He opened one lock after another until he'd opened seven.

"Again seven," I let slip out, half asleep, remembering the letters and the crosses on Abi-Ruj's body.

"The doors opened with a loud screech. The interior was as dark as the inside of a wolf's mouth, but the worse part was the smell. You can't even imagine the smell... It was nauseating."

"It smelled like rotten leather and old rags," clarified Boswell.

"We inched along in the shadows along rows of bookcases full of Byzantine manuscripts whose letters were decorated with gold leaf which sparkled in the light of Father Sergio's lamp. Finally, we stopped in front of a display cabinet. 'This is where we keep some of the oldest codices. You can take a look at whatever you want,' said the monk, but I thought it was joke. It was so dark in there, you couldn't see a thing!"

"That was when I tripped over something and bumped into the corner of one of the cabinets," interjected the professor.

"Yes, that's right."

"I said to Father Sergio that if they wanted the foreign guest to give them money for the restoration of the library"—he cleared his throat forcefully and again pushed his glasses in place—"the least they could do was show him around in the light of day and hold nothing back. Father Sergio said that they had to protect the manuscripts because they'd been robbed before, and that we should be grateful that he was even showing us the most valuable things in the monastery. But since I kept protesting, the monk finally walked over to one corner of the room and flipped a light switch."

"The library has a glaring electric light, but it's never used," the captain explained. "The monks of Saint Catherine of Sinai protected their manuscripts by only showing them to those who get previous authorization from the archbishop himself. Furthermore, they always show them in the dark so no one can get a clear idea of what's there. When some researcher shows up with permission, they take him to the library at night and keep him in the shadows while he consults the manuscript that interests him. That way, he never suspects what's around him. I imagine that the robbery of the Codex Sinaiticus by Tischendorff in 1844 left a painful and indelible mark on them."

"Our robbery will leave the same mark, Captain," murmured Boswell.

"You stole a manuscript from the monastery?" I asked alarmed, waking abruptly from the sweet stupor I'd been lulled into by the story.

The most profound silence answered my question. I looked at them, one by one, confused, but the four faces around me were blank, wax masks.

"Captain...," I insisted, "answer me, please. Did you steal a manuscript from Saint Catherine of Sinai?"

"Judge for yourself," he said coldly, pushing toward me the linen-wrapped package. "Then tell me you wouldn't have done the same in my place."

Unable to react, I looked at the wrapper as if were a rat or a cockroach, not daring to put my hands on it.

"Open it," ordered Monsignor Tournier abruptly.

I turned to Cardinal Colli for protection, but he was staring at the floor. As for Professor Boswell, he was cleaning his glasses with the hem of his jacket.

"Sister Salina," demanded Monsignor Tournier's impatient voice again, "I just told you to open that package. Did you not hear me?"

I had no choice but to do what he asked of me. It wasn't the time to get cold feet or have an attack of conscience. The white linen cloth turned out to be a bag, and as soon as I managed to loosen the ribbons that sealed it, I began to make out the corner of an ancient codex. I couldn't believe my eyes. My confusion grew as I extracted the heavy volume from its package. Finally, I held in my hands a thick, bulky primitive square-shaped Byzantine manuscript. Its wood binding was covered in leather and embossed with the seven crosses of Saint Catherine—two columns of three on each side and one below, aligned with the crosses on the lower ends. The monogram of Constantine was on the upper central part and below it was the seven-letter Greek word that seemed to be the key: ΣΤΑΥΡΟΣ (STAUROS), or *cross*. Looking at the codex, my hands trembled so badly I nearly sent it tumbling to the floor. I tried to get ahold of myself but couldn't. I suppose that was largely due to how exhausted I was, but Monsignor Tournier had to snatch the volume from me to safeguard its integrity.

I remember that at that very moment I heard something that took me completely by surprise: Captain Glauser-Röist was laughing for the very first time.

*I*t seems obvious that it's not in our hands to revive the dead; that thaumaturgical ability belongs to God only. We cannot make blood circulate through dry veins again nor thoughts return to a lifeless brain. We can, however, recover the pigments on parchments that time has erased and, thus, the ideas and thoughts that someone had shaped and once articulated onto the vellum. It is a marvel of science to breathe life into the sleeping, lethargic spirit of a medieval codex.

As a paleographer, I could read, decipher, and interpret any written ancient text. What I couldn't do was guess what had been written on those stiff, translucent, yellowed parchments whose letters, worn away over the centuries, were practically illegible.

The Iyasus Codex, named in honor of our Ethiopian man, was in a truly lamentable state. According to the captain, after they explored the monastery's library for two days, in a corner next to piles of wood the monks used to heat the monastery during the winter they discovered a pile of baskets filled with cast-off parchment and papyruses used as kindling. To distract Father Sergio while Glauser-Röist examined the contents of the baskets, Professor Boswell took out a bottle of superb Omar Khayam Egyptian wine, a luxury reserved only for non-Muslims and tourists. (The professor had brought several bottles from Alexandria to give Archbishop Damianos as a farewell gift.) Delighted, Father Sergio returned the favor with a bottle of the wine made there at the monastery. One thing led to another, and both men ended up tipsy and lost, happily singing old Egyptian songs. (It turned out that Father Sergio had been a sailor before becoming a monk.) They whooped for joy when they saw the missing Glauser-Röist reappear. By then, he had the Iyasus Codex hidden under his shirt.

The codex was in a straw basket, under a jumble of loose parchment and torn sheets, along with other codices rejected by the monks because they were in bad shape or because they had no value. When the captain brushed a thick layer of dust and dirt off the cover and saw the engravings on the cover of the codex, he let out a yelp of surprise that he thought would awaken the entire community of Saint Catherine. Luckily, not even Father Sergio and Professor Boswell noticed.

The next day, at first light, they left the monastery. The monks must have figured something was up when they saw Father Sergio with a hangover, because a few kilometers from Cairo, as it was just beginning to get dark, Professor Boswell's cell phone rang. It was the secretary to His Beatitude Stephano II Ghattas, warning them not to enter Cairo—or any Egyptian city. They needed to head east toward Israel along back roads and try to cross the border as quickly as possible. The police had been alerted and were pursuing them.

They went to Bilbays, crossed the Suez Canal at Al Quantara, and drove all night to Al'Arish, near the Israeli border. There, a representative of the apostolic delegation of Jerusalem was waiting for them with diplomatic passports from the Holy See. They crossed the border at Rafah, and in less than two hours they were resting at the delegation's office. At exactly the same time that I was flying to Ireland, they were taking off from Ben Gurion Airport in Tel Aviv. Three and a half hours later they were arriving at the Roma Ciampino Military Airport, just as I was boarding my return flight from Dublin.

If we then thought those hurdles large, we were in for a shock—for we had no clue of what was to come.

Leafing through the codex that night, I realized its deterioration was so advanced that we would have great difficulty extracting a couple of paragraphs in acceptable condition. You could barely make out a few spots and shadows. The codex resembled a watercolor on which several glasses of water had been spilled. Parchment, like the smooth skin of a drum, is less permeable to ink than paper. With time, it gets worn down and can be erased completely depending on the ink used. If that manuscript had once contained useful information on why Abi-Ruj Iyasus and others like him were stealing fragments of the True Cross, it no longer did… Or so I thought. After all, I was just a paleographer in the Vatican Classified Archives, not an archeologist from the famous Greco-Roman Museum of Alexandria. My knowledge of the techniques used to recover old words from papyruses and parchments left a lot to be desired, as Professor Farag Boswell had kindly pointed out.

*F*riday morning, while I was still asleep in a room at the Domus Sanctae Martae, Reverend Father Ramondino went to the Hypogeum and told the directors of Information Services, Document Restoration, Paleography, Codicolography, and Reproduction Photography that, for now, they and their staff should forget about returning to their respective convents, seminaries, and communities. Martial law had been declared and nobody would leave until the task was completed. As soon as he had described the nature of the project, they protested that that would take a minimum of a month of hard, focused work—to which Prefect Ramondino replied that they had just one week. In one week, if they had not finished they could pack their bags and forget about their careers at the Vatican. Later on, it became clear that such urgency wasn't necessary; but at that moment, nothing seemed to be enough.

Under Professor Boswell's directions, the Department of Document Restoration started by unbinding the codex, separating the in-folio sheets and uncovering its small square boards that turned out to be cedar, customary in Byzantine manuscripts. The type of binding clearly placed it around the fourth or fifth century. Once the parchment folios were separated (182 pieces altogether—that is, 364 pages), you could see that it was made from the skin of an unborn gazelle that must have been perfectly white when new. The photographic reproduction lab then made proofs to determine which of two techniques—infrared or high resolution digital with refrigerated telecamara CCD—would allow us, in the end, to recover the most text. We adopted a combination of both, since once the manuscript was passed through a stereomicroscope and scanner, the images obtained could be easily superimposed onto a computer screen. Thus the fragile, yellowed vellum began to reveal its dazzling secrets. An empty space or at most one covered in shadows, slowly became a magnificent sketch of Greek uncial letters,* without accents or breaks between words, in two wide columns of thirty-eight lines each. The margins were wide and evenly spaced, and the letters at the beginning of the paragraph were clearly distinguishable. They stretched toward the left border of the page and were written in purple, in contrast to the rest of the text, which was written in smoke black ink.

When we finished the first folio, it was still impossible to make out its text completely. It had a multitude of words and phrases that were truncated and nonrecoverable at first glance. There were long fragments where the infrared light, the stereomicroscope, and the high quality digitalization we used were unable to pick anything up. Then the Department of Computer Analysis took its turn. With the aid of a sophisticated graphic design program, the technicians selected a set of characters from the recovered material. Since the writing was done by hand and therefore was variable, they extracted five different representations of each letter. They patiently measured the vertical and horizontal outlines, the curves, diagonals, and spaces in the center of each character; the width and height of the body, the depth under the base lines, the descending outlines, and the elevation of the ascending outlines. When this was done they called me to take a look at one of the most curious sights I'd ever had the chance to study. With the complete image of the folio on screen, the program automatically showed us, at a dizzying speed, all the possible characters that fit in the empty spaces. When the system completed the chain, it verified that a word existed in the dictionary of the magnificent Ibycus program that contained all well-known Greek literature—biblical, patristic, and classical. If a word had appeared previously in the text, the system also collated it to verify its exactness.

The process was very fast but labor intensive. After only one day of work, we could provide a complete image of the first folio in almost perfect condition, with 95 percent of the text recovered. The lethargic

---

* Capital letters modified by curved and angular lines that were easier to write.

sleeping spirit inside the Iyasus Codex had come back to life. The moment would come when I would read its message and interpret its content.

I was deeply moved to be back at work at the Hypogeum. After Mass on the fourth Sunday of Lent at Saint Peter's, I sat down at my work table, put my glasses on my nose, and was ready to begin. My staff also got ready to start the paleographic analysis, based on the study of the different elements in the writing: morphology, angles and inclination, *ductus*,* ties, nexuses, rhythm, style, and other elements. Luckily, Byzantine Greek used very few of the abbreviations and contractions that are so common in Latin and in medieval transcriptions made by classical authors. However, the peculiarities of a language as evolved as Byzantine Greek could cause significant confusions, for neither the writing nor the meaning of words were the same as in the days of Aeschylus, Plato, or Aristotle.

Reading the first folios of the Iyasus Codex was an utter thrill for me. The scribe was named Mirogenes of Neapolis, but in the text he repeatedly referred to himself as Cato. He explained that, by the will of God the Father and his son Jesus Christ, a few brothers of good will, deacons† of the Basilica of the Holy Sepulchre in Jerusalem and devoted worshippers of the True Cross, had designed a brotherhood under the name of *ΣΤΑΥΡΟΦΙΛΑΚΕΣ* (STAUROFILAKES), or guardians of the Cross. He, Mirogenes, had been chosen archimandrite of the brotherhood, and given the title of Cato, the first day of the first month of 5850.

"5850?" Glauser-Röist said, surprised. The captain and the professor were seated across from me, listening to my transcription of the folio.

"That year corresponds to the year 341 of our era," I explained, raising my glasses and holding them in the folds of my forehead. "The

---

* Order, succession, and meaning of the movements that the scribe executed to trace the letters.
† In the the ecclesiastic hierarchy, the deacons follow the presbyters or priests and carried out liturgical and administrative duties.

Byzantines' calendar began on September 1 of the year 5509, the day when they believed God created the world."

"So on the first day of September of the year 341"—the professor laced his fingers together tightly as he spoke—"this Mirogenes was a Byzantine and deacon of the basilica of the Holy Sepulchre of Jerusalem. If I remember correctly, that's fifteen years after Saint Helen discovered the True Cross."

"Yes," I added, "and on this date, he was rebaptized as Cato and began to write this chronicle."

"We need to look for more information on that brotherhood," proposed the captain, springing from his seat. Despite being the coordinator of the operation, he had less work than anyone and wanted to feel useful. "I'm on it."

"Good idea," I agreed. "We need to demonstrate the historical existence of the Staurofilakes other than in the codex."

We heard a few discreet little taps on my lab door. It was Prefect Ramondino, smiling from ear to ear.

"I came to invite to you to dinner at the Domus's restaurant, if you like. To celebrate the good work."

But things weren't going as well as we thought. That same afternoon, while I was returning with my head held high, to the tiny apartment at the Piazza delle Vaschette, the important *Lignum Crucis* of the Convent of Sainte-Gudule, in Brussels, disappeared from its silver reliquary.

*C*aptain Glauser-Röist was gone all day Monday. As soon as he received the news of the robbery, he left for Brussels on the first plane, and didn't return until noon on Tuesday. Meanwhile, Professor Boswell and I continued working in the Hypogeum lab. The restored folios began to land on my desk at greater and greater speed. The technicians had perfected a way to accelerate the process, to the point that sometimes I barely had two or three hours to complete the reading and transcription of the manuscript before the next batch of data arrived.

I believe it was that early April night, that Monday, when Professor

Boswell and I had supper all alone in the employees' cafeteria of the Classified Archives. In the beginning I feared it would be particularly hard to keep up a conversation with somebody so bashful and quiet, but the professor proved to be very pleasant company. We talked a lot and about many things. After telling me, once again, the complete story of the robbery of the codex, he asked about my family. He wanted to know if I had brothers and sisters and if my parents were still living. At first surprised by that personal turn in the conversation, I gave him a brief description, but when he heard the number of members of the Salina tribe, he wanted to know more. I even drew a family tree on a napkin so he could follow who I was talking about. It's always strange to find someone who knows how to listen. Professor Boswell did not ask directly; he didn't even show much curiosity. He just watched me attentively, nodding or smiling at just the right moment. Of course I fell into his trap. By the time I realized what had happened, I'd already told him my life story. He laughed, very amused, and I thought the moment had come for a counterattack, because suddenly I felt very vulnerable and even guilty, as if I'd said too much. I asked him if he was worried about losing his job at the Greco-Roman Museum in Alexandria. He frowned and took off his glasses, pinching the bridge of the nose, looking tired.

"My work...," he murmured and retreated into his thoughts for several seconds. "You don't know what's happening in Egypt, do you, Doctor?"

"No, I don't know," I answered, disorientated.

"I am Coptic, and being Coptic in Egypt means being a pariah."

"That surprises me, Professor Boswell. You Coptics are the true descendants of the ancient Egyptians. The Arabs arrived much later. In fact, your language, Coptic, comes directly from demotic Egyptian, spoken in the time of the pharaohs."

"Yes, but things aren't as rosy as you paint them. It would be great if the world saw things the way you do. We Coptics are a small minority in Egypt, divided into Catholic Christians and Orthodox Christians. Ever since the fundamentalist revolution began, the *irhebin*...I mean the terrorists from the Islamic guerrilla group Al-Gama'a al-Islamiyya have murdered members of our small communities. In 1992 they shot and killed fourteen Coptics from the province of Asyut for refusing to pay 'protection services.' In 1994 a group of armed terrorists attacked the Coptic monastery of Deir ul-Muharraq, near Asyut, killing the priests and the faithful," he sighed. "There are assaults, robberies, death threats, beatings…They've started setting off bombs in the entrances to churches in Alexandria and Cairo."

I silently deduced that the Egyptian government must not be doing anything to stop the violence.

"I'm fortunate, I realize," he said, laughing suddenly. "I'm a bad Catholic-Coptic. It's been years since I've been to church, and that has saved my life." He kept smiling and put his glasses back on, adjusting them carefully around his ears. "Last year, in June, Al-Gama'a al-Islamiyya put a bomb in the doorway of Saint Anthony Church in Alexandria. Fifteen people died—among them, my younger brother, Juhanna; his wife, Zoë; and their five-month-old son."

I was speechless with shock and horror and lowered my eyes to the table.

"I'm so sorry…," I managed to stammer with difficulty.

"Well they…they are no longer suffering. My father is now the one suffering. He'll never get over it. Yesterday when I called him, he begged me not to return home to Alexandria; he begged me to stay here in Rome."

I didn't know what to say. In light of such unfortunate events, what are the right words to say?

"I liked my job. But if I've lost it, as I most likely have, I will start over. I can do so in Italy, as my father wishes, far from danger. In fact, I also happen to be an Italian citizen. On account of my mother, as you already know."

"Oh yes! Your mother was Italian!"

"From Florence. In the mid-1950s, when Pharaonic Egypt came back into vogue, my mother had just finished her studies in archeology and got a grant to work on the excavations at the birthplace of Oxirrinco. My father, also an archeologist, spent a day visiting the site, and they met. And here I am! Life can be so strange… My mother always said she married my father because he was a Boswell. She was joking, of course." He smiled again. "My parents had a very happy marriage. She adapted well to her new country and her new religion, but deep down she always preferred the Roman Catholic rituals."

I was very curious to know if he'd inherited those deep navy blue eyes from his mother—many northern Italian women have blue eyes— or from some distant English relative. But it didn't seem like the right time to ask.

"Professor Boswell," I started to say.

"Why don't we call each other by our first names, Doctor," he broke in, looking me straight in the eye, as always. "Everyone stands on such ceremony around here."

I smiled. "That's because here in the Vatican, personal relationships are developed within very strict boundaries."

"Well, what do you say we jump over those boundaries? Do you think Monsignor Tournier or Captain Glauser-Röist will be scandalized?"

"I'm sure they will!" I said between hiccups of laughter. "But let them!"

"Then it's . . . Ottavia?"

"Pleased to meet you, Farag."

And we shook hands over the table.

That day, I discovered that Professor Boswell—Farag—was a delightful person in private, completely different from the public Professor Boswell. I understood that what intimidated the professor wasn't people, but groups. The bigger they got, the worse he was. He stuttered, choked, blinked, pushed up his glasses over and over, doubted himself, lost his voice, and was simply a social mess.

*G*lauser-Röist returned from Brussels the next day. He showed up at the lab with a forbidding look on his face, his brow knit into a frown and his lips pressed into a practically imperceptible thin line.

"Bad news, Captain?" I asked. I looked up from the folio I'd just received when I saw him come in.

"Bad, very bad."

"Please, sit down and tell me."

"There's nothing to tell," he muttered as he let himself fall in a chair that groaned under his weight. "Nothing. I didn't find a clue, not one sign of violence, no forced doors, no clues of any kind. It was an impeccable robbery. I was unable to find out if any Ethiopian citizen entered the country over the last weeks, either. The Belgian police will question the residents of Ethiopian heritage to see if they can supply any information. They'll call me if there's any news."

"It's possible that this time the thief wasn't Ethiopian."

"We thought of that. But we have nothing else." He looked around, distracted. "How's it going here?" he finally asked, looking at the folio that lay on my table. "Gotten very far?"

"We're getting faster and faster," I answered, satisfied. "Really, I'm the bottleneck of the operation. I can't transcribe and translate and keep up with the rest of the team. These are very complicated texts."

"Could any of your staff help you?"

"They have enough on their hands with the paleographical problems! Right now, they are working on the second Cato."

"The second Cato?" he asked, raising his eyebrows.

"Oh yes. Mirogenes died in the year 344. The Brotherhood of the Staurofilakes elected a certain Pertinax as archimandrite. Now we're working on him. According to my staff, Cato II (as he called himself) was a very cultivated man, with an exquisite vocabulary. The Greek used in Byzantium had a very different pronunciation from the classical Greek that was ultimately the one that set the linguistic and lexigraphic norm." The captain looked puzzled, so I gave him an example. "What happened then was what is happening now to modern English. Kids have to learn to spell words and then memorize them because they are pronounced nothing like they are spelled. After so many centuries of modifications, Byzantine Greek was equally complicated."

"Ah, okay."

Not too shabby, I thought to myself, relieved. The Swiss Rock was catching on.

"Pertinax, or Cato II, must have received a very nice education in some monastery where the manuscripts were copied. His grammar is impeccable and his style is very refined compared to Cato I, who seemed to have little formal education. Some of my staff believe Pertinax was more than any old monk. He could have been a member of the royal family or a cartier in Constantinople, because his *ductus* is elegant, far too elegant for that of a monk."

"So, what does Cato II say?"

"I've just finished his chronicle. During his rule, the brotherhood grew unexpectedly. A large number of pilgrims poured into Jerusalem during religious festivals, and many of them took root in the Holy Land. Some of these pilgrims joined the brotherhood, and Cato II refers to the difficulties he faces in governing such a large and diverse community. He proposed imposing restrictions on admitting new members but apparently nothing was approved because the patriarch of Jerusalem was very satisfied with the growth of the brotherhood. Given the dates, the patriarch must have been Maximos II or Kyril I. I've already asked the Archives to review their biographies, in case we may find something."

"Has anyone searched for direct information through our databases?"

"No, Captain. That's your job. Don't you remember you offered to do it?"

Glauser-Röist slowly rose to his feet. His elegant suit, wrinkled from his trip, was disconcertingly sloppy, completely out of character. He almost looked depressed.

"I'm going to shower at the barracks. I'll be back this afternoon so I can get started."

"In a few minutes the prefect, Professor Boswell, and I are going to the cafeteria. Would you like to join us?"

"Don't wait for me. I have an urgent audience with the secretary of state and His Holiness."

After Cato II came Cato III, Cato IV, and Cato V... For some reason, the archimandrites of the Staurofilakes had chosen that strange name to symbolize the highest authority in their order. To the well-recognized titles of Pope and Patriarch, they seem to have added the lesser-known title of Cato. Professor Boswell locked himself away in the library for a day with the seven thick volumes of *Parallel Lives* by Plutarch. He studied the biographies of the only Catos known in history, the Roman politicians Marcus Cato and Cato of Utica. After several hours, he returned with a relatively plausible theory. Lacking anything better, we considered it.

"I think there's no doubt that one of the Catos served as a model for the archimandrite of the Staurofilakes."

We were in my lab, gathered around my old wooden desk, covered with hundreds of loose papers and notes.

"Marcus Cato, called Cato the Elder, was a damned fanatic, a defender of the most debauched and traditional Roman values. In the way the stereotype of a southerner in America believes in the superiority of the white race and is a sympathizer of the Ku Klux Klan, Marcus Cato despised Greek culture and language and everything foreign because he said it weakened all Romans. He was as hard and cold as a stone."

"What an image," I commented, amused. Glauser-Röist looked at me. He seemed to notice how friendly Farag and I had gotten.

"He served Rome as a quaestor, aedile, praetor, consul, and censor from 204 to 184 B.C. Although he had a large fortune, he lived with the greatest austerity and considered any useless expense frivolous. For example, he refused to give food to any slave who was too old to work, killing them instead, as a scheme to save money. He advised Roman citizens to follow his example for the good of the Republic. He considered himself perfect and exemplary."

"I don't like this Cato," affirmed Glauser-Röist, elegantly folding one of my sheets of notes into fours.

"No. Me neither," Farag agreed, shaking his head. "Without a doubt, the brotherhood focused on the other Cato, known as Cato the younger and also as Cato of Utica, great-grandson of the first Cato and an admirable man. As quaestor of the Republic, he restored honor to the Roman treasury after many centuries of corruption. He was decent and honest. As a judge he was impartial and couldn't be bribed, for he was convinced that in order to be fair, one must simply desire to be so. His sincerity was so proverbial that in Rome, when you wanted to refute something soundly, you'd say, 'This isn't true, even if Cato says so.' He ardently opposed Julius Caesar, whom he rightly accused of corruption, ambition, and manipulation for wanting to exert full dominion over the Roman Republic. He and Caesar hated one another. They were locked in a feud for years: One wanted to become the exclusive lord of a great empire and the other was committed to stopping him. When Julius Caesar finally triumphed, Cato retired to his home in Utica, where he committed suicide by falling on his sword. He said he wasn't coward enough to beg Caesar for his life nor brave enough to apologize to his enemy."

"That's strange." Glauser-Röist was paying close attention to Farag's story. "Caesar's name, Cato's great enemy, became the title for Roman emperors, the Caesars, the same way Cato became the title for the archimandrites of the brotherhood, the Catos."

"That *is* very strange," I agreed.

"Cato of Utica exemplified the essence of freedom. For example, Seneca says, 'Neither did Cato, freedom dying, nor was there freedom anymore when Cato died.'* Valorous Maximous asks, 'What will freedom be without Cato?'"†

"Could the word *Cato* be synonymous with honor and freedom, just as the word *Caesar* was synonymous with power?" I hinted.

"Most certainly," replied the professor as he pushed his glasses onto the bridge of his nose, just as I had done.

"Strange," Glauser-Röist repeated, looking from one of us to the other.

"We're starting to find some interesting pieces of this incredible puzzle," I said, breaking the silence. "The most fantastic part is what I've figured out in the chronicle of Cato V. The Catos wrote their chronicles in the Monastery of Saint Catherine of Sinai."

"Are you serious?"

I nodded. "I already suspected something like that because a codex like the Iyasus had to have been written in a monastery or some great

* Lucius A. Seneca, *De Const. II.*
† Val. Max. VI:2.5.

library in Constantinople. The vellum had to be cut and perforated with tiny needles that marked the first and last of the text on each page. They had to draw lines so that the text was straight and didn't swerve. They had to draw or paint in miniature the large letters at the beginning of each paragraph. It was meticulous work that required expert personnel. And don't forget, they also had to bind the folios. Clearly the Catos used the services of some specialized center. Since the content was supposed to be secret, it could only be a monastic retreat, as isolated as possible."

"But there are hundreds of monasteries that could've done that!" exclaimed Farag.

"Yes, that's true, but Saint Catherine's was erected by the will of Saint Helen, the empress who found the True Cross. And don't forget, that was where you found it. It's safe to say that the codex remained in Saint Catherine's and either the Catos traveled there to write their chronicle or the codex was dispatched to them, then later returned to the monastery. That would explain why it was later abandoned. Perhaps the Staurofilakes stopped writing their chronicles, or perhaps something happened that stopped them. The fact is, Cato V explains that his trip to Saint Catherine's was particularly hazardous and difficult but that he couldn't delay it any longer because of his advancing age."

"The relationship between the brotherhood and the monastery must have been very close," commented Farag. "I don't think we'll ever know just how close."

"What else have we figured out?"

"Well…" I consulted my scribbled notes, taken from the dense reports my staff had passed me. "There's still a lot to translate, but I can tell you that the majority of the Catos fill just a few lines with their chronicles, others a page or a folio, still others a double sheet, and the rest a set of three sheets. But every Cato, without exception, travels to Saint Catherine in the last five or six years of his life. If one Cato happens to leave out something important, the next Cato tells it at the beginning of his chronicle."

"Do we know how many Catos there were in all?" Glauser-Röist asked.

"We can't be sure, Captain. The Department of Computer Analysis hasn't finished reconstructing the complete text. But up to the capture of Jerusalem by King Cosroes II in the year 614, there had been a total of thirty-six Catos."

"Thirty-six Catos!" the captain said admiringly. "And what happened to the brotherhood during all that time?"

"Oh, nothing major, apparently. Their main problem was the Latin pilgrims who arrived by the thousands. They had to organize a type of praetorian guard of Staurofilakes around the True Cross. Among other barbarities, as many pilgrims kneeled to kiss the cross, they ripped out splinters with their teeth to take as relics. Around the year 570, during the rule of Cato XXX, there was an important crisis. A group of corrupt Staurofilakes organized the theft of the reliquary. They were veteran pilgrims who had entered the brotherhood years before, people who never would have been suspected of boldly looting the relics if it hadn't been for the fact that they had been caught in action. The old debate about admitting new members was reopened. Apparently, the brotherhood needed to filter out the Latin rabble ready to take a cut of the profits and prosper. But in the end, nothing was done, not on this occasion or in the following years. The patriarchs of Jerusalem, Alexandria, and Constantinople pressed for the Staurofilakes to continue on as they were, for the Staurofilakes filled a much appreciated political function and no one wanted them to become a sort of private, restrictive club.

"So, Captain," Farag asked abruptly with a lot of interest, "have you found that additional information you were going to look for on the Staurofilakes?"

Over the last several days we'd seen Glauser-Röist working feverishly at the computer, printing page after page then reading them over and over. I had expected him to tell us about some interesting discovery at any moment; but days went by, and the Swiss Rock had gone back to being the *old* Swiss Rock, silent and unalterable as ever.

"I have looked, but haven't found anything at all…" He plunged into very deep reflection. "Well, I guess that isn't entirely the truth. I did find a reference, but so insignificant that I didn't think was worth mentioning."

"Captain, please," I protested, full of self-righteous indignation.

"Well, okay, let's see," he began, and tugged at his jacket. "The brotherhood was alluded to in a curious manuscript by a Galician nun."

"The *Itinerarium* of Egeria?" I interrupted, sarcastically. "We talked about that work when we were investigating the monastery of Saint Catherine of Sinai."

The captain nodded. "Yes, the *Itinerarium* of Egeria, written between Easter 381 and Easter 384. Well, in the chapter that describes the offices of Holy Friday in Jerusalem, she affirms that the Staurofilakes oversaw the care of the relic and watched over the faithful who approached it. The Spanish nun saw them with her own eyes."

"Confirmed!" Farag declared full of joy. "The Staurofilakes existed! The Iyasus Codex is telling the truth!"

"Well, let's get to work," Glauser-Röist grunted. "The secretary of state is very dissatisfied with our slow progress."

*F*or the first time in my life, Holy Week arrived without my realizing it. I didn't celebrate Palm Sunday or Holy Thursday or Resurrection Monday. I didn't even attend the penitential commemoration or the Easter Vigil. Not having participated in any of that, I also didn't make my weekly confession with good Father Pintonello. Since we were submerged in our work at the Hypogeum, we received dispensation from the pope, who exonerated us from our religious obligations. While His Holiness appeared in all the media celebrating the offices of Holy Week (proving to the world that he was in excellent health), he wanted us to continue working uninterruptedly until we solved the problem. Despite being tired, we continued with true zeal. We stopped going to the employee cafeteria because meals were brought down to us in the lab. We stopped going back home to sleep because they put us up in the Domus. We stopped taking breaks and days off because we simply didn't have time. We were voluntary prisoners besieged by the fever of our impassioned discovery of a secret guarded for centuries.

The only one who left with any frequency was the captain. Besides his regular meetings with the secretary of state, Angelo Sodano, to update him on our investigation, Glauser-Röist slept in the Swiss Guard barracks (officials and subofficials had rooms of their own). At times he stayed there for several hours, doing shooting practice and attending to other matters about which we had no idea. He was a mysterious guy—reserved, silent, nearly always taciturn, and once in a while even a bit sinister. At least that's how he seemed to me, because Farag had a different opinion. He was convinced that Glauser-Röist was a simple, affable person, tormented by the type of work he had fallen into. In Egypt they had talked for long hours in the ATV as they crossed the desert, and although the captain hadn't divulged the details of his position within the Vatican, Farag intuited that he wasn't much a fan of his own job description.

"But didn't he tell you anything else?" I asked, dying of curiosity one afternoon when just the two of us were in the lab working on one of the last folios. "Did he give you any details on his life? Did he share any interesting tidbit of information?"

Farag laughed easily. His white teeth stood out against his dark complexion. "All I recall," he began, amused, trying to eradicate his Arabic accent, "is that he said that he entered the Swiss Guard because everyone else in his family had done so since his ancestor Commander Kaspar Röist saved Pope Clement VI from Charles V's troops during the sack of Rome."

"Wow! So the captain's from a family of nobles!"

"He also told me he was born in Berne and studied at the University of Zurich."

"What did he study?"

"Agricultural engineering."

My jaw dropped. "Agricultural engineering?"

"What's so strange about that? I'm pretty sure he said he also had a degree in Italian literature from the University of Rome."

"I can't picture him constructing greenhouses for fruits and vegetables," I said.

Farag laughed so uproariously he had to wipe away his tears. "You're impossible!" He looked at me for a second, his eyes shining. Then he shook his head and pointed to the folio we'd been examining. "What do you say we get back to work?"

"Yes, that would be best. We left off here," and I pointed with a pen to a place midway down the second column.

With the occupation of Jerusalem by Cosroes II, king of Persia, in 614, the Brotherhood of the Staurofilakes plunged into a crisis. After his victory, Cosroes took the True Cross to Ctesiphon, the capital of his empire, and laid it at the foot of his throne as a symbol of his own divinity. The weaker members of the brotherhood disappeared, terrified, and the few who remained (under the rule of Cato XXXVI), feeling responsible for the loss of their relic, dedicated themselves to purging their supposed incompetence with terrible fasts, penitence, flagellations, and true sacrifices. Some even died as a result of the wounds they inflicted upon themselves. Fifteen painful years went by, during which Byzantine emperor Heracles continued to fight Cosroes II and finally defeated him in 628. A while later, in an emotional ceremony celebrated on September 14 of that year, the True Cross was returned to Jerusalem, carried through the city by the emperor himself. The Staurofilakes actively participated in the procession and in the solemn act of restoring the relic to its place. From then on, September 14 was commemorated on the liturgical calendars as the Exaltation of the True Cross.

But the era of anguish hadn't ended. Only nine years later, in 637, another powerful army arrived at Jerusalem's doors: the Muslims, commanded by Caliph Omar. By then, the order had a new Cato, the thirty-seventh, originally named Anastasios, who decided he wasn't going to stand quietly by when danger arrived. When news of the invasion began to spread through the city, Cato XXXVII sent a small team of well-known Staurofilakes to negotiate with the caliph. A pact was signed in secret, and the safety of the True Cross was guaranteed in exchange for the brotherhood's collaboration in locating the Christian and Jewish treasures that had carefully been hidden as the advance of the Muslims became known. Omar kept his word, and so did the Staurofilakes. For many years there was peace and cohabitation between the three monotheistic religions, Christianity, Judaism, and Islam.

During this peaceful period, the order went through a deep transformation. Having learned from the loss of the True Cross during the Persian invasion and by the good that came from their later accord with the Arabs, the Staurofilakes became more convinced than ever that their strict, simple mission was to protect the Holy Wood. They started to become more withdrawn, more independent from the patriarchs, more invisible, and also much more powerful. Among their ranks they started to enlist men from the best families of Constantinople, Antioch, Alexandria, and Athens, and from the Italian cities of Florence, Ravenna, Milan, and Rome. They were no longer a group of henchmen, ready to skin alive any pilgrim who dared touch the True Cross. They were clever and intelligent men, more soldiers and diplomats than deacons or monks.

They succeeded in strengthening the organization by doing what Cato II had proposed back in the fourth century: They set out requirements for admittance. The new aspirants had to know how to read and write, have a command of Latin and Greek, know mathematics, music, astrology, and philosophy; more important, they needed to pass a series of physical tests of resistance and strength. Slowly, the Staurofilakes became an important, estranged institution, always attentive to its sole mission.

The problems returned with the waves of European pilgrims, people of all classes and conditions—mostly vagabonds, beggars, thieves, hermits, adventurers, and mystics; a picturesque group of people looking for a place to live and die. During the ninth and tenth centuries, the situation grew worse: The caliphs of Jerusalem were no longer as magnanimous as Omar, forbidding Christians to enter the holy sites. In 1009, Caliph al-Hakem, a demented man with whom the patriarch of Jerusalem and the brotherhood had had serious problems, ordered the destruction of all religious sanctuaries that weren't Muslim. While al-Hakem's soldiers destroyed church after church, temple after temple, the Staurofilakes scrambled to save the Cross. They hid it in the place they'd prepared in advance for just such an occasion: a secret crypt under the Basilica of the Holy Sepulchre itself, where the relic was usually housed. They managed to save it from destruction but at a cost of the lives of several Staurofilakes who fought off the soldiers so their brothers could get to the hiding place.

The photographic reproduction lab completed the last folio, number 182, on the afternoon of the second Easter Sunday. My staff finished its paleographic analysis two days later, the first week in May. All that was missing was my part, the slowest and least systematic of them all, so we decided to reorganize the team and have the members of my department take care of the translations, allowing me to sit down with Glauser-Röist and Farag to read and interpret the pages that were brought to us from the lab.

In 1054, to no one's surprise, the Great Schism in the Christian church came about. Romans and Orthodox Christians openly confronted each other over futile theological questions and distribution of power. Rome insisted that the pope was the only direct successor to Peter. The patriarchs rejected that idea, stating that *they* were the apostle's legitimate successors. The Staurofilakes didn't align themselves with either group, despite the untenable position that left them in. Their sole allegiance was to themselves and to the Cross, and increasingly their attitude toward the rest of the world was one of profound mistrust.

While Cato LXVI urgently studied ways to protect the order from its critics and from attacks by the two Christian factions, the Holy Land was once again on the brink of war. In the spring of 1097, four large armies of crusaders were concentrated in Constantinople, planning to advance all the way to Jerusalem and liberate the Holy sites from Islamic dominion.

Again a group of Staurofilakes negotiators surreptitiously left the city, to meet the vast European troops commanded by Gottfried of Bouillon. They caught up with them two months later, laying siege to Antioch after conquering the Turkish troops in Nicea and Dorilea. According to Cato LXVI's chronicle, Gottfried of Bouillon didn't accept the brotherhood's proposal. He told them that the True Cross of the Savior was the real objective of that crusade, whose symbol the soldiers proudly displayed on their clothes. They were not willing to renounce that cross for any Islamic, Jewish, or Christian treasure. He told them that because the Staurofilakes hadn't joined the Church of Rome during the Great Schism, as soon as he took the city, he would have them excommunicated and dissolve the brotherhood for good.

The negotiators returned to Jerusalem with the bad news, causing real distress among the guardians of the Cross. On the night of July 3, 1098, Cato LXVI announced the coming dangers to all the Staurofilakes at an assembly in the Basilica of the Holy Sepulchre. With the unanimous support of those present, he proposed hiding the relic and keeping silent the order. At that moment, the Staurofilakes ceased to exist publicly.

A year later, after a month of siege, the crusaders took Jerusalem and literally massacred its entire population. There was so much blood in the streets that the frightened horses reared and whinnied and the soldiers couldn't walk. In the middle of this carnage, Gottfried of Bouillon went to the Basilica of the Holy Sepulchre to take the True Cross with his own hands, but he didn't find it. He ordered all surviving Staurofilakes to be brought to him, but there were none to be found. He tortured the Orthodox priests until they confessed that there were three disguised Staurofilakes in their midst: Three very young monks—Agapios, Elijah, and Teofanes—had remained in Jerusalem to watch over the relic. Gottfried tortured them, whipping, burning, and dismembering them. Teofanes, the weakest, could not hold out. With his arms and legs tied to horses, in his last moment he shouted that the Holy Wood was hidden in a secret crypt under the basilica. Practically senseless and dragged by Bouillon's soldiers, he pointed out the place with great difficulty. He was left in the street, to his own fate, where he died, stabbed to death by unknown hands.

The True Cross became the most important relic of the crusaders who carried it into battle. For more than a hundred years, it was shown to soldiers before battles in order to rouse them; and, for a hundred years, thanks to the Wood of Christ, they remained undefeated. A number of *Lignum Crucis* were sent to Europe as a gift to kings and popes, monasteries and the noble families of the West. The Holy Wood was divided and distributed as if it were a pie, for wherever there was one of its splinters, riches flowed in the form of pilgrims and devotees. The Staurofilakes watched from a distance, powerless to do anything to stop it. Their concern turned to anger, and they swore to recover what was left of the True Cross at any cost. But at the time the task seemed impossible.

According to Cato LXXII's chronicle, some of the brothers infiltrated the crusades so they could watch the movements of the Wood. They feared it would fall into Muslim hands during some major battle or skirmish, for the Arabs and the Turks knew perfectly well the meaning it held for the Christians. They knew that if they seized it, the Christians' victories would dwindle. At that same time (around 1150), other groups of Staurofilakes left for the principal Christian cities of the East and West. Their plan was to establish relations with influential, powerful people who could mediate in their favor or demand the return of the relic. In time, those who left made contact with some of the many organizations and religious orders that proliferated in medieval Europe and whose foundations were firmly rooted in Christianity. From the European Knights Templar and the Catharists to the Fede Santa, the Massenie du Saint Graal, the Compagnonnage, the Minnesänger, or the Fidei d'Amore—almost all were contacted by Staurofilakes, resulting in an exchange of information or shared interests. Many Staurofilakes entered these orders or organizations, and vice versa. The Staurofilakes also recruited the most prominent, most important young men and princes from the cities where they were based, planning for these boys to mature in the shadow of the brotherhood before occupying the positions of power to which they were destined by family and birth. But for these youngsters to be guardians of the True Cross was something intangible; the Holy Wood was still in Jerusalem, a city that was too far away. Many of them left the brotherhood only a few years after they joined. It was precisely one of those deserters who informed the ecclesiastic authorities of Milan of what he knew about the Staurofilakes. A year later, in Jerusalem and Constantinople, the members of the brotherhood, including Cato LXXV, were arrested in their homes and sent to prison. There they were excommunicated and reminded that Gottfried of Bouillon had dissolved their brotherhood one hundred years before. They were classified as lapsed, and therefore were sentenced to death. All, without exception, were executed.

The next Cato, who referred to these sad events at the beginning of his portion of the codex, was one of the Staurofilakes from Antioch. He summoned all the brothers to an assembly in that city at the end of 1187. He began his address with the terrible news that was on everyone's lips: The Ayyubi strongman, Saladin, had defeated the crusaders in the battle of Hattina, in Galilee. According to the Staurofilakes present at the battle, he snatched the relic of the True Cross from the hands of the defeated king, Guy de Lusignan. The Cross of Jesus Christ had fallen into Muslim hands.

Many important things were decided in that meeting. They selected the brothers who would infiltrate Saladin's armies (Nikephoros Panteugenos, Sophronios of Teila, Joachim Sandalya, Dionisios of Dara, and Abraham Abdounita) to watch over the True Cross and, if possible, steal it. They agreed that they needed to be more careful about selecting the aspiring Staurofilakes, so that the treason that caused the death of the brothers from Jerusalem and Constantinople and Cato LXXV never took place again. A group of fifteen brothers from the cities of Rome, Ravenna, Athens, Antioch, and Alexandria were put in charge of devising an initiation process sufficiently rigorous so that only the best and most devoted could enter the brotherhood. There was no mercy for those who did not pass these tests; their mouths were sealed forever. A group of twelve Staurofilakes were commissioned to find a safe place where the relic could be hidden as soon as it was recovered. Once the True Cross was back in the brotherhood's hands, it would never be taken again, and never would any lay person be allowed to touch it or see it. The hiding place would be impregnable. Twelve brothers traveled the world until they found the suitable site. Meanwhile, the rest of the Staurofilakes were focused on urgently recovering the relic. They proudly concluded that eight hundred years of their existence must not end in failure.

After a few months, the Holy Land had fallen into Saladin's power and the crusaders were forced to fall back to the coast of Tyrus, in Lebanon. The Staurofilakes were in fact the secret organizers of the Second Crusade.

In August 1191, Richard the Lionhearted put an end, finally, to the Muslim armies, defeating them in numerous battles. The Muslims agreed to negotiate the return of the True Cross, and a group of envoys from the Christian king, including an undercover Staurofilax, were able to see and venerate the relic. But then Richard, in an absurd and inexplicable gesture, killed two thousand Muslim prisoners, and Saladin broke off talks.

The Staurofilakes in charge of organizing the initiation tests concluded their work in July 1195. The information was taken to all the brothers via emissaries who traveled to the main cities of the world. A short time later, the first candidate began the tests. Cato LXXVI described them thus:

So that their souls arrive pure to the True Cross of the Savior and are worthy of prostrating themselves before it, they must purge themselves of all their faults until they are free of all stain. The expiation of the Seven Deadly Sins will take place in the seven cities that boast the terrible distinction of being known to practice them perversely: Rome, for its pride; Ravenna, for its envy; Jerusalem, for its wrath; Athens, for its sloth; Constantinople, for its greed; Alexandria, for its gluttony; and Antioch, for its lust. In each one of these cities, as if they were an earthly purgatory, an aspirant will suffer for his faults in order to enter the secret place we Staurofilakes will call the earthly paradise. The Archangel Michael gave Adam a branch from the Tree of Good and Evil which he planted, and from it was born the tree whose wood was used to build the Cross on which Christ died. So the brothers of one city know what happened in the previous cities, upon finishing each step, the supplicant's flesh will be marked with a cross, one for each deadly sin erased from his soul, as a souvenir of his expiation. The crosses will match those on the wall of the Monastery of Saint Catherine, in the Holy Place of Sinai, where Moses received from God the Tablets of the Law. If the supplicant arrives at the earthly paradise with seven crosses, he will be admitted as one of us, and he will always display on his body the chrismon and the sacred word that gives meaning to our lives. If he does not, may God have mercy on his soul.

Seven tests in seven cities," whispered Farag, impressed. "And Alexandria is one of them, for the sin of gluttony."

We had spent two days studying the last portion of the manuscript that covered the tumultuous twelfth century. Everything we read pointed to Abi-Ruj Iyasus: the scarifications of the seven crosses of Saint Catherine, the chrismon, and the word *Stauros*. It was frightening to think that the Staurofilakes still existed 1,659 years after their creation. None of us doubted they were the ones behind the theft of the *Ligna Crucis*.

"Where could that earthly paradise be?" I asked, taking off my glasses and rubbing my tired eyes.

"Perhaps the last folio has the answer," suggested Farag, picking up the transcript. "Come on. We're almost finished. Captain?"

But Captain Glauser-Röist did not move. His eyes were glazed with distraction.

"Captain..." I looked at Farag, amused. "I believe he's fallen asleep."

"No, no...," murmured the Rock, "I'm not asleep."

"Then what's wrong?"

Farag and I studied him, astonished. The captain had a haggard, dazed look. He jumped to his feet and peered down on us. His mind seemed racing with thoughts.

"You go ahead. I have to check something."

"What's wrong?" I started to ask, but Glauser-Röist had already run out the door. I turned to Farag, who also had an incredulous look on his face. "What's wrong with him?"

"That's what I'd like to know."

The truth is, there was an explanation for the captain's odd behavior: We were working under a lot of pressure many hours a day. We hardly slept, and we spent all our time in the artificial atmosphere of the Hypogeum, not seeing the sun or breathing fresh air. What we really needed was a healthy walk in the country or a day at the beach, but we were in a hurry, we pushed the limits of the humanly possible, fearing that at any time we would get the bad news of some new theft of *Ligna Crucis.* We were simply exhausted.

"Let's keep going, Ottavia."

The last Cato, curiously number LXXVII on the list, began his chronicle with a beautiful prayer of thanks: The brotherhood had rescued the True Cross in 1219.

"They got it back!" I exclaimed, delighted. I'd completely forgotten that the Staurofilakes were the bad guys.

"That was obvious, don't you think?"

"Well, I don't know why...," I responded, offended.

"Well, because the True Cross disappeared! Or don't you remember history? No one ever found out what became of it."

Farag was right, of course. The truth is I was exhausted; my brain seemed to be nothing but neuron juice. The True Cross mysteriously disappeared between the Fifth and the last Crusade, at the beginning of the thirteenth century. Cato LXXVII narrated it, of course, from a very different point of view. According to him, the emperor of the Germanic Holy Roman Empire, Frederick II, besieged the port of Damietta, in the Nile Delta. Sultan al-Kamil offered to give back the True Cross if the Christians left Egypt. Shortly before that, following great dangers and difficulties, the Staurofilax Dionysius of Dara, one of the five brothers who thirty-two years before had infiltrated Saladin's army, was named treasurer by the sultan. He was so assimilated to his role as an important Mameluke diplomat that, on the night he showed up at Nikephoros Panteugeno's humble hut holding a large package in his hands, Nikephoros didn't even recognize him. Both prostrated themselves before the relic of the Cross and cried tears of joy, and then departed to search for the three missing brothers. At first light, the five Staurofilakes, in disguise, set off on foot for the Monastery of Saint Catherine of Sinai, where they hid until Cato LXXVII arrived with a jubilant group of brothers. Cato LXXVII wrote his happy chronicle, at the end of which he announced that the Brotherhood of the Staurofilakes was going to retreat forever to the earthly paradise, which the other brothers had finally found.

"But he doesn't say where!" I protested, turning over the sheet of paper in my hands.

"I think we must read to the end."

"He's not going to say, you'll see."

Surely enough, Cato LXXVII did not say where the earthly paradise was. He only mentioned that it was in a very distant country and that with preparations for the long journey already completed, he had to bring his story to a close because they were leaving immediately. They left the codex in the care of the monks of Saint Catherine's, where it remained for nine centuries, and he announced the history of the brotherhood would cease to be written there. "My successors will continue in our new refuge. There we will protect what little the evil of men has left of the Holy Cross. Our fate is sealed. May God protect us."

"And that's it," I said, disheartened, letting the paper fall from my hands.

Like two statues of salt, Farag and I were mute and immobile for a good long time, incapable of believing that everything had ended and that we didn't know much more than when we started. Wherever the Staurofilakes' happy earthly paradise was, there too were the *Ligna Crucis* stolen from the Christian churches. Aside from the satisfaction of having information on the thieves, we had no other joy.

Several months of investigation, all the resources of the Classified Archives and the Vatican Library, hours and hours closed up in the Hypogeum with all the staff working diligently. All that for nothing.

I sighed deeply. My head flopped over and my chin rested on my chest. My tired vertebrae cracked like trampled glass.

*E*ver since this whole story had started, I hadn't managed to get a good night's sleep. If it wasn't the insomnia, it was every little sound I heard in the Domus room (the little refrigerator, the creaking of the wood, the clock on the wall, the wind hitting the blinds); it was the never-ending and exhausting dreams that kept me awake. They weren't quite nightmares, but oftentimes I was truly afraid, like that night when I dreamed that I was walking down an enormous avenue under construction filled with dangerous holes that I had to avoid by crossing weak planks of wood or by hanging from a rope.

After the frustrating and anticlimactic end of our work, and our not knowing what had happened to the captain, Farag and I went to the Domus, had supper, and retired to our rooms with a leaden, disheartened look wrought deeply in our faces. We were disappointed, and although Farag tried to comfort me by telling me that as soon as we rested, we'd feel up to extracting what we needed from the Catos' history, I got into bed deeply discouraged.

I felt like I was dangling from a rope, with an abyss beneath my feet, when the sound of my telephone made me bolt up in bed and open my eyes in the dark. I didn't know where I was or what that roar was or how to stop my heart from leaping out of my mouth, but I was wide awake, with my senses completely alert. When I was able to react and locate myself in space and time, I swatted at the light switch and answered the telephone.

"Yes?" I grunted.

"Doctor?"

"Captain? My God! Do you know what time it is?" I focused desperately on the clock on the opposite wall.

"Three thirty," answered Glauser-Röist, unperturbed.

"Three-thirty in the morning, Captain!"

"Professor Boswell will be down in five minutes. I'm in the Domus meeting room. I beg you to hurry, Doctor. How long will it take you to get ready?"

"Ready for what?"

"To go to the Hypogeum."

"The Hypogeum? Now?"

"Are you coming or not?" The captain was losing his patience.

"I'm coming! I'm coming! Give me five minutes."

I walked to the bathroom and turned on the lights. A blast of cold fluorescent light struck my eyes. I washed my face and brushed my teeth, passed the brush through my matted hair and returned to my room. I quickly put on a black skirt and a heavy beige wool cardigan. I grabbed my jacket and purse and went into the hall, still stunned by a surreal sense, as if I had gone directly from the scaffolds of the road in my dreams to the elevator in the Domus.

Farag and Glauser-Röist were waiting for me in the enormous and brightly lit vestibule, speaking in anxious whispers. Farag, half asleep, smoothed down the locks of matted hair with a nervous gesture, whereas the captain was impeccable and looked surprisingly fresh and clear-eyed for such an early hour.

"Let's go," he barked as soon as he saw me, and started off in the direction of the street without checking if we were following him.

The Vatican is the smallest state in the world, but if you cross a good bit of it on foot, at almost four in the morning, in the cold and through its silence, it seems like a nonstop road trip across the United States. We passed some black limousines with their *Se Cristo Videsse* license plates; their headlights fleetingly shone upon us and were soon lost down side streets of the City.

"Where are those cardinals going at this hour?" I asked, surprised.

"They're not going anywhere," Glauser-Röist answered dryly. "They're coming back. And if I were you, I wouldn't ask where they've been. You won't like the answer."

I closed my mouth as if it had been sown shut and told myself that, in the end, the captain was right. The depraved lives of the cardinals of the Curia were certainly unruly and indecorous; but then again, they were the ones who had to live with their consciences.

"Aren't they worried about scandal?" Farag wanted to know, in spite of the captain's sharp tone. "What would happen if some newspaper told all?"

Glauser-Röist kept walking in silence for a few moments. "That's my job," he spit out finally. "To prevent the Vatican's dirty laundry from coming to light. The church is holy, but some of its members can be very sinful."

The professor and I looked at each other and kept our lips glued shut until we got to the Hypogeum. The captain had the keys to all the doors of the Classified Archives, and watching him go from place to place, you could tell it wasn't the first night he'd come to these offices alone.

We finally entered my lab, which no longer resembled anything like the tidy office it had been a few months ago. A heavy book lying on my desk caught my eye. I was drawn to it like a magnet, but Glauser-Röist was fast and got the book before me. He grabbed it with his huge hands, his hulking body not letting me see it.

"Doctor, Professor...," began the Rock. We rushed to take a seat so we could pay attention. "I have in my hands a book, a type of travel guide that will take us to earthly paradise."

"Don't tell me the Staurofilakes published a Baedeker!"* I commented sarcastically. The captain struck me down with a look.

"Something like that," he replied, turning to show us the title page.

For an instant, Farag and I were in complete shock, unable to utter a single word.

"The *Divine Comedy* by Dante?" I queried. Either the captain was making fun of us or he'd gone completely mad.

"Yes indeed, the *Divine Comedy*," he replied.

"Dante Alighieri?" Farag was more surprised than I, if that were possible.

"Is there any other *Divine Comedy*, Professor?" argued Glauser-Röist.

"It's...," babbled Farag, incredulous. "Captain, that doesn't make much sense." He gave a little laugh, as if he'd just heard a joke. "Come on, Kaspar, quit pulling our legs!"

Glauser-Röist sat down at my desk and opened the book to a page marked with a red sticky note.

"*Purgatory*," he recited like a diligent schoolboy. "Canto I, lines thirty-one and beyond. Dante arrives with his guide Virgil at the gates of Purgatory and says:

"I saw near me an ancient man, alone,
whose face commanded all the reverence
that any son could offer to his sire.

---

*Famous paperback travel guidebooks, published in Germany since 1829.

"Long-flowing was his beard and streaked with white,
as was his hair, which in two tresses fell
to rest upon his chest on either side.

"The rays of light from those four sacred stars
struck with such radiance upon his face,
it was as if the sun were shining there."

The captain looked at us expectantly.

"Very nice, sure," commented Farag.

"Truly poetic," I agreed, dripping with cynicism.

"Don't you see?" Glauser-Röist said, exasperated.

"Well, what do you want us to see?" I exclaimed.

"The old man! Don't you recognize him?" Before our astonished eyes and our look of total incomprehension, the captain sighed, resigned, and adopted the air of a patient elementary-school teacher. "Virgil forces Dante to prostrate himself before the old man, and the old man asks who they are. Then Virgil tells him that, on a petition from Jesus Christ and Beatrice (Dante's dead beloved), he is showing Dante the kingdom of the underworld."

He skipped a page and read again:

"Already I have shown him all the Damned;
I want to show him now the souls of those
who purge themselves of guilt in your domain.

"May it please you to welcome him—he goes
in search of freedom, and how dear that is,
the man who gives up life for it well knows.

"You know, you found death sweet in Utica
for freedom's sake; there you put off that robe
which will be radiant on that Great Day."

"Utica! Cato of Utica!" I cried. "The old man is Cato of Utica!"

"Finally! That was what I wanted you to figure out!" explained Glauser-Röist. "Cato of Utica, who is the namesake for the archimandrites of the Staurofilakes brotherhood, is the guardian of Purgatory in Dante's *Divine Comedy*. Don't you think that means something? As you know, the *Divine Comedy* is composed of three parts: *Inferno*, *Purgatory*, and *Paradise*. Each one was published separately. Observe the coincidences in the text by the last Cato and Dante's text in *Purgatory*." He turned pages back and forth, and searched my desk for the transcript of the last folio of the Iyasus Codex. "In line eighty-two, Virgil says to Cato, 'Allow us to go through your seven realms,' so that Dante should purge himself of the seven deadly sins, one in each circle or cornice of the mountain of *Purgatory*: pride, envy, wrath, sloth, greed, gluttony, and lust," he enumerated. Then he grabbed up the copy of the folio and read: "The expiation of the Seven Deadly Sins will take place in the seven cities that boast the terrible distinction of being known to practice them perversely: Rome, for its pride; Ravenna, for its envy; Jerusalem, for its wrath; Athens, for its sloth; Constantinople, for its greed; Alexandria for its gluttony; and Antioch, for its lust. In each of these cities, as if it were an earthly purgatory, they will suffer their faults in order to enter in the secret place we Staurofilakes will call the earthly paradise."

"And does the Mountain in Dante's *Purgatory* have at its peak earthly paradise?" asked Farag, intrigued.

"That's right," confirmed Glauser-Röist. "The second part of the *Divine Comedy* ends when Dante purifies himself of the Seven Deadly Sins and arrives at the earthly paradise. From there he can now reach the heavenly paradise, which is the third and last part of the *Divine Comedy*. Now, listen to what the guardian angel at the door of Purgatory tells Dante when he begs him to let him pass:

> "*Then with his sword he traced upon my brow*
> *The scars of seven P's. 'Once entered here,*
> *Be sure you cleanse away these wounds,' he said.*"*

* *Purgatory*, Canto IX, 112–14.

"Seven *P's*—one for each deadly sin!" the captain continued. "Do you understand? Dante will be free of them, one by one, as soon as he expiates his sins in the seven cornices of purgatory. The Staurofilakes marked the aspiring Staurofilakes with seven crosses, one for each deadly sin overcome in the seven cities."

I didn't know what to think. Could Dante have been a Staurofilax? It sounded absurd. I had the feeling we were sailing on stormy seas. Could it be that we were simply tired and lacked perspective?

"Captain, how can you be so sure?" I said, unable to hide the doubt in my voice.

"Look, Doctor, I know this work like the back of my hand. I studied it in depth at the university. I guarantee that Dante's *Purgatory* is the Baedeker guide, as you put it, that will lead us to the Staurofilakes and the stolen *Ligna Crucis.*"

"But how can you be so sure?" I insisted stubbornly. "It could all just be a simple coincidence. All the material Dante used in the *Divine Comedy* is a part of medieval Christian mythology."

"Do you recall that in the middle of the eleventh century various groups of Staurofilakes departed from Jerusalem bound for the main Christian cities in the East and West?"

"Yes, I do."

"Do you recall that those groups made contact with the Catharists, the Fede Santa, the Massenie du Saint Graal, the Minnesanger, or the Fidei d'Amore, just to mention some of the Christian organizations?"

"I recall that too."

"Well, let me tell you that from a very young age, Dante Alighieri was part of the Fidei d'Amore, and he came to occupy a very prominent position in the Fede Santa."

"Are you serious?" stammered Farag, blinking. "Dante Alighieri?"

"Why do you think people don't understand a thing when they read the *Divine Comedy*? They think it's a beautiful yet extremely long poem loaded with metaphors students always interpret as allegories for the Holy Catholic Church, the Sacraments, or some crazy thing like that. Everyone thinks that Beatrice, his beloved Beatrice, who died at the age of twenty, was the daughter of Folco Portinari. However, that's not true, and that's why people don't understand what the poet is saying, because they critique it from a mistaken perspective. Beatrice Portinari isn't the Beatrice Dante refers to, and the Catholic Church isn't the protagonist of the work. The *Divine Comedy* has to be read in code."

He walked away from my desk and took out a piece of meticulously folded paper from the inside pocket of his jacket. "Did you know that each one of the three parts of the *Divine Comedy* has exactly thirty-three cantos? Did you know that each one of those cantos has exactly 115 or 160 lines, the sum of whose digits is seven? Do you think that's merely a coincidence in a work of such magnitude as the *Divine Comedy*? Did you know that the three parts, *Inferno*, *Purgatory*, and *Paradise*, end with the exact same word, *stars*? This is but a small part of the mystery contained in this colossal work. I could mention dozens of examples, but we would be here forever."

Farag and I looked at each other, stupefied. It never would have occurred to me that the pinnacle of Italian literature, one I abhorred in high school because it was required reading, could also be a compendium of esoteric wisdom. Or was it?

"Captain, are you telling us that the *Divine Comedy* is a type of guide book to initiation into the Staurofilakes?"

"No, Doctor, I'm not saying it is *that type* of book. I am saying it *is* THE book. Without any doubt. Do you want me to prove it to you?"

"Yes, I do," exclaimed Farag, clearly frustrated.

The captain picked up the book he'd left on the table and opened it to a section he'd already marked.

"Canto IX of the *Inferno*, lines sixty-one through sixty-three:

"Men of sound intellect and probity,
Weigh with good understanding what lies hidden
Behind the veil of my strange allegory!"

"Is that it?" I asked, disappointed.

"Observe, Doctor, that these lines are found in the ninth canto—nine being a number of great importance for Dante. According to all his writings, Beatrice is the number nine; and nine, in medieval numerical symbolism, represents wisdom, supreme knowledge, and the science that explains the world beyond faith. What's more, this mysterious affirmation is found in lines sixty-one through sixty-three of the canto. Add the digits of those numbers—six plus one is seven, six plus three is nine. Remember that in Dante, nothing is by chance, not even a comma. *Inferno* has nine circles where the souls of those condemned are lodged according to their sins, *Purgatory* has seven cornices, and *Paradise* again has nine circles... Seven and nine, don't you get it? But I promised I would prove it to you, and that's exactly what I'm going to do."

All his pacing was making me nervous, but it wasn't the right time to ask him to stand still. He was deeply engrossed in what he was telling us.

"As most experts confirm, Dante was inducted into the Fidei d'Amore in 1283, when he was eighteen years old, a little while after his second supposed meeting with Beatrice (according to his very own account in *La Vita Nuova*, the first encounter occurred when they were both nine. As you will see, the second encounter took place nine years later, when they were both eighteen). The Fidei d'Amore was a secret society interested in the spiritual renewal of Christianity. We are talking about an era in which corruption had already made inroads into the Church of Rome: riches, power, ambition... It was the time of Pope Boniface VIII, with his terrible legacy. The Fidei d'Amore tried to combat this depravity and restore Christianity back to its primitive purity. Some actually believed that the Fidei d'Amore, the Fede Santa, and the Franciscans were three distinct branches of the same Tertiary Order of the Templar. This, of course, can't be proven. What's certain is that Dante was raised by the Franciscans, and that he always maintained close ties with them. Well-recognized poets such as Guido Cavalcanti, Cino da Pistoia, Lapo Gianni, Forese Donati, Dante himself, Guido Guinizelli, Dino Frascobaldi, Guido Orlandi, and many others were members of the Fidei d'Amore. Cavalcanti, who had the reputation of being extravagant and heretical, was the Florentine head of the Fidei d'Amore, and was the one who admitted Dante into this secret society. As cultured men, intellectuals of a new, unfolding medieval society, they were nonconformists. At the top of their lungs, they denounced the ecclesiastic immorality and Rome's efforts to stop nascent freedoms and scientific knowledge. Could the *Divine Comedy* be, as they claim, a great religious work that glorifies the Catholic Church for its values and virtues? I don't think so. In fact, the simplest reading of the text reveals Dante's rancor toward numerous popes and cardinals, toward the corrupt clerical hierarchy and the riches of the church. Yet certain scholars have twisted the poet's words and made them say what they don't say."

"But what does Dante have to do with the Staurofilakes?" Farag insisted.

"Sorry," mused the captain. "I got carried away. Dante did indeed have a relationship with the Staurofilakes. He knew them and he may even have belonged to the order for a while. But of course, later he betrayed them."

"He betrayed them?" I was surprised. "Why?"

"Because he revealed their secrets, Doctor. Because, in *Purgatory*, he explained in detail the order's initiation process. The same way Mozart revealed the Masons' initiation ritual in his opera *The Magic Flute*. In fact, Mozart's death also presents numerous enigmatic aspects, still unsolved. There's no doubt Dante Alighieri was a Staurofilax. He took advantage of his knowledge of the brotherhood to triumph as a poet and to enrich his literary work."

"The Staurofilakes wouldn't have allowed it. They would have broken off ties with him."

"Who said they didn't?"

I opened my mouth wide. "They did?"

"Do you know that after the publication of *Purgatory* in 1315 Dante disappeared for four years? Nothing is known of him until January 1320 when"—he took a deep breath and stared at us—"when he reappeared, by surprise, in Verona, and delivered a lecture on the sea and earth in the Church of Saint Helen! Why there after four years of silence? Was he asking for forgiveness for what he had done in *Purgatory*? We'll never know. What we do know is as soon as he ended his lecture, he departed at full gallop for Ravenna, a city governed by his great friend Guido Novello da Polenta. Clearly he was seeking protection.

That same year, he received an invitation to teach some classes at the University of Bologna; but he rejected the offer, alleging he was afraid that if he left Ravenna, he would be in grave danger, a danger he never specified and that, historically speaking, seems completely unjustified." The captain stopped for a moment, reflecting. "Sadly, a year later his friend Novello asked a very special favor of him, to intercede with the doge in Venice, who was about to invade Ravenna. Dante set off, but on the road he became mortally ill with a terrible fever. He died a short while later. Do you know what day he died on?"

Farag and I didn't say a word. I think we weren't even breathing.

"September 14, the day of the Exaltation of the True Cross."

CHAPTER

3

either the professor nor I showed
up at the Hypogeum the next morning. We had gone home to sleep
around six in the morning, on edge
thanks to the captain's incredible discoveries. By
noon, we were back, gathered around a table in
the Domus dining room. Our sleepy faces would
have frightened ghosts. Glauser-Röist was the
last to arrive. He looked more than sleepy; his
lips were contracted into an icy smile that worried me.

"Has something happened, Captain? You
don't look so good."

"No," he barked. He took a seat and spread
a napkin over his knees. That said it all. Farag and
I read each other's thoughts: Don't push him. Instead, we talked about Professor Boswell's future
in Italy while the Swiss Rock remained mute.
Only during dessert did he deign to pry his lips
apart. Naturally, it was to give us some bad
news.

"His Holiness is very upset," he sprung
on us.

"I don't think he's justified," I protested. "We've been working as fast as we can."

"That isn't good enough, Doctor. The pope was clear that he is completely dissatisfied with our work. If we can't get results in short order, he'll put another team on the project. Besides, the press is about to leak the news of the thefts of the *Ligna Crucis*."

"How's that possible?" I said, alarmed.

"People all over the world already know about it. Someone has been talking too much. We managed to stop the story for now, but who knows for how long."

Farag pinched his lower lip, deep in thought. "I think your pope is wrong. I don't understand how can he threaten us with another team. Does he think that will make us work harder? I wouldn't mind sharing what we know with another team. Four eyes see more than two, right? Either your pontiff is extremely upset, or he's treating us like children."

"He's very upset," answered Glauser-Röist, "so let's get back to work."

In less than half an hour, we were in the Hypogeum, seated around my desk. The captain suggested we each read the *Divine Comedy* all the way through, take notes on anything that caught our attention, and re-group at the end of the day to compare notes. Farag argued that we were only interested in *Purgatory* and that, instead of wasting time, we should skim the *Inferno* and *Paradise*, focusing only on the relevant material. Seeing that as my only chance, I came up with an even more definitive approach. With heart in hand, I admitted I detested the *Divine Comedy*. In high school my literature teachers had really made me hate it, and I felt absolutely incapable of reading that hulking bundle of papers, and that the best I could do was jump into the heart of it and skip over the rest.

"But Ottavia, we might inadvertently overlook too many important details," said Farag.

"I disagree. That's what we have the captain for! He's passionate about this book. He knows it and the author well. Let him read it clear through while we focus on *Purgatory*."

Glauser-Röist pursed his lips but didn't say a word. He seemed annoyed.

With that we got to work. That afternoon, the secretary general of the Vatican Library gave us two more copies of the *Divine Comedy*. I sharpened my pencils and arranged my notebooks, ready to tackle, for the first time in over twenty years, what I considered the biggest literary bore in the history of mankind. I'm not exaggerating when I say I got goose bumps just thinking about that book resting threateningly on my desk, Dante's skinny, aquiline profile staring at me from its cover. Sure, I could read Dante's magnificent text (I'd read much harder things—complete volumes of tedious scientific journals or medieval manuscripts of tiresome, patristic theology); it's just that it reminded me of the long afternoons back in high school when they made us read famous excerpts over and over while they repeated to us ad nauseam that that tiresome, incomprehensible work was a great source of pride for Italy.

Ten minutes later, I sharpened my pencils again. After that, I decided to go to the restroom. I sat back down, but five minutes later I was nodding off. So I went to the cafeteria, ordered an espresso, and drank it calmly. I dragged myself back to the Hypogeum, and it struck me that right then was an excellent time to straighten up my office, sort through a huge stack of papers and worthless odds and ends that seemed to have magically accumulated over the years. At seven that evening, racked with guilt, I gathered up my things and went home to the Piazza delle Vaschette. I didn't even say good-bye to Farag and the captain, both of whom were absorbed and profoundly moved by that great work of Italian literature.

During the short trip home, I lectured myself severely about responsibility and fulfilling one's obligations. I had deserted those poor men—that's how I saw them—toiling away dutifully while I fled like a terrified schoolgirl. I swore there'd be no excuses the next day. Bright and early, I'd sit down at my desk and get busy.

When I opened the door to my house, the strong aroma of spaghetti sauce attacked my nose. My gastric juices awoke with a vengeance and my stomach began to rumble. Ferma appeared at the end of the apartment's narrow hallway and smiled in welcome, attempting to hide the worried look on her face.

"Ottavia? We haven't seen you in days!" she exclaimed overjoyed. "I'm so glad you're home."

I sniffed the delightful aroma wafting from the kitchen. "Can I have some of that deliciously scented sauce you're making?" I asked, taking off my jacket, heading straight for the kitchen.

"It's just some spaghetti sauce I whipped up," she protested with false modesty. Ferma was probably cooking up something marvelous and grand.

"Well, then I need a plate of that spaghetti."

"Relax. We're just about to have dinner. Margherita and Valeria will be here any minute."

"Where did they go?"

Ferma looked at me reproachfully and stopped a couple of steps from me. She looked grayer every day, as if her gray hairs were multiplying by the hour.

"Ottavia… Don't you remember what happens next Sunday?"

Sunday, Sunday… What did we have to do on Sunday?

"Don't make me guess, Ferma!" I complained, forgetting dinner for a moment and heading for the living room. "What happens on Sunday?"

"It's the Fourth Sunday of Easter!" she exclaimed as if the world were coming to an end.

I stood there frozen, not reacting. Sunday was meant for our renewal of vows, and I had forgotten all about it.

"My God," I whispered with a moan.

Ferma left the living room, wagging her head in sorrow. She didn't dare reproach me, knowing that my disgraceful carelessness was due to the strange work I was immersed in, the work that kept me away from home and kept them and my family on my periphery. But I recriminated myself. On account of my failings that day, God was punishing me with a new guilt. Crestfallen and alone, I forgot about dinner and the pangs of hunger from my stomach, and went directly to the chapel to pray and ask for forgiveness. Forgetting the renewal of my vows wasn't so much a legal problem, it was a mere formality really. I'd forgotten the very important ritual that had been enjoyable and fulfilling all the years since I professed my faith. True, my work and my order's preferential treatment made me an atypical nun, but none of that would matter if my relationship with God weren't the foundation and focus of my life. So, I prayed, my heart weighed down with pain. I promised to strive to follow Christ so that my upcoming renewal of vows was indeed a new chapter, filled with jubilation and happiness.

When I heard Margherita and Valeria come in, I crossed myself and got up off the floor, leaning on the floor cushions, aching in all my joints. Maybe it was time to substitute regular chairs and kneeling pads for the modern decorations in the chapel. My sedentary life was taking its toll: Besides my destroyed vertebrae, my knees were starting to hurt when I sat still for small periods at a time. Whether I liked it or not, I was quickly becoming a feeble old woman.

After dinner with my sisters, I retired to my small room, which seemed less and less familiar, and called home to Sicily. I talked to my sister-in-law, Rosalia, Giuseppe's wife. Then Giacoma grabbed the phone and gave me a good scolding for being so out of touch. Suddenly, without bothering with niceties, she blurted out a sturdy "Good-bye!" Next, I heard my mother's sweet voice.

"Ottavia?"

"Mama! How are you, Mama?"

"Fine, my dear, fine… Everything is fine here. How are you?"

"Working a lot, as always."

"Well, keep up the good work." Her voice sounded happy, not a care in the world.

"Yes, Mama."

"Well, dear, take care. Will you do that?"

"Of course."

"Call again soon, I love to hear from you. By the way, next Sunday is your renewal of vows, right?" My mother never forgot important dates in her children's lives.

"Yes."

"I hope you're happy, my darling! We will all pray for you at Mass here at home. Kisses, Ottavia."

"A kiss to you, Mama. Bye."

That night I slept with a happy smile on my lips.

*T*he next morning, at eight on the dot, just like I promised myself, I was at my desk, my glasses jammed on my nose, pencil in hand, ready to read the *Divine Comedy* without procrastinating. I opened to page 270, and in the middle of the page, in tiny letters, was the word *Purgatory*. Sighing and armed with courage, I turned the page and started to read.

> *For better waters, now, the little bark*
> *Of my poetic powers hoists its sails,*
> *And leaves behind that cruelest of the seas.*
>
> *And I shall sing about the second realm*
> *Where man's soul goes to purify itself*
> *And become worthy to ascend to Heaven.**

Thus Dante's first lines pointed out the way. According to a footnote, the trip through the second kingdom started on April 10, 1300—Easter Sunday—around seven in the morning. In Canto I, Virgil and Dante have just arrived from the Inferno and are in the antechamber of Purgatory, a deserted plain. They immediately meet the guardian of that place, Cato of Utica, who reproaches them bitterly for being there. Just as Glauser-Röist said, once Virgil offers him an explanation and tells him that Dante must be instructed about the kingdoms from the other world, Cato gives them all the help he can to start them on their difficult journey.

> *Go with this man, see that you gird his waist*
> *with a smooth reed; take care to bathe his face*
> *till every trace of filth has disappeared,*

---

* *Purgatory,* Canto I, 1–6.

*for it would not be fitting that he go
with vision clouded by the mists of Hell,
to face the first of Heaven's ministries.*

*Around this little island at its base,
down there, just where the waves break on the shore,
you will find rushes growing in soft sand.**

Virgil and Dante head off on the lower plain toward the sea. The great poet of Mantua brushes his palms over the dewy grass, then washes the dirt off his face left by his trip though the Inferno. After that, they come to a deserted beach. Across from it is a little island where Dante wraps a reed around his waist, just as Cato had ordered.

In the next seven cantos, from that dawn till nightfall, Virgil and Dante cross Pre-Purgatory, running into and having conversations with old friends and acquaintances. In Canto III they finally reach the foot of Purgatory Mountain. It has seven circles or terraces where souls are cleansed of their sins so they can enter heaven. Dante observes that the stone walls are so rocky it would be very difficult to climb them. As he looks on in awe, a mob of souls walks slowly toward him and Virgil. They are the excommunicated who repented their sins before they died and are condemned to walk very slowly around the mountain for eternity. In Canto IV, Dante and Virgil come across a narrow path and start their ascent. They have to struggle on all fours, but they finally reach a wide landing. As soon as they catch their breath, Dante complains of terrible fatigue. Suddenly, a mysterious voice beckons to them from behind a rock, and as they approach it, they discover a second group of souls, those who tarried in repenting. A short distance down the road, in Canto V, they run into the souls of those who died a violent death and recanted their sins at the last second. In Canto VI an extremely emotional meeting takes place: Dante and Virgil find the soul of the famous poet Sordello de Gioto who, in Canto VII, accompanies them all the way to the valley of irresponsible princes, and explains to them that on Pur-

* *Purgatory*, Canto I, 94–102.

gatory Mountain they must stop their journey and seek shelter as soon as evening light disappears since "at night it is forbidden to ascend."

After some conversations with the princes in the valley, Canto IX begins. True to his favorite number, nine, Dante places the real entrance to Purgatory in this canto. Needless to say, it's not easy. Apparently it's around three in the morning, and Dante, the only mortal there, can't stay awake, and he falls asleep on the grass like a little boy. In his dream he sees an eagle swoop down like lightning, grab him with its claws, and lift him to the sky. Terrified, he awakens to discover it's already the next morning and he is looking out at the sea. Calmly Virgil warns him not to be alarmed; they have finally come to the longed-for door to Purgatory. He tells him that while he was asleep a woman named Lucia* came and carefully carried him in her arms to where they were now. After setting him on the ground, she looked toward the road they should follow. I liked the mention of the patron saint of vision; she's one of Sicily's patron saints, along with Saint Agueda, which is where the names of my two sisters come from.

Dante, his mind clear from the shadows of his dream, continues on with Virgil in the direction Lucia pointed, and they come before three steps. At the top of those steps, behind a door, is the guardian angel of Purgatory, the first of the ministers of Paradise that Cato had told them about.

> He said to us: "Speak up from where you are.
> What is it that you want? Where is your guide?
> Beware, you may regret your coming here."
>
> "A while ago, a lady sent from Heaven
> acquainted with such matters," said my guide,
> "told me: 'Behold the gate. You must go there.'"†

Clutching a gleaming sword, the guardian angel invites them to climb to where he stands. The first step was made of gleaming white

---

*Saint Lucia.
† *Purgatory*, Canto IX, 85–90.

marble, the second of a rough, black stone, the third of blood-red porphyry. According to a footnote, this landscape was an allegory of the
sacrament of the confession: The angel represented the priest and the
sword symbolized the priest's words that move us to repent. At that moment I thought of Sister Berardi, one of my high school teachers, who
explained that landscape to us. She used to say, "The white marble step
signifies the examination of conscience; the black stone, the pain of
contrition; the red porphyry, the satisfaction of repentance." The mind
retains such strange things! After all these years, I could recall Sister
Berardi and her soporific literature classes.

Just then, the captain and Farag poked their heads in my door.
"How's it going?" the professor asked sarcastically, wearing a big grin.
"Have you overcome your childhood traumas?"

"No, I haven't." I flopped back in my chair and rested my glasses on
my forehead. "This work is still an unbearable bore."

He studied me in a strange way I couldn't put my finger on. Then
like someone awakening from a long dream, he blinked and got tongue-
tied. "Where…where have you gotten to?" He jammed his hands into
the pockets of his old jacket.

"The conversation with the guardian of Purgatory, the angel with
the sword standing on the steps."

"Terrific! That's one of the most interesting parts! The three steps
of alchemy."

"The three steps of alchemy?" I parroted, wrinkling my nose.

"Oh, come on, Ottavia! Surely you know that those steps represent
the three steps in the alchemic process: Albedo, Nigredo, and Rubedo.
The Work in White, or *Opus Album*; the Work in Black, or *Opus Nigrum*;
and…" Seeing the surprised look on my face, he stopped and smiled. "It
must ring a bell… You're probably more familiar with the Greek names:
Leucosis, Melanosis, and Iosis."

"Of course it sounds familiar, but I never would have imagined that
the steps of Purgatory had anything to do with alchemy. What I remember is that they were a symbol for the sacrament of the confession…"

"The sacrament of the confession? Look what he wrote: The guardian angel's feet rest on the step of porphyry and he is seated at the

threshold of a door made of diamonds. With the Work in Red, which is sublimation, the last step of the alchemic process, one reaches the philosopher's stone which is made of diamonds, remember?"

"Yes..." I couldn't shake my astonishment. I would never have suspected it. This interpretation was much more plausible than the one about confession.

"I see you're bewildered! I'll leave you to your work. Keep reading."

"Yeah, sure. See you at dinner."

"We'll come by for you."

But I wasn't listening to him anymore, I couldn't do a single thing. I gazed, stunned, at the text of *Purgatory*.

"I said, Kaspar and I will come get you for lunch," Farag repeated from the door, in a really loud voice. "Okay, Ottavia?"

"Yeah, sure...lunch, right."

Dante Alighieri had just been reborn in my eyes. I was starting to think maybe the Swiss Rock had been right, that the *Divine Comedy* was a book for initiates. But, dear God, how could that be linked to the Staurofilakes? I massaged the bridge of my nose and put my glasses back on, ready to read the rest of the verses with greater interest and new eyes.

Farag interrupted me when Virgil and Dante were at the steps. Once they climbed them, Virgil tells his pupil to humbly ask the angel to open the latch.

Falling devoutly at his holy feet,
In mercy's name I begged to be let in;
But, first of all, three times I smote my breast.

Then with his sword he traced upon my brow
The scars of seven P's. "Once entered here,
be sure you cleanse away these wounds," he said.

From beneath his ash- or earth-colored robes, the angel takes out two keys, one made of silver and the other, gold. The angel opens the locks first with the white, then the yellow, explains Dante:

*"Whenever either one of these two keys
fails to turn properly inside the lock,"
the angel said, "the road ahead stays closed.*

*"One is more precious, but the other needs
Wisdom and skill before it will unlock,
For it is that one which unties the knot.*

*"I hold these keys from Peter, who advised:
'Admit too many, rather than too few,
if they but cast themselves before your feet.' "*

*Then, pushing back the portal's holy door,
"Enter," he said to us, "but first be warned:
to look back means to go back out again."*

Well, I said to myself, if that isn't a guide for entering Purgatory, I don't know what is. I had to admit Glauser-Röist was completely right. But we were still missing the main point: Where in the real world would we find the Pre-Purgatory, the three alchemic steps, the guardian angel, and the door with two locks?

At noon as we headed for the cafeteria, I realized I should mention my temporary absence from the team to Glauser-Röist.

"On Sunday, I celebrate my renewal of vows, Captain. I need to go on a retreat for a couple of days. Without fail, I'll be back on Monday."

"We've really fallen behind," he muttered angrily. "Couldn't you take just Saturday?"

"What is renewal of vows?" Farag asked.

"Well," I answered bewildered. "We in the Order of the Blessed Virgin Mary renew our vows every year." For a nun, talking about these things was the most private, intimate part of her life. "Other orders take perpetual vows or they renew them every two or three years. We do it every year on the fourth Sunday of Easter."

"The vows of poverty, chastity, and obedience?" Farag insisted.

"Strictly speaking, yes..." I replied growing more and more uncomfortable. "But not just that... Well, yes it's that, but..."

"Don't you Coptics have ordained people as well?" Glauser-Röist
came to my rescue.

"Yes, sure. Forgive me, Ottavia. I was just being curious."

"No, it's okay, really."

"I thought you were a nun forever," Farag added rather inappropri-
ately. "An annual renewal of vows is a good thing. If you decide you
don't want to go on being a nun someday, you can leave."

The strong sunlight coming through the windows blinded me for a
moment. For some reason, I didn't explain to him that throughout the
entire history of my order, no nun had ever quit.

*G*od's designs are so hard to understand! We are immersed in total
blindness from the day we're born till the day we die. During the
brief interval we call life, we have no control over what happens around
us. On Friday the phone in our apartment rang. I was in the chapel with
Ferma and Margherita, reading some passages by Father Caciorgna, the
founder of our order, trying to prepare for the ceremony on Sunday. I
don't know why, but when I heard the phone ringing, I knew instinc-
tively that something serious had happened. Valeria answered the phone.
Seconds later, the door to the chapel half-opened softly.

"Ottavia, it's for you."

I got up, crossed myself, and left. My sister Agueda's voice wailed on
the other end of the phone line.

"Ottavia. Papa and Giuseppe..."

"Papa and Giuseppe?" I asked when my sister had grown quiet.

"Papa and Giuseppe are dead."

"What do you mean, Papa and Giuseppe are dead?" I was finally
able to ask. "What are you saying, Agueda?"

"Yes, Ottavia," my sister began to cry softly. "They're dead."

"My God! What happened?"

"An accident. A horrible accident. They were driving on the highway, and..."

"Calm down, please. Don't cry in front of the children."

"They're not here," she wailed again. "Antonio took them to his parents' house. Mama wants everyone to meet at the estate."

"And Mama? How's Mama?"

"You know how strong she is... But I'm worried about her."

"And Rosalia? And Giuseppe's children?"

"That's all I know, Ottavia. They're all at the villa. I'm leaving right away."

"Me, too. I'll catch the ferry tonight."

"No," my sister scolded me. "Don't catch the ferry. Get on a plane. I'll ask Giacoma to send some men to pick you up at the airport."

*W*e spent the entire night holding a wake and praying the Rosary in the living room, by the light of tall wax candles set on tables and the hearth. My father's and brother's bodies were still in the forensic offices in Palermo, although the judge assured my mother that, first thing the next morning, they would bring them to us so they could be exhumed in the cemetery at our villa. My brothers Cesare, Pierluigi, and Salvatore, who went to the depository at dawn, told us that Papa and Giuseppe were very disfigured and it wouldn't be wise to have open caskets in the candlelit chapel. My mother called the funeral home—it turns out we own it—to tell the makeup artists to compose the bodies as much as possible before bringing them home.

Giuseppe's wife, Rosalia, was shattered. Her children clung to her, inconsolable, worried something would happen to her. She couldn't stop crying, a blank look in her unfocused eyes, like that of a crazy woman. My sisters, Giacoma, Lucia, and Agueda, stayed with my mother, who led the Rosary, her brow furrowed, her face a waxen mask. My other sisters-in-law, Letizia and Livia, attended to the numerous family visitors who, despite the late hour, came to extend their condolences and join in the prayers.

And me? I drifted around the mansion, going up and down the stairs, my heart in such pain. I couldn't stay still. When I got to the roof-top terrace, I was surprised to see the sky through the attic window. I turned around and went back down to the reception, letting my hand trail along the soft, shiny wood banister we'd slid down so many times as kids. My mind kept going back to childhood memories of my father and brother. I repeated to myself that my father had been a good father, an unbeatable father, and my brother Giuseppe, despite becoming taciturn over the years, had been a good brother. When I was little, he'd tickle me and hide my toys to make me mad. The two of them had spent their lives working, maintaining and enlarging a family patrimony we were deeply proud of.

The condolences and weeping kept up till the next day. Villa Salina was filled with sadness and pain. Dozens of vehicles were parked by the garden. Hundreds of people took my hand, kissed my face, and hugged me. Only the Sciarra sisters were missing, which pained me deeply, for Concetta Sciarra had been my best friend for years. However, I can't say I was surprised that Doria, the youngest, was not there. The last thing we'd heard was that she'd left Sicily before she turned twenty and wandered here and there in who knows what foreign country. Now she was working as a secretary in some remote embassy. But I knew Concetta loved my father at least as much as I loved hers. Despite business squabbles between our families, I never thought she'd stay away.

The funeral took place on Sunday morning; Pierantonio couldn't get home from Jerusalem until late Saturday night, and my mother was determined to have him celebrate the Mass. I don't recall much until Pierantonio arrived. My brother and I hugged each other tight, then other mourners took him aside, kissed his hand, and paid him the reverences required by his position and circumstance. When they left him in peace, he grabbed a bite to eat, then shut himself away with Mama in her bedroom. As for me, I fell asleep on the sofa where I had sat down to pray.

Very early Sunday morning as we entered our church for the funerals, I received an unexpected phone call from Captain Glauser-Röist. Heading for the nearest phone, I grumbled, annoyed, wondering why he could possibly be calling me at such a bad time. I told him what happened and said good-bye before I left Rome. His call seemed disrespectful and woefully awkward. Given the circumstances, I wasn't one for courtesy.

"Is that you, Dr. Salina?" he asked when he heard my curt hello.

"Of course it's me, Captain."

"Doctor," he ignored my unpleasant tone of voice. "Professor Boswell and I are here in Sicily."

"Here? In Palermo?"

"Actually, we're at the airport in Punta Raisi, thirty miles outside the city. Professor Boswell is renting a car."

"What are you doing here? If you've come for my father and brother's funeral, you're a little late. You won't get here in time."

I felt uncomfortable. On the one hand, I appreciated his goodwill and his desire to be with me during such a sad time; but on the other, his gesture was unwarranted and somewhat inappropriate.

"We don't want to bother you, Doctor." I heard Glauser-Röist's booming voice over the squawk of loudspeakers calling passengers to board various flights. "We will wait until the funerals are over. What time do you think you could meet us?"

My sister Agueda stopped in front of me and pointed insistently to her watch. "I don't know, Captain. You know how these things are. Maybe noon."

"Not before?"

"No, Captain, not before!" I got even madder. "If you remember well, my father and brother just died and we are trying to have a funeral here!"

I could just imagine him, on the other side of the line, breathing deeply and trying to hold his composure.

"You see, Doctor, we've found the entrance to Purgatory. It's here, in Sicily. In Syracuse."

I stood there, hardly breathing. We'd found the entrance.

I didn't want to look at my father and brother when they opened the caskets for us to say good-bye. My mother, armed with courage, approached the coffins. First she leaned over to kiss my father on the forehead, but when she tried to kiss my brother, she fell to pieces. I saw her stagger and grip the edge of the casket, grabbing her cane with the other. Giacoma and Cesare were right behind her and rushed forward to hold her, but she fended them off with a threatening look. She bent her head and started to cry silently. I'd never seen my mother cry. Nobody had, but I think that pained us more than what was happening. Disconcerted, we looked at each other, not knowing what to do. Agueda and Lucia started to cry, too, and everyone, including me, started toward my mother to support and console her. The only one who reached her was Pierantonio; he ran around the altar and down the stairs, putting his arms around her shoulders and wiping away her tears. She was comforted by him, and for a moment looked like a little girl. We all realized that the day had produced an irreparable fissure that took its toll on her. She would never recover from the emotional toll of the deaths of her husband and son.

When the ceremony concluded and the burial ended and we were entering the house and they were starting to set the table, I asked Giacoma to lend me her car so I could go to Palermo. I was meeting with Farag and Glauser-Röist, at twelve-thirty, at La Gondola Restaurant on Via Principe di Scordia.

"Are you crazy?" my sister exclaimed, her eyes incredulous. "This isn't the day to go out to a restaurant!"

"This is work, Giacoma."

"That makes no difference! Call your friends and tell them to come here. You can't leave, do you hear me?"

I called Glauser-Röist on his cell phone and explained that I couldn't leave the villa. He and the professor were invited to have lunch at our home. I explained as best I could how to get there. I detected a note of reticence in his tone of voice that made me impatient.

They arrived just as we were about to sit down to the table. The captain was impeccably dressed as always, a somber look on his face. Farag, who usually dressed like a dignitary from some remote African country, now looked like a brave adventurer and hardened Jeep driver. The minute they walked in, I began the introductions. The professor looked disconcerted and restrained, but in his eyes you could detect the curiosity of a scientist who's studying a new animal species. Glauser-

Röist, on the other hand, was master of the situation. His aplomb and steadfastness were gratifying. My mother received them affably, and to my surprise, Pierantonio greeted the captain in a standoffish manner, as if he already knew him. After the greeting, they scurried apart like the same poles of two magnets.

I had been wanting to talk to Pierantonio since the moment he arrived, but hadn't gotten the chance. I suddenly found myself corralled in a corner of the garden where we were having coffee, to take advantage of the nice weather. My brother was not his usual good-natured self. He had dark circles under his eyes, wrinkles on his brow. He shot me a piercing look and then grabbed me by the wrist.

"Why are you working with Captain Glauser-Röist?" he said point-blank.

"How do you know I work with him?" I replied, surprised.

"Giacoma told me. Answer my question."

"I can't give you any details, Pierantonio. It has to do with what we talked about on Papa's saint day."

"I don't remember. Refresh my memory."

With my free hand I shrugged, raising my palm and holding it in the air. "What's wrong with you, Pierantonio? Are you sick in the head or what?"

My brother seemed to wake up from a dream. He looked at me, disconcerted. "Forgive me, Ottavia," he babbled, letting go of me. "I'm a bit nervous. Forgive me."

"Why are you nervous? Is it about the captain?"

"I'm sorry. Forget it," he replied, moving away.

"Come back here, Pierantonio," I ordered, sternly. He stopped abruptly. "Don't walk away without an explanation."

"Is little Ottavia rebelling against her big brother?" he crowed, wearing a very strange smile. But I wasn't laughing.

"Out with it, Pierantonio, or I'll really get angry."

He looked very surprised and took two steps toward me, frowning again. "You know who Kaspar Glauser-Röist is? You know what his job is?"

"I know he's a member of the Swiss Guard, but he works for the Sacred Roman Rota. He's coordinating the investigation I'm participating in."

My brother slowly shook his head several times. "No, Ottavia, no. Don't be fooled. Kaspar Glauser-Röist is the most dangerous man in the Vatican, the black hand who carries out every single one of the church's disgraceful acts. His name is associated with… This is great. Why is my sister working with the person most feared by heaven and earth?"

I was frozen and couldn't react.

"What do you have to say for yourself? Can you not give me an explanation?" my brother insisted.

"No."

"Well, this conversation is over, then." He walked away to join some cousins chatting around the table in the garden. "Be careful, Ottavia. That man is not what he seems."

When I recovered from my shock, I glimpsed over at my mother and Farag off in the distance, in an animated chat. With a faltering step, I headed their way. Before I could reach them, the captain's huge mass blocked my way.

"Doctor, we should leave as soon as possible. It's getting very late, and soon there won't be any light."

"How do you know my brother, Captain?"

"Your brother?"

"Look, don't put on an act. I know you know Pierantonio. Don't lie to me."

The Rock looked around, nonchalant. "I gather Father Salina didn't tell you, so neither will I, Doctor," he looked down at me. "Can we please go?"

I nodded and rubbed my face in consternation.

I said good-bye to everyone, one by one, and got in the car that the captain and Farag had rented, a silver Volvo S40, with tinted windows. We crossed the city and got on Highway 121 headed for Enna, in the heart of the island. From there, we took the A19 to Catania. Glauser-Röist really enjoyed driving. He turned on the radio and played music till we left Palermo. Once we were on the highway, he turned the volume down, and Farag, who was sitting in the backseat, leaned forward over the front seats and rested his arms close to each of our shoulders.

"Actually, Ottavia, we don't know why we're here. We came to check out a hunch, but we may be completely mistaken."

"Don't pay any attention to him, Doctor. The professor has found the entrance to Purgatory."

"Don't pay any attention to the captain, Doctor," the professor interjected, "I seriously doubt that we'll find the entrance in Syracuse, but the captain is hell-bent on verifying it in situ."

"Okay." I sighed. "At least give me a convincing explanation. What's in Syracuse?"

"Santa Lucia!" celebrated Farag.

I turned toward him, annoyed. "Santa Lucia?"

I was so close to the professor that I could feel his breath. I was paralyzed. A terrible feeling of shame suddenly suffocated me. I made a superhuman effort to turn back around to watch the highway in an attempt to hide my distress. Boswell had to have noticed, I told myself fearfully. It was an awkward situation. His silence was unbearable. Why didn't he continue telling his story?

"Why Saint Lucia?" I finally asked.

"Because..." Farag cleared his throat, dumbstruck. "Because..."

I couldn't see his hands, but I was sure they were trembling.

"I can explain, Doctor," intervened Glauser-Röist. "Who takes Dante to the door of Purgatory?"

I ran through my memory of the text. "Saint Lucia. She transports him through the air from Pre-Purgatory while he's asleep and leaves him by the sea. What does that have to do with Sicily? Okay, Saint Lucia is the patron saint of Syracuse, sure, but..."

"Syracuse looks out onto the sea," the professor observed, seemingly recovered from our momentary awkwardness. "Also, after setting Dante on the ground, Saint Lucia looks in the direction to the door with the two keys."

"Well, sure, but..."

"You know, of course, that Lucia is the patron saint of sight?"

"What a question! Naturally!"

"All images of her show her carrying her eyes on a small plate."

"She ripped her eyes out when she was martyred. Her pagan fiancé, who denounced her as a Christian, adored her eyes, so she ripped them out and had them delivered to him."

"May Saint Lucia preserve our sight," recited Glauser-Röist.

"Yes, that's the popular refrain."

"Nevertheless, the patron saint of Syracuse is always depicted with her eyes wide open. On the tray, she seems to be carrying an extra pair."

"Well, that's because no one is going to paint her with empty, bloody eye sockets."

"You think so? In my opinion, Christian iconography never seems to have shied away from emphasizing the blood and physicality of pain."

"Well, that's another matter. Where are you going with this?"

"It's simple. According to all the Christian martyrologies that describe the saint's torture, Lucia never plucked out her eyes nor lost them in any way. The truth is, Roman authorities who served Emperor Diocletian tried to rape her and burn her alive; but because of divine intervention, they were unable to, so they finally stabbed a sword in her throat to kill her. That was December 13, 300. But there was nothing about her eyes, nothing at all. Why, then, is she patron saint of sight? Could it be another type of sight—not of the body, but a vision that leads to a higher knowledge? In fact, in the language of symbols blindness symbolizes ignorance, and vision equals knowledge."

"That's just an assumption," I answered. I didn't feel well. Farag's long-winded commentary burdened me deeply. My father's and brother's deaths were still very much on my mind, and I didn't feel like listening to enigmatic subtleties.

"Just an assumption? Listen to this: The celebration of Saint Lucia honors the supposed day of her death, December 13."

"Yes, I know. It's my sister's saint day."

"Maybe you don't know that before the ten-day adjustment introduced by the Gregorian calendar in 1582, her day was celebrated on the winter solstice, December 21. Since ancient times, the winter solstice was when light's victory over darkness was commemorated, because the days started growing longer."

I didn't say a word. I couldn't grasp any of that rigmarole.

"Ottavia, please, you're an educated woman. Use all your knowledge and you'll see that what I'm saying is not some foolish notion. Dante made Saint Lucia his mysterious porter all the way to the entrance of Purgatory. After she left him on the ground, still asleep, she points out *with her eyes* the path to the door where they find the three alchemic steps and the guardian angel with the sword. Isn't that crystal clear?"

"I don't know. Is it?"

Farag remained silent.

"The professor isn't sure," murmured Glauser-Röist, pushing down on the accelerator. "That's why we're going to check it out."

"There are many Saint Lucia sanctuaries in the world," I grumbled. "Why the one in Syracuse?"

"Besides being the saint's birthplace, where she lived and was martyred, there are other facts that make us suspect Syracuse is the correct place," the Swiss Rock emphasized. "Cato of Utica suggests to Dante that, before appearing before the guardian angel, he wash the dirt off his face and gird his waist with rushes growing around a little island near the shore."

"Yes, I remember."

"The city of Syracuse was founded by the Greeks in the eighth century," continued Farag. "At that time it went by the name Ortygia."

"Ortygia?" I replied, trying not to turn around to look at him. "But isn't Ortygia the island across from Syracuse?

"Aha! Right! Across from Syracuse there's an island named Ortygia. The famous papyruses and rushes still grow there abundantly."

"But today, Ortygia is a suburb of the city. It's totally developed, and joined to land by a huge bridge."

"True. That doesn't take away one iota from the importance of the clue Dante put in his work. And you still don't know the best part."

"Really?" I had to admit they were beginning to make sense. As I listened to that string of theories, I was putting off the pain I felt over the tragic deaths in my family and, little by little, without realizing it, was getting back to reality.

"After the Roman Empire disappeared, Sicily was captured by the Goths. In the sixth century, Emperor Justinian, the same one who had the fort built around the Monastery of Saint Catherine of Sinai, commanded General Belisario to retake the island for the Byzantine Empire. The moment the troops from Constantinople arrived in Syracuse, do you know what they did? They built a temple in the place where the saint was martyred. And that temple—"

"I'm familiar with it."

"—is still standing today after many restorations over the centuries, of course." Farag was unstoppable. "But the old Saint Lucia Church's greatest attraction is located in its catacombs."

"Catacombs? I had no idea there were catacombs under the church."

Our car had just sped onto Highway 19. The sun began to set.

"Remarkable catacombs from the third century. Some of the main sections have hardly been examined. They were extended and modified during the Byzantine period, when there were no longer any persecutions and Christianity was the faith of the empire. Unfortunately they are only open to the public during the celebrations of Saint Lucia, from December 13 to the 20th, and, even then, the access isn't open to all of them. There are several floors and galleries left to explore."

"So how are we going to get in?"

"Maybe we won't have to. We don't actually know what we'll find. We don't know what we're looking for, the way we did in Saint Catherine of Sinai. We'll look around and then decide. Maybe we'll get lucky."

"I refuse to gird myself with rushes and wash my face with the dew from the grass of Ortygia."

"Don't be so stubborn," Glauser-Röist's angry voice reverberated. "That is, indeed, the first thing we'll do when we get there. In case it hasn't occurred to you, if indeed we are right, we'll be completely immersed in the Staurofilakes' initiation process before nightfall."

I kept my lips zipped the rest of the way.

*J*t was late when we arrived in Syracuse. I was afraid the Swiss
Rock would want to descend right then into the catacombs. Thank
God, he drove across the city, directly to the island of Ortygia, at whose
center, a short way from the famous Aretusa Fountain, was the archbishopric.

The church of the duomo was quite beautiful despite its unique
blend of architectural styles piled on top of one another over the centuries. Its huge baroque façade had six enormous white columns and an
upper vaulted niche with an image of Saint Lucia. But we didn't go in.
We parked the car in front of the church and followed Glauser-Röist on
foot, headed for the nearby archbishopric, where His Excellency Monsignor Giuseppe Arena received us in person.

That night we were feted by the archbishop with an exquisite dinner. After chatting about matters concerning the archdiocese and paying
a very special tribute to our pontiff, who would turn eighty that next
Wednesday, we retired to our rooms.

At four in the morning, with not one lousy ray of sunlight entering
the window, I was snatched from a deep sleep by loud knocks on the
door. It was the captain, ready to get started. I heard him knocking on
Farag's door as well. Half an hour later, we were all in the dining room,
eating a big breakfast served by a Dominican nun. As usual, the captain
was his alert and ready self, while Farag and I could barely utter a few
words. We wandered around the dining room like zombies, bumping
into chairs and tables. There was absolute silence in the building, broken
only by the nun's soft steps. After a few sips of coffee, my brain began
to process information again.

"Ready?" asked the imperturbable Swiss Rock, setting down his
napkin.

"I'm not," mumbled Farag, grabbing hold of his coffee cup the way
a sailor grabs the mast of a ship during a storm.

"I don't think I'm ready either," I answered with a conspiratory
look.

"Good, I'll go get the car, and I'll pick you up in five minutes."

"Okay, but I don't think I'll be here," warned the professor.

I laughed as Glauser-Röist left the dining room, oblivious to us.

"That man is impossible," I said as I noticed that Farag hadn't shaved that morning.

"We'd better hurry. He's capable of leaving without us. What can you and I do in Syracuse at five o'clock on a Monday morning?"

"Catch a plane and go home," I said, determined, as I got to my feet.

It wasn't cold outside. The weather was springlike, although humid and with a stiff breeze that ruffled my skirt. We got into the Volvo and drove all the way around the plaza, then down a street that led us directly to the port. We parked and walked to the end of the road to a spot where, by the light of the streetlights, you could make out very fine, white sand and where, of course, there were hundreds of rushes. The Rock carried with him a copy of the *Divine Comedy*.

"Professor, Doctor...," he murmured, visibly moved by the moment. "It's time to start."

He set the book down on the sand and headed for the rushes. With a reverent gesture, he passed his hands over the grass and wiped his face with the dew. Then, he yanked out the tallest of those flexible stems, pulled his shirttail out of his slacks, and tied it around his waist.

"Okay, Ottavia," Farag whispered, "it's our turn."

The professor marched over and repeated the process. Wet with dew, his face took on a special glow, as if he were in the presence of the divine. I felt troubled, uncertain. I had doubts about what we were doing, but I had no choice but to follow their lead; any rejection on my part would be ridiculed. I set my shoes in the sand and walked over to them, brushing my palms over the grass and then rubbing them on my face. The dew was cool, and it woke me up and left me lucid and full of energy. Then, I chose the rush that looked the greenest and prettiest, and tore it at the root, hoping it would some day grow back. I raised the hem of my sweater and held the plant against my waist, above my skirt. I was surprised by how delicate it felt. Its fibers were so elastic that I was able to easily tie it around my waist.

We had completed the first part of the ritual. Now we needed to know if it had served any purpose. If we were lucky, I told myself, trying to be calm, nobody had seen us. Back in the car, we left the island of Ortygia by the bridge and got on Avenue Umberto I. The city was beginning to stir. You could see lights lit in apartment windows and the traffic was already getting snarled. A few hours later it would be as chaotic as in Palermo, especially around the port. The captain turned right and headed toward the Via dell'Arsenale. Suddenly, he seemed surprised by what he saw.

"Do you know what this street is called? Via Dante. Isn't that strange?"

"In Italy, Captain, every city has a Via Dante," I replied, trying not to laugh. Farag's laughter, however, clearly pierced the morning air.

We arrived at the Plaza of Saint Lucia next to the soccer stadium, in no time. Instead of a plaza, it was an ordinary street that circumvented the rectangular church. Adjacent to the solid, white stone building and its modest three-story bell tower was a very small octagonal baptistery. Despite the Norman reconstruction of the twelfth century and the Renaissance rosette on its facade, this building was as Byzantine as Constantine the Great himself.

A man of about sixty, dressed in old trousers and a worn jacket, paced the sidewalk in front of the church. When he saw us get out of the car, he stopped and looked us over carefully. He had beautiful, thick gray hair and a small face covered with wrinkles. From the opposite side of the street, he waved his arm high over his head and broke into an agile run toward us.

"Captain Glaser-Röi?"

"Yes, that's me," the Rock said amiably, not correcting him and squeezing his hand. "These are my companions, Professor Boswell and Dr. Salina."

The captain had a small canvas backpack slung over his shoulder.

"Salina?" the man smiled amiably. "That's a Sicilian name, not from Syracuse. Are you from Palermo?"

"Yes, I am."

"Ah, I knew it! Well, come with me, please. His Excellency the archbishop called last night to advise of your visit. This way."

With an unexpectedly protective gesture, Farag took me by the arm until we reached the sidewalk.

The sacristan stuck an enormous key into the church's wood door and pushed it open, without entering. "His Excellency the archbishop asked us to leave you alone, until seven o'clock Mass. Our patron's church is all yours. Go on in. I'm going back home to have breakfast. If you need anything, I live over there." He pointed to the second floor of an old stucco building. "Aye, I almost forgot! Captain Glaser-Ro, the fuse box is on the right, and here are the keys to the entire place, including the chapel of the tomb and the baptistery next to it. Be sure to visit it, because it's really special. Well, so long. At seven o'clock sharp I'll come by to get you." He took off running back across the street. It was 5:30 a.m.

"Well, what are we waiting for? Doctor, you first."

The temple was completely dark, except for some overhead emergency lights. No light was coming in yet through the rosette or the large windows. The captain flipped the switches, and suddenly, electric lights hanging from the ceiling on long cables cast a diaphanous glow over everything. There were three richly decorated naves separated by pilasters, and a wood-trimmed caisson ceiling bearing the shields of the Spanish kings of Aragon who governed Sicily in the fourteenth century. Under a triumphal arch, there was a crucifix painted in the twelfth or thirteenth century and another one at the back from the Renaissance. On a magnificent silver pedestal was the processional image of Saint Lucia, with a sword sticking through her neck. In her right hand was a glass holding her pair of spare eyes.

"The church is ours." The Rock's voice sounded like a thunderclap inside a cave. The acoustics were fabulous. "Let's look for the entrance to Purgatory."

It was much colder inside than on the street, as if a current of frozen air bubbled out of the ground. I walked down the central corridor toward the altar. I felt an urgent need to kneel before the shrine and pray for a few moments. My head sunk between my shoulders, I covered my face with my hands and tried to reflect on all the strange things that had happened to me in the last several weeks. In just over a month, I had completely lost control of my once ordered life. In the last week, the situation had run even more amuck. Nothing was the same. I begged God to pardon me for having abandoned him, and with a desolate heart, I begged him to be merciful with my father and my brother. I also prayed that my mother find the strength she needed in these terrible times, and for the rest of my family. My eyes filled with tears, I crossed myself and stood up. Farag and the captain were examining the lateral naves. I walked up to the presbytery and looked at the red granite column. According to tradition, the saint lay there, dying from her wounds. Over the centuries the hands of the faithful had polished the stone. Its importance as an object of adoration was clear by how often this symbol was repeated on the church's decoration. Her eyes were depicted to the point of overkill. Hanging everywhere were hundreds of those strange ex-votos in the shape of small loaves of bread. They were called "Saint Lucia's eyes."

When we finished exploring the church, we headed down a narrow stairway that took us to the chapel of the sepulchre. Both buildings were connected by an underground tunnel carved out from solid rock. The octagonal baptistery contained the rectangular niche, or loculus, where the saint was buried after she was martyred. The truth is, her body wasn't in Syracuse, nor in Sicily. When Lucia died, her remains traveled halfway around the world and came to rest in San Jeremiah Church in Venice. In the eleventh century, the Byzantine general Maniace took them to Constantinople, where they were venerated until 1204. In that year, the Venetians brought them back to Italy for good. The people of Syracuse had to resign themselves to honoring an empty grave that was wonderfully decorated with a beautiful wood painting placed on an altar. Below that was a marble sculpture by Gregorio Tedeschi representing the saint at the moment of her funeral.

That was the end of our visit to the church. We had seen everything and examined it all in great detail. There was nothing strange or significant to connect it to Dante or the Staurofilakes.

"Let's recap," the captain proposed. "What caught your attention?"

"Absolutely nothing," I said, very convinced.

"So," declared Farag, pushing up his glasses, "we have only one option."

"That's exactly what I'm thinking," the Swiss Rock observed, as he went back down the corridor that led to the church.

Thus, against my deepest wishes, we descended into the catacombs.

According to the sign by the door, the catacombs of Saint Lucia were closed to the public. If anyone was curious, the poster added, he could visit the nearby catacombs of Saint Giovanni. Terrible images of earthquakes and cave-ins flashed before my eyes but I brushed them aside. Using one of the keys the sacristan had given him, the captain opened the door and squeezed himself inside.

Contrary to popular belief, the catacombs didn't serve as a refuge for the Christians in time of persecutions. To begin with, the persecutions were very brief and very limited in time. In the middle of the second century, the first Christians started to buy land to bury their dead, because they were against the pagan practice of cremation, believing in the resurrection of their bodies on Judgment Day. In fact, they didn't call these underground cemeteries *catacombs*, the Greek word meaning "cavity." They called them *koimeteria*, "bedrooms"—from which we get the term *cemetery*. They believed they would simply sleep until the resurrection of the flesh. Since they needed more and more space, the galleries of the *koimeteria* grew underground in every direction, becoming true labyrinths up to several kilometers long.

"Let's go, Ottavia." Farag cheered me on from the other side of the door, seeing I had no intention of entering.

A naked lightbulb hung from the ceiling of the grotto, casting a dim glow of shadows on a table, a chair, and some tools covered with a thick layer of dust located next to the entrance. Luckily, the captain had brought a powerful flashlight that lit the space up as though it was a thousand-watt beam. Some stairs, excavated in the rock many centuries before, tumbled toward the depths of the earth. Without hesitating, the Rock began his descent, while Farag stood to one side to let me pass and brought up the rear. Along the walls, lots of graffiti carved in the rock recalled the dead: *Cornelius cuius dies inluxit*, "Cornelius, whose day dawned"; *Tauta o bios*, "This is our life"; *Eirene ecoimete*, "Irene went to sleep." After a cramped space, the stairs turned left. There, several head-stones were piled, some of which were only fragments. Finally we came to the last stairway and found a small, rectangular-shaped sanctuary decorated with magnificent frescos that must have dated from the eighth or ninth century. The captain shined his flashlight on them, and we were fascinated to discover the prayer of the forty martyrs of Sebastia. According to legend, these young men made up the Twelfth Legion and loaned their services in Sebastia, Armenia, during the reign of Emperor Licinius, who ordered that all his legionnaires make sacrifices to the gods for the good of the empire. The forty soldiers of the Twelfth Legion flatly refused, since they were Christian. They were condemned to death by numbness—that is to say, they died frozen, hung by a rope, naked over an icy pond.

We admired how that whitewashed plaster wall had stayed in nearly perfect condition all those centuries, while later works done with more advanced techniques were in lamentable condition today.

"Don't shine your flashlight on the frescos, Kaspar," Farag begged, from the dark. "It could damage them forever."

"Sorry." The Rock quickly pointed the light toward the ground. "You're right."

"What do we do now? Do we have a plan?"

"Keep walking, Doctor. That's all."

On the other side of the sanctuary, we came to a cavity that seemed to be the beginning of a long corridor. We continued for a long stretch in complete silence, passing other galleries on the right and left in which you could see an endless line of tombs dug into the walls. The only sound we heard was that of our footsteps. Despite the vents in the ceiling, I felt I was suffocating. At the end of the tunnel, there was a new stairway, blocked off by a chain with a sign prohibiting entrance. The captain went around it and led us to the second level underground; there, the atmosphere was even more oppressive, if that were possible.

"Let me remind you," whispered the Rock, "these catacombs have hardly been explored. This level has never been studied, so be really careful."

"Why don't we study the upper level?" I felt the blood racing in my temples. "We have passed many galleries. The entrance to Purgatory might be there."

The captain walked forward a few steps and stopped, shining his light on something he saw on the floor. "I don't think so, Doctor. Look."

At our feet, enclosed in an intense circle of light, you could clearly make out a monogram of Constantine with the horizontal traverse line, identical to the one on Abi-Ruj Iyasus's body and on the cover of the codex of Saint Catherine. There was no doubt that the Staurofilakes had been there. What we couldn't know, I told myself in anguish, was how long ago they had been there, since most of the catacombs had fallen into disuse during the early Middle Ages right after, little by little, the saints' relics had been removed for security reasons and the vegetation had sealed the entrances, many of which had disappeared completely.

Farag couldn't contain his delight. As we advanced at a good pace through a very low tunnel, he celebrated the fact that we had deciphered the Staurofilakes' mysterious language. From now on, he said, we would be able to understand all their secret clues and hidden signs. His voice rose from the darkness that closed in behind me; only the captain's flashlight lit up that cavern a good meter in front of me. In the reflection of the light on the rock walls, I examined the three rows of loculi—many of them obviously occupied—that meandered at the height of our feet, our waists and our heads. I read the names of the dead engraved in the small headstones: Dionisio, Puteolano, Cartilia, Astasio, Valentina, Gorgono. Each one had a symbol for the work they did (priest, farmer, housewife) or for the primitive Christian religion they professed (the Good Shepherd, the dove, the anchor, the loaves and fishes). Encrusted in the plaster were the deceased's belongings, from coins to tools or toys, if they were children. That place was a priceless historical resource.

"A new chrismon," the captain announced, stopping at the intersection of two galleries.

To the right, at the back of a narrow passageway, was a cubicle with an altar at its center; on the walls were various loculi and large niches, each shaped like an oven, in which an entire family was usually buried.

To the left was another gallery with a high ceiling identical to the one we had just passed. In front of us was a new stairway dug into the rock. It was a spiral stairway that twisted and turned down around a thick central column of polished stone that then disappeared into the dark depths of the earth.

"Let me have a look," begged Farag, stepping in front of me.

The monogram of Constantine was chiseled right on the first step.

"I believe we need to keep going down," the professor murmured, passing his hands nervously over his hair and pushing up his glasses.

"I don't think that's such a good idea," I objected. "It's dangerous to keep descending."

"We can't turn back now," affirmed the Rock.

"What time is it?" asked Farag looking at his own watch.

"Six forty-five," the captain announced, starting to descend.

Given the chance, I'd have tromped back to the surface. But who was brave enough to backtrack alone, in the dark, through that labyrinth full of dead people? I had no choice but to follow the captain and descend, with Farag close behind me.

The spiral stairway seemed endless. We continued down into that pit, step by step, breathing air that grew heavier and more stifling, as we held on to the column to keep from losing our balance. Soon the captain and Farag had to walk stooped over, as their foreheads grazed the stairs overhead. The steps began to grow narrower, and the wall and the central column started to close in, making that dreadful funnel more suitable for children than adults. The captain had to stoop over and walk sideways, since his wide shoulders no longer fit through the opening.

If the Staurofilakes had thought up those stairs, they had twisted minds. The place was claustrophobic. The air was dwindling; and the thought of returning to the surface seemed just short of impossible. It seemed as though we'd bidden farewell to the real world (its cars, lights, people) forever. I felt like we'd entered one of those niches and we could never leave. Time stood still, and there was apparently no end to that diabolical stairway, which grew smaller and smaller at each step.

At one point, I was seized by a panic attack. I couldn't breathe, I was choking. I just wanted to get out of there, leave that hole, get back to the surface immediately. I was gasping like a fish out of water. I stopped, closed my eyes, and tried to calm the ferocious, hurried beats of my heart.

"Wait, Captain," Farag said. "Doctor Salina isn't well."

The place was so narrow that Farag could barely reach me. He softly stroked my hair and then my cheek. "Are you better, Ottavia?"

"I can't breathe."

"Yes you can. Just calm down."

"I have to get out of here."

"Listen to me," he said firmly, taking my chin and raising my face to where he stood a few steps above me. "Don't let claustrophobia get the best of you. Take several deep breaths. Forget where we are and look at me, okay?"

I did as he said. I fixed my eyes on him, and as if by magic, his eyes gave me breath and his smile expanded my lungs. I calmed down and regained control. He stroked my hair again and gave the captain a sign to keep descending.

Five or six steps farther down, Glauser-Röist abruptly stopped. "Another chrismon."

"Where?" asked Farag. Neither he nor I could see it.

"On the wall, level with your head. It's etched deeper than the others."

"The others were on the floor," I pointed out. "As the steps wore away, the engravings could have worn down."

"That's absurd," added Farag. "Why here? It doesn't point to any path."

"It could be confirmation to the aspiring Staurofilax that he's going the right way. A sign of encouragement."

"Maybe." Farag wasn't convinced.

We resumed our descent, but we had barely gone two or three steps when the captain stopped again. "Another chrismon."

"Where is it this time?" The professor was very annoyed.

"The same place as the last one." The previous chrismon was at the level of my face. I could see it perfectly.

"I still think this makes no sense," insisted Farag.

"Let's keep going down," the Rock said laconically.

"No, Kaspar, wait! Examine the wall. See if you notice anything. If not, let's keep descending. But please check it over carefully."

The Swiss Rock turned the flashlight on me, momentarily blinding me. I covered my eyes with one hand and cried out a muffled protest. Just then I heard an exclamation louder than my own.

"There's something here, Professor!"

"What have you found?"

"Between the two chrismons, you can make out another eroded shape in the rock. It looks like a small gap. I can barely see it."

My blindness was passing. Suddenly I could detect the shape the captain was talking about. It wasn't a gap at all. It was a sliver of stone perfectly embedded into the wall.

"It looks like the work of *fossores*,* a reinforcement in the wall or a masonry frame," I commented.

"Push it, Kaspar!" the professor urged.

"I don't think I can. I'm all twisted up."

"Then you push it, Ottavia!"

"You want me push that rock? It isn't going to move an inch."

As I was protesting, I rested my palm on the block. With just a nudge, it gently moved inside. The hole it left in the wall was smaller than the rock itself. The front face of the rock was chipped away along the edges so it would fit into a frame about five centimeters thick.

"It moved! It moved!"

It was strange. The ashlar stone slid away noiselessly and without any resistance, as if it had been greased. My arm wasn't long enough to push the rock to the end of its track. We were clearly surrounded by several meters of rock, and the small square passageway it slid down seem endless.

"Take the flashlight, Doctor," yelled Glauser-Röist. "Get into the hole! We have to follow it."

"Do I have to go first?"

The captain snorted. "Listen, the professor and I have nowhere to

---

* Excavators specialized in opening galleries of the catacombs.

move. You are right in front of it. Get in the damn hole! The professor will enter after you, and then I will backtrack to where you are now."

So there I was, making my way down a narrow corridor barely two feet high and about a foot wide. I pushed the stone with my hands and pushed the flashlight with my knees. I nearly fainted when I realized that Farag was behind me and that I was on all fours, my skirt probably failing to cover me entirely. I told myself it was no time for foolishness. Still, in the future, when I returned to Rome—*if* I returned to Rome— I would buy some pants, even if my sisters, my order, and the entire Vatican had a heart attack.

Luckily for my hands and feet, the passageway was as smooth as a newborn baby's skin. It was like walking on glass. The sides of the stone cube that touched the walls must have been planed too, and that's why it was so easy to move. When I lifted off my hands, it slid back toward me a bit, as if the tunnel were on a slight incline. I had no idea how far we'd gone—fifteen or twenty meters, maybe more. It seemed like an eternity.

"We are ascending," the captain's voice announced from far away.

That was true. That corridor was tilting more and more. The stone was starting to weigh on my tired wrists. It wasn't a place where any human being could get through. A dog or cat, maybe, but definitely not a person. The thought that at some point I'd have to go back the way I'd come, ascend the sinister spiral stairway, and climb two levels of catacombs made me long for sunlight and fresh air.

Finally I noticed that the far end of the stone was out of the tunnel. The slope was very steep. I could barely push the block; it kept falling back against me. With my last effort, I gave it a big push, and the stone fell into the void, immediately hitting something metallic.

"Done!"

"What can you see?"

"Wait till I catch my breath."

I shined the flashlight through the hole. I didn't see anything, so I inched forward and stuck my head in. It was a cubicle identical to the one we had seen in the catacombs, but this one was completely empty.

At first glance, it was just four empty walls, dug right into the rock, with an even lower hung roof and a floor covered by a strange plank of steel. Right then, I didn't register that everything was spotless, and I didn't notice I was leaning on the same rock I had pushed up that long ramp. The rock's height was approximately equal to the distance from the floor to the hole I'd emerged through.

Taking a deep breath like a pole-vaulter about to jump, I twisted myself into an outlandish knot and threw myself inside the cubicle, clattering onto the ground. Then Farag made his way through the hole, immediately followed by the captain. He looked pretty foolish—his body was too big, so he had to slither down the path, dragging his back-pack. Farag was almost as tall as he, but he was thinner and moved through it more easily.

"A very unusual floor," mused the professor, tapping his shoe on the steel plank.

"Give me the flashlight, Doctor."

"It's all yours."

Then something shocking happened. No sooner had the captain come through the hole than we heard a rough screech, like a painful twisting of old rope and gears slowly being set in motion. Glauser-Röist spun around, lighting up the entire cubicle, but we didn't see a thing. It was the professor who discovered it.

"The stone! Look at the stone!"

My beloved stone, the one I had so lovingly followed for the length of the corridor, was lifting off the floor on a platform and was deposited at the mouth of the tunnel. It slid back down and disappeared faster than you could say amen.

"We're trapped!" I shouted in anguish. The stone slid nonstop down the conduit until it fit back into the stone frame at the entrance. From the inside it was impossible to get back out. At that point I realized that that frame was not made to hide the entrance, but rather to seal up the exit.

Another mechanism had also started up. In the center of the wall across from the opening, a slab of stone turned on its hinges like a door, revealing a human-size, vaulted niche. You could clearly see three colored steps: white marble, black granite, and red porphyry. Above the steps, carved into the rock, was the enormous figure of an angel lifting his arms in prayer; over his head, pointing to the heavens, was a sword. The figure must have been painted once. In the *Divine Comedy*, the angel's long robe was the color of ashes or dry earth; his skin, pale pink; and his hair, a very dark black. Sticking out of holes in the angel's palms, which were raised imploringly, were two chains of equal length. One was clearly gold, and the other was silver. Both were clean and shiny and sparkled in the light of the flashlight.

"What does this all mean?" Farag walked up to the figure.

"Hold on, Professor!"

"What's the matter?" The professor jumped, startled.

"Don't you recall Dante's words?"

"His words?" Boswell scowled. "Didn't you bring a copy of the *Divine Comedy?*"

The Rock had already taken it out of his backpack and opened it to the right page.

"Falling devoutly at his holy feet," he read *"in mercy's name I begged to be let in; but, first of all, three times I smote my breast."*

"Please! Are we going to mimic each and every one of Dante's gestures?" I protested.

"The angel then takes out two keys, one silver and one gold," Glauser-Röist continued. "Using the silver key first, then the gold, he opens the locks. He says very clearly that when one of the keys doesn't work, the door won't open. *One is more precious, but the other needs wisdom and skill before it will unlock, for it is the one which unties the knot.*"

"My God!"

"Come on, Ottavia," Farag cheered me. "Try to enjoy this. After all, it's still a beautiful ritual."

Well, he was partly right. If we hadn't been so many meters underground, buried in a crypt with our exit sealed up, maybe I would have seen the charm Farag was talking about. But captivity upsets me, and a sense of danger rose sharply up my spine.

"I suppose," Farag continued, "the Staurofilakes chose the three alchemic colors in a purely symbolic sense. For them, as for anyone who got this far, the three phases of the great alchemic work matched the process the aspirant was to go through on his journey to the True Cross and earthly paradise."

"I don't understand."

"It's simple. Throughout the Middle Ages, alchemy was a very highly regarded science, and the number of wise men who practiced it was vast: Roger Bacon, Ramon Llull, Arnau de Vilanova, Paracelsus... The alchemists spent a good part of their lives closed up in their labs surrounded by water pipes, chemical retorts, crucibles, and stills. They were searching for the philosopher's stone, the elixir of eternal life." Boswell smiled. "Alchemy was really a road to inner perfection, a type of mystic practice."

"Can you be specific, Farag? We're trapped in a crypt with no way out."

"I'm sorry...," he stuttered, pushing his glasses onto his forehead. "The great students of alchemy, such as the psychiatrist Carl Jung, supported the idea that it was a path to self-knowledge, a process of searching for one's self, that went through the stages of dissolution, coagulation, and sublimation—in other words, the three works or alchemic steps. Perhaps the aspiring Staurofilakes had to suffer a process similar to destruction, integration, and perfection. The brotherhood may have gotten its symbolic language from that."

"In any case, Professor," the captain cut him short, crawling over to the guardian angel, "we too are now aspiring Staurofilakes."

Glauser-Röist bent down before the figure and touched his forehead to the first step. I have to admit it was quite a sight, to the point that I even felt a bit embarrassed for him; but then Farag imitated him, and I had no other option but to follow his lead to avoid starting an argument. We each struck our chest three times as we begged the angel to be merciful and open the door. But of course it didn't open.

"Let's try the keys," murmured the professor. He got to his feet and climbed those impressive steps. He stood face to face with the angel, but his eyes fell on the chains in the angel's hands. They were thick; three links hung from each palm.

"Try pulling the silver first, then the gold," the Rock said.

The professor did as he was told, and with the first tug, another link came out. Now there were four in the left hand and three in the right. Farag took the gold one and tugged on it, too. The same thing happened: A new link appeared. But that wasn't all that happened. We heard a new screech, under our feet, under that cold steel floor, much louder than the one from my stone's platform. It gave me goose bumps, although nothing seemed to happen.

"Pull again," urged the Rock. "First the silver and then the gold."

I couldn't see clearly. Something wasn't right. We were missing some important detail, and I sensed it wasn't a good idea to go on playing with the chains. But I didn't say anything, so Boswell repeated the process. The angel now had five links in each hand.

Suddenly I felt very hot, unbearably hot. Glauser-Röist, unaware of what he was doing, took off his jacket and dropped it on the ground. Farag unbuttoned his collar and started to breathe hard. The heat increased at a dizzying speed.

"Something strange is happening, don't you think?" I asked.

"The air is almost unbreathable," warned Farag.

"It's not the air...," murmured the Rock, looking down. "It's the floor. The floor is heating up!"

He was right. The iron plank was radiating heat. Were it not for our shoes, our feet would have been burning as if we were walking on hot sand at the beach in the middle of summer.

"We have to hurry, or we'll be roasted alive!" I exclaimed horrified.

The captain and I jumped precipitously to the steps, but I kept climbing to the porphyry stone and joined Farag. We stared at the angel. A light spark of clarity began rattling around in my brain. The solution was there. It had to be. But God knows where. In a matter of minutes the chamber was turning into a crematory oven. The angel wore a slight smile, like the Mona Lisa's, as if what was happening was a joke. With his hands raised toward heaven, he was enjoying himself ... His hands! I had to focus on his hands. I carefully examined the chains, but they didn't seem to have anything special. They were thick, normal, everyday chains. But his hands...

"What are you doing, Doctor?"

His hands weren't normal. Not at all. His right hand was missing the index finger. The angel was mutilated. What did that remind me of?

"Look at that corner of the floor!" Farag shouted. "It's turning red!"

A muffled bellow, a roar of furious flames, rose from the lower floor.

"There's a fire down there," muttered the Rock. Infuriated, he demanded, "What the devil are you doing, Doctor?"

"The angel is mutilated," I explained, my brain functioning at top speed, searching for a distant memory I could not quite recall. "He's missing the index finger on his right hand."

"So what?"

"Don't you get it?" I shouted, turning toward him. "This angel is missing a finger! It can't be a coincidence! It's got to mean something!"

"Ottavia's right, Kaspar." Farag took off his jacket and unbuttoned his shirt all the way. "Let's use our brains. It's the only way to save ourselves."

"He's missing a finger. Terrific."

"Maybe it's a kind of combination." I thought out loud. "Like a safe. Maybe we should put one link on the silver chain and nine on the gold chain. That would be ten fingers."

"Come on, Ottavia! We don't have much time!"

With each link I pushed back into the angel's hand, you could hear a metallic clack. I left one silver link showing, and tugged on the gold chain until there were nine links. Nothing.

"The corners of the floor are bright red, Ottavia!" Farag shouted.

"I can't go any faster. I'm going as fast as I can!"

I was dizzy. The air, almost like the strong odor of burning cleaning solution, was really getting to me.

"One and nine doesn't work," the captain ventured. "Maybe we need to look for a different answer. There are six fingers on one side and three on the one missing a finger, right? Try six and three."

I tugged on the silver chain like a possessed woman and left six links exposed. We're going to die, I told myself. For the first time in my life, I was sure the end had come. I prayed. I prayed desperately as I stuck six gold links back in the right hand, leaving only three hanging loose. Nothing happened.

The captain, Farag, and I looked at each other, panic entering our minds. A flame surged from the floor. The jacket the captain had dropped on the floor caught fire. Sweat poured over my body, but the worst was the buzzing in my ears. I took off my sweater.

"We're running out of oxygen," the Rock announced in a neutral voice. In his gray eyes I could see he also knew the end was near.

"We'd better pray, Captain," I said.

"You all at least have the consolation of …," sighed the professor, watching the jacket burn, his hands pushing locks of damp hair off his forehead, "believing that soon you will begin a new life."

Fear flooded me. "You're not a believer, Farag?"

"No, Ottavia, I'm not," he apologized with a shy smile. "Don't worry about me. I've been preparing for this moment for many years."

"Preparing?" I was scandalized. "You should turn to God and trust in his mercy."

"I'll simply go to sleep, that's all," he said with all the tenderness he could muster. "For a long time, I was afraid of death, but I didn't allow myself the weakness of believing in God to save me from that fear. Then, I realized that each night when I went to sleep, I died somewhat. The process is the same, don't you think? Do you recall Greek mythology?" he smiled. "The twin brothers, Hypnos* and Thanatos,† sons of Nyx, the Night… Remember?"

"For the love of God, Farag!" I moaned. "How can you blaspheme like that when we're about to die?"

I never would have dreamed Farag was not a believer. I knew he wasn't what you'd call a practicing Christian, but from that to not believing in God there was an abyss. I hadn't known many true atheists in my life, and I was convinced that everyone, in his own way, believed in God.

---

* *Hypnos,* Sleep.
† *Thanatos,* Death.

I was horrified to realize that his stupidity was gambling away eternal life.

"Give me your hand, Ottavia," he begged, extending his trembling hand. "If I'm going to die, I'd like to have your hand in mine."

"Captain, shall we pray?"

The heat was infernal. There was hardly any air. I could barely see, not just because of the sweat streaming in my eyes, but because I was feeling faint. A sweet stupor, a burning dream was overpowering me, leaving me weak. That cold steel plank that had received us was now an overpowering lake of fire. Everything glowed orange and red, including us.

"Of course, Doctor. Start the prayer and I will follow you."

But then I suddenly understood. It was so simple. It came to me as I cast a last glance at Farag's and my clasped hands: intertwined, wet with sweat and shining in the light, our fingers had multiplied. My thoughts went back, as if in a dream, to a childhood game, a trick my brother Cesare taught me, a way around learning the multiplication tables. For the nines table, he explained, all I had to do was extend both hands and count from the little finger of my left hand to get the multiplier and double that finger. The number of fingers remaining on the left hand was the first number of the answer, and the fingers remaining on the right, the second.

I turned loose from Farag, who didn't open his eyes, and rose to face the angel again. For a moment, I thought I'd fall over, but my hope sustained me. There weren't six and three links left hanging. There were sixty-three. But sixty-three wasn't a combination that opened that safe. Sixty-three was the product of multiplying another two numbers, like Cesare's trick. And they would have been so easy to simply guess! Dante's numbers, nine and seven! Nine times seven, sixty-three; seven times nine, sixty-three. Six and three. There were no other possibilities. I gasped, and started pulling at the chains. True, I was delirious—euphoric, even—due to lack of oxygen; but that euphoria had given me the solution: seven and nine. Or nine and seven! My hands couldn't push and pull the damp links, but a type of madness, a hallucinating fury, forced me to try again with all my strength until I got it right. A soon as the links fell into place, the stone slab that held the figure of the angel slowly sunk into the ground, uncovering a cool new corridor. The fire below us had stopped.

We dragged ourselves along the ground, out of that cubicle. We gulped mouthfuls of old and rancid air, but to us, at the moment, it seemed cleaner and sweeter than any we'd ever breathed. We didn't have a plan, but without realizing it, we had also followed the angel's final commandment to Dante: *"Enter, but first be warned: to look back means to go back out again."* We didn't look back. Behind us, the stone slab closed again with a thud.

*T*he path before us was wide and ventilated. A long passageway took us to the surface. We were exhausted—battered, even—and about to pass out. Farag coughed so hard he nearly broke in two. The captain leaned against the wall and took wobbly steps. As for me, I was disoriented. All I wanted was to get out of there, look at the bright blue sky, and feel the sun on my face. None of us made a sound. We walked along in complete silence, and except for Farag's coughs, we seemed powered by our mere instincts.

After more than an hour, Glauser-Röist turned off the flashlight; enough light was filtering through the narrow skylights above us so we could walk safely. The exit couldn't be very far. A few steps later, instead of reaching freedom, we came to a small, round esplanade, a type of landing about the size of my small bedroom in Rome. Its walls were covered with large Greek symbols carved in the stone. At first glance, the carving resembled a prayer.

"Ever seen this before, Ottavia?" Farag's cough had slowed.

"I'd have to copy it and translate it." I sighed. "It could be a common inscription, or maybe a Staurofilax text for those who made it into Purgatory."

The Rock, who no longer seemed as strong and invincible as usual, slumped to the ground, leaned against the epigraph, and took a bottle of water out of his backpack.

"Want some?" he offered us, laconic.

Did we want some! We were so dehydrated that, between the three of us, we gulped down every drop in the bottle.

Barely recuperated, the professor and I planted ourselves in front of the inscription and shined the flashlight on it:

Πᾶσαν χαρὰν ἡγήσασθε, ἀδελφοί μου, ὅταν πειρσμοῖς
περιπέσητε ποικίλοις, γιυώσκοντες ὅτι τὸ δοκίμιον ὑμῶν
τῆς πίστεως κατεργάζεται ὑπομονήν.

"Πᾶσαν χαρὰν ἡγήσασθε, ἀδελφοι μου...," read Farag in very correct Greek "'Consider, my brothers...' What is this?"

The captain took a notebook and pen out of his backpack and handed them to the professor to take notes.

"'Consider, my brothers,'" I translated, guiding my index finger over the letters, "'as motive for great joy to see you involved in all manner of tests, knowing that the test of your faith produces perseverance.'"

"Okay," the captain muttered sarcastically, without getting up, "I will consider it a reason for great joy that I was on the verge of dying."

"'But let your perseverance bring with it a perfect work,'" I continued, "'so you are perfect and fully integrated, without any flaw.' Wait a minute... I know this text!"

"Oh? So it's not a letter from the Staurofilakes?" asked Farag, disappointed, raising the pen to his forehead.

"It's the New Testament! The opening lines of Saint James's letter! The greeting Saint James of Jerusalem gave to the twelve tribes of the dispersion."

"Saint James, the apostle?"

"No, no. Although he calls himself Iacobos,* the author of this letter doesn't ever identify himself as the apostle. Besides, as you can see, he writes in a very scholarly and correct Greek that couldn't have come from Saint James the Elder."

"So, this isn't a letter from the Staurofilakes?"

"Of course it is, Professor," Glauser-Röist consoled him. "From

---

* *Iacobos* is Greek for James.

what you've read to us, I believe it's correct to surmise that the Stauro-filakes used sacred words from the Bible to compose their messages."

"'If any of you lacks wisdom,'" I continued, "'ask God for it, that he shall give wisdom to everyone in abundance, without flaunting it, and he will give it to you.'"

"I would translate this sentence," Boswell interrupted me, also putting his finger on the text, "as, 'If any of you is lacking in wisdom, ask it of the Lord, who gives to all generously and without reproach, and it will be granted to you.'"

I sighed, arming myself with patience.

"I don't see any difference," the captain concluded.

"There is no difference," I declared.

"Okay, okay!" wailed Farag, shrugging with fake indifference. "I'll admit my translations are a little baroque."

"A little?" I asked surprised.

"Depends on your point of view. One could also say they are very precise."

I was about to observe that, as dirty as his glasses were, it was impossible for him to see clearly, but I held my tongue because he was stuck with copying the text and I had no particular interest in doing that.

"We are getting off track here," ventured Glauser-Röist. "Would you experts focus on the meaning, not the form, please?"

"Of course, Captain." I looked at Farag over my shoulder. "'But ask with faith, without a single doubt. Doubt is like the waves of the ocean stirred up by the wind and carried from one place to another. Such a man should not think about receiving anything from the Lord. He is indecisive, inconstant in all his paths.'"

"Rather than *indecisive*, I would read here *a man of twisted spirit*."

"Professor!"

"Okay! I won't say another word."

"'Glory be to the humble man in his exaltation and the rich man in his humility,'" I was coming to the end of that long paragraph. "'Good fortune to he who endures the test, because once proven, he will receive the crown.'"

"The crown they will engrave in our skin, above the first cross," murmured the Rock.

"Well, the entrance test to Purgatory wasn't easy, and we don't have a mark on our bodies that we didn't already have," commented Farag, wanting to push aside the nightmare of future scarifications.

"This is nothing compared to what awaits us. What we have done is simply ask permission to enter."

"True," I said, lowering my finger and my eyes to the last words of the epigraph. "There's not much left to read. Just a couple of sentences."

καὶ οὕτως εἰς τὴν Ῥώμην ἤλθαμεν.

"'And with this, we head for Rome,'" the professor translated.

"That's what you would expect," affirmed the Rock. "The first cornice of *Purgatory* is about pride. According to Cato LXXVI, this deadly sin had to be expiated in the city known for its lack of humility: Rome."

"So, we're going home," I murmured gratefully.

"Yeah, if we ever manage to get out of here. But we won't be there very long, Doctor."

"We haven't even finished here," I said, turning to the wall. "There's still the last line. 'The temple of Mary is beautifully adorned.'"

"That can't be in the Bible." The professor rubbed his temples. His hair, grimy with dirt and sweat, fell in his face. "I don't recall any mention of the temple of Mary."

"I'm nearly positive it's from the Gospel of Luke, although modified by the mention of the Virgin. They must be giving us some kind of a clue."

"Let's study it when we get back to the Vatican," pronounced the Rock.

"It's from Luke, I'm sure," I insisted, proud of my good memory. "I can't say what chapter or verse, but it's the moment when Jesus prophesied the destruction of the Temple in Jerusalem and the persecutions of the Christians."

"Actually, Luke wrote those prophesies and attributed them to Jesus," pointed out Boswell. "Those events took place between A.D. 80 and 90. Jesus didn't prophesy any of it."

I looked at him coldly. "That was uncalled-for, Farag."

"I'm sorry, Ottavia. I thought you knew."

"I knew," I replied rather angry, "but why do you need to remind me of it?"

"Well…," he stuttered, "I've always thought it's better to know the truth."

Not wanting to get mixed up in our discussion, the Rock got to his feet, picked his backpack up off the floor, slung it over his shoulder, and headed down the hallway toward the exit.

"If the truth harms people, Farag," I snapped, enraged, thinking about Ferma, Margherita, and Valeria, and so many others, "they don't need to know it."

"We have different opinions on this, Ottavia. I've always preferred the truth to a lie."

"Even if it does harm?"

"That depends on the person. There are cancer patients who don't want to hear a thing about their disease. Others demand to know everything." He stared into me. "I thought you were of the latter."

"Doctor! Professor! The exit!" Glauser-Röist boomed, not very far away.

"Let's go, or we'll be stuck in here forever!" I exclaimed, and started off down the passageway, leaving Farag alone.

We surfaced through a dry well, in the middle of some rugged, wild mountains. Night was falling, it was getting cold, and we didn't have the slightest idea where we were. We walked for a couple of hours, following a river through a narrow canyon, and reached a dirt road that led to a private villa whose kind owner was used to opening his doors to lost hikers. He told us we were in the Anapo Valley, some 10 kilometers from Syracuse. We'd skirted the Iblei Mountains in the dark. After a short time, a car from the archbishopric picked us up at the villa and took us back to civilization. We couldn't tell His Excellency Monsignor Giuseppe Arena about our adventure, so we ate a quick dinner in the archdiocese, picked up our bags, and left as fast as we could for the Fontanarossa Airport, some 50 kilometers away, to hop on the first flight for Rome.

As we were fastening our seat belts in the plane, the old sacristan of Saint Lucia popped into my head. I asked myself what they might have told him at the archdiocese to keep him quiet. I wanted to mention the matter to the captain, but when I looked over, I noticed he was fast asleep.

When I opened my eyes the next day, it was well before dawn. I felt like one of those travelers cast adrift when they lose a day due to the earth's rotation. In that guest room in the Domus, I felt so drained, as if I hadn't slept through the entire night. In the silence, studying the silhouettes that the pale light from the street sketched all around me, I asked myself a thousand and one times what had I gotten myself into, what was happening, and why my life had come unhinged. Just hours before, I'd been on the brink of dying in the bowels of the earth. In less than two days, my father's and brother's deaths had become a distant memory. If that weren't enough, I hadn't taken my renewal of vows.

How could I adjust to the way I was living, a rhythm I so was completely unaccustomed to? The days, weeks, and months flew by. I became less and less conscious of my role and obligations as a religious person and as director of the Restoration and Paleography Laboratory of the Vatican's Classified Archives. I knew I shouldn't worry about my vows; situations like mine were provided for in my order's statutes. As long as I signed the petition as soon as I had a moment, my vows were automatically renewed *in pectore.* True, my order and the Vatican gave me dispensation for everything. True, I was doing a job of vital importance to the church. But did I give myself dispensation? Did God give me dispensation?

I rolled over, closed my eyes, and tried to go back to sleep for a few more minutes. I decided to abandon my morning reflections and instead let life lead me by the reins. But my eyelids refused to close, and my inner voice accused me of acting like a coward, always grumbling about everything and hiding behind some false fear or remorse.

Instead of weighing down my conscience with blame, why didn't I enjoy what life had offered me? I always envied Pierantonio's adventures: his jobs, his post in the Holy Land, his archeological excavations. Now, I was wrapped up in a similar project, and instead of unleashing my strong side, I was tangled up in my fears like a fly in a web. Poor Ottavia! Her whole life squeezed into books, prayers, and studying; trying to shine with her codices, scrolls, papyruses, and parchments. When God decides to snatch her from her studious work and take her out into the field, she trembles like a little girl.

If I wanted to keep investigating the theft of the *Ligna Crucis* with Farag and Captain Glauser-Röist, I had to change my attitude, and act like the privileged person I was. I had to be more spirited and decisive, learning to stop my laments and protests. Hadn't Farag lost everything without complaining—his home, his family, his country, his work in the Greco-Roman Museum in Alexandria? In Italy all he could rely on was a rented room in the Domus and the stingy hourly wage the secretary of state had allotted him at the captain's request. Yet he was ready to put his life on the line to clear up a mystery that was turning all Christian churches upside down. And he was an atheist!

Not an atheist, I told myself, as I turned on the light on the nightstand, poised to hop out of bed. For all he claimed to be, he just couldn't be an atheist. We all believed in God, in one way or another. At least that was what I'd been taught and what I firmly believed. Farag surely believed in his own way, no matter what he said. Deep down I knew, however, that my unbendable stance, so typical of believers, was intolerant

and arrogant: There certainly were people in the world who didn't believe in God, no matter how strange that seemed to me.

I couldn't help letting out a shriek as I swung my legs out from
under the covers. I felt pain all over my body. The adventure in the catacombs of Saint Lucia the day before had left me bruised and injured.
Nonetheless, I did feel proud of what we had accomplished in Syracuse.
I was deeply satisfied that we had solved the puzzle and come out of that
hole alive. It was highly likely that others had died in that very spot.

"And what about their remains?" I asked out loud.

I do not doubt that there are Staurofilakes in Syracuse," the captain
said hours later when we gathered in my lab for the first time since
Syracuse.

"Ask the archbishop about the sacristan of the church," Farag proposed.

"The sacristan?" the Rock asked.

"Yes, I'm sure he has something to do with the brotherhood," I
agreed. "Just my intuition."

"Why should I call? They're going to tell me he's a good man who
has spent many, many years generously helping out at Saint Lucia. Unless you don't have a better idea, let's drop it."

"Still, I'm sure he's the one who cleans up after the test and removes
the remains of those who don't pass. Remember how shiny the gold and
silver chains were?"

"So what if he was?" he replied sarcastically. "Do you think that if
we asked nicely, he would confess to being a Staurofilax? Maybe we can
get the police to lock him up, even though he has never committed a
single crime, even though he's Saint Lucia's honored elderly sacristan. In
that case, we could take off his clothes to see if he has scarifications on
his body. Though, if he isn't willing to strip, we can always get a court
order to force him to. And once we manage to get him naked at the police station—surprise! There are no marks on his body and he turns out
to be the person he says he is. Then he sues us, okay? He slaps a nice
lawsuit squarely on the Vatican, and the news hits all the papers."

"The question is, if the sacristan is a Staurofilax," Farag said to settle the argument and calm the captain, "besides doing the jobs Ottavia mentioned, he could also be the one to warn the brotherhood of anyone who has taken the first test."

"We can't ignore that possibility," conceded the captain. "We should keep our eyes peeled in Rome."

"Speaking of Rome...," I said. The men looked at me, questioningly. "We need to keep in mind that we could die in one of these tests. I'm not saying I'm scared or that we should backpedal, but the possibility should be on the table before we continue."

The captain and Farag looked at each other, then at me.

"I thought that was settled already, Doctor."

"What do you mean, it was settled already?"

"We're not going to die, Ottavia," Farag declared very decisively, raising his glasses. "Nobody says it won't be dangerous, but..."

"...But, as dangerous as it may be," the Rock continued, "why wouldn't we pass the tests, like hundreds of Staurofilakes over the centuries?"

"No, I didn't say we were going to die *for sure*. What I said is, we *could* die, that's all. We shouldn't forget that."

"We know that, Doctor. And His Eminence Cardinal Sodano knows that and His Holiness the Pope knows that. No one is forcing us to be here. If you don't feel capable of continuing, I'll understand. For a woman..."

"Don't start that!" I exclaimed, indignant.

Farag laughed under his breath.

"I'd like to know what you're laughing about!" I spit out.

"I'm laughing because you'll want to be the first woman to pass all the tests."

"Well, yes! What of it?"

"Nothing!" he answered, breaking out in a belly laugh. Before I had time to react, I heard another belly laugh. I couldn't believe what I saw. Farag and the Rock were laughing, both a chorus of unending chuckles. I sighed and smiled, resigned. If they were ready to follow that adventure to its end, I decided I'd be two steps in front of them. So, the matter was settled. Now I just had to get them to work.

"We should start studying our notes on the inscription," I suggested, patiently leaning my elbows on the table.

"Yes, yes...," babbled Boswell, drying his eyes with the back of his hand.

"Great idea, Doctor," said the captain, between hiccups of laughter.

"Well, once you recover, please read your notes, Farag."

"Just a moment," he begged, looking at me affectionately as he extracted his notebook from one of the enormous pockets in his jacket. He was hoarse. He pushed his hair off his face, raised his glasses, and took a deep breath. Finally locating what he was looking for, he started to read. "'Consider, my brothers, as motive for great joy to see you involved in all manner of tests, knowing that the test of your faith produces perseverance. But let your perseverance bring with it a perfect work, so you are perfect and fully integrated, without any flaw. If any of you lacks in wisdom, ask it of the Lord who gives to all generously and without reproach, and it will be granted to you. But ask with faith, without a single doubt. Doubt is like the waves of the ocean stirred up by the wind and carried from one place to another. Such a man should not think of receiving anything from the Lord. He is a man of twisted spirit...'"

"A man of twisted spirit? That isn't my translation."

"Actually, it's mine. Since I was the one taking notes...," he said, proud of himself. "'...He is a man of twisted spirit, inconstant in all his paths. Glory be to the humble brother in his exaltation and the rich man in his humility. Good fortune to he who endures the test, because once proved, he will receive the crown.' Then this part: 'And with this, we set off for Rome.' As the captain said, this is the clue to the city of the first test of *Purgatory*. And finally, 'The temple of Mary is beautifully adorned.'"

"Is beautifully adorned," I repeated, a bit vexed. "It refers to a beautiful temple dedicated to the Virgin. It's the clue to finding the spot, of course, but it's a pretty poor clue. The solution isn't a sentence; it's *in* the sentence. But how do we figure it out?"

"In Rome all the churches dedicated to Mary are beautiful, right?"

"Just those churches dedicated to Mary, Professor?" Glauser-Röist said ironically. "In Rome all the churches are beautiful."

Without thinking, I got to my feet and raised my right hand in the air. My mind pondered the words. "How did that phrase go in Greek, Farag? Did you copy down the original text?"

The professor noticed my hand mysteriously holding on to some nonexistent cable and furrowed his brow. "Something wrong with your arm?"

"Did you copy down the text, Farag? The original, did you copy it down?"

"Well, no, I didn't copy it down, Ottavia, but I remember it more or less."

"More or less does me no good," I exclaimed, lowering my hand to the pocket in my lab coat. I always put it on out of habit. I didn't know how to work in my lab without it. "I need to know how the words went exactly, the words 'beautifully adorned.' Was it *kalos kekosmetai?** I have a hunch."

"Let's see...Let me think...Yes, I'm sure it was 'το ιερον της Παναγιας καλως κεκοσμεται,' 'The temple of Her Holiness is beautifully adorned.' *Panagias,* 'All Holy' or 'Santisima,' is the Greek name for the Virgin."

"Of course!" I proclaimed. *Kekosmetai! Kekosmetai!* Santa Maria in Cosmedin!"

"Santa Maria in Cosmedin?" asked Glaucer-Röist, clueless.

Farag smiled. "Incredible! A church in Rome with a Greek name? Santa Maria the Beautiful, the Lovely. I thought everything here would be in either Italian or Latin."

"'Incredible' is an understatement," I murmured, pacing back and forth. "It's one of my favorite churches. I don't go as often as I'd like, because it's far from my apartment, but it's the only church in Rome that conducts Mass in Greek."

---

* *Kalos kekosmetai,* phonetic transcription of καλως κεκοσμεται "beautifully adorned."

"I don't think I've ever been there," the Rock said.

"Have you ever stuck your hand in the 'Mouth of Truth,' Captain? If you have, you know what church I'm talking about. According to legend, that horrific effigy bites off the fingers of liars."

"Oh, yes! Of course I've visited the 'Mouth of Truth.' It's a very important place in Rome."

"Well then, the 'Mouth of Truth' is located in the portico of Santa Maria in Cosmedin. People from all over the world descend upon the church in tourist buses that often crowd the plaza. They stand in line, walk up to the effigy, stick their hand in, take the obligatory picture, and leave. No one enters the church, no one even notices it, no one knows it exists. And yet it's one of the most beautiful churches in Rome."

"'The temple of Mary is beautifully adorned,'" recited Boswell.

"Okay, Doctor, but how do you know that church is the place? As I said, there are hundreds of beautiful churches in this city."

"No, Captain," I replied, stopping right in front of him. "Not just because it's beautiful, which it is, nor even because the Byzantine Greeks further adorned it when they fled to Rome in the eighth century to escape persecution over their worship of icons, but because the inscription in the catacombs of Saint Lucia points directly to it: 'The temple of Mary is beautifully adorned'—*kalos kekosmetai*... Don't you see? *Kekosmetai,* Cosmedin."

"He can't see it, Ottavia. Let me explain, Captain. Cosmedin is derived from the Greek word *kosmidion,* which means adorned, decorated, beautiful. For example, *cosmetic* is also derived from this word. *Kekosmetai* is the passive verb in our phrase. Take off the first syllable, *ke,* whose only function is to mark the perfect tense, and you're left with *kosmetai.* As you can see, *kosmidion* and *Cosmedin* share the same root."

"The Staurofilakes definitely mean Santa Maria in Cosmedin," I said, totally convinced. "Now all we have to do is go there and prove it."

"Before we go, let's review our notes on the first circle of *Purgatory,*" Farag said as he picked up my copy of the *Divine Comedy.*

I took off my lab coat. "Fine. While you're doing that, I'll run a few important errands."

"There is nothing more important, Doctor. This very afternoon we should go to Santa Maria in Cosmedin."

"Ottavia, you always duck out when we have to read Dante."

I hung up my lab coat and turned to look at them. "If I have to drag myself on the ground again, climb dusty stairs, and run all over unexplored catacombs, I need more appropriate clothes than what I wear at the Vatican."

"You're going shopping for clothes?" Boswell asked, surprised.

I opened the door and walked into the hall. "Actually, I'm just going to buy some pants."

The truth is, I never would have gone to Santa Maria in Cosmedin without reading Canto X of *Purgatory,* but the stores closed at noon, so I didn't have much time to buy what I needed. Besides, I wanted to call home to see how my mother and the rest of the family were doing. For that I needed some peace and quiet.

When I got back to the archives, I learned that Farag and the captain were having lunch at the Domus restaurant. So I ordered a sandwich from the cafeteria and shut myself up in the lab to read what would befall us that afternoon.

The trick with the multiplication table kept running around in my head. I could still see myself, seven or eight years old, sitting at the kitchen table, my homework in front of me, Cesare beside me explaining the trick. How could child's play be elevated to a thousand-year-old sect's initiation test? There were just two explanations. First, what was considered the *summum* of science centuries ago was reduced to the level of primary school. The other was astounding and hard to accept: The wisdom of the past had crossed the centuries hidden in popular customs, stories, children's games, legends, traditions, and seemingly innocuous books. To find it, we had to change the way we looked at the world. We had to accept that our eyes and ears are poor receptors of the reality that surrounds us. We had to open our minds and put aside our preconceived notions. I was starting to suffer through that surprising process, but I had no idea why.

I no longer read Dante as indifferently as before. Now I knew that his words hid a meaning more profound than what I first had thought. Dante had also stood before the guardian angel in the catacombs in Syracuse and had pulled those same chains. Among other things, I felt a certain intimacy with the great Florentine author. I was surprised he dared to write *Purgatory* knowing that the Staurofilakes would never forgive him. Maybe his literary ambition was so enormous that he needed to show that he was the new Virgil, to receive that crown of laurels, the poets' prize that adorned all his portraits. According to him, it was the only thing he truly coveted. Dante had felt the irresistible urge to go down in history as the greatest writer ever, and it must have been extremely painful for him to watch time passing, to see himself grow old without fulfilling his dreams. Just like Faust centuries later, he probably considered selling his soul to the devil in exchange for glory. He realized his dreams, but the price he had to pay was his life.

Canto X started as Dante and Virgil were finally crossing the threshold into Purgatory. They heard the door close behind them and figured there was no turning back. Thus began the Florentine's purification, his own process of internal cleansing. He had visited hell and had seen the punishments inflicted upon the condemned for eternity. Now he begged to be purified of his own sins. He wanted to enter the heavenly kingdom, totally renewed, to join his beloved Beatrice, who, according to Glauser-Röist, was just a symbol of Wisdom and Supreme Knowledge.

> *Then we were climbing through a narrow cleft*
> *along a path that zigzagged through the rock*
> *the way a wave swells up and then pulls back.*
>
> *"Now we are at the point," my guide began,*
> *"where we must use our wits: when the path bends,*
> *we keep close to the far side of the curve."*

My God, a rock in motion! The piece of bread I was chewing turned bitter. I was glad I'd bought those new pants. They hadn't cost very much and were really comfortable. Hidden in the store's dressing room in the store, alone in front of the mirror, I discovered they gave me a youthful look I never had before. I wished with all my heart there wasn't a ridiculous rule that forbade me from wearing them. In such case, I'd have to completely ignore it, without remorse. I suddenly remembered the celebrated North American nun, Sister Mary Dominic Ramacciotti, founder of Girls' Village in Rome. She got special permission from Pope Pious XII to wear fur coats, get a perm, wear Elizabeth Arden makeup, frequent the opera, and dress with exquisite elegance. I didn't aspire to all that; I was simply content to wear some simple pants.

After great hardships, Dante and Virgil finally reached the first cornice, the first circle of Purgatory.

> *From the plain's edge, verging on empty space,*
> *to where the cliff-face soars again, was room*
> *for three men's bodies laid out end to end;*

> *as far as I could take in with my eyes,*
> *measuring carefully from left to right,*
> *this terrace did not vary in its width.*

Suddenly Virgil admonishes Dante to stop snooping around and pay attention to the strange mob of souls headed their way, painfully and slowly.

> *"Master, what I see moving toward us there,"*
> *I said, "do not seem to be shades at all;*
> *I don't know what they are, my sight's confused."*

> *"The grievous nature of their punishment,"*
> *he answered, "bends their bodies toward the ground;*
> *my own eyes were not sure of what they saw.*

> *"Try hard to disentangle all the parts*
> *Of what you see moving beneath those stones.*
> *Can you see now how each one beats his breast?"*

These were in fact the souls of the sovereigns, crushed by the weight of enormous rocks to humble and purify them of worldly vanities. They advanced painfully through the narrow cornice, their knees pressed to their chests, their faces contorted by exhaustion. They were reciting a strange version of the Lord's Prayer befitting their situation: "Oh Father, who art in heaven, although not just in heaven…" is how Canto XI starts. Horrified by their suffering, Dante bids them a speedy journey through Purgatory so they can soon reach "the wheeling stars." Virgil, always more practical, asks the souls to point out the way to the second cornice.

> *Someone, however, said: "Follow this bank*
> *along the river with us, and you will find*
> *the road a living man can surely climb."*

As in Pre-Purgatory, Dante has long conversations with old acquaintances or famous people along the way. They warn him against vanity and pride, as if they guessed that this cornice might keep the poet from being purified on time. After a lot of talking and walking, he starts Canto XII. At the beginning, Virgil admonishes the Florentine to leave the souls of the prideful in peace and concentrate on finding the way up:

> *"Now, look down," he said. "You will be pleased,*
> *and it will make your journey easier,*
> *to see this bed of stone beneath your feet."*

Dante obediently looks at the road and sees the marvelously carved figures covering it. In a long passage of twelve or thirteen tercets, he gives succinct details of some of the scenes in the engravings: Lucifer falling from heaven like a bolt of lightning, Briareus agonizing after rebelling against the gods of Olympus, Nimrod crazed when he saw his beautiful Tower of Babel for the last time, the suicide of Saul after his defeat in Gelboe. A multitude of mythological, biblical, and historical examples of the punishment for pride. As he walks along, bent way over so he can see every single detail, the poet asks admiringly who the artist was who so skillfully depicted those shadows and poses.

Fortunately, I said to myself, Dante didn't have to carry a rock. That was a great consolation to me. Still, he still had to walk doubled over a long ways to see the reliefs. If that was the Staurofilakes' next test, I was ready to start. Yet something told me it wasn't going to be that easy. The experience in Syracuse had had a profound effect on me, and I no longer trusted Dante's beautiful verses.

The travelers finally come to the far side of the cornice. Virgil tells Dante to get ready, to adorn his face and attitude with reverence because an angel, dressed in white, shining like a morning star, is approaching to help them depart:

> He spread his arms out wide, and then his wings.
> He said: "Come, now, the steps are very close;
> henceforth, the climbing will be easier."

> To such an invitation few respond:
> O race of hen, born to fly heavenward,
> How can a breath of wind make you fall back?

> He led us straight to where the rock was cleft.
> Once there, he brushed his wings against my brow,
> then he assured me of a safe ascent.

Some voices intone the *Beautus paupers spiritu** while Virgil and Dante climb the steep stairs. Up until then, Dante has complained several times about how tired he is. Suddenly, he's surprised he feels as light as a feather. Virgil tells him that, although he hadn't realized it, the angel has erased, with a beat of his wings, one of those seven *P*'s engraved on Dante's forehead (one for each deadly sin). He's carrying less weight now. Dante Alighieri has just shed the sin of pride.

---

*First beatitude of Christ's Sermon on the Mount, *Beatitude of the poor in spirit*...(Matthew 5:3).

At this point, I fell asleep on my desk, completely worn out. The Florentine poet was saved from exhaustion; I was not so lucky.

My dream that night was full of disturbing images of the crypt in Syracuse. Always, Farag smiled and led me to safety. I took his hand in desperation, for it was my only chance to save myself. He called to me with an infinite sweetness.

"Ottavia... Ottavia. Wake up, Ottavia."

"Doctor, it's getting late." Glauser-Röist roared mercilessly.

I moaned, and couldn't shake my dream. I had a splitting headache that felt worse if I tried to open my eyes.

"Ottavia, it's three o'clock," Farag said.

"I'm sorry," I mumbled, struggling to get up. "I fell asleep. I'm so sorry."

"We're all exhausted," Farag agreed. "Tonight we'll rest, you'll see. When we leave Santa Maria in Cosmedin, we will head straight to the Domus and not get up for a week."

"It's getting late," the Rock insisted, lifting his backpack onto his shoulder. It looked much heavier today than on our last outing, in Syracuse. It looked so big that he could've had a fire extinguisher in it.

We left the Hypogeum, but not before I took something for my headache, the strongest thing I could find. We crossed Vatican City and got into Glauser-Röist's blue sports car parked on the Swiss Guard's lot. The fresh air helped clear my head and alleviate the pressure. What I really needed was to go home and sleep for twenty or thirty hours. Right then I understood our harsh reality—until our quest ended, rest, dreams, and an ordered life were impossible luxuries.

We crossed Porta Santo Spirito and drove down Lungotévere until we came to the Garibaldi Bridge, buried as usual in fierce traffic. After ten long minutes of delay, we crossed the river and sped straight down Via Arenula and Via delle Botteghe Oscure to the Piazza San Marco. We took a roundabout route that got us to Santa Maria in Cosmedin even faster. Scooters buzzed around and cut in front of us like clusters of crazed wasps. Miraculously, Glauser-Röist managed to dodge them. After several close calls, the Alfa Romeo pulled up at the sidewalk next to the Piazza Bocca della Verità parking lot. There was my little, ignored Byzantine church, with its wise, harmonious proportions. I studied it fondly as I opened the door of the car to get out.

The sky had clouded up throughout the day. A dark, gray light ran roughshod over Santa Maria in Cosmedin's beauty, but didn't diminish it entirely. I looked to the highest part of the seven-story bell tower rising majestically from the center of the church and reflected again on that old idea of the effects of time, inexorable time, that destroys us and turns works of art infinitely more beautiful.

Since antiquity, there had been an important Greek colony in that part of Rome (known as the Boario Forum, on account of the cattle fairs held there). There was an even more important temple dedicated to Hercules the Triumphant, erected in his honor for recovering oxen stolen by the thief Caco. In the third century A.D., a Christian chapel was constructed on the ruins of that temple. It grew in stages and was embellished until it became the wonderful church it is today. It was a defining moment for Santa Maria in Cosmedin when Greek artists came to Rome, fleeing Byzantium where they'd been persecuted by other Christians who thought it was a sin to create images of God, the Virgin, or the saints.

Farag, the captain, and I walked up to the church's portico, not without sidestepping the curlicue of tightly packed rows of retirees standing in line to have their pictures taken with their hand inside the enormous mask of the "Mouth of Truth." The captain advanced with the determination of a military flagship, indifferent to his surroundings. On the other hand, Farag's eyes were popping out of his head as he tried to memorize even the most insignificant details.

"That mouth…," he asked amused. "Has it ever bitten anyone?"

I broke out in laughter. "Never! If it ever does, I'll let you know."

I watched him laugh. His blue eyes grew darker in the light. Stray gray hairs here and there in the stubble of his beard highlighted his Semitic features and his dark Egyptian skin. Life took some strange twists and turns to bring together a Swiss Guard, a Sicilian nun, and a compendium of so many races.

Spotlights placed at the top of the lateral naves and columns lit up the interior of Santa Maria. The light filtering in from outside was too weak to celebrate Mass. The church's style was essentially Greek Byzantine. Although I liked everything about the church, what drew me like a magnet were its enormous iron candelabra. Instead of sheltering dozens of squat, white votive candles as in Latin churches, they held delicate yellow tapers, typical of the Eastern world. Without hesitating for a second, I walked to the candelabra leaning against the parapet of the schola cantorum, in the central nave in front of the altar. I tossed some coins into the alms box and lit one of the golden lights. I closed my eyes halfway and sank into prayer, asking God to take care of my poor father and brother. I also prayed that he protect my mother, who, apparently, was having trouble getting over their deaths. I gave thanks for being placed on a mission for the church, a mission that helped me put off the pain of losing them.

When I opened my eyes, I was completely alone. I glanced around for Farag and the captain, who were wandering around the lateral naves like baffled tourists. They were very interested in the frescos on the walls with scenes from the life of the Virgin and in the *cosmatesque*-style decorations on the floor. Since I was familiar with all that, I went to the presbytery to examine the most remarkable peculiarity of Santa Maria in Cosmedin. Under a Gothic baldachin from the end of the eighth century, an enormous bathtub made of dark, salmon-colored porphyry served as the church's altar. One would think that some rich Byzantine man—or woman—from imperial Rome had once taken some nice perfumed baths in that future Christian tabernacle.

Nobody noticed me walking in that presbytery. Except for during Mass and the Rosary prayers, there was no priest or sacristan in the church. Nor were there any dear little old ladies who would leave a few lire in the alms box and spend their afternoon in the church, as happily as my nieces and nephews spent their Saturday nights in Palermo nightclubs. Santa Maria in Cosmedin remained peaceful and solitary; only rarely did some lost visitor wander in.

I examined the bathtub at length. I tugged hard on the four large porphyry rings on its side to see what would happen. Nothing. Farag and Glauser-Röist weren't having any luck either. It was as if the Stauro-filakes had never been there. As I was inspecting the episcopal throne of the apse, my companions joined me.

"Anything special?" asked the Rock.

"No."

Wearing a solemn look, we headed for the sacristy, where we found the only living person in there: the old salesclerk of an odd gift shop filled with medallions, crucifixes, postcards, and slides. He was an old priest, unshaven, wearing a greasy soutane, his gray hair uncombed. That clergyman's hygiene was conspicuously absent. He observed us glumly when we entered, but his expression suddenly changed to that of a ser-vile amiability that instantly put me off.

"Are you the people from the Vatican?" he inquired as he came from behind the counter, planting himself in front of us. His body odor was repugnant.

"I am Captain Glauser-Röist. This is Dr. Salina and Professor Boswell."

"I've been expecting you! My name is Bonuomo, Father Bonuomo, at your service. How can I help you?"

"We've seen the church. Now we'd like to see the rest. I believe there's also a crypt."

The clergyman frowned, and I was more than surprised: a crypt? That was the first I'd ever heard of it. I had no idea there was such thing in Santa Maria.

"Yes," admitted the old man, annoyed, "but it's not visiting hours at the moment."

Bonuomo? . . . * He really was *Maluomo.* Glauser-Röist didn't budge. He stared at the priest, not moving a muscle in his face, not even blinking, as if the old man hadn't said a word and he could wait forever for an invitation. The priest squirmed, torn between his duty to obey and his wretched inability to alter the church's schedule.

---

* A common last name in Italy that translates as "good man."

"Is there a problem, Father Bonuomo?" Glauser-Röist asked in a cold, sharp voice.

"No," the old man groaned. He turned and led us to the stairs that descended into the crypt. He stopped at the door and flipped several switches on a panel to the right. "Here's some light. I regret I will not be able to accompany you, but I cannot leave the store. Let me know when you are finished."

With these curt words, he disappeared. Breathing the unpleasantly pungent smell he gave off made my stomach churn. I was glad he was gone.

"Once again, we're off to the earth's center!" Farag joked heartily as he took his first step.

"I hope to see sunlight again someday...," I muttered, following him.

"Not anytime soon, Doctor."

I turned to look at him glumly.

"As you well know...," the Rock said, as serious as ever. "The world might come to an end any day now. It might even happen while we're in the crypt."

"Ottavia!" Farag rushed to stop me. "Don't even think about starting an argument!"

I had no intention to. There are trivialities that do not deserve an answer.

That fatuous priest had tricked us about the light. We'd barely gotten to the end of the stairs when we were plunged into total darkness. Unfortunately, we had descended so far down that going back would be quite the chore. We must have been several feet below the level of the Tiber River.

"Isn't there is any light in this hole?" Farag's voice said, to my right.

"There is no light in the crypt," Glauser-Röist announced. "Don't worry. I already knew that. I brought a flashlight."

"Father Bonuomo could have told us that before he encouraged us to descend." I was surprised. "Besides, how do they light the way for tourists?"

"Didn't you notice, Doctor, that there's no poster announcing visiting hours?"

"I already thought about that. In fact, I've visited this church many times, and never knew there was a crypt."

Switching on the flashlight that splashed an intense beam of light on the place, Glauser-Röist said, "Isn't it strange that there's no light whatsoever, and that a priest of the church dares to challenge a direct order from the Secretariat of State, and that that same priest does not accompany the Vatican's envoys on their visit?"

The captain shined the light toward the bottom of the crypt. The first thing I noticed was a small altar right beneath the central nave. That place was shaped exactly like a scale model of a church, with little columns that divided it into three naves. It even had chapels on the side, all completely covered in darkness.

"Are you insinuating, Captain," Boswell asked, "that Father Bonuomo could be a Staurofilax?"

"I'm saying he just might be, just like the sacristan of Santa Lucia."

"Well, he is," I pronounced, as I entered the little church.

"We cannot be sure, Doctor. That's just a guess, and guessing gets us nowhere."

"How did you know this secret place existed?" I asked.

"I looked on the Internet. You can find almost anything on the Internet. But you already know that, don't you, Doctor?"

"Me? But I barely know how to work a computer!"

"Yet you went online to find all that information on the *Ligna Crucis* and the accident involving Abi-Ruj Iyasus, isn't that right?"

I was paralyzed by the point-blank question. There was no way I would confess to involving my poor nephew, Stefano, in the search. But I couldn't lie either. Besides, why lie? At this point my face revealed all the guilt I felt.

Glauser-Röist didn't wait for my answer. He passed me on the right, and as he did, he handed me a flashlight like the one he gave Farag. We split up, each one taking a side. With the light from three flashlights, the place became less forbidding.

"This crypt is known as the Crypt of Adriano, in honor of Pope Adrian I, who ordered its restoration in the eighth century," the Rock explained as we examined the enclosure, meter by meter. "The building dates to around the third century, during the persecutions of Diocletian, when the first Christians built a small secret church on the foundation of a pagan temple. The stones sticking out of the plaster walls are the ruins of the pagan temple and the altar of the apse is what's left of the Ara Maxima."

"It was a temple dedicated to Hercules the Triumphant," I clarified.

"Like I said, a pagan temple."

I shined my light into every corner of the three naves and some of the small lateral oratories on the left. There was dust everywhere, as well as broken urns containing the remains of saints and martyrs forgotten many centuries back. Aside from its obvious historical and artistic value, that modest chapel contained nothing worth mentioning. It was simply a strange underground church with no information and no clues to the first test of Staurofilakes purgatory.

After our fruitless search, we gathered in the apse and sat down on the ground, next to the Ara Maxima, to take stock. In my new pants, I felt completely at ease. In a large chest in the wall, the skull and the bones of one Saint Cirilla rested next to me ("Saint Cirilla, virgin and martyr, daughter of Saint Trifonia, died for Christ in the reign of Prince Claudius," read her epitaph in Latin).

"This time we haven't found any chrismon to point the way," Farag said, pushing his hair out of his face.

"There must be something," the captain replied, distressed. "Let's go back over everything we have seen since we got to Santa Maria in Cosmedin. What got your attention?"

"The Mouth of Truth!" exclaimed Boswell enthusiastically. I smiled.

"I'm not talking about tourist attractions, Professor."

"Well... That really got my attention."

"The cover of that Roman culvert is very interesting," I observed to cover his back.

"Fine. We will go back on top and start our inspection all over again."

That was more than I could bear. I looked at my watch and saw it was five thirty in the afternoon. "Can't we come back tomorrow, Captain? We're tired."

"Tomorrow, Doctor, we will be in Ravenna, facing the second circle of Purgatory. Don't you get it? At this very moment, somewhere in the world, there could be another theft of a *Lignum Crucis!* Maybe right here in Rome! No, we are not going to stop, and we are not going to rest, either."

"I'm sure it's not important," the professor blurted out, stuttering and pushing up his glasses again, "but I saw something strange over there." He pointed to one of the oratories on the right.

"What is it, Professor?"

"A word written on the ground… etched in the stone."

"What word?

"You can barely make it out; it's almost worn away. It seems to be *Vom.*"

"*Vom?*"

"Let's see." The Rock got to his feet.

In the left corner of the oratory, right in the center of a huge rectangular flagstone at right angles with the walls, you could make out the word *VOM.*"

"What does *Vom* mean?" the Rock asked.

I was just about to answer when, suddenly, we heard a dull crack and the ground began to tremble. I screamed as I fell like dead weight onto the stone slab. We were sinking into the earth, rocking furiously from side to side. One important detail stuck with me: seconds before the crack, I got a strong whiff of the unmistakably pungent smell of Father Bonuomo's sweat and dirt. He had to have been close by.

I was too panicked to think clearly; all I could do was try to grab onto the oscillating floor to keep from falling into the void. I lost my flashlight and purse. An iron hand was clutching me by the wrist, helping me keep my body glued to the stone.

We descended like that for a long time. Of course, what seemed like an eternity may have only been a few minutes, but finally the damned rock touched down and came to a halt. Nobody moved. All I could hear was Farag's and the Rock's ragged breathing under mine. My legs and arms felt like they were made of rubber, as if they'd never be able to support me again. I trembled uncontrollably from head to toe. My heart was beating wildly and I felt like I really needed to throw up. I recall a blinding light streaming through my closed eyelids. We must have looked like three frogs spread out facedown on some mad scientist's dissection tray.

"No. No, we didn't . . . we didn't do it right . . . ," I heard Farag say.

"What are you saying, Professor?" asked the Rock in a very low voice, as if he didn't have the strength to speak.

"Through a narrow cleft, along a path that zigzagged through the rock," the professor recited, gulping in air, *"the way a wave swells up and then pulls back. 'Now we are at the point,' my guide began, 'where we must use our wits: when the path bends, we keep close to the far side of the curve.'"*

"Blessed Dante . . ." I sighed with dismay.

My companions got to their feet, and the iron hand turned me loose. That's when I realized it was Farag. Standing in front of me, he timidly extended that same hand like a gentleman, offering me help getting to my feet.

"Where in the world are we?" pronounced the Rock.

"Read Canto X and you'll know," I murmured, my legs still trembling and my pulse racing. That place smelled damp and rotten, in equal parts.

A long line of torch holders, attached to the walls by iron rings, lit up what seemed to be an old culvert, a drainage ditch. We were on its ledge. From that ledge, where a trench of black and dirty water flowed, to the wall, there must have "room for three men's bodies laid out end to end," the exact width of the slab we had descended upon. The same vaulted tunnel extended as far as I could see, all the way to the right and to the left.

"I think I know what this is," the captain said, settling the backpack on his shoulder with a decisive gesture. Farag was brushing the dust and dirt off his jacket. "It's very possible we are in some branch of the Cloaca Maxima."

"Cloaca Maxima? It still exists?"

"The Romans didn't build things halfway, Professor. When it comes to engineering, they were the best. Aqueducts and culverts held no secrets for them."

"In fact, the Roman aqueducts are still in use in many European cities," I added. I had just found the remains of my purse scattered everywhere. My flashlight was destroyed.

"But the Cloaca Maxima!"

"It was the only way they could build Rome," I explained. "The entire area occupied by the Roman Forum was a swamp and had to be drained. They started building the sewer in the sixth century B.C., by order of the Etruscan king, Tarquin the Old. They expanded and reinforced it until it reached colossal dimensions. It was in perfect working order during the Roman Empire."

"Where we are standing was, no doubt, a secondary branch," Glauser-Röist said, "the branch the Staurofilakes use for their test of pride."

"Why are the torches lit?" asked Farag, taking one of them from its holder. The fire roared as it struggled against the air. The professor put his other hand up to protect his face.

"Clearly, Father Bonuomo knew we were coming."

"Well then, let's get going," I said, looking up toward the distant opening, which was nowhere to be seen. We must have descended quite a few feet.

"Right or left?" asked the professor, planting himself in the middle of the path, holding his torch high, resembling the Statue of Liberty.

"Definitely through here," indicated Glauser-Röist, pointing mysteriously toward the ground. Farag and I walked over to him.

"I can't believe it!" I murmured, fascinated.

Right where the ledge started to our right, the stone ground was wonderfully etched with scenes in relief, just the way Dante described it. The first was Lucifer's nosedive from heaven. You could see his beautiful angel face wearing a terrible look of anger as he reached toward God as he fell, begging for mercy. Such artistic perfection and attention to details gave me chills.

"It's Byzantine," commented the professor, impressed. "Look at that strict Pantocrator thinking over his favorite angel's punishment."

"The prideful punished...," I murmured.

"Well, that's the idea, right?"

"I'll get out the *Divine Comedy,*" announced Glauser-Röist. "We need to check out the similarities."

"Don't worry, Captain. They'll match, they'll definitely match."

The Rock leafed through the book, then looked up with a smile in the corners of his lips.

"Did you know that the tercets in these iconographic representations start in verse twenty-five of the canto. Two plus five, seven. One of Dante's favorite numbers."

"Don't get carried away, Captain," I implored. There was quite an echo.

"I'm not getting carried away, Doctor. For your information, the series in question started in verse sixty-three. Six plus three, nine, his other favorite number. We're back to seven and nine."

Farag and I weren't paying much attention to that spate of medieval numerology. We were too busy enjoying the beautiful scenes on the ground. After Lucifer came Briareus, the monster son of Uranus and Gaia, heaven and earth. He was easy to recognize by his one hundred arms and fifty heads. Believing he was stronger and more powerful, he rebelled against the gods of Olympus and died, pierced by a celestial arrow. Despite how ugly Briareus was, the image was incredibly beautiful. The light from the torches gave the reliefs a terrifying lifelike quality, while the flames from Farag's torch gave them greater depth and volume. Nuances stood out that might have gone unnoticed.

The next scene was the death of the proud giants who plotted to do away with Zeus. They, too, died dismembered by Mars, Athena, and Apollo. Next was crazed Nimrod standing before the ruins of his Tower of Babel. After that came Niobe, turned to stone for daring to have seven sons and seven daughters in the presence of Latona, who only had Apollo and Diana. The path continued on: Saul, Arachne, Roboam, Alcmaeon, Senaquerib, Cyrus, Holofernes, and the razed city of Troy, the last example of punished pride.

There we were, our heads bent like oxen in a yoke, not talking, avidly studying it all. Like Dante, we walked along admiring those artful pieces of mythology or history that promoted humility and simplicity. After Troy, there were no more reliefs, and the lesson ended. Or did it?

"A chapel!" exclaimed Farag, squeezing through an opening in the wall.

We made our way through and found another Byzantine church identical to the Crypt of Adriano in size, shape, and layout. This chapel was different from its bigger twin in one important way: The walls were covered by wooden platforms from which hundreds of empty eye sockets in as many skulls glared at us from those perches. Farag put his free arm around my shoulders.

"Did that startle you, Ottavia?"

"No," I lied, "I was just taken aback." The truth was, I was terrified, paralyzed with fear by those empty gazes.

"This is one big necropolis, right?" joked Boswell. He flashed me a smile and walked over to the captain. I scurried behind him. I didn't want to be separated by one centimeter.

Not all the craniums were intact. The majority were leaning directly on some upper teeth (if they had any) or on their base, as if somewhere they had lost the lower jaw. Many lacked a parietal bone, a temporal bone, pieces of the frontal bone, or even the entire frontal bone. To me, the worst part was the eye sockets. Some were totally empty, and others still had the orbital bones. All in all, it was hair-raising. There were literally hundreds of those remains.

"They are relics of Christian saints and martyrs," announced the captain, carefully examining a row of skulls.

"What?" I was shocked. "Relics?"

"Well, that's what they look like. There is an inscription engraved in front of each one with what looks like a name: Benedetto *sanctus*, Desirio *sanctus*, Ippolito *martyr*, Candida *sancta*, Amelia *sancta*, Placido *martyr*…"

"My God! And the church has no knowledge of this? Surely it gave these relics up for lost centuries ago."

"Maybe they're not authentic, Ottavia. Keep in mind, this is Staurofilax territory. Anything's possible. Besides, if you take a good look, the names aren't in classical Latin, but in medieval Latin."

"It doesn't matter if they're fake," warned the Rock. "That's something for the church to decide. In that case, is the True Cross we are so desperately looking for real?"

"The captain is right about that. That's up to the experts in the Vatican and the Reliquary Archives."

"What's the Reliquary Archives?" asked Farag.

"The Reliquary Archives is where they display, in cases and cabinets, the relics of the saints the church needs for administrative matters."

"Why do they need them?"

"Well... Every time a new church is built, the Reliquary Archives has to send some bone fragment to be deposited under the altar. It's mandatory."

"Wow! I wonder if we have the same thing in our Coptic churches. I admit my ignorance in these matters is endless."

"Surely your churches do. Although I don't know if you also keep—"

"How about we get out of here and continue our journey?" Glauser-Röist cut us off and started walking for the exit.

Like well-behaved students, Farag and I followed him out of the chapel.

"The reliefs stop here," the Rock pointed out, "right in front of the entrance to the crypt. I don't like that."

"Why?" I asked.

"It looks like this branch of the Cloaca Maxima has no exit."

"The water from the culvert is barely flowing," Farag pointed out. "It's practically still, as if it were dammed up."

"Of course it's flowing," I protested. "I saw it moving as we walked along. Very slowly, but it's moving."

"*Eppur si muove...,*"* said the professor.

"Exactly. If it weren't, it would be putrid. And it isn't."

"Boy, but it sure is dirty!"

We all agreed about that.

---

* "And, nevertheless, it is moving." Famous phrase spoken in 1632 by Galileo, after the church forced him to retract his theory that Earth turned around the sun, as Copernicus affirmed and demonstrated.

Unfortunately, when the captain went up ahead, he ascertained that the branch had no exit. Barely two hundred meters later, we came to a stone wall blocking the tunnel.

"But...the water is moving...," I babbled. "How is that possible?"

"Professor, raise the torch as high as you can and go over to the very edge of the ledge," said the captain as he lit up the wall with his strong flashlight. In the two sources of light, the mystery became clear. At the very center of the dike, about halfway up, you could make out a faint chrismon of Constantine scratched into the rock; a vertical line with irregular edges passed through its axis and divided the wall in two.

"It's a floodgate!" wailed Boswell.

"Are you surprised, Professor? Did you think it was going to be easy?"

"But how are we going to move those two slabs of stone? They must weigh a couple of tons each, at least!"

"Well, let's sit down and think it over."

"It's too bad this comes at dinnertime. I'm starting to get hungry."

"Well then, let's solve this puzzle in a hurry," I advised, plopping down on to the ground. "If we don't get out of here, there won't be any dinner tonight, no breakfast tomorrow morning, no meals for the rest of our lives. Life seems pretty short right about now."

"Don't start that again, Doctor! Let's use our brains. As we figure it out, we'll eat the sandwiches I brought."

"You knew we'd be spending the night here?" I was shocked.

"I wasn't sure what would happen. Just try to solve the problem, please."

We went round and round about the floodgate and examined it carefully many times. We even used a piece of wood from the platforms in the crypt to poke at the submerged part of the dike. A couple of hours later, all we'd figured out was that the stone slabs weren't perfectly squared off and that water escaped through that minuscule chink in the wall. We went back to the reliefs again and again, up and down, down and up, but that didn't clarify anything. They were beautiful, but nothing more.

Near midnight, exhausted and freezing, we returned to the church.

By then, we knew that branch of the Cloaca Maxima really well, as if we'd built it with our own hands. Clearly, there was no way out of there without some magic intervention or unless we passed the test. If only we could figure out what the test was. On one end were the floodgates; a couple of kilometers away was the bucking flagstone; and in-between was a pile of rocks, a cave-in where the water filtered through several gaps. In a corner, we found a wooden box filled with burned-out torches. We concluded that that wasn't a good sign.

We considered the possibility of moving those enormous boulders, since the prisoners of the first cornice suffered exactly that punishment for their pride. We decided that that was impossible; each one of those rocks must have weighed two or three times what we weighed. So we were trapped. If we didn't find a solution soon, we would be stuck there until we were food for the worms.

My headache had disappeared for a few hours; but now it was back with a vengeance. I was tired and sleepy. I didn't even have the energy to yawn, but the professor certainly did. He opened his mouth wide with growing frequency.

It was cold in the church, although not as cold as in the culvert. We carried all the torches we could to one of the oratories and built a bon-fire. That warmed the corner enough so we could survive the night. Being surrounded by watchful skulls, however, wasn't exactly conducive to sleep.

Farag and the captain got caught up in a long hypothetical discussion over the test we had to pass. They agreed that the only way was to open the floodgates. The problem was *how* to open them; they couldn't reach an agreement on that point. I don't recall much about that conversation. I was half-asleep, floating in an ethereal space lit up by a fire and surrounded by whispering skulls. The skulls *were* talking... or was that part of my dream? I was sure they were talking or whistling. The last thing I recall before slipping into a deep lethargy was someone helping me stretch out and putting something soft under my face. That was all until I opened my eyes halfway for a moment (it was a very peaceful rest) and saw Farag stretched out at my side, asleep. The captain was totally engrossed in reading Dante by the light of the fire. Not much time had passed when a voice woke me up. I stood up, startled, and saw the Rock on his feet, as tall as a Greek god, throwing his arms in the air.

"I've got it! I've got it!"

"What's going on?" Farag asked in a sleepy voice. "What time is it?"

"Get up, Professor! Get up, Doctor! I need you! I found something!"

I looked at my watch. It was four in the morning. "Lord!" I sobbed. "Will we ever get six or seven hours of sleep at one time?"

"Listen closely, Doctor," the Rock cried, rushing toward me like a force of nature. "*'I saw him who was supposed to be the noblest creature of creation.' 'I saw Briareus on the other side...' 'I saw Thymbraeus, saw Pallas and Mars...' 'I saw the mighty Nimrod by his tower...'* What do you think?"

"Aren't those the first verses that describe the reliefs?" I asked Farag, who gave the captain a puzzled look.

"But there's more!" continued Glauser-Roist. "Listen: *'Oh, Niobe, I saw your grieving eyes!' 'Oh, Saul, transfixed by your own sword...!' 'Oh, mad Arachne, I could see you there...!' 'Oh, Rehoboam, the image of you here no longer threatens...!'*"

"What's happening to the captain, Farag? I don't understand a thing he's saying!"

"Neither do I, but let's see where he's going with this."

"And, finally, *fi-nal-ly*..." He waved the book in the air, then looked at it again. "*'Verily, he pointed out the hard pavement...' 'Verily, he pointed out how they were sent...' 'Verily, he pointed out the crude example...' 'Verily, he pointed out how they fled defeated...'* Pay attention, now—this is very, very important. Lines sixty-one to sixty-three of the canto:

> *"I saw Troy gasping from its ashes there:*
> *O Ilium, how you were fallen low,*
> *Depicted on the sculptured road of stone."*

"It is a series of acrostic strophes!" Boswell exclaimed, snatching the book from the captain. "Four lines that begin with *'I saw,'* four with

'O,' and four with '*Verily, he pointed out.*'" In its original Italian, the first four lines started with a '*V,*' the second four with an '*O,*' and the third with an '*M.*'

"And a last tercet, the one about Troy, has the key!"

My head really hurt, but I understood what was happening. I even figured out before they did the acrostic relationship of those strophes with the mysterious word Farag found in the rocking slab: *VOM.*

"What could *Vom* mean?" the captain asked. "It has to mean something!"

"It does, Kaspar, it does. That brings to mind good Father Bonuomo. Right, Ottavia?"

"I already thought of him." I struggled to my feet, rubbing my face. "I ask myself how many poor aspiring Staurofilax have lost their lives trying to pass these tests. You have to be very shrewd to tie up all the loose ends."

"Would you two please kindly explain? Now, *I* don't understand *you.*"

"In Latin, Captain, the *U* and the *V* are written the same, like a *V.* So *Vom* is the same as *Uom*, 'man,' in medieval Italian. Our charming priest is named Bon-Uomo, or Bon-Uom—that is to say, *Good man.* See where I'm going with this now?"

"Will you consider locking this guy up, Kaspar?"

The captain shook his head. "Nothing has changed. Father Bonuomo will have a solid alibi and an inscrutable past. The brotherhood already has surely covered its back, especially that of the guardian of the Roman test. He would never voluntarily reveal he's a Staurofilax."

"Okay, gentlemen!" I said with a sigh. "Stop the chitchat. Since we're not going to get any sleep, let's stay focused. We have Dante's acrostic, the word *UOM*, and some stone floodgates. Now what?"

"Some of these skulls are labeled *Uom sanctus*," Farag suggested.

"Then, hop to it."

"But, Captain, the torches are almost burned out. It will take a while to look for more."

"Collect what coals are left, and begin. We don't have much time!"

"Hear me out, Captain Glauser-Roist!" I exclaimed, angry. "If we get out of this, I refuse to continue if we don't get some rest. Do you hear me?"

"She's right, Kaspar. We're worn out. We should stop for a few days."

"We'll discuss that when we get out of here. Now, please, look around, Doctor, start over there. Professor, you go to the opposite end. I will examine the presbytery."

Farag crouched down and grabbed the two torches still burning among the coals. He gave me one and kept the other. A while later, after checking out all the relics, we had found no saint or martyr named Uom. It was disheartening.

The sun was rising outside, when it finally dawned on us that maybe we should be looking for a name besides *Uom*. Maybe it was like the acrostics, every skull beginning with *V* or *U, O* or *M*. And we guessed right. After another long, tedious search, we found four saints whose names began with *V: Valerio, Volusia, Varrón,* and *Vero;* four martyrs whose name started with *O: Octaviano, Odenata, Olimpia,* and *Ovinio;* and four other saints whose name began with *M: Marcela, Martial, Miniato,* and *Mauricio.* There was no doubt we were on the right track. We marked the twelve skulls with soot, in case their location had anything to do with the answer, but they didn't seem to be in any order. All the twelve skulls had in common was that they were whole. In that warehouse of broken junk, that was proof enough. After this breakthrough, we still didn't know what to do. Nothing seemed to be the key to opening the floodgates.

"Are there any sandwiches left, Kaspar?" Farag asked. "When I don't sleep, I get ferociously hungry."

"There are some in my knapsack. Look and see."

"Want some, Ottavia?"

"Yes, please. I'm getting weak."

All that was left in the captain's knapsack was a miserable, dried-up salami and cheese sandwich. We split it up with our dirty hands and ate it. It was divine.

While Farag and I tried to deceive our stomachs with our food, the captain paced like a caged animal. He was focused, engrossed. From time to time, he repeated the tercets he had obviously learned by heart. My watch read nine thirty in the morning. Somewhere above us, life was rousing for the day. The streets were jammed with traffic and children were headed to school. Way underground, three exhausted souls tried to escape from a rat hole. The half sandwich had appeased my hunger. I felt more relaxed. I sat down and leaned against the wall, looking into the last embers of the fire. Very soon, they would go out for good. I felt a deep stupor, and I closed my eyes.

"Sleepy, Ottavia?"

"I need to rest my head. Do you mind, Farag?"

"Me? No. Why would I mind? Just the opposite, I think it's a good idea for you to rest a while. I'll wake you up in ten minutes, okay?"

"Your generosity overwhelms me."

"We have to get out of here, Ottavia. We need your input," chimed the captain

"Ten minutes. Not one minute less."

"Go ahead. Sleep."

Sometimes ten minutes can feel like eternity. I rested more during those ten minutes than I had in the four hours we slept the night before.

We inspected everything again and lit a couple of torches from the box next to the cave-in. Clearly the Staurofilakes had meticulously programmed the entire process and knew exactly how long the test would last.

Desperate and crestfallen, we returned to the church.

"It has to be here!" Glauser-Röist shouted, crouching on the ground. "I am sure the solution is here, damn it! But where, where?"

"In the skulls?" I suggested.

"There is nothing in the skulls!" he roared.

"Well, actually...," the professor said, pushing his glasses up to his eyes, "we haven't looked inside them."

"Inside?" I was surprised.

"Why not? What other possibility do we have? Let's at least check it out. Shake the skulls of those twelve saints and martyrs—give them each a rattle."

"Touch them?" That seemed to me very irreverent and loathsome. "Touch the relics with our hands?"

"I'll do it!" Glauser-Röist shouted. He went up to the first skull with a soot mark and raised it in air, shaking it with little respect. "There's something in there!"

Farag and I hopped around as if we were on a trampoline. The captain studied the skull carefully.

"It's sealed up. All its orifices are sealed up: the neck hole, the nasal cavity, and the eye sockets. It's a container!"

"We need to empty it somewhere," Farag said, looking around.

"In the altar," I proposed. "It's concave, like a bowl."

It turned out that Valerio and Ovinio contained sulfur (unmistakable by its scent and color); Marcela and Octaviano, a gummy, resinous black substance we identified as fish; Volusia and Marcial, two sticks of fresh butter; Miniato and Odenata, a whitish dust that burned the captain's hand slightly (he deduced it was quicklime); Varrón and Mauricio, a thick, shiny black grease that, given its intense smell, had to be crude oil, or rather, naphtha. Finally, Vero and Olimpia contained a fine ocher-colored dust we couldn't identify. We put all those substances into separate small piles. The altar became a lab table.

"I believe I am right when I say," began Farag, with the intense look of someone who has reached a worrisome conclusion, "that what we have here are the components of Greek fire."

"My God," I raised my hand to my mouth, in horror.

Greek fire was the Byzantine armies' most lethal and dangerous weapon. Thanks to it they were able to keep the Muslims at bay from the seventh to the fifteenth centuries. For hundreds of years, the formula for Greek fire was the best-kept secret in history. Even today we aren't completely sure what it was made of. According to the legend, in the year 673, Constantinople was besieged by the Arabs and on the verge of surrendering when, one day, a mysterious man named Callinicus appeared, offering the worried Emperor Constantine IV the most powerful weapon in the world: Greek fire. It had the strange property of catching on fire on contact with water and burning mightily. Nothing could extinguish it. The Byzantines hurled Callinicus's mixture through tubes erected on their boats, completely destroying the Arab fleet. The surviving Muslims fled in fear of the flames that seemed to burn even under water.

"Are you sure, Professor? Couldn't it be something else?"

"Something else? No way. These are the elements that the most recent studies show are the ingredients of Greek fire: gasoline or crude oil, which floats on water; calcium oxide or quicklime, which ignites on contact with water; sulfur, which gives off a toxic steam when it burns; fish or resin, to set off the combustion; and fat, to hold it all together. The ocher-colored dust that we couldn't identify must be potassium nitrate—in other words, saltpeter. When it comes in contact with combustion, it gives off oxygen and keeps the fire burning under water. Not too long ago, I read an article on this in a magazine called *Byzantine Studies.*"

"What good is Greek fire to us?" I asked, remembering I had read the exact same article.

"All we're missing is one element," Farag said, looking at me. "We could mix all this together and absolutely nothing would happen. Can you guess what ingredient would catch the mixture on fire?"

"Water, of course."

"And where is water in this place?"

"Do you mean the water in the channel?" I said, frightened.

"Exactly! If we mix up a batch of Greek fire and throw it into the water, it will catch fire with incredible force. It's very likely that the floodgates are opened by heat."

"If it's not too much trouble," the Rock looked worried, "before we perform such a dangerous task, I would like to know how heat opens the floodgates."

"Ottavia, correct me if I'm wrong. Weren't the Byzantines big fans of all mechanical things, hinged toys and automated machinery?"

"Sure. The biggest fans in history. One emperor made a pair of roaring mechanical lions that paraded single file in front of foreign ambassadors. Other rulers had devices in their thrones that triggered lightning and thunder to frighten courtiers. There was the fantastic Golden Tree of the royal garden, with its mechanical singing birds. It was very famous back then; it's all but forgotten now. There were priests—Christian priests, I mean—who made 'miracles' happen during Holy Mass, such as opening and closing church doors and things like that. In Constantinople there were coin-operated fountains that dispensed water. I could go on and on. There's a very good book on the subject."

"*Byzantium and Its Toys*, by Donald Davis."

"That's the one. I believe we have the same taste in reading materials, Professor Boswell," I exclaimed with a wide smile.

"True, Dr. Salina," the Professor replied, also smiling.

"Okay, okay... You are twin souls, great. Would you mind getting to the point, please? We have to get out of here."

"What Ottavia is saying, Kaspar, is that there were priests who voluntarily opened and closed the doors of the temples. The faithful thought it was a miracle, but in fact it was a very simple trick. It was triggered—"

"—by lighting a fire." I took the words out of Farag's mouth, I knew the subject so well. Byzantine machinery had always fascinated me. "The heat expanded the air in a container that was filled with water. The expanded air forced the water through a siphon into another container suspended by some springs. This second container descended under the weight of the water, and the springs that held it up turned cylinders that moved the axes of the doors. How's that sound?"

"Sounds like gobbledygook!" the captain snorted. "We're going to set off a fiery bomb on the chance that that opens the floodgates? You two are nuts!"

"Well, give us an alternative if you can," I said in an icy tone.

"Don't you understand?" he repeated, desolate. "The risk is enormous."

"Could it be I'm not the only one who's afraid to die?" I said.

He muttered a few abominations and swallowed his rage. Slowly but surely that man was losing his grip on his emotions. He'd come a long way from the phlegmatic, cold captain of the Swiss Guard to the visceral, demonstrative human being standing before me.

"Fine! Go ahead! Get it over with! Hurry!"

Farag and I didn't wait for him to change his mind. While the Cracked Rock shined the flashlight on us, we used the burned-out torches like shovels to scoop up and mix all those elements together. I felt some irritation in my eyes, nose, and throat because of the quicklime, but it was so slight I wasn't alarmed. Soon, a grayish, viscous mass, very similar to bread dough, was stuck to our rudimentary wood spatulas.

"Should we divide it into several pieces or throw it in one block at the channel?" Farag asked, indecisive.

"Let's divide it. We can cover more surface area that way. We don't know exactly how the floodgates' mechanism works."

"Well, let's get on with it. Grab the stick like a spoon, and let's go."

The mass didn't weigh much, but it was much easier if the two of us carried it. We walked over to the floodgates. Once there, we set our projectile on the ground, careful to keep it very dry, and divided it into three identical sections. The Rock scooped one of them up with another burned-out torch. Once we were set, we threw those sticky, disgusting projectiles into the center of the stream. We were probably part of just a handful of individuals who, in the last five or six centuries, had had the chance to witness Byzantine Greek fire, and I was almost excited about it.

Tremendous flames leaped toward the stone vault almost instantly. The water burned with such extraordinary force that a hot hurricane-like wind forced us against the wall as if we'd been punched. In the middle of that blinding light, the horrible roar of the fire, and the dense black smoke over our heads, we watched the floodgates to see if they were opening. They didn't budge.

"I warned you, Doctor," the Rock shouted at the top of his lungs. "I warned you this was madness!"

"The mechanism will start up!" I answered. I was also going to say that we just had to wait for a little, when a coughing fit took all the air out of my lungs. The black smoke from our projectiles began to fill the room.

"Get down!" Farag shouted, letting all his weight fall on my shoulder to knock me over. The air was still clear at ground level. I gulped air, as if I'd just pulled my head out of the water.

Then we heard it—a sound that got stronger and stronger until it was louder than the roar of the fire. The axes of the floodgates were turning, grinding stone against stone. We sprang to our feet. Jumping together, we threw ourselves down into the dry side of the channel and ran toward the narrow opening through which the water was filtering to the other side. The fire floating on the water followed dangerously on our heels. I don't think I've ever run that fast in all my life. I was half-blinded by smoke and tears, with no air to breathe, begging God to let my legs be nimble enough to make it across that threshold as fast as possible. I was on the verge of a heart attack when I got to the other side.

"Don't stop!" the captain shouted. "Keep running!"

The fire and smoke crossed the floodgates too, but we were much faster. After three or four minutes, we had moved far enough out of danger and were slowing down to a complete stop. Huffing and puffing, our arms outstretched like athletes when they cross the finish line, we looked back at the long path we'd left behind. You could make out a distant glow behind us.

"Look, there's daylight at the end of the tunnel!" Glauser-Röist exclaimed.

"We know, Captain. We see it."

"No, Doctor, for the love of God! At the other end!"

I pivoted on my toes like a spinning top and saw the light the captain pointed out.

"Oh, Lord!" I blurted, on the brink of tears again, although these were from sheer joy. "The way out, finally! Let's go, please, let's go!"

We hurried out of there, half walking, half running. I couldn't believe that the sun and the streets of Rome were on the other side of the entrance to that mine. Just the thought of going home put rockets in my shoes. Freedom lay just ahead. Less than twenty meters away!

My relief at being freed was the last thought I had. A sharp blow to my head left me unconscious in the blink of an eye.

I saw lights inside my head before I came to completely. Intense jabs of pain accompanied those lights. Whenever one of them went off, I felt the bones in my skull crack, as if a tractor were squashing it.

Slowly, that unpleasant sensation eased, and I perceived another just-as-delightful feeling. A burning sensation, like a hot red fire, shot through me, from my right forearm, and brought me back to harsh reality. With plenty of groaning, I struggled to put my left hand on the intensely throbbing spot where I felt a sharp pain when I barely brushed against my sweater. I pulled my hand away with a shout, my eyes wide open.

"Ottavia?..." Farag's voice sounded far off. "Ottavia? Are you... Are you okay?"

"Oh, my God, I don't know. How about you?"

"My...my head hurts really bad."

I made out his figure several meters away, tossed on the ground like a teddy bear. Still further away, the captain was also unconscious. On all fours, I crawled over to the professor, trying to keep my head up.

"Let me see, Farag."

He tried to turn to show me the part of his head where he had received the blow. He moaned suddenly and lifted his hand to his right forearm.

"Gods!" he howled. That pagan exclamation shocked me for a few seconds. I was going to have to have a serious talk with Farag. Soon.

I ran my hand through the hair on the back of his neck. Although he moaned and pulled away, I felt a sizable bump.

"They whacked us good," I whispered, sitting beside him.

"And they marked us with the first cross, right?"

"I'm afraid so."

He smiled as he took my hand and squeezed it.

"You are as brave as *Augusta Basíleia!*"

"The Byzantine empresses were brave?"

"Oh yes! Very!"

"I never heard that...," I murmured, freeing my hand from his. I tried to stand up to see how the captain was.

Glauser-Röist had been hit much harder. The Staurofilakes must have thought that to bring down that huge Swiss, they really needed to let him have it. You could clearly see a spot of dried blood on his blond head.

"Let's hope they change their method in the future...," Farag murmured as he slowly rose to his feet. "They'll finish us off if they have to knock us out six more times."

"They may have already finished off the captain."

"Is he dead?" The professor was alarmed, hurrying toward him.

"Fortunately not. But he's really bad off. I can't get him to wake up."

"Kaspar! Hey, Kaspar, open your eyes! Kaspar!"

Farag tried to revive him, and I resumed my mental alacrity. We were still in the Cloaca Maxima, right where we'd lost consciousness, or maybe a bit closer to the exit. The outside light had disappeared, though. A torch illuminated the corner where they'd left us. I raised my wrist to see what time it was and felt that terrible burning on my forearm again. According to my watch, it was eleven at night; we'd been out for more than six hours. They couldn't have managed that with just a blow to the skull; they must have used something else to keep us asleep. However, I didn't feel any of the aftereffects of anesthesia or sedatives. I felt pretty good, considering.

"Kaspar!" Farag kept shouting and slapping the captain in the face.

"I don't think that'll wake him up."

"We'll see!" Farag said over and over, slapping the Rock.

The captain moaned and opened his eyes halfway. "Holiness?" he stammered.

"Holiness? It's me, Farag! Open your eyes right now, Kaspar!"

"Farag?"

"Yes, Farag Boswell. From Alexandria, Egypt. And this is Dr. Salina, Ottavia Salina, from Palermo, Sicily."

"Oh, yes...," he murmured. "Now I remember. What happened?"

The captain went through the same instinctive motions we did. He frowned as he felt the first painful throb from his head, then he tried to raise his hand to the nape of his neck. When he did that, the wound on his forearm brushed against his shirt.

"What the...?"

"They marked us, Kaspar. We still haven't seen our new scars, but there's no doubt what they did to us.

Hobbling like elderly cripples, we held up the captain as we made our way to the exit. As soon as the fresh air hit us, we could see that we were on the bank of the Tiber River, about two meters above water level. If we dropped down the embankment and swam a bit, we would come to a dock and some stairs on our right, about ten meters away.

On our left, farther away, we saw the Ponte Sisto, so we surmised we were halfway between the Vatican and Santa Maria in Cosmedin. Overhead, the streetlights and the upper floors of elegant buildings spurred us on despite our fatigue. We fell into the river, letting the smooth current of the freezing water carry us to the stairs. Since it hadn't rained in several months, the river was low, but it was enough to revive Farag and me almost completely. Glauser-Röist was worse off; he didn't regain consciousness completely, even with our river dunking. It was like he was drunk; he was unable to coordinate his movements or his words very well.

When we finally got out of the river and climbed up the dock's stairs, soaked, numb, and exhausted, the traffic in Lungotévere and the normal rhythm of the city at that hour made us smile. A couple of late-night runners, in shorts and T-shirts, happened by and couldn't hide their bewilderment. We must have looked strange and pitiful.

Holding onto both of the captain's arms, we made it to the edge of the sidewalk, intending to stop the first taxi we saw—by force, if necessary.

"No, no...," Glauser-Röist murmured with difficulty. "Cross the street at the next crosswalk. I live right over there."

I looked at him in surprise. "You have a house in the Lungotévere dei Tebaldi?"

"Yes... Number fifty."

Farag signaled to me not to make him talk, and we headed for the crosswalk. We crossed the street, under the surprised and scandalized gaze of drivers stopped at the traffic light, and we came to a beautiful vestibule with stone and wrought iron. When we searched for the key in Glauser-Röist's jacket pocket, a wet piece of paper fell to the ground.

"What is it?" the Rock asked, as I lagged behind.

"I don't know. A piece of paper, Captain."

"Let me see it."

"Later, Kaspar. Right now, let's get inside."

I put the key in the lock and opened the door with a shove. The vestibule was elegant and spacious, lit up with great stone crystal lamps; mirrors on the walls multiplied the light. The elevator was old, made of polished wood and wrought iron. The captain must be very rich if he had an apartment in the building.

"What floor, Kaspar?" Farag asked.

"The top one. The penthouse. I need to throw up."

"Not here, for God's sake!" I exclaimed. "Wait till we get you home! We'll be there in just a minute."

We went up in the elevator fearing that at any moment the Rock would hurl his soul out his mouth. But he behaved himself and held back until we entered his house. Unable to wait any longer, he shook us off and staggered down a dark hall. We heard him vomit through the door of the bathroom.

"I'm going to help him," Farag said as he turned on the lights. "Look for a phone and call a doctor. I think he needs one."

I crossed the wide house with the creepy feeling I was invading Captain Glauser-Röist's privacy. A man that reserved, quiet, and prudent about his private life surely didn't let many people in his house. Up until that moment, I'd assumed the captain lived in the Swiss Guard barracks right there, between the right side of Saint Peter's Square and the Porta Santa Ana. It hadn't occurred to me he would have his own flat in Rome. While the halberdiers—the enlisted soldiers—had to live in the Vatican, it was highly likely that high-ranking officers didn't. Still, I never imagined that someone whom I presumed got miserable pay—the Swiss

Guards' wages were famous for being incredibly low—had an elegant flat in the Lungotévere dei Tebaldi that was furnished and decorated with such good taste.

In a corner of the living room, next to the drapes, I found the telephone book and the captain's address book. On the same table, in a silver frame, was a photograph of a smiling girl. The girl was very pretty; she wore a brightly colored ski cap and had black hair and dark eyes. She couldn't be the Rock's blood relative; they looked nothing alike. Maybe she was his fiancée? I smiled. What a surprise that would be!

When I opened the address book, a stack of papers and loose cards slipped to the floor. I gathered them up and quickly looked for the number of the Vatican's health services. Doctor Piero Arcuti was on call, someone I was acquainted with. He assured me he'd be right over. I was surprised when he asked if I thought he needed to notify the secretary of state, Angelo Sodano.

"Why should you call the cardinal?"

"There's a note in Captian Glauser-Röist's file that says, in a situation like this, we're to notify the secretary of state. If he can't be reached, we're to call the archbishop secretary of the Second Section, Monsignor François Tournier."

"I don't know what to say, Dr. Arcuti. Do what you think is right."

"In that case, Sister Salina, I'm going to call His Eminence."

"Very well, Doctor. We'll be expecting you."

I'd just hung up when Farag appeared in the hall with his hands in his pockets and a quizzical look. He was as dirty and unkempt as a homeless man who had just rummaged around in the garbage.

"Did you talk to the doctor?"

"He'll be here right away."

He searched through his pockets and pulled something out. "Look, Ottavia. It's the paper you found in the captain's jacket."

"How's Glauser-Röist?"

"Not very well," he said, walking toward me with the note in his hand. "I'd say he's unconscious, not resting. He keeps passing out. What drugs do you think they gave us?"

"Whatever it was, it only affected him. You're okay, aren't you?"

"Not entirely. I'm starving. Look at this first, then I'll go to the kitchen to see what I can find."

I examined the piece of paper. It wasn't normal paper. Even though it was soaking wet, it was still thick and rough, with jagged edges, definitely not cut by a machine. I flattened it out on my palm and I saw some sentences in Greek scarcely blurred by the Tiber River.

"From our friends, the Staurofilakes?"

"Of course."

τί στενὴ ἡ πύλη καὶ τεθλιμμένη ἡ ὁδὸς ἡ ἀπάγουσα εἰς τὴν ζωήν, καὶ ὀλίγοι εἰσὶν οἱ εὑρίσκοντες αὐτήν.

"'How narrow is the door and how narrow the path that leads to life.'" I translated, with a lump in my throat. "'And how few are those who find it.' It's from the Gospel of Saint Matthew."

"Everything in the Bible sounds the same to me," Farag whispered. "The meaning is what scares me."

"It means that the brotherhood's next initiation test has to do with narrow doors and narrow paths. What's this below it?..."

"*Agios Konstantinos Akanzon.*"

"Saint Constantine of the Thorns...," I murmured, pensive. "It can't refer to Emperor Constantine, although he is also a saint, because he has no title after his name, much less *Akanzon.* Could it be the name of some important Staurofilax patron or perhaps the name of a church?"

"If it's a church, it's in Ravenna. The second test takes place there, the sin of envy. And that part about the thorns..." He raised his glasses and ran his hands through his filthy hair, then looked down. "I don't like the part about the thorns one bit. In Dante's second cornice, the bodies of the envious souls are covered with hairshirts and their eyes are sewn shut with wires."

Suddenly, a cold sweat covered my forehead and cheeks, as if my blood had instantly drained from my face.

"Please!" I begged, scared of the thought of what was to come. "Not tonight!"

"No… Not tonight," Farag agreed, coming over and putting his arm around my shoulders. "Tonight let's attack Kaspar's refrigerator, then sleep for several hours. Come with me to the kitchen."

"I hope Dr. Arcuti gets here soon."

The captain's kitchen was a sight. The moment we entered it, my first thought was for poor Ferma. With only a third of space and a tenth of the appliances, she took great pains to prepare delicious meals. What would she do with the captain's household version of NASA? An amazing stainless-steel refrigerator, with a water and ice dispenser in its door; next to that, a computer panel. When we opened the door, it beeped softly and told us it was time to buy more veal.

"How do you think he manages to pay for all this?" I asked Farag, who was taking out a loaf of bread and a pile of cold cuts.

"It's none of our business, Ottavia."

"Why not? I've worked with him for over two months and all I know is he has the emotions of a stone and he reports to the Sacred Roman Rota and Tournier. Go figure!"

"He no longer reports to Tournier."

Leaning on the red marble counter, Farag fixed mouth-watering sandwiches.

"Fine, but he still has the emotions of a stone."

"You've always seen him in a bad light, Ottavia. Deep down, I think he's just unhappy and lonely. I'm convinced he's a good person. Life has dragged him into the unsavory place he now finds himself in."

"Life doesn't drag you along if you don't let it," I pronounced, convinced I'd said a great truth.

"Are you sure?" he asked, sarcastically, as he cut the crusts off the bread. "I know someone who wasn't very free when it came time to choose her destiny."

"If you're talking about me, you're wrong." I was offended.

He laughed and brought two plates and a couple of brightly colored napkins to the table. "Do you know what your mother told me on Sunday after the funeral?"

Something poisonous was twisting around my heart by the second. I said nothing.

"Your mother said that of all her children, you were the brightest, the smartest, and the strongest." Without missing a beat, he sucked hot sauce off his fingers. "I don't know why she talked so frankly to me. In any case, she said you would only be happy living the life you're living, giving yourself to God, because you were never made for marriage and could never have borne a husband's demands. It seems like your mother measures the world according to the values of her day."

"My mother measures the world however she pleases," I replied. Who was Farag to judge my mother?

"Please, don't get mad. I'm just telling you what she told me. Now, let's eat these greasy, spicy sandwiches. They have a bit of nearly every-thing there was in the refrigerator on them. Dig in, empress of Byzan-tium, and you'll experience one pleasure in life you're not familiar with."

"Farag!"

"Sorry," he said. With his mouth so full, he could barely close it when he chewed. He didn't seem the least bit apologetic.

How could he be so wide-awake when I was so dead on my feet? Some day, I told myself as I chewed the first bite and admired how good it was, someday I'd commit to some type of healthy exercise. The days of spending long hours in the lab, never moving my legs, were over. I would walk, I'd work out in the mornings and take Ferma, Margherita, and Valeria with me for a run through the Borgo.

We'd almost finished eating when the doorbell rang. "Stay here and finish," Farag said, getting to his feet. "I'll get the door."

I knew the minute he headed for the door I'd fall asleep right there, right on top of that table, so I gulped down the last bite and followed him. I greeted Dr. Arcuti as he walked in. While he examined the cap-tain, I headed for the living room, to stretch out for a few minutes on the sofa. As I passed by a half-closed door, I couldn't resist temptation. I turned on the light and found myself in an enormous office, decorated with modern office furniture that somehow went perfectly with the an-tique mahogany bookshelves and the portraits of Captain Glauser-Röist's military ancestors. On the table was a sophisticated computer that looked like it could run circles around the one in my lab. To its right, next to a window, was a stereo with more buttons and digital screens than an airplane control panel. Hundreds of CDs were stacked in strange, tall, twisted cabinets; from what I saw, there was everything from jazz to opera, including folk music (there was a CD of music by actual pygmies) and Gregorian chants. The Rock was quite a music lover.

The portraits of his ancestors were another story. With slight variations, Glauser-Röist's face was repeated over the centuries in his great-great-grandparents or his great-uncles. They were all named Kaspar or Linus or Kaspar Linus Glauser-Röist. They all had the same stern expression the captain often wore—serious, grave faces; soldiers' faces; the faces of officers or commanders of the Vatican's Swiss Guard who dated back to the sixteenth century. I noticed that only his grandfather and father—Kaspar Glauser-Röist and Linus Kaspar Glauser-Röist—appeared in the fancy uniform designed by Michelangelo. The rest wore metal armor, breast- and backplates, as was the custom of armies in the past. Was it possible that the famous colorful uniform was actually a modern design?

A photograph much larger than the rest stood between the computer and a splendid iron cross resting on a stone pedestal. I walked around the desk to get a better look and came face to face with the same brunette whose framed picture I'd noticed in the living room. Now I was sure she was his girlfriend. Nobody has so many photographs of a friend or a sister. So, the Rock had a delightful house, a beautiful girlfriend, a noble family; he was a big fan of music and also a book lover, for there were many books in every room, not just in that office. You would have expected to find the typical collection of antique weapons that all military men value, but the Rock didn't seem interested in that. Except for the portraits of his ancestors, that home said its owner was anything but an army officer.

"What're you doing, Ottavia?"

I jumped and turned toward the door. "My God, Farag, you scared me!"

"What if I had been the captain? What would he have thought?"

"I didn't touch anything. I was just looking around."

"If I'm ever in your house, remind me to 'look around' in your room."

"You wouldn't do that."

"Get out of there right now—let's go," he said to me, ushering me out of the office. "Dr. Arcuti needs to examine your arm. The captain is going to be fine. They must have given him a very strong sleeping pill. He, too, has a nice cross on his upper right forearm. You can see it now. His and mine are a Latin design, framed by a vertical rectangle with a little seven-pointed crown on its upper half. Maybe they gave you a different model."

"I don't think so…," I murmured. To tell the truth, I'd already forgotten about my arm. It had stopped bothering me quite a while ago.

We entered the Rock's bedroom, where he was fast asleep, and still as dirty as when we left the Cloaca Maxima. Dr. Arcuti asked me to lift up the right sleeve of my sweater. The upper inside part of my forearm was a bit swollen and red, and you couldn't see the cross because they'd put a bandage over it. For a thousand-year-old sect, they were very up-to-date in the practice of tribal scarifications. Arcuti carefully pulled off the bandage.

"It's fine," he said, looking at my new tattoo. "It's not infected and it's clean, despite this greenish coloration. Some herbal antiseptic, perhaps—I couldn't say. It's a professional job. Would it be too much to ask…"

"Don't ask, Dr. Arcuti," I replied, looking at him. "It's a new fashion trend called body art. David Bowie is one of its most ardent followers."

"And you, Dr. Salina?"

"Yes, Doctor, I too follow the trend."

Arcuti smiled. "I suppose you can't tell me anything. His Eminence Cardinal Sodano told me not to be surprised by anything I see tonight, and not to ask. You must be on an important mission for the church."

"Something like that," Farag mused.

"Well, in that case," he said putting a new dressing on my cross, "I'm done here. Let the captain sleep until he wakes up. You both should get some rest, too. You don't look so good. Sister Salina, I think you'd better come with me. I have a car downstairs, and I can take you to your community."

Dr. Arcuti was a numerary member of Opus Dei, the religious organization with more power inside the Vatican since the election of the current pope. He didn't look favorably upon my staying overnight in a house with two men. To make matters worse, those men weren't priests. They say the pope doesn't do anything without Opus Dei's blessing. Even the strongest, most independent members of the powerful Curia Romana avoided openly opposing the politico-religious directors of that conservative institution. Its members, such as Dr. Arcuti or the Vatican's spokesman, the Spaniard Joaquin Navarro Valls, were omnipresent in every branch of the Vatican.

I looked at Farag, disconcerted, not knowing how to answer the doctor. There were plenty of bedrooms in that house. It was late, and, as tired I was, it hadn't occurred to me that I needed to go back to the apartment at the Piazza delle Vaschette to sleep. But Dr. Arcuti insisted.

"You want to get out of those dirty clothes, right? Don't give it another thought! How could you take a shower here? Oh no, sister."

I realized it would be crazy to resist. Besides, if I refused, the next day or that same night my order would be severely reprimanded. And I couldn't risk that. So I said good-bye to Farag, who was more dead than alive, and left with the doctor. He let me out at the Piazza delle Vaschette, smiling like someone who has done his duty. Ferma, Margherita, and Valeria were scared to death when they saw the state I was in. I know I showered, but I have no idea how I got to bed.

True to his Swiss-German nature, the captain refused to rest a single day, and despite Farag's and my insistence, he showed up the next afternoon at my lab, his head bandaged, ready to risk his life again. To him there was more to that demented story than hunting down and capturing some relic thieves. Captain Glauser-Röist seemed consumed by the idea of getting the jump on the Staurofilakes and their earthly paradise. Maybe for him those initiation tests represented more than a personal challenge. For me they were only a provocation, like a glove flung at my feet which I chose to pick up.

I awoke on Thursday around noon, recovered from the terrible spiritual and physical wear and tear from the previous week. It felt good to open my eyes and find myself in my own bed in my own room, surrounded by my own things. The eleven or twelve hours of uninterrupted sleep felt marvelous. Despite all the bruises, the muscle spasms in my legs, and my strange new tattoo, I felt at peace and relaxed for the first time in a long time, as if everything were in order.

But this pleasant feeling barely lasted a moment. From my bed, the covers pulled all the way up to my ears, I could still hear the phone ring and I figured the call was for me. But not even when Valeria came in to wake me up did my good mood change. There really was nothing like a good night's sleep.

It was Farag on the phone. In an uncharacteristically furious voice, he told me that the captain wanted us to meet at the lab after lunch. I insisted the Rock stay in bed for at least a day, but Boswell, angrier than I was, shouted that he'd tried everything. I begged him to calm down and not worry so much about someone who didn't take his own health seriously. I asked how he was feeling, and in a much calmer and gentler tone he said he had just woken up a couple of hours ago. He said aside from the scar on his arm, still green but less swollen, if he didn't touch the bump on his head, he was fine. He had rested and eaten a huge breakfast.

So, we decided to meet in my lab at four. In the meantime, I had lunch with my sisters, prayed in our chapel, and called home to see how everyone was doing. I couldn't believe I had three whole hours all to myself. I needed it to get my feet back on the ground.

Fresh as a rose, a happy smile on my lips, I walked from my house to the Vatican, enjoying the fresh air and the afternoon sun. How little we value things until we lose them! The light on my face infused me with the joy of living. The streets, the noise, the traffic, and the chaos brought me back to my normal daily routine. That's how the world was, so why complain when anything could be beautiful, depending on your point of view? If you look at things the right way, even dirty asphalt or an oil spot or a piece of paper thrown on the ground can seem beautiful. Especially if you had been sure you'd never see them again.

I ducked into the Al Mio Caffè to get a cappuccino. Being so close to the Swiss Guards' barracks, it was always packed with young guards talking loudly and laughing raucously. People like me also came and went on their way to work or home. Besides being a very pleasant place, it served a terrific cappuccino.

I finally arrived at the Hypogeum five minutes early. Work was back to normal on the fourth level of the basement, as if the craziness brought on by the Iyasus Codex had been wiped from everyone's mind. I was surprised when my staff greeted me congenially; some even waved. With a timid, awkward gesture, I responded to everyone, then flew into my lab to hide, asking myself what strange miracle might have caused such a change of attitude. Perhaps they had finally discovered that after all I was human and that my feeling of well-being was contagious.

I was just hanging my coat and purse when Farag and the captain showed up. A lovely bandage covered the captain's huge blond head, but from under his eyebrows, metallic flashes forecast stormy weather.

"I'm enjoying the beautiful day, Captain," I warned him as a greeting, "and I don't feel like seeing gloomy faces."

"Who's gloomy?" he answered dryly.

Farag wasn't in a good mood either. Apparently whatever had happened at the Rock's house had been apocalyptic. The captain didn't even take off his jacket or make a move to sit down.

"In fifteen minutes I have an audience with His Holiness and His Eminence Cardinal Sodano. It's very important, so I will be gone for a couple of hours. In the meantime, I need you to read Dante's next cornice. When I get back, we'll finalize our plans."

Without another word, he disappeared out the door. A heavy silence lingered in the lab. I didn't know if I should dare ask Farag what had happened.

"You know something, Ottavia?" He was still looking at the door. "Glauser-Röist is coming unhinged."

"You shouldn't have insisted he rest. When someone as stubborn as the captain wants to do something, you have to let him do it, even if it kills him."

"If that were all it was!" He gave me a strange look. "Am I my brother's keeper? I get it that Kaspar is a grown-up and can do what he likes. It's just… Look, I don't know, but this story about the Staurofilakes is driving him crazy. Either he's trying to win a medal or he wants to prove to himself that he's Superman or something. Maybe he's using this adventure the way other people drink—to forget or to self-destruct."

"I was thinking the same thing this morning. I mean this afternoon." I took my glasses out and put them on. "For you and me, this is an adventure we were drawn into voluntarily, out of interest and curiosity. For him it's something more. He doesn't give a damn about anything—getting rest, my father's and brother's deaths, the fact that you lost your life and your job in Egypt. He has us racing against time as if the theft of one relic was a major catastrophe."

"I don't agree. I think he was deeply sorry about your father and brother's accident and he's worried about my situation. But he *is* obsessed with the Staurofilakes. The moment he woke up this morning, he called Sodano. They talked for a long time, and during the conversation he had to lie down a couple of times, because he was on the verge of collapsing. He still hadn't had breakfast when he shut himself away in his office (the one you were poking around in, remember?), opening and closing drawers and files. While I ate and showered, he staggered around the house, shouting in pain, sitting down a moment to recover, then getting up to do more. He hasn't had breakfast or lunch since the sandwich in the Cloaca."

"He's going nuts."

We grew silent again, as if there were nothing more to say about Glauser-Röist. I'm sure we both were thinking the same thing. Finally I sighed deeply.

"Shall we get to work?" I asked, trying to get his spirits up. "Ascent to the second comice of *Purgatory.* Canto XIII."

"You could read it out loud," he proposed, stretching out in an easy chair propping his feet up on the computer box sitting on the floor. "Since I've already read it, we can comment on it."

"Do I have to read it?"

"I can, if you like; but the thing is, I'm comfortable here and I like the view."

I ignored his flip comments, so I started to recite Dante's verses.

"Now we are standing on the highest step,
where, for a second time, we saw a ledge
cut in the mount that heals all those who climb . . ."*

"Our alter egos, Virgil and Dante, come to a new cornice that was smaller than the previous one. They walk quite a way, looking for some soul to tell them how to keep climbing. Suddenly Dante hears voices saying *'Vinum non habent,'†* *'I am Orestes,'* and *'Love those who do you harm.'"*

"What does that mean?" I asked Farag, looking over the pile of boxes.

"They refer to classic examples of loving your fellow man. That is what the protagonists of this circle are suffering from. Keep reading and you'll see."

Curiously, Dante asks Virgil the same thing, and the Mantuan answers:

Then my good master said: "The Envious
This circle scouges—that is why the whip
Used here is fashioned from the cords of love.

"The curb must sound the opposite of love:
You will most likely hear it, I should think,
Before the pass of pardon has been reached.

---

* Canto XIII, 1–3.
† "We don't have any wine"—a reference to the wedding at Cana.

"Now look in front of you, look carefully
And you will see some people over there,
All of them with their backs against the cliff."

Dante examines the wall and discovers some shadows dressed in shawls the color of stone. He gets closer to them and is terrified at what he sees:

Their cloaks seemed to be made of coarsest cloth,
The nature of the penance they endured,
The sight squeezed bitter tears out of my eyes.

. . . .

Just as the blind cannot enjoy the sun,
So, to the shades I saw before me here,
The light of Heaven denies its radiance:

The eyelids of these shades had been sewn shut
With iron threads, like falcons newly caught,
*Could not stare back.**

I looked at Farag, who was looking at me with a smile. I shook my head. "I don't think I can bear this test."

"Did you have to carry rocks in the first cornice?"

"No."

"Who says they're going to stitch wire through your eyelids?"

"But what if they do?"

"Did they harm you when they marked you with the first cross?"

"No," I admitted again, although I mentioned the small matter of the blow to my head.

"Well, come on, keep reading. Don't worry so much. Abi-Ruj Iyasus didn't have holes in his eyelids, did he?"

"No."

*This was a common practice in falconry to tame the birds.

"Did you stop to think that the Staurofilakes had control over us for six hours and that all they did was give us a little tattoo? Has it dawned on you that they know perfectly well who we are and yet they are allowing us to pass the tests? For some reason, they're not afraid of us. It's as if they said, 'Go ahead, come to our earthly paradise, if you can!' They are very sure of themselves. They even left the clue for our next test in the captain's jacket. They didn't have to do that. Actually, if they hadn't, we'd be wracking our brains right now."

"Are they daring us?"

"I don't think so. More like inviting us." He ran his hand over his beard, which was lighter than his skin. He winced, annoyed. "Are you going to finish reading the second cornice or not?"

"I'm fed up with Dante, the Staurofilakes, and Captain Glauser-Röist! Really! I'm fed up with everything about this!"

"Are you also fed up with...?" he started to ask, following the train of my complaints; but he stopped short, letting out a big belly laugh which almost sounded forced and looked at me sternly. "Ottavia, please keep reading!"

Docily, I lowered my eyes to the book and continued.

Next came a long, tedious segment in which Dante strikes up a conversation with all the souls who tell him about their lives and why they are on this mountain ledge: Sapia dei Salvani, Guido del Duca, Rinier da Calboli... All were terribly envious; other peoples' bad fortune made them happier than did their own good fortune. Finally, canto XIV ends, and canto XV starts with Dante and Virgil alone again. A very bright light shines in Dante's eyes, forcing him to cover them with his hand. It's the guardian angel from the second circle. He erases another *P* on the poet's forehead and guides them to the foot of the stairs leading to the third cornice. As he does this, the angel recites some strange lyric: *Beati misericordes* and *Conqueror, rejoice...*

"And that's that," I said.

"Well, so now we have to figure out what *Agios Konstantinos Akanzon* is."

"We need the captain for that. He knows how to work the computer."

Farag looked at me surprised. "Isn't this the Vatican's Classified Archives?" he asked, glancing around.

"You're right!" I jumped to my feet. "What are those people out there for?"

I flung the door open and went out, resolved to recruit the first staff member I crossed paths with. Instead, I ran smack dab into the Rock, who was just about to storm into the lab like a bulldozer.

"Captain!"

"Were you going somewhere important, Doctor?"

"Well, really, no. I was going…"

"Well, come back in here, then. I have something important to tell you two."

I backtracked and sat down again. Farag frowned again in disgust.

"Professor, before you say anything, I want to apologize for my behavior this morning," the Rock said humbly, sitting down between Farag and me. "I felt pretty bad, and I am an awful patient."

"I figured that out."

"When I'm not feeling well, I become unbearable. I'm not used to staying in bed, not even with a 105-degree fever. I've been a horrible host and I'm so sorry."

"Okay, Kaspar, case closed," concluded Farag, waving a hand that meant that he'd closed that door forever.

"Okay, so," sighed the Rock, unbuttoning his jacket and getting comfortable, "I'll just jump right in. I told the pope and the secretary of state everything that happened to us in Syracuse and here in Rome. His Holiness was visibly impressed. Today, in case you don't recall, is his birthday. His Holiness turns eighty. Despite his many engagements, he made time to receive me. See how important this matter is to the church? Despite the fact that he was very tired and couldn't express himself clearly and had to speak through His Eminence, he let me know he is satisfied and is going to pray for us every day."

An emotional smile flickered across my lips. If my mother only knew! The pope, praying for her daughter, every day!

"Well, the next question is, what's next? We still have six tests to pass before reaching the Staurofilakes' earthly paradise. Should we survive those six tests, our mission is, of course, to recover the True Cross. We must also offer forgiveness to the members of the sect when they are ready to be integrated into the Catholic Church as another religious order. The pope is especially interested in meeting the current Cato, if he exists, so we'll have to bring him to Rome, voluntarily or by force. Cardinal Sodano told me that since the remaining tests take place in Ravenna, Jerusalem, Athens, Istanbul, Alexandria, and Antioch, the Vatican will loan us one of the Dauphin 365 along with His Holiness's own Westwind. As far as our diplomatic credentials…"

"Just a moment!" Farag raised his hand like a schoolboy. "What are a Dauphin and a Westwind?"

"I'm sorry," said the Rock, calm as lake water. "I didn't realize you don't know a thing about helicopters and airplanes."

"Oh no!" I mused, letting my head fall heavily between my shoulders.

"Oh yes, dear *Basileia!* We're going to keep running against time!"

Fortunately, Glauser-Röist didn't understand the inappropriate Greek qualifier that Farag had lately regaled me with.

"We have no choice, Professor. This matter must be settled as soon as possible. Christian churches everywhere have been robbed of their *Ligna Crucis.* The few remaining fragments have disappeared, despite being carefully guarded. For your information, three days ago a *Lignam Crucis* was stolen from Saint Michael's Church in Zweibrucken, Germany."

"They keep stealing them even though they know we're pursuing them."

"They're not afraid, Doctor. Saint Michael's Church was guarded by a private security service hired by the dioceses. The church is spending a lot of money to protect the relics. With no luck, as you can see. That's another reason Cardinal Sodano, with His Holiness's blessing, gave us one of the Vatican's helicopters and the pope's own Alitalia Westwind II."

Farag and I looked at each other.

"So, here's the plan: Tomorrow at seven a.m. we will meet at the Vatican heliport. It's at the far west side of Vatican City, right behind

Saint Peter's—directly across from the Leonine mural. The Dauphin will be waiting for us there, and we'll set off for Ravenna. Have you figured out the clue for the next test?"

"No," my voice cracked. "We needed your help."

"My help? Why?"

"You see, Kaspar, we know the city is Ravenna, we know the sin is envy, we know that the test has narrow doors and tortuous paths. The definitive clue seems to be a name we aren't at all familiar with: *Agios Konstantinos Akanzon.* Or Saint Constantine of the Thorns."

"The second circle is the one about hairshirts," said Glauser-Röist, pensively.

"We already know how things are going to go—or how we think they'll go. We need to figure out who this Saint Constantine is. Maybe his life can show us what we have to do."

"Or maybe," I proposed, *"Agios Konstantinos Akanzon* is a church in Ravenna. That's what you have to figure out, with that marvelous invention called the Internet."

"Very well," replied the Rock, taking off his jacket and hanging it carefully on the back of his chair. "Let's get to work."

He turned on the computer, waited a moment to let the system boot up. Next, he connected to the Vatican's server.

"What was that saint's name?"

"Agios Konstantinos Akanzon."

"No, Captain," I said. "First try Saint Constantine of the Thorns. It's more logical."

After a little while, just when Farag and I were tired of standing still, staring at the screen as countless documents whizzed by, Glauser-Röist let out a triumphant shout.

"We've got it!" he said, flopping back in his chair and loosening his tie. "Saint Constantine Acanzzo, in the providence of Ravenna. Listen to what this tourist guide says about its green routes."

"Green routes?" asked Farag.

"Ecotourism, Professor, itineraries for nature lovers—hiking and rock-climbing off the beaten track."

"Ah!"

"'Saint Constantine Acanzzo is an ancient Benedictine abbey located north of the Po delta, in Ravenna Province. It's a monastic complex, built before the tenth century. It includes a highly esteemed Byzantine church, a refectory decorated with splendid frescoes, and a bell tower from the eleventh century.'"

"I'm not surprised the Staurofilakes chose Ravenna as one of the cities for their tests," I commented. "It was the capital of the Byzantine Empire in the West from the sixth to the eighth century. What I don't understand is why they considered it the most representative of the sin of envy."

"During its period of greatest splendor, those two centuries of Exarchate you just mentioned, Ravenna established a real rivalry with Rome."

"I know Rome's history," I glowered at him. "I'm the only Italian here, remember?"

The captain didn't even look at me. He turned to Farag, ignoring me entirely. "As you know, the Roman Empire in the West fell in the fourth century, and the barbarians then controlled the entire Italian peninsula. When the Byzantines won it back in the sixth century, they handed it over to Ravenna instead of returning it to the Western capital, Rome, because Rome was the pope's territory and the enmity between Byzantium and the Roman pope had gone on for years."

"As I recall, the Roman pope was and still is considered the only true successor to Saint Peter," Farag pointed out in a singsong voice. "If it weren't for that small detail, the union of all Christians throughout the world might be a bit easier."

Glauser-Röist studied him in silence, void of expression.

"Since Byzantium left Rome in the dust," he continued, as if Professor Boswell hadn't said a word, "the city declined as Ravenna grew richer and stronger. Not content with its glory, it focused all its efforts on overshadowing the past grandeur of its enemy. Besides filling itself with magnificent Byzantine structures that are the pride of the city and all of Italy even today, they added one more humiliation, the worship of Saint Apollinar, patron saint of Ravenna, to Saint Peter's Basilica itself."

Farag gave a long, soft whistle. "Yes," he admitted, astonished. "I have to say envy was the great characteristic of Byzantine Ravenna. That business with Saint Apollinar was a really bad idea. How do you know all that?"

"Do you think there's no diocese in Ravenna? At this moment, people all over the world are digging up those details for us, especially in the six cities we still have to visit. You can be sure that in those six cities, they are already prepared for our arrival." He loosened his tie even more. "Stopping the Staurofilakes is a grand-scale undertaking in which we are no longer alone. All Christian churches have a lot at stake in this."

"Okay, but I don't see any of them joining us to risk their lives in *Agios Konstantinos Akanzon.*"

"Now it's called Saint Constantine Acanzzo," I reminded him.

"Exactly, and with all this chitchat we haven't finished reading about that ancient abbey," grumbled the captain, turning back to the screen. "The old monastic complex is very run-down, but there is still a small community of Benedictines who run an inn for travelers. It's situated in the center of the Palu Forest, which it owns and which extends more than five thousand hectares."

"'How narrow is the door and how narrow the road that brings life. And how few are they who find it,'" I recalled.

"Are we going to have to cross that forest?" Boswell asked.

"The forest is the monks' private property. You need their permission to enter it," the Rock explained, looking at the screen. "Either way, we'll get there by helicopter."

"Now that's more like it!" I said, amused at the thought of crossing the sky in an eggbeater.

"Well, you're not going to like what I'm going to say next, Doctor. I need you to pack your bags. We won't return to Rome until we are in the presence of the current Cato. As of tomorrow evening, Alitalia's Westwind II will be waiting for us at the Ravenna airport to take us straight to Jerusalem. Those are His Holiness's orders."

CHAPTER

5

The Vatican heliport was a narrow
rhomboid hemmed in on all sides
by the sturdy Leonine Wall, which
had separated the city from the
rest of the world for over eleven centuries. The
sun had just risen in a beautifully radiant, light
blue cloudless sky.

"We're going to have first-rate visibility!"
shouted the pilot of the Dauphin AS-365-N2
to Captain Glauser-Röist. "It's a splendid morning."

The Dauphin's engines were running and its
blades were moving gently. It sounded like a gigantic fan, not at all like in the movies. The pilot,
a young, robust, blond guy with a rosy complexion, was decked out in a gray flight suit that was
covered with pockets. He had a pleasant, frank
smile. He looked us over, probably asking himself who we might be to deserve a ride in his
shiny white Dauphin.

I was a bit nervous, since I'd never flown in a
helicopter before. Farag was carefully examining
everything with the curiosity of a foreign tourist
visiting a Chinese pagoda.

The night before, I had packed my bags feeling somewhat uneasy. Ferma, Margherita, and Valeria helped me out. They rushed around the apartment putting everything in the washing machine; ironing, folding, and packing. They cheered me up with jokes and a good meal. I wanted to feel like a heroine off to save the world; instead, I was terrified, and crushed by a weight I couldn't identify. I felt like these were the last minutes of my life—my last supper. The worst part was definitely going to our chapel. When my sisters prayed for me and the mission I was about to undertake, I couldn't hold back my tears. I had the feeling I was never coming back to the apartment again. I tried to shake off such useless fears and tell myself to be brave, not to be so cowardly. If I didn't come back, it would be for a good cause and for the good of the church.

Now here I was, at the heliport, dressed in my freshly washed and ironed pants, about to climb into a helicopter for the first time. I crossed myself when the pilot and the captain said it was time to board. I was surprised at how comfortable and elegant the interior was; there were no hard metal benches or military gear. Farag and I sat down in overstuffed white leather seats in an air-conditioned cabin, with wide windows and in a church-like silence. Our luggage was stowed in the lower part of the helicopter, while Captain Glauser-Röist took the copilot's seat.

"We're taking off," Farag announced, looking out the window.

The helicopter rocked slightly as it lifted off the ground. If it weren't for the strong vibration of the engines, I wouldn't have known I was in the air.

Flying in a helicopter was incredible. The sun to our right, we executed some maneuvers that were clearly impossible to perform in a steadier, more conventional airplane. The sky was so dazzling that looking out the window hurt my eyes. Farag reached over and hooked something around my ears.

He said, "Keep them," and smiled. "You're such a bookworm, I knew you wouldn't have any."

He had put a pair of sunglasses on me so I could look out the window comfortably. I took notice of how the bright sunlight filtered through the windows and reflected off his hair.

The sun climbed higher and higher. Our helicopter flew over the town of Forli, twenty kilometers from Ravenna. Glauser-Röist told us over the loudspeaker we'd be arriving at the Po Delta in fifteen minutes. We'd disembark and the helicopter would fly to the Spreta airport, in Ravenna, to await our instructions.

Those fifteen minutes passed in a sigh. Suddenly the machine tipped forward, and we started a dizzying descent that made my heart race.

"We have descended about five hundred feet," the captain's metallic voice announced. "We are flying over the Palu Forest. Notice how dense it is."

Our faces were glued to the window. We saw a green carpet with no beginning or end, formed by enormous trees. My vague mental image of five thousand hectares was unimaginably off.

"Good thing we don't have to cross it on foot," I mused, entranced.

"Let's not get ahead of ourselves," replied Farag.

"To the left is the monastery," said the captain's voice. "We'll land in that clearing there, in front of the main entrance."

Boswell sat beside me, studying the abbey. It must have been a beautiful place for reflection and prayer many centuries before with its unassuming four-story cylindrical bell tower and a cross above its eaves. All that remained was the thick oval wall that enclosed the complex. From our bird's-eye view, the rest was a pile of broken rocks and a wall here and there that struggled to remain upright. Only when we started our descent, the air from the blades stirring up the woodlands, did we make out some small structures near the abbey's walls.

The helicopter landed gently. Farag and I opened the cabin door. We didn't take into account that the propellers were still rotating; their wild force flung us around like hapless plastic bags in a hurricane. Farag grabbed me by the elbow and helped to steady me.

The captain stayed in the cockpit for a few minutes, talking to the pilot, now just a helmet with an impenetrable black visor. The man nodded and gunned the engines as Glauser-Röist, with less effort than we had needed, cut through the whirlwind. The machine rose back into the air, and in seconds, it was just a white speck in the sky. My first flight in a helicopter had been thrilling, something I'd do again first chance I got, but in a split second, it was old news. Farag, the captain, and I found ourselves standing in front of an iron gate at the entrance of the *Agios Konstantinos Akanzon.* With the copter out of earshot, all we heard were the birds singing.

"Well, here we are," the Rock said, glancing around. "Let's go find the friendly Staurofilax in charge of this test."

We didn't have to look too far. From out of nowhere, two elderly monks in black Benedictine habits appeared on the gravel road that led to the main gate.

"Hello! Good morning!" exclaimed one of them, waving his arm in the air, as the other opened the gate. "Are you seeking shelter?"

"Yes, Father!" I answered.

"Where are your bags?" the older of the two asked, folding his hands over his chest and covering them with his sleeves.

The Rock lifted his backpack to show them. "This is all we need."

The monks were much older than I had guessed, but they had pleasant, jovial spirits and nice smiles.

"Have you had breakfast?" asked the only one of the two with a small tuft of hair.

"Yes, thank you," answered Farag.

"Well, let's go to the inn and get you some rooms." He looked us over and added, "Three, right? Or is one of these men your husband, young lady?"

I smiled. "No, Father. Neither of them is my husband."

"Why did you come in a helicopter?" the other nonagenarian asked with childlike curiosity.

"We don't have much time," the Rock explained, walking very slowly so his long strides didn't leave the old men behind.

"Oh! Then you must be very rich. Not just anyone travels in a helicopter."

Both monks laughed heartily, as if this was the funniest joke in the world. We exchanged furtive, perplexed looks. Either those Staurofilakes were first-rate actors, or we were completely wrong about the place. I studied them for any sign of deception, but their wrinkled faces were so innocent; their frank smiles seemed completely honest. Had we made a mistake?

As we headed toward the inn, the monks told us a succinct history of the monastery. They were very proud of the Byzantine frescoes that decorated the refectory and the well-preserved church, to which they had dedicated their entire lives in a place in the middle of nowhere and visited by just a few hikers. They wanted to know what made us decide to visit Saint Constantine Acanzzo and how long we were going to stay. Of course, they said, we were welcome to share their table; and if their services pleased us, would we mind, since we were so rich, leaving a nice tip for the abbey when we departed. With that they laughed again like happy children.

As we walked and chatted, we came to a small garden where another elderly Benedictine monk was bent over, plunging a shovel into the earth with great effort.

"Father Giuliano, we have visitors!" shouted one of our companions.

Father Giuliano put his hand over his eyes to see us better and grunted.

"Father Giuliano is our abbot. Go over and say hello," one of our companions urged under his breath. "Most likely he'll detain you a while with questions, so we'll wait for you at the inn. When you are finished, follow that path over there and take a right. You can't miss it."

The captain was getting impatient and was out of sorts. Clearly he thought we were mistaken, and that this was all just a waste of our time. Those monks bore no resemblance to the image we had of the Staurofilakes. But as we walked over to the garden, I asked myself, what image did we really have of the Staurofilakes?

We'd only seen one we could be sure of—our young Ethiopian man, Abi-Ruj Iyasus. The other two, the sacristan at Saint Lucia and the foul-smelling priest at Santa Maria in Cosmedin, might have been just what they appeared to be.

The monks disappeared down the path while the abbot awaited us, leaning on his shovel, rigid as a king on his throne.

"How long do you plan on staying?" he asked point-blank when we got close to him.

"Not long," answered the Rock, obviously skeptical of our decision to be there.

"What brings you to Saint Constantine Acanzzo?" he asked. We couldn't see his face; his head was covered by the wide hood of his habit.

"The flora and fauna," the captain answered gruffly.

"The countryside, Father, and the peace and quiet," the professor rushed in to add.

The abbot grabbed his shovel with both hands, turning his back on us, and resumed digging. "Go to the inn. They're expecting you."

Confused and surprised by the brief conversation, we set off, single file, through the garden, down the road the others had pointed out. The trail penetrated a shadowy stretch of forest and grew narrower until it was little more than a path.

"What are those tall trees, Kaspar?"

"There's a bit of everything," explained the Rock, without looking up at them, as if he'd already examined them. "Oaks, ash, elms, white poplars. But those species don't usually grow so tall. Maybe the soil is very rich or maybe the monks of Saint Constantine have developed some special fertilizer over the centuries."

"Impressive!" I exclaimed, raising my eyes to the dense, leafy dome which cast a shadow on the path.

After walking a few minutes in silence, Farag asked, "Didn't the monks say we should go right at the fork in the road?"

"It can't be much farther," I answered.

But it was a long way. Several minutes passed with no sign of a fork in the road.

"I think we're on the wrong path," said the Rock, looking at his watch.

"I said that a while ago."

"Let's keep walking," I objected, sure we had gone the way we were told.

After a half an hour, I had to admit my mistake. We were headed into the deepest part of the woods. The road was barely visible and the foliage was very thick. The lack of sunlight due to the dense treetops kept us from determining the direction in which we were going. Luckily, the air was fresh and clean, making the hike somewhat pleasant.

"Let's go back," ordered Glauser-Röist, scowling.

Neither Farag nor I argued. We clearly weren't getting anywhere. The strange thing was, when we doubled back, we had barely gone a kilometer when we found the fork. How had we missed it?

"This is annoying," bellowed the Rock. "We didn't pass this junction before."

"Want my opinion?" asked Farag, smiling. "This is the start of our journey through the second cornice. They must have covered up those trails and then cleared them off so we could find them. One of them leads to the right place."

That seemed to pacify the captain. "In that case, let's proceed as if this was just what we were expecting."

"Which way? Right or left?"

"What if this isn't the test?" I objected, pursing my lips. "What if we're just lost and imagining things?"

Their reply was an indifferent silence. They both began to snoop around, kicking and pushing aside the gravel with their shoes. They were like two Boy Scouts, or two hunting dogs looking for fallen prey.

"Here! Over here!" shouted Farag.

He'd found a little Constantine chrismon, tiny as a fingernail, on the trunk of a tree growing next to the road to the left.

"What did I tell you?" he said smugly. "It's this way!"

"This way" turned out to be a very long path that led to a hedge nearly three meters tall blocking our path. We stopped, as surprised as a Tuareg would be if he came upon a skyscraper in the middle of the Sahara.

"I think we've arrived," murmured the professor.

"Now what do we do?"

"Follow it, I guess. Maybe there's an opening. Maybe there's something for us on the other side."

We skirted it for about twenty minutes, until its perfectly regular shape finally gave way. An entrance some two meters wide invited us to enter. An iron chrismon nailed into the ground left no doubt about what we had to do.

"The circle of the envious," I murmured, a bit cowardly, putting my left hand on my forearm where the tattoo of the first cross was still tender.

"Come on, *Basileia*, don't let them think we're cowards," Farag uttered, elated, as he thrust himself through the hole.

A second hedge extended in front of us. We couldn't see the end in either direction; the two formed a path that seemed to go on forever.

"Would the lady and gentleman prefer the right or the left?" Boswell said in the same good-humored voice.

"Which way does Dante go?" I asked.

The captain quickly pulled his well-thumbed copy of the *Divine Comedy* out of his backpack and scanned it.

"Listen to what he says in the third strophe of the canto," he said, visibly excited. " '*No sign of any souls or carvings here. The cliff face is all bare, the roadway bare...*' Four lines later he observes of Virgil: '*Then, looking up and staring at the sun, he made of his right side a pivot point bringing his left side of his body round.*' Could you ask for any clearer directions?"

"So, where's the sun?" I inquired, looking around. The gigantic trees grew so close together they covered the sky.

The captain looked at his watch, took out a compass, and pointed to a spot in the sky. "It should be about there."

Sure enough, once we knew where it was, it was easy to detect the source of the light coming through the branches.

"But we can't be sure what time of day Virgil looked at the sun," replied Farag. "That could completely change the direction."

"Let's take a chance," I reasoned. "If the Staurofilakes wanted us to take a certain direction, they would have shown it to us."

Glauser-Röist, still reading the *Divine Comedy*, raised his head and looked at us with shining eyes. "Well, Doctor, this time chance is on our side, for Virgil and Dante arrived at the second cornice just past noon. About the same time we did."

With a satisfied smile, I lifted my face to the sun, planted my right

foot on the ground, and turned to my left. My left foot landed on the
path on the right. We started down the "bare roadway" between the bare
walls that only appeared seamless because they were formed by a dense
bower. The "bare roadway" wasn't completely smooth, either: Every
couple of hundred meters, firmly anchored in the ground, was a wooden
star. At first those stars really caught our eye, and we speculated about
what they meant. After more than an hour of walking, we decided that
however incorrect we might be, whatever they were, they were all the
same and were therefore insignificant as clues.

Fatigue was starting to take its toll. My feet were burning and aching. What I wouldn't have given for a chair—better yet, a comfortable
leather armchair like the one in the helicopter. Like Dante and Virgil, we
walked a long way before we found anything noteworthy.

"This reminds me of a line by Borges," said Farag, "which says: 'I
know a Greek labyrinth that is a unique, straight line. So many philosophers have gotten lost on this line that even a mere detective could get
lost.' I think it's from *Artificios*."

"And don't you remember the part about that 'infinite circle whose
center is everywhere and whose circumference is so great that it appears to be a straight line'?" I too had read Borges, so why not show it
off a bit?

At about five in the afternoon, with nothing to appease our hunger
or thirst, we came upon a gap in the hedge: an iron door, as tall as the
enclosure it sealed, and some eighty centimeters wide. When we pushed
it and crossed the threshold, we discovered some interesting things.
First, our enormous hedges were solid stone walls nearly a meter thick
and entirely covered by vines. Second, the door was designed so that it
could only be opened from the outside. As soon as we turned our backs,
we couldn't open it again.

"We need something to prop it open," proposed Farag.

There were no rocks lying around, and we couldn't spare anything
we were carrying. On top of that, the vines were as strong as hemp rope
and pricked like the devil. The only solution was to use Farag's watch.
He offered it generously, saying that it was made of titanium and would
easily hold up. We leaned the iron slab on it very gently. The poor watch

held out for a few seconds, then buckled under the door's weight and shattered into a thousand pieces.

"Sorry, Farag," I said, to console him. More than downhearted, he was incredulous.

"Don't worry, Professor—the Vatican will compensate you. The bad part is, the door is now closed and there's no way for us to get out."

"That means we're on the right path," I replied, nervous about what might be next.

We were all thinking the same thing, so we started walking again. The second path was narrower than the first, and darkness made walking dangerous. There may have still been plenty of light outside the forest; but under that thick sky of branches, visibility was very poor.

We hadn't walked a hundred meters when we stumbled upon a new symbol on the ground. This one was much more original.

$$ \hbar $$

It seemed to be made of lead, although we couldn't be sure. Whoever put it there had made certain we couldn't pry it loose. It was as if it had sprung from the earth.

"It looks familiar." I squatted down to examine it. "Is it a zodiac sign?"

The captain just stood there, as if waiting for the two classics experts to decide what it is.

"No. It looks like one, but it isn't," said Farag, brushing back the weeds. "It's an ancient symbol for the planet Saturn."

Furtively, I bared my teeth in a scornful grimace only Farag could see. He smiled. We stood up and kept walking. Night was filtering down on us. From time to time we heard the cry of some bird and the sound of leaves rustling in the gusts of wind. As if that weren't enough, it was starting to get cold.

"Will we have to spend the night here?" I asked, turning up the collar of my jacket. At least it was leather and had a thick flannel lining.

"I'm afraid so, *Basileia*. Kaspar, I hope you foresaw this possibility."

"What does *Basileia* mean?" asked the captain.

Suddenly, my legs started to tremble.

"It was a very common word in Byzantine, meaning 'worthy woman.'"

What a liar! I sighed silently with relief. *Basileia* would never have been translated as 'worthy woman' and it wasn't a common Byzantine word. Its literal meaning was "empress" or "princess."

It was only six thirty in the evening, but the forest was so dark that the captain had to switch on his powerful flashlight. We'd walked all day down long dirt paths and had gotten nowhere. Finally, we stopped and sat on to the ground to eat our first meal since we had had breakfast back in Rome. We chewed the infamous salami and cheese sandwiches (the captain's menu never varied), and recapped what we'd learned. We came to the conclusion that we were missing several pieces of the puzzle. The next day we'd figure out what we'd gotten ourselves into. A Thermos of hot coffee got us back into a good mood.

"Why don't we sleep right here? We can set out at dawn," I ventured.

"Let's go on a bit longer," countered the Rock.

"But we're tired, Captain."

"Kaspar, I think we should do what Ottavia suggests. It's been a very long day."

The Rock gave in, utterly disgusted. We set up an improvised tent, and the captain handed us a couple of heavy woolen hats. We laughed, and looked at him as if he were crazy.

"Your ignorance is shameful!" he thundered. "Haven't you ever heard the saying 'If you're feet are cold, put on a hat'? A good part of body heat is lost through the head. The human organism is programmed to sacrifice the extremities if the torso and back get cold. If we don't lose heat through our heads, we will maintain our body temperature and keep our feet and hands warm."

"That's too complicated! I'm just a simple man of the desert!" joked Farag. Nonetheless, he and I jammed the caps down to our ears. The one the captain gave me looked vaguely familiar. I didn't recall why until later.

Then, the Rock took from his magic backpack what looked like a pouch of tobacco and tried to give one to each one of us. Of course we rejected the offer in the nicest way possible. Glauser-Röist, steeling himself with patience, explained that the pouches contained survival blankets, a sheet of plastic that weighed practically nothing but kept you really warm. Mine was red on one side and silver on the other, Farag's was yellow and silver, and the captain's was orange and silver. They were indeed very warm. Between the cap and the blanket (which rustled every time you moved), we barely noticed we were out in the middle of an open forest. I sat down between the two men, carefully leaning my back against the wall, the captain switched off his flashlight. I must have slid down without realizing it until I was leaning against Farag, my head on his shoulder. In between dreams, it came to me that my woolen cap was the same one the brunette girl wore in the photograph in the captain's living room.

*I*t started to grow light—going from utter blackness to a dark gray—at about five in the morning. We all woke up at the same time, surely on account of the bird's deafening arias. Half-asleep, I remembered it was Saturday, and that just the week before, I had been in Palermo with my family, at my father and brother's wake. I silently prayed for them and tried to accept the demented reality around me before I opened my eyes for the day.

We stumbled around, drank some cold coffee, gathered up our supplies, and set off down the path. We walked without a break until nine or nine thirty; we counted some thirty symbols of Saturn. Suddenly, in front of us, we came across an enormous wall that cut into the path.

"Attention!" announced Farag. "We're there!"

We picked up the pace, animated by the crazy desire to reach the last step. But the truth was, we weren't even near the end. Although that bramble-covered wall closed off the path we had traveled, to our left we noticed an iron door, identical to the one we had walked through the day before. Knowing there was nothing we could do to keep it open, we pushed on it and walked through with an air of resignation, guessing that on the other side we would find a panorama similar to what we were leaving behind. If it weren't for the fact that the new path was narrower than the previous one, we'd have thought we hadn't gone anywhere at all.

"I get the feeling we're walking across parallel paths that are getting closer to one another." Farag extended his arms from side to side; the tips of his fingers were just a palm's width from the hedges. The hedges had changed too; the walls weren't just covered by tangled stalks and leaves. Interlaced were huge thickets of thorns, brambles, thistles, and nettles that pricked us if we just lightly brushed up against them.

"The paths are much narrower," the Rock agreed, looking at his compass, "but I don't think we're headed down straight, parallel lines. We seem to have veered about seventy degrees to the left."

"Are you serious?" Farag said, surprised. He walked over to the captain to check out his measurements.

"Borges once spoke of 'infinite circle whose center is everywhere and whose circumference is so great that it appears to be a straight line,'" I said, as my fingertips touched one of the pointy-tipped spines protruding through the wall. If it weren't so clearly a plant, I would have bet it was the sharpest needle ever made. Its thorn oozed a soft black goo. Seconds after touching it, my skin got red and burned as if I'd touched a burning match. "My God, these nettles are terrible! We must stay away from them."

"Let me see."

As the captain studied my hand, the redness and stinging slowly subsided. "Fortunately, the poison of the nettle you touched is short-lived; but all the species around here may not be the same. Be careful."

Trying not to brush up against the thorny plants, whose rapiers were strong enough to tear our clothes, we walked about a hundred or hundred and fifty meters more until the captain stopped short.

"Another strange design," he said.

Farag and I leaned over to look at it. It resembled an artistic numeral 4, made with a metal that shone with a bluish glint.

4

"The symbol for the planet Jupiter," Farag pointed out. "I won-der... If we are in fact turning and a planet appears on each new path, it's possible all this is in fact a large rendition of the cosmos."

· "Perhaps," admitted the Rock, touching the design. "But an image made of tin."

"Saturn was made of lead, as I recall," I said.

"I don't know...," repeated Farag, irritated. "This is all very strange. What kind of game are they playing this time?"

We found the next door about five hours later.

We sat down on the ground and ate something before entering. The next path—or gigantic circle, if you like—was narrower, and the thorny plants seemed to be denser and more dangerous. Here, the symbol was the planet Mars, and it was made of iron.

$$\male$$

"Now there's no doubt," commented the captain.

"We're walking through the solar system."

"We shouldn't think in contemporary terms," Farag corrected me, leaning over the figure. "Our knowledge of the planets and the universe today has nothing to do with what was known in antiquity. If you look closely you'll see that the sequence we have followed has been Saturn–Jupiter–Mars. I'd say we're moving through the universe as it was per-ceived from the time of classical Greece until the Renaissance: The sphere of the stationary stars on the first path, then the seven planets and Earth."

"That's the same concept Dante has of the universe."

"That's right, Captain. Dante, like everyone before him and many more after him, believed the universe was a series of nine concentric spheres. The outermost enclosed all the rest as well as the stationary stars, while the innermost was Earth, where humans lived. Neither of these two spheres moved; their position was fixed. The spheres that did turn were one inside them, the seven known planets—Saturn, Jupiter, Mars, Mercury, Venus, the sun, and the moon."

"Nine spheres and seven planets," observed Glauser-Röist. "Seven and nine again."

I couldn't hide my deep admiration for Farag. He was the most intelligent man I'd ever met. Everything he said was completely right; his memory was excellent, even better than mine. I'd never met anyone I could say that about.

"So, the next orbit will be Mercury."

"I'm sure, Kaspar. I also think we are advancing more and more quickly, since the circles are contained within each other. The perimeters should be smaller."

"And the paths, narrower," I added.

"Let's get walking," ordered the Rock. "We've got four more planets to visit."

We came to the door of Mercury by sunset, when I was thinking to myself that Abi-Ruj Iyasus must have been a kind of Colossus, a true Hercules, if he had passed the brotherhood's tests. The rest of the Staurofilakes—Dante and Father Bonuomo included—what kind of faith or fanaticism propelled them to bear all these calamities? If the Staurofilakes are so special, and so incredibly wise, why did they agree to remain in humble outposts, living out innocuous, hidden lives?

We stopped for the night at one of the Mercury symbols, made this time from a sparkly, highly polished violet-colored metal we were unable to recognize. We had to stretch out single file to sleep. The edge between the path's thorny walls no longer allowed for any niceties.

On the morning of the next day, Sunday, we awoke once again startled by the birds' deafening song, and set out at first light, every one of our bones and muscles aching.

We reached the orbit of the fifth planet when the sun was at its zenith. The captain announced that we had turned more than two hundred degrees from our original point, so we'd covered more than half a complete circle. On Venus's path we found only twenty-two symbols, made of red-brown copper. The big surprise awaited us on the next path. Unlike the previous paths, it no longer had straight convergent lines, but lines that clearly curved to the left. As soon as we crossed the threshold and delved into the circle of the sun, we were shocked to see that the thorny cover of brambles and thistles now formed an arch above our heads. The side walls were so close together that Captain Glauser-Röist had to walk sideways. The sleeves of Farag's jacket had torn even before we'd found the first symbol, and I had to keep my eyes peeled if I didn't want to get jabbed by hundreds of those horrendous needles.

The first symbol appeared almost immediately—a simple circle with an even simpler dot at its center. It was made of gold—a gold so pure that, even in the shadowy enclosure, it twinkled in the faint light filtering through the canopy. If we hadn't been so rushed, with large spines threatening us on all sides, ripping our clothes and scratching our skin, we certainly would have stopped to study such riches. (We counted fifteen solar symbols.) But we were in a hurry to get out of there, to get somewhere we could move around without wearing ourselves out, without incurring rashes from nettles. Besides, night was falling.

As we advanced, we worried about what we would find once we crossed the threshold of the seventh and last planet, the moon. Once we finally got there, the iron plate in front of us barely opened enough to let us squeeze through, as if there were something behind it blocking the door. The obstacle turned out to be nothing less than the hedges. The path was so narrow at this point that only a child could have walked through it without getting scratched. The thorns on the walls and the roof had been pruned to form a human-shaped hole in its center. We had to walk with our heads caged, as if a brambly trap had closed in around our necks, preventing us from moving anywhere but the path. Since Farag and the captain were taller and wider than the hole in the hedge—it fit my body like a tailored suit—I gave them my jacket and sweater to avoid as many of the wretched scratches as possible. Farag flatly refused to cover up.

"We're all going to get scratches, *Basileia!*" he argued. "Don't you see? That's part of the test! Why should you suffer more than we do?"

I stared at him, trying to telegraph all the determination I felt. "Listen to me, Farag. I'll only get some scratches, but you two will have more serious wounds if you don't cover up with all the clothes you can."

"Professor Boswell," added the Rock, "the doctor is right. Put on her jacket."

"And the caps," I added. "Put the caps on your heads."

"We'll have to cut holes for our eyes."

"You'll have to protect your face with a cap, too, Ottavia. I don't like this one bit…," jabbered Boswell.

"I know. Don't worry—I'll cover up too."

The path of the seventh planet was a nightmare. The captain said that the moon's symbols—silver crescent moons shaped like bowls— were the most beautiful of all. He could see them, since he went first and was carrying the flashlight. But even if I could have tilted my head to see them—touching them was out of the question—I have to say I couldn't have cared less. I had the desire, in my desperation, to impale myself against the foliage, to stop once and for all those hundreds of unbearable tiny nips, pinpricks, and cuts that made my arms, my legs, and even my cheeks bleed. There was no wool nor any other cloth that could stop the assault from those natural daggers. I tried to stay calm thinking about how Christ suffered as he walked to Calvary wearing his crown of thorns. I recall being on the verge of desperation, of uncontrollable hysteria. But above all, I recall Farag's dirty, bloody hand reaching for mine. And I think it was in those moments, when I had no control over myself, that I realized I was falling in love with that strange Egyptian who was always at my side and who secretly called me *empress*. It seemed impossible, and yet I felt it could only be love, although I had nothing to compare it with. I'd never been in love, not even when I was a teenager. I never understood the meaning of the word. Not once had I had my heart broken. God had always been my center, and I had always protected myself from the emotions that drove my older sisters and my friends crazy, making them say and do silly, stupid things. Now here I was, Ottavia Salina, a nun of the Order of the Blessed Virgin Mary, nearly forty years old, falling in love with a blue-eyed foreigner. I no longer felt the thorns. And if I did, I now no longer remember it.

The rest of the path of the seventh planet was a losing battle with myself. I thought I could still do something to block what was happening to me; at least, that was what I had decided to do before we came to the last door of that diabolical labyrinth. I said to myself that that unknown feeling that bewildered me, making my heart race while I felt like both crying and laughing at the same time, was no more than the product of the terrible circumstances we were living through. When this Staurofilakes adventure ended, I would go back home and be the same person I was before—no more rash behavior. Life would get back on track, and I would go back to the Hypogeum and bury myself among my codices and my books. Bury myself? The truth was, I couldn't bear the idea of returning home without Farag Boswell. I said his name in a low voice so no one would hear me, and a childish smile spread across my lips. *Farag.* No, I couldn't go back to my former life without Farag. But I couldn't go back with him either! I was a nun. I couldn't stop being a nun! My whole life, my work, revolved around this central fact.

"The door!" exclaimed the captain.

I wanted to turn around toward the professor, smile at him, and let him know I was there. I needed to see him and tell him that we had made it, even though he already knew we had; but if I'd turned my head even a centimeter, I probably would have lost my nose. Thankfully, that thought saved me. Those last seconds before we left the path of the moon brought me back to my senses. Perhaps it was coming to the end of the path or the certainty I would lose myself forever if I gave in to those intense emotions... My rational side won that first battle. Without hesitation, I ripped the danger out by the root, and smothered it mercilessly.

"Open it, Captain!" I cried, dropping the hand that an instant before was all that mattered. As I pulled away, though it pained me, everything I had felt was erased.

"Are you okay, Ottavia?" Farag asked me, worried.

"I don't know." My voice trembled a little, but I got control of it. "As soon as I can breathe without getting myself jabbed, I'll tell you. Right now, I just need to get out of here."

We'd come to the center of the labyrinth. I thanked God for the wide, circular space in front of us, where we could move, stretch our arms, and even run if we felt like it.

The captain set the flashlight on a table in its center. We gazed around as if it were the most beautiful palace in the world. What wasn't so charming was how we looked: like miners coming out of the mines. We had a multitude of small cuts on our foreheads and cheeks; our necks and hands were dripping with blood and sweat. We even had bloody wounds under our pants and sweaters, as well as numerous bruises and rashes caused by the fluid that had oozed from many of the plants.

Luckily, the captain had a small first-aid kit in his backpack. With a little cotton and sterile water, we cleaned the blood off our wounds—which were all superficial, thank God. In the glow of the flashlight, we applied a coat of iodine. When we were finished, slightly composed, and comforted by our new situation, we took a moment to look around the enclosure.

The first thing that got our attention was the rudimentary table where we'd first set the flashlight. After a quick inspection, we saw something else: an ancient, large iron anvil, its top battered by many years of service in a blacksmith's shop. Yet the strangest thing was not the anvil, but an enormous pile of hammers of various sizes piled carelessly in a corner.

We stood there in silence, unable to figure out what to do. If we'd had a forge and some metal to mold, we would have understood. But there was just an anvil and a mountain of hammers. That wasn't much to go on.

"I suggest we eat something and get some sleep," said Farag, letting himself fall to the ground, leaning against the soft, lush vines that now covered the circular stone walls. "Tomorrow is another day. I'm exhausted."

Without another word, in complete agreement, the captain and I sat down next to him and followed his lead. Tomorrow would be another day.

We had no more cold coffee in the Thermos, no water in the canteen, no salami and cheese sandwiches in the backpack. We had nothing, except our wounds, exhaustion, and creaking joints. We couldn't even stay warm with the survival blankets, because they'd been shredded the day before in our trek around the labirynth. As the sun rose in the sky, I said to myself that if God didn't help us get out of there, we would most certainly end up like the numerous Staurofílakes aspirants who'd failed.

Despite appearances, I realized our situation hadn't changed much from when we were in the circle of the moon. While there, we were forced to stay on the outlined path of that vegetal jail. Here—in this seemingly free, diaphanous center—all we could do was solve the problem of the anvil and the hammers. It was that simple.

"We have to move around," murmured Farag, still sleepy.

I wanted to turn and look at him. With an iron will, I lowered my head and resisted a foolish need to cry. I was starting to get sick of my childish emotions.

Glauser-Röist got to his feet and did some jumping jacks to get the blood flowing. I didn't move an inch.

"Call room service and have them send up a big breakfast."

"I want a steaming hot espresso and a chocolate biscotto," I begged, my palms pressed together.

"What do you say we get to work?" The Rock cut us short, his arms behind his head. He looked like he was trying to pull his head out by the root.

"Let's forge a sculpture with the iron hammers," I joked.

The captain stood right in front of them, totally focused. Then he crouched down. At that point, I lost sight of him because he was hidden behind the anvil. Farag sat up to watch him, then he finally stood up and walked toward him.

"Find anything, Kaspar?" he asked. The Rock got to his feet and I could see the upper half of his body again. He had a hammer in his hand.

"Nothing special. They're just regular hammers," he said, hefting the tool. "Some have been used and others haven't. There are big ones, little ones, and medium-size ones. But there doesn't seem to be anything extraordinary about them."

Farag jumped up immediately, carrying one of those iron mallets. He raised it in the air, flipped it, threw it up, and caught it with ease.

"Nothing extraordinary, indeed," he lamented. Then he stepped up to the anvil and struck it. The sound boomed like a huge bell in the forest. We froze, but the birds didn't. Flocks of them flew away, squawking from the highest treetops. Seconds later, when the clamor stopped, none of us dared move, still alarmed by what had happened, frozen like statues.

"Lord...," I babbled, blinking nervously and swallowing hard.

The Rock let out a huge laugh. "Well, *that* was extraordinary, Professor."

But Farag wasn't laughing. He was serious and expressionless. Without saying a word, he turned around and snatched the hammer out of the captain's hands. Before we could stop him, he struck the anvil again with all his might. I covered my ears, but it didn't help. The blow of iron against iron drilled into my brain through the bones of my skull. I jumped to my feet and marched over to him. I preferred an argument a thousand times over to suffering that abominable sound again.

"What on earth are you doing?" I snapped, confronting him over the anvil. He didn't answer. He went back to the pile of hammers, about to grab another one. "Don't even think about it!" I shouted. "Are you crazy?"

He looked at me as if he'd never seen me before. Then he ran around the anvil, planted himself in front of me, and grabbed me by the shoulders.

"*Basileia, Basileia!* Think, *Basileia!* Pythagoras!"

"Pythagoras?..."

"Pythagoras, Pythagoras! Isn't it wonderful?"

My brain replayed what had happened since we climbed out of the helicopter. Then I quickly ran through all I knew about Pythagoras: the labyrinth of straight lines, the famous theorem (the square of the hypotenuse of a right triangle is equal to the sum of the square of the other angles, or something like that). The seven planetary circles, the Harmony of the Spheres, the Brotherhood of the Staurofilakes, the secret sect of the Pythagoreans... The Harmony of the Spheres and the anvil and the hammers... I smiled.

"Do you get it?" Farag smiled, not taking his eyes off me. "Now you see!"

I nodded. Pythagoras of Samos, one of the most preeminent Greek philosophers of antiquity, born in the sixth century B.C., established a theory in which numbers were the fundamental principle of all things and the only possible way to decipher the enigma of the universe. He founded a type of scientific-religious community that considered the study of mathematics a way to spiritual perfection. He put all his effort into teaching deductive reasoning. His school had a number of followers; from it originated a line of wise men that continued through Plato and Virgil—Virgil!—up until the Middle Ages. In fact, today he is considered to be the father of medieval numerology; in the *Divine Comedy*, Dante followed him with mathematical precision. It was Pythagoras who first classified the different types of mathematics according to a system that has lasted for over two thousand years in the quadrivium of the sciences—arithmetic, geometry, astronomy, and... music. Yes, music. Pythagoras was obsessed with explaining the musical scale mathematically. It was a great mystery for people back then. He was convinced that the intervals between the notes of an octave could be represented through numbers. He focused on this theme for the greater part of his life, until one day, legend has it that—

"Would one of you please explain it to *me*," Glauser-Röist grumbled.

Farag turned, like someone waking out of a trance, with a guilty look on his face. "The Pythagoreans were the first to define the cosmos as a series of spheres that functioned as circular orbits. The theory of the nine spheres and the seven planets is the basis for the labyrinth we just came through, Captain. It was Pythagoras who exposed it for the first time..." He grew pensive for a moment. "Why didn't I realize that before? You see, Pythagoras maintained that as the seven planets followed their orbits, they emitted a series of sounds, the musical notes that created what he called the Harmony of the Spheres. That sound, that harmonious music, cannot be heard by us humans because we are inured to it from birth. According to this theory, each one of the seven planets emitted one of the seven musical notes, from *do* to *ti*."

"And what does that have to do with the hammers?"

"Can you please explain it to him, Ottavia?"

I felt a knot in my throat. I was looking at Farag, and all I wanted was for him to keep talking. So I gently turned down his offer by shaking my head. The old Ottavia had died, I said to myself in shock. Where had my taste for intellectual boasting gone?

"One day," continued Farag, "as Pythagoras was walking down the street, he heard some rhythmic blows that grabbed his attention. The noise was coming from a nearby blacksmith. Wise Pythagoras was attracted by the musicality of the blows on the anvil. He stood there for a long time, observing how the blacksmiths worked and how they used their tools. He realized that the sound varied according to the size of the hammers."

"It's a well-known story," I said, making a superhuman effort to seem normal, "that appears to be true, because Pythagoras did discover the numerical relationship between the musical notes, the same musical notes emitted by the seven planets as they rotated around the earth."

The bright sun appeared from behind the hedge, casting sheets of light on that earthly circle we were trying to escape. Glauser-Röist was impressed.

"We're on that earth," Farag happily concluded, "the center of the Pythagorean cosmology. That's where the planetary symbols in the previous circles came from."

"I suppose you've already surmised that your beloved Dante derived his numerology directly from Pythagoras," I said with irony.

The Rock looked at me. He had reverence in his steely eyes. "You don't understand, Doctor. All this deepens my conviction that we have lost so much beautiful, profound wisdom throughout history."

"Pythagoras was wrong, Captain. To begin with, the moon isn't a planet; it's the earth's satellite. No star emits musical notes as it orbits. And the orbits aren't round, but elliptical."

"Are you sure, Doctor?"

Farag listened to us very attentively.

"What do you mean *am I sure?* For the love of God! Don't you remember what you learned in high school?"

"From so many possible paths," the captain reflected, "it seems like humanity chose the saddest of all. Wouldn't you like to believe there's music in the universe?"

"Well, to tell you the truth, it's all the same to me."

"Not to me," he declared, turning his back on me, silently facing the hammers. It never ceases to amaze me how such a tough guy could harbor such a tender nature.

"Remember," Farag whispered, "romanticism was born in Germany."

"And what does that have to do with it?" I was getting annoyed.

"Sometimes one's reputation or public side doesn't necessarily jibe with the truth. I told you Glauser-Röist is a good person."

"I never said he wasn't!"

Just then a frightening hammer blow boomed. The captain had struck the anvil with all his might. "We have to find the Harmony of the Spheres!" he shouted at the top of his lungs as the ringing subsided. "You're wasting time!"

"None of us will have our head on right when all this ends," I lamented, observing the Rock.

"I hope *you* do, at least, *Basileia.* Yours is the most valuable."

As I turned around, I collided with the glare of his smiling blue eyes. Dear God, how wrong Farag was! My head was already lost.

"Please!" the captain insisted. "Can you please explain what Pythagoras did with these damned hammers?"

Farag turned to him and smiled. "He had the blacksmiths bring him a pile just like ours. He hit them on an anvil until he found the ones that played the notes on the musical scale. Actually the Greeks divided the notes in tetrachords. Our *do, re, mi, fa, so, la, ti* actually came from the first syllable of the verses of a medieval hymn dedicated to Saint John, but in the end, they're exactly the same thing."

"I used to know that hymn," I said. "But right this minute, I can't recall it."

"And what else did Pythagoras do with all those hammers?" the captain snorted.

"He found the numerical relationship between the weight of the ones he had and then deduced the weight of those he was missing. He had them made, and the seven sounded as if they had just been tuned."

"Okay, so what is that numerical relationship?"

Farag and I looked at each other, and then looked at the captain.

"Not a clue," I said.

"I suppose mathematicians and musicians would surely know it," Farag said. "But we're neither."

"Maybe we need to figure them out."

"Maybe we do. I just recall one thing, but I'm not sure it's right. The weight of the hammer that makes the *do* sound was exactly twice that of one that made the *do* sound an octave lower.

"In other words," I continued, "the hammer that produced the highest *do* weighs half what the hammer that produced the lowest *do* weighs. Yes, that sounds right to me too."

"It's one of those historical oddities you always remember."

"You half remember," I quickly objected. "If we weren't standing here, I would never have dredged it out of my memory."

"Well, the fact is, we've been in this place for three days. We have to use the Harmony of the Spheres if we ever want to see the world again."

Just the thought of having to strike all those hammers over and over again until we found the seven we were looking for made me completely ill. How I loved silence.

I proposed we group the hammers according to their weight. That task took longer than we thought. In most cases, the difference between a kilo hammer and a kilo-and-a-half hammer, for example, was imperceptible. At least we enjoyed the daylight as the sun rose to its highest point. What we didn't have was food or water. I was braced for a hypoglycemic attack at any moment.

After a couple of hours, we discovered it was easier to line the hammers up, from largest to smallest. By the time we finally did that, we were sweating and as parched as the desert sands. But after that it got much simpler. We softly struck the largest hammer on the anvil. Then we chose the eighth hammer from it and struck that one. Since we weren't quite sure if the notes were exact, we tried the seventh and the ninth, too, but

that just added to our confusion. After plenty of debate and hefting the
hammers back and forth, we decided to switch the eighth for the ninth.
After that simple adjustment, the notes sounded much better.

Unfortunately, the hammer that was supposed to be the *re* note, the
second in line, didn't sound like *re* at all. However, in the second octave,
the one we had obtained by exchanging the *do* hammer, the second hammer did sound like the correct *re*. We were making progress, just like the
day was passing without our realizing. But in the second scale the *mi*
didn't fit—or so we thought after trying them all. So we had to locate a
third *do* and find its corresponding *re* and *mi*—which, of course, were
out of order.

The situation was absolutely insane. We had no way of assembling
a complete octave. Either the hammers were in the wrong place or the
hammers we needed just weren't there. Because of our desperation, the
blows on the anvil, the hunger and thirst, I was starting to get one of my
headaches, which steadily got worse and worse. Finally, by midafternoon, we thought we had completed the scale. Almost all the notes
sounded fine, but I wasn't sure they were absolutely right. Some hammers seemed to be missing a few grams of iron; some seemed to have
had too much. Farag and the captain, however, were convinced we had
completed the task.

"Fine, so why hasn't anything happened?" I asked.

"What's supposed to happen?" Glauser-Röist argued.

"We're supposed to get out of here, Captain, remember?"

"Well, let's sit down and wait. They'll come and get us out."

"Why can't I convince you two that this musical scale isn't totally
correct?"

"It's correct, *Basileia*. You're the one who's insisting it's not."

Upset on account of the pain in my head and their pigheadedness,
I flopped down on the ground, leaned against the anvil, and closed myself off in a stormy silence they ignored. Minutes turned into a half
hour. They started to look chagrined, thinking I might be right after all.
With my eyes closed, and taking slow, measured breaths, I thought back
and realized that taking some rest was doing us good. When you listen
to noises all day, noises that were supposed to sound like musical notes,

there comes a time when you simply can't hear a thing. After silence had refreshed their ears, maybe Farag and the Rock would change their minds if they listened to their precious musical scale one more time.

"Try again," I encouraged them, without getting up.

Farag didn't move a muscle, but the captain, irreducible, tried again. He played the seven notes, and a slight error was clearly detectable in the *fa* tone.

"The doctor is right, Professor," the Rock admitted grudgingly.

"I heard it," Farag replied, shrugging his shoulders and smiling.

The captain went down the line until he found the hammers immediately before and after the defective *fa*. Once again, there was an error, and once again, he tried and tried until he came up with the right tool, the one that sounded right.

"Play them all again, Kaspar."

Glauser-Röist struck the anvil with the seven definitive hammers. Night was falling. The sky was dimming with warm, golden light. All was harmony and quiet in the forest when the silence returned. I felt sleepy. I realized it wasn't my normal way of falling asleep; something seemed to be off. An immense lassitude was taking over my body, carrying me slowly into a dark well of lethargy. I opened my eyes and saw Farag, glassy-eyed, and the captain who was leaning against the anvil, his arms as taut as ropes, trying to stay on his feet. There was a soft aroma of resin in the air. My eyelids fluttered closed again, against their will. I began to dream. I dreamt about my great-grandfather Giuseppe directing the construction of Villa Salina, which surprised me. The part of me that was conscious warned me that the dream wasn't real. I struggled to open my eyes, and a delicate cloud of white smoke filtered into the circle from under the wall, rising off the ground. I watched Glauser Röist fall to his knees, murmuring a soliloquy I couldn't make out. He clutched the anvil, trying not to lose his balance, and shook his head to stay awake.

"Ottavia...," Farag called out. I roused myself enough to stretch my hand toward him, although I couldn't answer. My fingertips brushed his arm, and immediately his hand found mine. United again, our joined hands were the last clear memory I had.

I awoke to an intense cold and a strong white light shining in my eyes. I felt as if my essence were all that existed, and that I had no past, no memories, not even a name. I returned to life slowly, floating like a bubble rising in a sea of oil. I wrinkled my forehead and noticed how rigid my facial muscles were. My mouth was so dry that I couldn't unglue my tongue from the roof of my mouth or separate my jaws.

The noise of a nearby car and an intense cold helped make me lucid. I opened my eyes wide, and still with no identity or conscience, I saw before me the facade of a church, a street lit up by lampposts, and a paltry bit of green under my feet. The white light shining on me in fact came from one of those tall lampposts. I could have been in New York or Melbourne. Instead of being Ottavia Salina, I could just as well have been Marie Antoinette. And then I remembered. I took a deep breath, filling my lungs, and it all came back to me—the labyrinth, the spheres, the hammers, and *Farag!*

I quickly sat up and searched around me. There he was, to my left, fast asleep between me and the captain, who was also still asleep. Another car came down the street. The driver didn't shine his light on us. If he had, he probably would have thought we were three bums sleeping on a park bench. The grass was wet with dew. I told myself I had to wake the sleeping beauties next to me so we could figure out where we were and what had happened. I shook Farag's shoulder gently, but was hit by a pain on the inside of my left forearm, like the one I felt when I woke up in the Cloaca Maxima. I pulled up my sleeve and found another bandage covering a new, cross-shaped tattoo. In their strange way, the Staurofilakes had certified that we had passed the second test. We had conquered envy.

Farag opened his eyes. He looked at me and smiled. "Ottavia...," he murmured and ran his dry tongue over his lips.

"Wake up, Farag. We're out."

"Out of what? I don't remember. Oh, yeah! The anvil and the hammers."

He glanced around him. Still groggy, he brushed his palms over his shaggy cheeks. "Where are we?"

"I don't know," I said, my hand still on his shoulder. "In a park, I think. We have to wake the captain."

Farag tried to stand up, but couldn't. His face registered surprise. "Did they hit us very hard?"

"No, Farag, they didn't hit us this time—they put us to sleep. I remember some white smoke."

"White smoke?..."

"They drugged us with something that smelled like resin."

"Resin? I swear, Ottavia, I don't remember a thing after Kaspar struck the anvil with the seven hammers."

He was puzzled for a moment and then started to laugh, raising his hand to his left forearm. "They marked us, right?" He seemed delighted.

"Yes. Now, please wake up the Rock."

"The Rock?" he asked, puzzled.

"The captain, I mean. Wake the captain up."

"You call him the Rock?" he asked, utterly amused.

"Don't even think about telling him."

"Don't worry, *Basileia*," he said, dying of laughter. "He'll never hear it from me."

Poor Glauser-Röist was once again the worst off. We had to shake him hard and slap him a couple of times to get him to come around. We were thankful no police happened by right then, or we would have ended up in the jail for sure.

By the time the Rock came to, the traffic had picked up, although it was only five in the morning. Fortunately, nearby was a sign pointing to the Gala Placida Mausoleum. That confirmed we were in downtown Ravenna. Glauser-Röist made a call on his cell phone and talked for several long minutes. When he hung up, he walked over to where we were patiently waiting and looked at us, bewildered.

"Want to know something funny? Turns out we are in the gardens of the National Museum, near the Gala Placida Mausoleum and the

Basilica of Saint Vitale, between the church of Saint Mary Maggiore and this church right here."

"Why is that so funny?" I asked.

"This is the Church of the Holy Cross."

We were getting used to those kinds of coincidences. And we'd get even more accustomed to it, I told myself.

Time passed very slowly while we tried to clear our heads. I paced back and forth, looking down at the grass.

"Hey, Kaspar! Look in your pockets, let's see if they left us a clue for the next cornice."

The captain patted himself down. In his right pants pocket, just like after the previous test, he found a folded piece of thick, lumpy homemade paper.

ἐρώτησον τὸν ἔχοντα τὰς κλεῖδας· ὁ ἀνοίγων
καὶ κλείσει, καὶ κλείων καὶ οὐδεὶς ἀνοίγει.

"'Ask he who has the keys: that which is open, no one closes, and that which is closed, no one opens,'" I translated. "What do they want us to do in Jerusalem?" I was confused.

"I'm not worried, *Basileia*. Those people know our every move. They'll let us know."

A car with its headlights on came racing down the street.

"Right now we have to get out of here," muttered the Rock, running his hand through his hair. The poor man was still somewhat groggy.

A gray Fiat pulled up. The driver's side window rolled down. "Captain Glauser-Röist?" asked a young priest wearing a cleric's collar.

"That's me."

The priest looked like he'd been rousted out of bed. "The archbishop sent me. I'm Father Iannucci. I'm to take you to La Spreta Airport. Please get in." He got out of the car and graciously opened the doors for us.

We arrived at the airport a few minutes later. It was a minuscule place that didn't resemble the large airport in Rome at all. Even the airport in Palermo seemed enormous next to this one. Father Iannucci dropped us off at the entrance and vanished as politely as he had appeared.

Glauser-Röist interrogated the lone counter agent. The young woman, her eyes still swollen with sleep, directed us to a separate area, next to the Francesco Baracca Aeroclub, where the private airplanes were parked. Back on his cell phone, Glauser-Röist called the pilot, who informed him that the Westwind was ready to take off as soon as we boarded. Over the phone, the pilot guided us to the plane, a short distance from the small aeroclub planes. Its engines were running and its lights were on. Compared to the other mosquito-like planes around us, the Westwind seemed like a gigantic Concorde jet. It was actually a small airplane, with five windows; and of course it was white. A young flight attendant and a couple of pilots from Alitalia were waiting for us at the foot of the stairs. After they greeted us with a certain professional coldness, they invited us to climb aboard.

"Can this plane really get us to Jerusalem?" I asked under my breath, somewhat doubtful.

"We aren't going to Jerusalem, Doctor," the Rock announced at the top of his lungs as we climbed the stairs. "We're landing in Tel Aviv From there we will take a helicopter to Jerusalem."

"But can this little plane get us across the Mediterranean?"

"We have priority to take off," one of the pilots said to the captain. "We can leave whenever you like."

"Let's go now," ordered Glauser-Röist laconically.

The flight attendant showed us to our seats, pointing to the life jackets and the emergency doors. The cabin was very narrow and the roof was very low, but the space was perfectly laid out, with a couple of long sofas on one side and four appealing easy chairs at the back, upholstered in a leather as white as snow.

A few minutes later, the plane gently took off. The sun flooded the cabin's interior with its first rays. Jerusalem, I said to myself, excited. I'm going to Jerusalem! To the place where Jesus lived, made his predictions, and died to rise on the third day! It was a trip I'd wanted to take my entire life; but I had never been able to go, because of my job. Now, that very job was taking me there. I felt my emotions grow, and closing my eyes, I gave thanks for the gentle rebirth of my strong, steadfast religious vocation. How had I allowed some irrational feelings to betray the most sacred part of my life? In Jerusalem I would beg forgiveness for that fleeting foolishness, hoping that in the holiest place in the world I would be free of my ridiculous passions once and for all. Besides, in Jerusalem I had a more important matter: my brother Pierantonio. I'm certain he would never imagine I was flying in this dinky little plane toward *his* domain. As soon as I set foot on land—if I ever did—I would let him know I was in Jerusalem and have him set aside all his obligations for the day and dedicate all his time to me. The upstanding guardian was in for a big surprise.

It took less six hours to get to Tel Aviv. During the trip, the flight attendant took great pains to making our trip pleasant. Every time we saw her coming down the aisle, we started to laugh. Every five minutes or so, she offered us food and drink, music, videos, or newspapers and magazines. Finally, Glauser-Röist dispatched her so we could doze in peace. Jerusalem. Beautiful, holy Jerusalem! Before day's end I would be walking down its streets.

Shortly before we landed, the Rock took out his worn copy of the *Divine Comedy.* "Aren't you curious to read about what awaits us?"

"I already know. An impenetrable curtain of smoke," said Farag.

"Smoke!" I let escape, stupefied.

The captain leafed through it quickly. A radiant light streamed in through windows.

"Canto XVI of *Purgatory,* verse one and following:

"The gloom of Hell or of a night bereft
Of all its planets, under barren skies,
and totally obscured by dark, dense clouds,

"never had wrapped my face within a veil
so thick, made of such harsh and stinging stuff,
as was that smoke that poured around us there.

"It was too much for open eyes to bear,
and so my wise and faithful guide drew near,
offering me his shoulder for support."

"Where will they lock us up this time?" I asked. "It'll have to be some place they can fill with a dense cloud of smoke.

"With us inside, of course," Farag pointed out.

"That goes without saying. What else happens in the third cornice, Captain? How do they get out of there?"

"They walk. That's it."

"That's it? Don't they nail them to anything or fall down a cliff?..."

"No, Doctor, nothing happens. They walk through the cornice and meet the souls of the wrathful, traveling around the circle completely enveloped by smoke. They talk and then ascend to the next circle after the angel wipes a new *P* off Dante's forehead."

"That's it?"

"That's it. Right, Professor?"

Farag nodded. "But there are some strange things," he added in his slight Arab accent. "For example, this circle is the shortest in *Purgatory*. It only lasts a canto and a half. Canto XVI, as the captain said, lasts just a few pages, and a short fragment of the XVIIth." He sighed and crossed his legs. "Here's the second strange part: Uncharacteristically, Dante doesn't end the circle at the end of the canto. The cornice of the wrathful begins in Canto XVI, as the captain said; but how far does it go, Kaspar?"

"To verse seventy-nine of Canto XVII. Seven and nine again."

"And in verse seventy-nine, literally in the middle of nowhere, starts the fourth circle of Purgatory, the circle of the slothful. The fourth cornice doesn't start at the beginning of the following canto either. For some reason, Dante fuses the end of one circle to the beginning of the next in the same canto, something he hasn't done before."

"Does that mean something?"

"Who knows, Ottavia. But don't worry; I'm sure you'll find out on your own."

"Thanks a lot."

"You're welcome, *Basileia.*"

We landed at Ben Gurion International Airport in Tel Aviv at around noon. An El Al vehicle took us to the nearest heliport, where we boarded an Israeli military helicopter that flew us to Jerusalem in just twenty-five minutes. The minute we landed, an official car with black-tinted windows rushed us to the apostolic delegation.

From what little I saw along the way, Jerusalem disappointed me. It was like any other city, with wide streets, traffic, and tall buildings. Barely distinguishable in the distance, some Muslim minarets pointed to the sky. The populace included Orthodox Jews with black hats and curly sideburns, as well as dozens of Arabs dressed in kaffiyeh* and *akal.*† Farag saw the disappointment in my face and tried to console me.

"Don't worry, *Basileia.* This is modern Jerusalem. You'll like the old city better."

I didn't see any sign, as I'd hoped, of God's presence on earth. I had dreamed of visiting Jerusalem someday, and I was sure that the moment I set foot in such a special place, I would feel God's unmistakable presence. But he was not there, at least not right then. The only thing that really got my attention was the mishmash of Eastern and Western architecture and the street signs in Hebrew, Arabic, and English. The large number of Israeli soldiers, armed to the teeth, strolling down the streets, also sparked my curiosity, reminding me that Jerusalem was a city endemically at war. The Staurofilakes had returned for the adjudication of a sin. Jerusalem was filled with wrath, blood, resentment, and death. Surely Jesus could have chosen another city to die in, and Muhammad, another city from which to ascend to heaven.

My biggest surprise, however, came at the apostolic delegation, a building no different from its neighboring buildings, except for its immense size. Several priests of all ages and nationalities received us at the door, headed by the apostolic nuncio, Monsignor Pietro Sambi. He led

---

* Cloth with which Arabs cover their heads.
† Cord that holds the kaffiyeh on the head, usually black.

us through several offices to an elegant, modern meeting room where, along with other dignitaries, was my brother Pierantonio!

"Little Ottavia!" he exclaimed the minute I came through the door behind the captain and Monsignor Lewis.

My brother rushed over and we hugged long and hard. This caused an amused outcry from the rest of the assistants.

"How are you?" he asked, at last pulling away from me and looking me over from head to toe. "Aside from being dirty and injured, I mean."

"Tired," I replied, on the verge of tears, "very tired, Pierantonio. But very happy to see you."

As always, my brother was a magnificent, imposing presence, in spite of his simple Franciscan habit. I rarely saw him dressed that way; at home, he wore secular clothes.

"You've become quite a celebrity, little sister! Look at all the important people here to meet you."

Glauser-Röist and Farag were being introduced to the gathering by Monsignor Sambi, so my brother did the honors for me: the archbishop of Baghdad and vice president of the Conference of Latin Bishops, Paul Dahdah; the patriarch of Jerusalem and president of the Assembly of Ordinary Catholics in the Holy Land, His Beatitude Michel Sabbah; the archbishop of Haifa, the Greco-melkita Boutros Mouallem, vice president of the Assembly of Ordinary Catholics; the Orthodox patriarch of Jerusalem, Diodoros I; the Armenian Orthodox patriarch, Torkom; the Greco-melkita exarches, Georges El-Murr. A true pleiad of the most important patriarchs and bishops in the Holy Land. After each introduction, my discomfort increased. Was our mission no longer a secret? Didn't Cardinal Sodano tell His Eminence that we had to keep complete silence about what we were doing and what was happening?

Farag greeted Pierantonio warmly, whereas I noticed Glauser-Röist stayed a discreet distance away. I no longer doubted that some deep antagonism must exist between my brother and the Rock. During the small talk that ensued, I also saw that many of those present approached the Rock with a certain fear and some even with visible scorn. I promised myself I'd solve that mystery before I left Jerusalem.

The meeting was long and boring. One after another, the patriarchs and bishops of the Holy Land expressed their great concern over the thefts of *Ligna Crucis.* They told us that the smaller Christian churches were the first to suffer thefts by the Staurofilakes. Often, it was just a tiny sliver or a little sawdust in a reliquary. What began as an obscure accident on some out-of-the-way mountain in Greece had turned into an international incident of outlandish proportions. Everyone was extremely worried about the effect the thefts could have on public opinion if the scandal popped up in the media. I wondered how long it could be kept silent when so many important people were already involved. In the end, the sole purpose of that meeting was for the curious patriarchs, bishops, and delegates to get to know us. Neither Farag nor the captain nor I had anything to gain. At best, we found out we could count on the help of all those churches for anything we might need. So I took advantage of that.

"With all due respect," I said in English, using the same formulaic courtesy they used, "do any of you know anyone who guards keys here in Jerusalem?"

They all looked at each other, disconcerted.

"I'm sorry, Sister Salina," Monsignor Sambi answered. "I don't believe we completely understood your question."

"We must locate," Glauser-Röist interrupted, "someone in this city who has keys. Whatever it is he opens, nobody can close, and vice versa."

They looked at each other, clearly showing that they didn't have a clue about what we meant.

"Ottavia!" My brother scolded me good-naturedly, ignoring the Rock. "Do you know how many important keys there are in the Holy Land? Every church, basilica, mosque, and synagogue has its own historical collection of keys! What you're saying makes no sense in Jerusalem. I'm sorry, but it's just ridiculous."

"Try to take this seriously, Pierantonio!" For a moment, I forgot where we were. I forgot I was addressing the respectable guardian of the Holy Land in the middle of an ecumenical assembly of prelates, some of whom were equal to the pope in esteem. I just saw my older brother with a sarcastic attitude about a matter that three times had nearly cost me my life. "It is very important to locate 'he who has the keys,' do you understand? Whether there are a lot or a few isn't the issue. There's somebody in this city who has the keys we need."

"Very well, Sister Salina," Pierantonio replied. I froze when I saw, for the first time, a look of respect and comprehension on his great princely face. Could it be that, for once, "little Ottavia" was more important than the guardian? Oh, dear, that was great news! For once I had the upper hand over my brother?

"Well…" Monsignor Sambi didn't know how to end that unusual family squabble at such a distinguished meeting. "I think we must take note of what Captain Glauser-Röist and Sister Salina are telling us and begin our search for that bearer of the keys, as you say."

There was a general consensus, and the conclave dissolved amicably for lunch, which was served in the luxurious dining room. They told me it was where the pope had lunched on several occasions during his recent trip to the Holy Land. I could not help an ironic smile when I remembered how we had gone for three days without a shower and realized that we probably smelled pretty bad.

When I went to my room, I discovered that a couple of Hungarian nuns had already unpacked my bags and had neatly arranged my things in the closet, the bathroom, and desk. They shouldn't have gone to so much trouble, I thought. The next day, probably at daybreak (or some other inopportune time), we would be flying to Athens for more bruises, wounds, and tattoos. Thinking about the tattoos, I went to the bathroom, took off my clothes above my waist and carefully removed the two bandages covering the inner part of my forearms. The marks were still swollen, the one from Rome much less than the one from Ravenna, just a few hours old. Like it or not, those two beautiful crosses would be with me for the rest of my life. Both had green lines deeply grooved into my skin, as if they'd been injected with some extract of plants and grass. I decided it wasn't a good idea to worry, so I took a long, glorious shower. Once I'd dried off, I doctored myself with what I found in a medicine cabinet and bandaged my forearms. Fortunately, if I wore long sleeves, it was impossible to notice the assault on my body.

In the middle of the afternoon, after we'd rested for barely an hour, Pierantonio offered to take us to old Jerusalem for a brief sightseeing trip. The nuncio was pretty worried about our safety, for just days before, the worst skirmishes since the end of the Intifada had taken place between Palestinians and Israelis. We were so engrossed in our own problems that we hadn't even heard the news. In the fighting, at least a dozen people had been killed and more than four hundred wounded. The Israeli government was forced to return three districts of Jerusalem—Abu Dis, Azaria, and Sauajra—to the Palestinian Authority with the hope of reopening negotiations and ending the revolt in the independent territories. The mood was tense, and everyone feared new attacks in the city; Because of this as well as because of Pierantonio's position, the nuncio insisted we drive one of the delegation's more low-key vehicles to get to the old city. He also provided us with one of the best guides: Father Murphy Clark, from the Biblical School of Jerusalem. A big barrel of a man, with a lovely, trimmed white beard, he was one of the world's foremost specialists on biblical archaeology. We parked the car near the Wailing Wall, and from there, went on a trip back through two thousand years of history.

I wanted to see it all and didn't have enough eyes to take it all in at once: the vast beauty of those stone streets, the T-shirt and souvenir shops, the strange populace dressed in the fashion of the city's three cultures. But most exciting was crossing the Via Dolorosa, the road Jesus took to Golgotha, a cross on his shoulders and a crown of thorns stuck on his head. There are no words to describe what I felt at that moment. Pierantonio, who could read me like a book, lagged behind me, while the captain, Father Clark, and Farag led the way. It was clear my brother wasn't exactly thinking about praying the Via Crucis with me. He really wanted to draw out as much information as he could about our mission.

"Let's see, Pierantonio," I protested, "don't you know it all already? Why don't you stop asking me so many questions?"

"Because you won't tell me a thing. I have to pry it out of you!"

"What do you want to get out me? There's nothing more!"

"Tell me about the tests."

I sighed and looked to heaven for help. "They're not exactly tests, Pierantonio. We are crossing a type of purgatory and we must purify our souls so we'll be worthy of entering the Staurofilakes' earthly paradise. That's our only goal. Once we locate the True Cross, we'll call the police and they'll take over."

"But what about Dante? My God, it's incredible! Come on, please tell me more!"

I stopped short, in the midst of a parade of North Americans praying the stations of the Via Crucis, and turned toward him. "I'll make a deal with you. You tell me about Glauser-Röist and I'll tell you the story in detail."

My brother's face was transformed. I would swear I saw a flash of hatred cross his holy eyes. He shook his head.

"In Palermo you told me Glauser-Röist was the most dangerous man in the Vatican. If memory serves me, you asked what I was doing working with somebody feared by heaven and earth, that he was the black hand of the church."

Pierantonio started walking again, leaving me behind. "If you want me to tell you the story of Dante Alighieri and the Staurofilakes," I baited him when I got to his side, "you'll have to tell me everything you know about Glauser-Röist. Remember, you yourself taught me how to get information by even ignoring my own conscience, if necessary, to do so."

My brother stopped in the middle of the Via Dolorosa. "You want to know about Captain Kaspar Linus Glauser-Röist?" he asked, giving off sparks of anger. "Your dear colleague is in charge of making all of the church's important members' dirty laundry disappear. For about thirteen years, Glauser-Röist has dedicated himself to destroying anything that might taint the Vatican's image. When I say destroy, I mean destroy: He threatens and extorts, and it wouldn't surprise me if he has gone as far as murdering someone to carry out his duty. Nobody escapes the long arm of Glauser-Röist: journalists, bankers, cardinals, politicians, writers. If you have some secret in your life, Ottavia, you'd better not let Glauser-Röist know it. He might use it against you someday, in cold blood, without one bit of pity."

"That can't be!" I argued, not because I doubted his allegations, but because I knew that would keep him talking.

"You don't think so?" he was furious. We started walking again because Father Clark, Farag, and the Rock were way ahead. "Do you need me to prove it to you? Remember the Marcinkus case?"

I did know something about the case, but not much. Customarily, anything that was against the church stayed out of my life and the life of all priests and nuns. It's not that we couldn't know, it's that we simply didn't want to. A priori, we didn't like to hear those types of accusations, and we more or less ignored any sort of anticlerical scandal.

"In 1987, Italian judges ordered the arrest of Archbishop Paul Casimiro Marcinkus, then director of the IWR, the Institute for Works of Religion, also known as the Vatican Bank. After seven months of investigations, he was accused of fraudulently leading the Ambrosian Bank of Milan to bankruptcy. It was proven that the Ambrosian Bank was controlled by a group of foreign corporations, with headquarters in the fiscal paradises of Panama and Liechtenstein, and that in fact it served as a cover for the IWR and Marcinkus himself. The Ambrosian Bank was 'missing' $1.2 billion, of which, after a lot of pressure, the Vatican gave back just $250 million to its creditors. In effect, the Vatican 'swallowed' more than $900 million. Do you know who was in charge of keeping Marcinkus from falling into the hands of the law and for covering up this murky subject?"

"Captain Glauser-Röist?"

"Your friend managed to get Marcinkus transferred to the Vatican, using a diplomatic passport that stopped the Italian police from arresting him. The danger past, he created a smokescreen to confuse the public, somehow getting some journalists to call Marcinkus a naïve, negligent, and very absent-minded manager. Then he made Marcinkus disappear and established a new life for him in a small North American parish in the state of Arizona. He's still there today."

"I don't see anything criminal in that, Pierantonio."

"No—see, that's the point—he never does anything outside the law, he simply ignores it! A cardinal is stopped at the Swiss border with a suitcase full of millions, which he wants to pass off as a mere briefcase.

Glauser-Röist goes there to remedy the offense. He goes and gets the cardinal, brings him back to the Vatican, gets the border guards to 'forget' the incident, and erases all traces of the matter as if the mysterious currency evasion never existed."

"I still say I see no reason to fear Glauser-Röist."

But Pierantonio was just getting started. "An Italian publishing house publishes a scandalous book on corruption in the Vatican. Glauser-Röist quickly identifies the monsignors who betrayed the Vatican's law of silence, gags them with who knows what threats, and gets the press to completely bury the matter after the initial scandal. Who do you think writes up the reports that have salacious details on the private lives of the members of the Curia, leaving these men no choice but to silently agree to egregious reversals of fortunes? Who do you think was the first to enter the apartment of the commander of the Swiss Guard, Alois Estermann, the night he, his wife, and Corporal Cedric Tornay were killed, supposedly by shots fired by the corporal? Kaspar Glauser-Röist. He was the one who removed proof of what really happened and who invented the official version of the corporal's 'temporary insanity,' so that both the church and the press accused the corporal of drug use and 'hate filled instability.' He's the only one who knows what really happened that night. A prelate from the Vatican organized a risqué nocturnal outing, and a journalist plans to publish scandalous photographs in the press... Not to worry. The article never sees the light of day and the journalist is silenced for the rest of his life after a visit from Glauser-Röist. Can you guess why? I bet you can guess. At this moment, there is an important prelate, the archbishop of Naples, who is being investigated by the judicial prosecutor of the basilica for usury, criminal association, and unlawful appropriation of wealth. You can bet he'll be absolved. From what they tell me, your friend has already intervened in the matter."

A very sinister thought popped into my mind, a thought I didn't like one bit and that caused me distress.

"So what do you have to hide, Pierantonio? You wouldn't talk that way about the captain if you hadn't had some problem with him yourself."

"Me?" he acted surprised. Suddenly all his fury disappeared and he was as innocent as the Easter lamb. But he couldn't fool me.

"Yes, you. Don't feed me some line about how you know all this because the church is one big family and everybody talks about everything."

"But it's true! We insiders who occupy top jobs *do* know everything about everything."

"That may be," I murmured mechanically, looking at the back of Murphy Clark's, the Rock's, and Farag's necks in the distance. "But you can't fool me. You've had problems with Captain Glauser-Röist, and you're going to tell me all about it right now."

My brother laughed. Just then, a ray of sun cut through the clouds and lit up his face. "Why should I tell you anything, dear Ottavia? What would compel me to confess sins that can't be revealed, especially to my little sister?"

I shot him a cold look, a fake smile on my lips. "Because if you don't, I'm going right over to Glauser-Röist and I'll tell him everything you said and have *him* explain it to me."

"He would never say a thing," he asserted. His Franciscan habit didn't humble him. "A man like him would never talk about that type of thing."

"Oh no?" If he could play chicken, so could I. "Captain! Hey, Captain!"

The Rock and Farag turned around. Father Murphy turned his immense belly toward me a few seconds after they did.

"Captain! Could you come here a minute?"

Pierantonio turned livid. "I'll tell you," he muttered, seeing Glauser-Röist backtracking. "I'll tell you, but tell him not to come over!"

"Sorry, Captain! My mistake... Please go on!" I waved him back with the others.

The Rock stopped, looked at me straight in the eye, then pivoted and continued on. A strange group of six or seven women dressed in black pushed past us. They were dressed in long robes that covered them from their necks to their feet. Each wore a curious headdress, a tiny round hat, pulled down over her forehead, held in place by a scarf tied around her head. I deduced they must be Orthodox nuns, although I couldn't figure out what church they belonged to. Oddly enough, another group of women passed by, right behind them, wearing the same robes, but without the hats, carrying long yellow tapers in their hands.

"Little Ottavia, you're becoming very stubborn."

"Speak."

Pierantonio was silent and meditative for a several minutes. Finally he sighed deeply and started in. "Do you remember the time I told you about my problems with the Holy See?"

"Yes, I remember."

"I mentioned schools, hospitals, nursing homes, archaeological excavations, a way station for pilgrims, biblical studies, the reestablishment of Catholic worship in the Holy Land..."

"Yes, yes, you said the pope ordered you to buy the Holy Cenacle without giving you the money to do it."

"Exactly. That's the problem."

"What have you done, Pierantonio?" I asked, pained. Right then, the Via Dolorosa was actually turning out to be truly painful.

"Well...," he waffled. "I had to sell some things."

"What things?"

"Things we found in our excavations."

"Oh my God, Pierantonio!"

"I know, I know," he admitted, contrite. "If it's any consolation to you, they were sold to the Vatican itself, through a front man."

"What are you saying?"

"Among the princes of the church, there are great art collectors. Before Glauser-Röist meddled, a lawyer working for me in Rome sold something to a prelate you know personally. He used to work in the Classified Archives. He paid nearly $3 million for an eighth-century mosaic discovered in the excavations of Banu Ghassan. I think it's hanging in his living room."

"Oh my God!" I moaned. I was floored.

"Do you know how many good things we did with all that money, little Ottavia?" My brother felt no remorse. "We founded more hospitals, fed more people, created more nursing homes and more schools for little kids. What's so wrong about that?"

"You illegally trafficked in holy relics, Pierantonio!"

"But I sold them to the church! Nothing ended up in hands that weren't blessed by the priesthood. I poured all the money into the urgent needs of the Holy Land's poor. Some of the princes of the church have incredible amounts of money, while here we need as much help as we can get…" He took shallow breaths. I saw the hate fill his eyes again. "One day, your friend Glauser-Röist showed up at my office. He'd done some research on my activities. He forbade me to continue the sales and threatened to leak the scandal, tarnishing my name and my order. 'I can make you front page news tomorrow in the most important newspapers in the world,' he told me without wavering. I told him about the hospitals, the shelters, the soup kitchens, the schools. But he didn't care. Now we are drowning in debt, and I have no idea how I'm going to fix the problem."

What was it that Farag had said in the catacombs of Saint Lucia? "The truth hurts, but it's always better than a lie." Now I asked myself if my brother's goodness, even if it did harm, wasn't preferable to injustice. Or maybe I felt doubt because this concerned my brother and I was desperately searching for a way to justify his actions. Maybe life wasn't black and white, but a multicolor mosaic with infinite combinations. Wasn't life full of ambiguities, interchangeable hues we tried to constrain in a ridiculous structure of norms and dogmas?

As I pondered this, our group abruptly turned a corner and entered the plaza of the Basilica of the Holy Sepulchre. I began to choke up. Before me was the place where Jesus was crucified. I felt my eyes welling up with tears, my emotions overwhelming me.

The basilica Saint Helen had built exactly where she had found the True Cross of Christ was impressive—sharp angles, solid, millennia-old stone, large windows covered with grillwork, square redbrick towers. The plaza was crowded with people of all races and stations in life. Groups of tourists roamed around us wearing thin wooden crosses and singing hymns in several languages. All the songs mixed together in that echo chamber, sounding like one big, discordant buzz. In the portico were the Orthodox nuns we'd crossed paths with, their backs to the Catholic nuns who were dressed in light-colored habits with knee-length skirts. Many women wore beautiful rosaries around their necks and prayed, their knees on the hard, rocky ground. There were also many Catholic priests and other religious people from a diverse array of orders. Long beards abounded, typical of the Orthodox monks who wore all manner of black tubular hats: some were plain, some were trimmed with a little lace; some were chimney-shaped; some even had a large headdress that hung down their backs to their waists. Above this human chaos, a multitude of white doves floated from one cornice to another, one window to another, searching for the best view.

The facade of the basilica was quite unusual. Its matching doors were located under two counterpoint arch windows that also matched, although oddly enough, the door on the right seemed to be sealed up with large stones. And the interior... The interior was dazzling. You entered through the side of the nave, so you couldn't get a complete view until you'd walked inside pretty far. Hundreds of Oriental oil lamps lit up the walkway. It was such an exciting moment, I can hardly recall everything I saw. Father Murphy explained in detail the particulars of each plaque we passed. In the atrium at the entrance, surrounded by candelabras and lamps was the Stone of Unction, a large rectangular slab of red limestone where it's said they placed the body of Jesus after lowering him from the Cross. In a frenzy, people threw holy water on the stone, and dozens of hands holding handkerchiefs and rosaries shot forward. There was no way to get near it. In the center of the basilica was the catholicon, the place where the Holy Sepulchre was said to be. Its facade was covered with lovely hanging lamps inside silver globes, and above the door there were three paintings that told of Jesus's Resurrection, each one in a different style—Latin, Greek, and Armenian. Past the door of the catholicon, you came to a small vestibule called the Chapel of the Angel, because it was said to be where the angel announced the Resurrection to the holy women. Behind another small door, you came to the Holy Sepulchre itself, in a small, narrow enclosure in which you could make out a marble bench that covered the original stone on which the body of Jesus was placed. I knelt down for a second—the influx of people didn't allow much more—and left with less unction than when I came in. The atmosphere may have been hypnotic and disposed to a certain type of religious Stockholm syndrome, but the throng's anguish cooled my ardor.

Down the stairs, we came to the place where Saint Helen found the three crosses, according to Jacopo della Voragine in his *Golden Legend*. The chamber was a wide, empty stone room, and in one corner an iron railing protected the exact spot where the relics appeared. Father Murphy tugged on his beard and started to tell us the story, but soon we discovered we knew much more than one of the most highly regarded experts in the world. When the affable archaeologist realized he was in the company of experts, he humbly listened to our comments.

We toured every inch of the basilica, including the Anastasis rotunda. Along the way, Pierantonio and Father Murphy told us that the Latin, Greek Orthodox, and Armenian Orthodox communities were equal co-owners of the church. It was governed by a status quo, that is, a fragile agreement, for lack of a better solution. The agreement tried to bring peace to the Christian churches of Jerusalem. They said the Orthodox Coptics, the Syrian-Orthodox, and the Ethiopians could also conduct their ceremonies in the basilica, to which Farag protested vehemently that the Coptic-Catholics didn't enjoy a similar right, but Father Murphy begged him, half joking, half serious, not to fan the fire.

When we finished the tour, my brother and Father Murphy proposed we continue by visiting other holy places in the city.

"There's still something we haven't seen," I answered back. "The underground crypt."

Pierantonio looked puzzled. Father Clark flashed a knowing smile.

"How do you know of the crypt's existence, Doctor?"

"It's a long story, Murphy," Farag answered, taking the words out my mouth, "but we're very interested in seeing it."

"That's going to be complicated...," he murmured, deep in thought, tugging at his beard again. "That crypt is the property of the Greek Orthodox Church. Just a few Catholic priests—you can count them on one hand—have seen it. Only your brother, Guardian Salina, could get permission."

"I didn't even know it existed!" my brother said, disconcerted.

"I haven't seen it either, Father," Murphy replied. "Like your sister, I would be delighted to do so. You can ask permission from the Orthodox patriarch of Jerusalem; a phone call ought to do it."

"Is this absolutely necessary?" my brother asked, clearly put off by the idea of asking for politically compromising favors.

"I assure you it is."

Pierantonio headed for the exit. Sheltering himself from the multitude outside the doors in a corner of the atrium, he took his cell phone out of the pocket of his habit. He was only gone a few minutes.

"Done," he announced happily. "Let's go find Father Chrysostomos. Let's just say it wasn't easy! It seems there is a secret vault, hidden in the deepest part of the basilica. You should have heard the surprised and incredulous exclamations that came through the phone. How do you know about it?"

"It's a long story, Pierantonio."

My enthused brother approached the first Orthodox priest who crossed his path. A few minutes later we found ourselves before a pope with a gray beard who wore the "chimney stack"–style hat, just like men wore in Florence during the Renaissance. Father Chrysostomos, whose glasses hung down his chest from a thin chain, looked completely disconcerted. His expression very clearly revealed that he still hadn't recovered from the phone call that warned him of our arrival and the reason for our visit. Pierantonio introduced himself, citing all his offices, and Father Chrysostomos held out his hand with respect, still with a look of surprise that seemed frozen on his face. Then the rest of us were introduced. Finally the Orthodox priest expressed the anguish weighing on his heavy heart.

"I don't want to be rude, but can you tell me how you knew of the existence of the chamber?"

"From some ancient documents that described its construction," replied the Rock.

"Is that right? If you don't mind, I would like to know more. Father Stephanos and I have spent our whole lives watching over the relics of the True Cross preserved in the crypt. We had no idea that it was known, nor that there were documents that spoke of its construction."

As we descended, step-by-step, into the depths of the earth, Farag, the Rock, and I told him what we knew about the Crusades and the secret chamber, but we didn't mention the Staurofilakes. After going down hundreds of stone steps, we came to a rectangular enclosure used for storage. Paintings of ancient patriarchs hung on the walls, and furniture covered by sheets of plastic seemed to sleep a slumber of the righteous. There was also an old Orthodox habit on a hanger, immobile as a ghost. In the back, an iron grate protected a second wooden door that seemed to be our objective. An old man with a long white beard got up from a chair when he saw us enter.

"Father Stephanos, we have visitors," announced Father Chrysostomos.

The two curates exchanged a brief dialogue in a low voice and then they turned to us. "Go ahead."

The old Orthodox curate took a ring of iron keys from inside the pleat of his soutane, turned toward the grate, and opened it in slow motion. Before doing the same with the wooden door, he pressed an antediluvian button located in the lintel.

I was really surprised when I entered in the Staurofilakes' secret vault, built around the year 1000 to protect the True Cross from the destruction ordered by the crazed caliph, al-Hakem, and I found myself in a type of military barracks furnished like a kitchen. After taking a second look, I made out a small altar in the center of the room, along with a beautiful icon bearing the image of the Crucifixion. Directly across from it was a pair of small crosses that turned out to be reliquaries holding the holy sliver. To my left, some old metal file cabinets, folding chairs, and wooden tables were scattered throughout the room. It was just a mess. If the Staurofilakes could see that! After thinking it over, maybe it was the smartest way to protect something so valuable.

Father Stephanos and Father Chrysostomos crossed themselves repeatedly in the Orthodox style. With great reverence, they pointed to tiny pieces of the Cross behind the windows of the reliquaries. We all then kissed those objects, except the Rock, who turned his back and stood as still as a statue. When Father Stephanos saw that, he slowly walked over to the Rock to see what the captain was studying with such interest.

"It's beautiful, isn't it?" he said in very correct English.

The rest of us walked over, too. What a surprise! We saw a beautiful Constantine chrismon painted on a large dark wooden board; a long Greek text was inscribed on it. The board rested on the ground, leaning against the wall.

"It's my favorite prayer. I've meditated on it for fifty years. Believe me, each day I find new treasure in its simple wisdom."

"What is it?" Farag asked, and bent down to get a better look.

"Thirty years ago, some English scholars told us it was a very old Christian prayer, from the twelfth or thirteenth century. The text contains many errors, so the penitent or artist who did the work probably wasn't Greek. The scholars told us it was probably a Latin heretic who visited this place. In gratitude he presented this beautiful board to the basilica, inspired by the True Cross."

I squatted down beside Farag and, in a low voice, translated the first words: "You have overcome pride and envy, now overcome wrath with patience." I stood up and gave the captain a meaningful look.

"'You who have overcome pride and envy, now overcome wrath with patience.'" I repeated in Italian.

Understanding what I was saying, the captain's eyes widened. Any Staurofilax aspirant who passed the tests in Rome and Ravenna must have known that the message was meant for him.

"That is what the first sentence says. Its ancient letters are outlined in red."

Father Stephanos looked at me fondly. "Has the young lady understood the meaning of the prayer?"

"Forgive me!" I apologized quickly. "I didn't realize I'd switched languages. I'm deeply sorry."

"Oh, don't worry! The emotion in your eyes when you read the text makes me very happy. I think you have grasped the importance of the prayer."

Farag stood up and the three of us exchanged meaningful looks. Not wanting to miss a thing, the three of us immediately looked at Father Stephanos... Father Stephanos or Stephanos the Staurofilax? I wondered.

"Do you like it?" the old man wanted to know. "I can give you a pamphlet printed shortly after the scholars visited. It includes a full-length photograph of the tablet and several smaller detailed photos. Unfortunately, the publication is rather old and the photos are in black and white. But it contains a translation of the prayer." He added with a proud smile, "I must warn you, I was the one who translated it." Deeply moved, he started to recite from memory. "'You who have overcome pride and envy, can now overcome wrath with patience now. Just as the plant thrives through the will of the sun, implore God that his divine light falls on you from the heavens. Christ says: fear nothing but the fear of sinning. Christ fed you in groups of one hundred and fifty hungry souls. His holy word did not say groups of ninety or two. Then trust justice as the Athenians did and do not fear the grave. Have faith in Christ as he had faith even in the wicked tax collector. Your soul, like the soul of the bird, races and flies to God. Do not hinder your soul by committing sins, and it will arrive at Christ's side. If you conquer evil, you will reach the light before dawn. Purify your soul, bow down before God as a humble supplicant. With the help of the True Cross, strike down your earthly appetites without mercy. Cleave to the Cross alongside Jesus with seven nails and seven blows. If you do this, Christ, in his majesty, will receive you at the sweet door. May your patience be filled to the brim by this prayer. Amen.' Beautiful, isn't it?"

"It's ... beautiful, Father Stephanos," I murmured.

"I see it has touched you!" he exclaimed, happy. "I'll go look for those pamphlets and give one to each of you!"

And in a slow, unsteady step, he left the crypt and disappeared.

The tablet was indisputably very old. The wood had been darkened by the smoke from the candles that had burned before it over the centuries, though it held no candles at the moment. It was about a meter high and a meter and a half long. The letters were ancient Greek, and the text was written in black ink; the first and last sentences were decorated with a red border. At the top, like a shield or a crest, was the emperor's chrismon and its faithful horizontal bar.

My brother quickly detected that this was something important. He struck up a trivial conversation with Father Murphy and Father Chrysostomos so Farag, the Rock, and I could talk.

"This tablet," the Rock observed, "is what we are in Jerusalem for."

"The message couldn't be any clearer," agreed Farag. "We will have to study it carefully. The content is very strange."

"Strange?" I exclaimed. "Extremely unusual! We'll fry our eyes trying to understand it!"

"What do you two think about Father Stephanos?" asked the Rock.

"Staurofilax," Farag and I answered simultaneously.

"Yes, definitely."

Father Stephanos reappeared, holding his pamphlets tightly so he wouldn't drop them. "Pray this prayer every day," he said as he handed them to us, "and you'll discover the beauty hidden in its words. You can't imagine the devotion it will inspire if you recite it patiently."

An absurd anger toward that cynical Staurofilax was growing inside me. I rejected the fact that he was an old, old man and couldn't be a member of the brotherhood. I wanted to grab him by the soutane and tell him to stop mocking us, for we had nearly died several times on account of his strange fanaticism. Then I recalled that the new test dealt with wrath. I tried to stifle my fury, brought on, I was sure, by physical and mental fatigue. I wanted to cry when I realized that those diabolical millenary deacons had devised that initiation process meticulously.

In a daze, we left the crypt with the old priest's affection and Father Chrysostomos's friendship and thanks. We promised to send him the historical documentation on the crypt. It was late in the afternoon, yet waves of tourists were still entering the basilica of the Holy Sepulchre.

We were given a modest office in the delegation so we could work on the prayer. The captain insisted on getting Internet access, while Farag and I requested several dictionaries from the library of the Biblical School of Jerusalem on classical Greek and Byzantine Greek. After a frugal dinner, Glauser-Röist settled down in front of the computer and began tapping away. To him, computers were like musical instruments that must be perfectly tuned or powerful machines that should be well oiled. While he began furiously typing on his new toy, Farag and I spread the pamphlets out on the desk and got to work on decoding the prayer.

Father Stephanos's translation could be called meritorious. His reading of the Greek text was irreproachable; however, grammatically it left a lot to be desired. The old man had clearly done his best, given how deficient the material was. Its author didn't seem to have a command of the Greek language: Even considering that Greek verb tenses are extremely complicated, some verbs were misspelled and some words were in the wrong place. Normally, one would have deduced that whoever wrote the prayer had put his soul into expressing his thoughts in a language he didn't know well, driven by some social or religious need. But knowing this was in fact a Staurofilax message, we couldn't overlook those errors. The first thing that got our attention was the sentences that contained numbers, partly because they didn't make contextual sense and partly because we were almost positive they were some sort of code. "Christ fed you in groups of one hundred and fifty hungry souls. His holy word did not say groups of ninety or two. Cleave to the Cross along with Jesus with seven nails and seven blows." We were pretty clear that the number 7 wasn't a coincidence, but 100, 50, 90, and 2?

That night we didn't get much farther. We were so tired we could hardly keep our eyes open. So we went to bed, convinced that a few hours of sleep would do wonders for our intellectual capacities.

The next day we didn't get good results either. We went over the text front and back and analyzed it word by word. Except for the first and last sentences outlined in red, nothing in the prayer directly alluded to the Staurofilakes' tests. Late in the afternoon, however, we figured out something that further clouded the few ideas that had occurred to us. The sentence "Christ fed you in groups of one hundred and fifty hungry people" could only refer to the evangelical passage about multiplying the loaves and fishes. The evangelist Mark talks about the multitude "placed in groups of one hundred and fifty."* Once again, we found ourselves empty-handed.

We soon outgrew the office the delegation had given us. The reference books, our notes, the dictionaries, the reams of pages printed off the Internet were *peccata minuta* in comparison to the boards we set up over the weekend. Farag thought we might see something—or see more—if we worked on an enlarged photograph of the prayer. The captain scanned the image from the pamphlet at high definition. Just as with the silhouette of Abi-Ruj Iyasus, he printed out sheets and taped them to a piece of cardboard the same size as the original tablet. He placed that reproduction on a large tripod that simply didn't fit in the office. So on Sunday we moved all our gear to a more spacious room with a large chalkboard where we could draw diagrams or analyze prayers.

Sunday afternoon I deserted my companions—desperation had dampened our spirits—and went alone to the Franciscan church in the Old City where Picrantonio celebrated Mass every Sunday at six. I couldn't miss something that special while I was there. (Besides, my mother would have killed me.) Since the Franciscan church stood next to the Basilica of the Holy Sepulchre, once I got out of the delegation's car just outside the walls, I walked the same route as the first day to get refocused. Where better than Jerusalem? I felt truly blessed to be elbowed and shoved on the Via Dolorosa.

According to the directions Pierantonio had given me over the phone, the Franciscan church was directly across from the entrance to the basilica. I didn't need to go all the way to the plaza but veered a couple of alleyways to the right before I took a strange roundabout route, all by myself, to reach my destination.

---

* Mark 6:40.

I piously attended Mass and received communion from Pierantonio's hands. Afterward, we went for a stroll and talked. I told him the entire story of the theft of the *Ligna Crucis* and the Staurofilakes. When it grew dark, he offered to walk me back to the apostolic delegation. We retraced our steps—I saw the Cupola of the Rock, Al-Aqsa Mosque, and many other things. We stopped in the plaza of the Basilica of the Holy Sepulchre, drawn by a small crowd gathered to take pictures and videotape the daily closing of the doors.

"It's incredible! Anything gets people's attention!" my brother said ironically. "How about you, Miss Tourist? Do you want to see it too?"

"You're very kind," I answered sarcastically, "but no thank you."

Yet, I headed in that direction. I suppose I couldn't tear myself away from the enchantment of nightfall in the Christian heart of Jerusalem.

"So, Ottavia, there's something I've been meaning to talk to you about, but I hadn't found the right time."

Like a circus performer, a little man climbed up a very tall ladder that leaned against the doors. He was lit up by the lights and flashes from the cameras below. The man toiled away with a heavy iron lock.

"Please, Pierantonio, don't tell me you have more disturbing news for me."

"No, this has nothing to do with me. It's about Farag."

I whipped around to face him. The little man on the ladder began his descent. "What about Farag?"

"To say the truth, there's nothing wrong with Farag," he said. *"You're* the one who seems to be having problems."

My heart stopped. The blood rushed to my face. "I don't know what you're talking about, Pierantonio."

Some shouts and an alarmed murmur arose from the spectators. My brother spun around to watch, but I was paralyzed by Pierantonio's words. I'd tried to keep my feelings in check, I'd done everything I could to hide my emotions, but Pierantonio had found me out.

"What happened, Father Longman?" I heard my brother ask. I looked up and saw he was addressing another Franciscan monk passing by.

"Hi, Father Salina. The Guardian of the Keys fell off the ladder. He injured his foot and was knocked out. Fortunately he was close to the ground."

I was so numb by the pain and shock it took me a few seconds to react. Thank God my brain started functioning and a voice repeated in my head: "The Guardian of the Keys, the Guardian of the Keys." I struggled to come out of the fog as Pierantonio thanked his fellow Franciscan.

"The man on the ladder took a tumble. Now, let's get back to our talk. I promised myself I would talk to you today without fail. If I'm not mistaken, you have a serious problem, little sister."

"What exactly did that monk from your order say?"

"Don't try to change the subject, Ottavia," Pierantonio rebuked me sternly.

"Enough of this foolishness! What did he say exactly?"

My brother was very surprised by my sudden change of mood. "That the basilica doorman tripped and fell as he was climbing down the ladder."

"No!" I shouted. "He didn't say doorman!"

A light must have switched on in my brother's mind. The look on his face changed and I saw he understood. "The Guardian of the Keys!" he stammered. "The one who has the keys!"

"I have to talk to that man!" I exclaimed as I left him standing there open-mouthed and the tourists made way for me. Someone called the "Guardian of the Keys" of the Basilica of the Holy Sepulchre of Jerusalem had to be pretty close to "the one who has the keys: the one who opens and no one closes and closes and no one opens." It wasn't exactly right, sure, but I had to give it a try.

By the time I reached the center of the crowd, the little man had gotten to his feet and was brushing dirt off his clothes. Like many other Arabs I had observed, he was dressed in a shirt and no necktie, the collar unbuttoned and his sleeves rolled up. On his upper lip he had a thin moustache. He wore a look of annoyance and contained rage.

"Are you the one they call the 'Guardian of the Keys'?" I asked in English, slightly embarrassed.

The little man looked at me with indifference. "I believe that's obvious, ma'am," he replied, looking quite exasperated. He immediately turned his back on me and set to work on the ladder, which was still leaning against the church doors. I felt the opportunity slipping away, and I simply couldn't let that happen.

"Listen!" I shouted to get back his attention. "I was told to ask for 'the one who has the keys'!"

"Sounds like a good idea to me, ma'am," he answered without turning around, assuming I was a poor crazy woman. He pounded on a box concealed in one of the doors, and it opened.

"Sir, you don't understand," I insisted, pushing aside a couple of pilgrims who were taking pictures of the ladder ceremony. "I was told to ask the one who opens and nobody closes, and the one who closes and nobody opens."

The man stood there stunned, for several seconds. He then turned and fixed his gaze on me. For a moment, he observed me the way an entomologist studies an insect. He showed his surprise. "A woman?"

"Am I the first?"

"No," he said, after thinking it over. "There've been other women, but not with me."

"Can we talk?"

"Of course," he said, tweaking his mustache. "Meet me right here in a half an hour. If you don't mind, I must finish this."

I let him continue his work. I turned to Pierantonio, who was waiting impatiently.

"That was the guy?"

"Yes. We arranged to meet back here in half an hour. He wants to meet when he's through and we can talk."

"Good, then let's take a walk."

Half an hour was not much time, but if my brother insisted on getting back to the subject of Farag, the time would feel like an eternity. To eat up some time, I asked for his cell phone and called the captain. The Rock was satisfied with the news of the Guardian of the Keys, but also alarmed, since there was no way he and Farag could get there in time. So he ticked off a long list of questions to ask the Guardian, then repeated himself like a broken record, reminding me to do or say what he'd just told me to do or say. After four days of delay and uncertainty, this important clue was a light in the dark. Now we could carry out the test of Jerusalem, whatever that was, and leave for Athens as soon as possible.

I talked at length with the captain and wasted as much of the half hour as I could, not giving my brother the chance to ask me any more compromising questions. When I finally gave him back his cell phone, Pierantonio smiled. We were in front of his church.

"I'll bet you think we can't talk about your friend Farag anymore," he said, taking me by the elbow and guiding me toward the rocky side street that led to the Via Dolorosa.

"Exactly."

"I just want to help you, dear Ottavia. If things are going badly, you can count on me."

"Things are going very badly, Pierantonio," I admitted, crestfallen. "Surely all nuns and priests have crises like this. We're not superhuman and we're not immune to human emotions. Hasn't this ever happened to you?"

"Well...," he mumbled, looking away. "The truth is, yes. A long time ago. Thank God, my vocation prevailed."

"Then I have trust, Pierantonio." I wanted to hug him, but this wasn't Palermo. "I trust God. If he wants me to follow his call, he will help me."

"I will pray for you, little sister."

We had reached the plaza of the Holy Sepulchre. The Guardian of the Keys was waiting for me in front of the church door, as he had said he would. I approached very slowly and stopped a few steps from him.

"Repeat the phrase for me, please," he asked me amiably.

"They told me: 'Ask the one who has the keys: the one who opens and nobody closes, and the one who closes and nobody opens.'"

"Very well, ma'am. Now listen carefully. The message I have for you is this: 'the seventh and the ninth.'"

"The seventh and the ninth?" I repeated, dumbfounded. "What seventh and what ninth? What are you talking about?"

"I don't know, ma'am."

"You don't know?"

The little man shrugged. "No, no ma'am. I don't know what it means."

"So, what do you have to do with...with the Staurofilakes?"

"Who?" He arched his eyebrows and brushed back his black hair. "I know nothing about that, forgive me. You see, my name is Jacob Nusseiba. Mujik Jacob Nusseiba. The Nusseiba family has been in charge of opening and closing the doors of the Basilica of the Holy Sepulchre ever since 637, when Caliph Omar gave us the keys. When the caliph entered Jerusalem, my family was part of his army. To avoid conflicts among the Christians, he gave the keys to us. For thirteen centuries, the eldest son of each generation of Nusseibas has been the Guardian of the Keys. At some point, this long tradition joined another. Each father says to his son when he passes the keys to him: 'When they ask if you are the one who has the keys, the one who opens and nobody closes and the one who closes and nobody opens, you answer: "the seventh and the ninth."' We memorized it and have been saying it for many centuries when somebody asks us, just like you did today."

The seventh and the ninth. Seven and nine again, Dante's numbers—but what could they refer to this time?

"Is there anything else I can do for you, ma'am? It's late."

I shook my head gently, waking from my daydream. I looked at Mují Nusseiba. That little man's family tree was older than many European royal houses. To look at him, you'd guess he was a waiter at a café.

"Have many people come like me?" I asked him. "I mean..."

"I understand. I understand," he hurriedly answered, waving his hand to shut me up. "My father gave me the keys ten years ago. Since then, I have repeated the answer nineteen times. Counting you, twenty."

"Twenty!"

"My father repeated it sixty-seven times. I believe five were women."

The Rock wanted me to ask about Abi-Ruj Iyasus, but the Guardian of the Keys didn't give me a chance. "I'm really sorry, ma'am, but I must go. They are expecting me at home. It's very late. I hope I've been of some help. May Allah protect you."

With that, he disappeared at a fast clip, leaving me with as many questions as I had had before I talked to him.

Suddenly Pierantonio appeared right in front of me, with a cell phone in his hand. "Want to call to your pals?" he asked.

"The seventh and the ninth?" the captain exclaimed, taking giant steps from one side of the office to the other. He was a caged lion. He'd been locked up for four days, keying phrases from the prayer into the computer, searching for a match with other documents around the world. All he'd managed to do was to miss out on the meeting with the Guardian of the Keys. He lost what little patience he had listening to the enigmatic instructions the Guardian gave me.

"Are you sure he said 'the seventh and the ninth'?"

"I'm absolutely sure, Captain."

"'The seventh and the ninth,'" Farag repeated, pensive. "The seventh test—but there's no ninth test. The seventh word and the ninth word of the prayer? The seventh and the ninth strophes of the circle of the wrathful? The Seventh and Ninth Symphonies of Beethoven? The seventh and ninth of something we don't know?"

"What are the seventh and ninth strophes of this cornice in Dante?"

"Didn't I tell you that there's nothing of interest in the fourth circle aside from the smoke?" Glauser-Röist roared, without stopping his desperate pacing.

Farag picked up the copy of the *Divine Comedy* and began to look for Canto XVI of *Purgatory*. The captain looked at him scornfully.

"Isn't anybody paying attention to me?"

"The seventh strophe of the sixteenth canto," Farag said, "verses nineteen through twenty-one, says:

'Each prayer they sang began with Agnus Dei;
The same words, sung in unison, produced
An atmosphere of perfect harmony.'"

"What's Dante talking about?" I asked.

"About the souls that approach them. About how they can't see the souls coming because they're blinded by the smoke. They know they're close by because they hear them singing the *Agnus Dei.*"

"The *Agnus Dei?*" shouted the Rock.

"What we pray during Mass as the priest divides the Bread: 'Lamb of God, who takes away the sins of the world, have mercy on us.'"

"I already told you—those strophes have nothing to do with this!"

Farag lowered his eyes to the book. "The ninth strophe of the same canto says:

> '*And who are you whose body cleaves our smoke?*
> *You speak of us as though you still belonged*
> *With those who measure time by calendars.*'"

"The souls are surprised to find a live person in their cornice," I deduced. "Nothing too interesting."

"No, of course not." Farag mulled it over, rereading the strophes.

Glauser-Röist let out an impatient bellow. "I had already said so! The only important thing is the smoke, and the smoke is this damn prayer that keeps us from seeing anything."

"What other options did you mention, Farag?"

"Options?"

"When you said that the seventh and the ninth could be strophes of Canto XVI, you mentioned other possibilities."

"Ah, yes! I said they could be the tests we're taking. That's out, since there're only seven tests. I don't think Beethoven's symphonies are an option, do you? I also said they could be the seventh and the ninth word of Father Stephanos's prayer!"

"That sounds good," I said, getting to my feet and walking over to the life-sized photograph of the panel. After four days of intensive work, I had memorized it and didn't need to look at it to know what it said:

*You who have overcome pride and envy, overcome wrath with patience
now. Just as the plant thrives through the will of the sun, implore God
that his divine light fall on you from heaven. Christ says: fear nothing but
the fear of sinning. Christ fed you in groups of one hundred and fifty
hungry souls. His holy word did not say groups of ninety or two. Then
trust justice as the Athenians did and do not fear the grave. Have faith in
Christ even as he had faith even in the wicked tax collector. Your soul,
like the soul of the bird, races and soars to God. Do not hinder it by
committing sins and it will arrive at Christ's side. If you conquer evil you
will reach the light before the dawn. Purify your soul bowing down before
God like a humble supplicant. With the help of the True Cross, strike
down your earthly appetites without mercy. Cleave to the Cross alongside
Jesus with seven nails and seven blows. If you do this, Christ, in his
majesty, will receive you at the sweet door. May your patience be filled to
the brim by this prayer. Amen.*

I sighed. There was no doubt about one thing: just as Glauser-Röist
had said, it was truly a smokescreen.

"Grab a marker, Ottavia," Farag said. "Something just occurred
to me."

I got right on it. When Farag had an idea, it was always a good one.
I grabbed a thick black marker and stood stock-still, like a diligent stu-
dent, waiting for the teacher to share his wisdom.

"Let's suppose that the two sentences written in red and black ink
have a special meaning on their own."

"We studied that several times this week." The Rock sulked.

"'You who have overcome pride and envy, overcome wrath with
patience now.' That statement is meant to grab our attention. The aspiring Staurofilax arrives at the crypt of Holy Sepulchre. Standing before
the relics, he finds the tablet warning him that what's coming next is part
of the next test."

"What I don't understand," I murmured, "is how aspirants who
come to Jerusalem discover that secret vault and how they manage to get
in it."

"How long ago did we begin the tests?" The Rock suddenly stopped his pacing and leaned on the back of the armchair.

"Exactly two weeks ago," I answered. "Sunday, May 14. I was in Palermo at my father's and my brother's funeral when you and Farag called me. Today is Sunday, May 28. Exactly two weeks have passed."

"Two weeks? Suppose that, instead of going from city to city in a helicopter or a plane, instead of having computers and the Internet and the inestimable aid of its vast knowledge and people in the respective cities helping us out, only one of us had to make all the moves on foot or horseback and find the test of Santa Lucia or the test of Pythagoras. How long do you think that would have taken?"

"It's not the same, Kaspar," protested the professor. "Remember, what for us is out-of-synch, historical knowledge, for someone in the twelfth to eighteenth centuries was a normal part of their studies. Back then, education guided a person to become well-rounded, to be a painter, sculptor, poet, architect, astronomer, musician, mathematician, athlete, minstrel—all at the same time! Science and art weren't separate the way they are today. Remember Hildegard von Bingen, Leon Batista Alberti, Trotula Ruggiero, or Leonardo da Vinci. From childhood, any medieval or Renaissance aspirant to Staurofilax, such as Dante, studied all these things that we have to salvage from a keepsake chest. Dante was also a doctor, did you know that?"

"Well, but Abi-Ruj Iyasus," I objected, "the only present-day case we know of, didn't get that classical education you're talking about."

"How can you be so sure?"

"Well, I'm not—but Ethiopia is a country where people die of hunger, where half of the population lives in refugee camps..."

"Don't be so quick to judge, Ottavia," Farag contradicted me. "Ethiopia is a country with a history, a tradition, and a culture that Europe and America would have envied. Before the catastrophe it's living through today, Ethiopia—Abyssinia—was rich, strong, powerful, and, above all, cultured, very cultured. Today, TV images show us a miserable country in a remote part of Africa. Just think, the queen of Sheba was Ethiopian, and Ethiopia's royal family was thought to have descended from King Solomon."

"Please, Professor!" the Rock interrupted. "Don't get off the subject! I asked you two a simple question and you haven't answered me. How long would it take one of us to get through these tests without any help?"

"Months probably," I answered. "Years even."

"That's what I'm saying! The Staurofilakes aspirants weren't in any hurry. They go from one city to another, from one test to another, with all the time in the world. They study, ask questions, use their brains. In Jerusalem, the logical thing is to live here for several months until…"

"Until they lose their patience—that's what this test is all about," pointed out Farag, with a smile.

"Exactly! But we don't have that kind of time. In two weeks we have completed pre-Purgatory and the first two circles."

"With a little luck, Kaspar, if we work all night, in a few days we may have completed the first part of the third circle."

Farag's words were a wake-up call, so I grabbed the marker again. He continued.

"As I was saying before this pleasant chat: When the aspiring Staurofilax arrived at the crypt of the True Cross, he finds the tablet decorated with the Constantine chrismon and a couple of sentences outlined in red. That gets his attention. The first sentence marked in red points out that he has finally found the test of wrath, which he must be patient to solve—very patient. Patience is the theological virtue that counters the deadly sin of wrath. The last sentence says, 'May your patience be filled to the brim by this prayer,' and advises him to look for the solution in the prayer, since it will fill his search to the brim. Eliminating the two sentences outlined in red, we're left with the text in black. I think that's where we'll find 'the seventh and the ninth.'"

"So, the seventh and the ninth words?" I asked, turning to the photograph.

"Let's try it, for lack of a better idea." Farag looked at the Rock who remained stock-still.

"The seventh word is *οταν*—'when,'" I said circling it, "and the ninth, *ελιος*—'sun.'"

"Οταν ο ελιος...," pronounced Farag with satisfaction. "'When the sun...' I believe we are right, *Basileia!* At least it means something."

"Don't be so fast to celebrate," Glauser-Röist scolded him. "Besides, those words don't match the words in the translation."

"No translation can ever match, Kaspar. But those words are in keeping with the literal translation. In the first sentence that should be, 'Like the plant that thrives when it desires the sun.'"

"Okay, supposing we look at the seventh and the ninth words of each sentence," I said, to stop them from arguing. "The following are *κατεδυ* and *εκ*—'to set' and 'at.'"

"There we have the test, Kaspar! *'Οταν ο ελιος κατεδυ εκ*—or, 'When the sun sets at...' It's the Greek expression for 'at sunset.' What do you think?"

I kept counting words and circling them until I'd distilled the complete message from the prayer.

"'When the sun is setting,'" I read, "'from where the grave of one hundred and ninety two Athenians to the tax collector. Run and arrive before dawn. As a supplicant knock seven times on the door.'"

"That makes sense!" shouted Farag.

"Oh, sure!" the Rock joked. "Explain it to me. I don't get it."

Farag came over and stood beside me. "At sunset, from the tomb of the 192 Athenians to the tax collector. Run and get there before dawn..."

"Why do you punctuate it the way it is in the prayer?" I added. "Take out the periods and the sentence works better."

"You're right. Let's see. At sunset, hmm... At sunset, run from the tomb of the 192 Athenians to the tax collector and get there before dawn. As a supplicant, knock seven times on the door. In Greek, 'calling at the door' and 'knocking at the door' mean the same thing."

"That's very good. The translation is correct."

"Are you sure, Doctor? Because I don't understand that part about running from the 192 Athenians to the tax collector. Hope you don't mind me saying so."

"I think we ought to go have lunch and continue later," Farag proposed. "We're worn out. We'll do better if we rest, get back our energy, and refresh our brains. What do you think?"

"I agree," I chimed in. "Come on, Captain. Let's stop for a while."

"You two go ahead. I have some things to do."

"Like what?" I asked, grabbing my jacket off the back of the chair.

"I could say it's a personal matter," he answered in a grouchy tone of voice. "But I want to investigate those Athenians and their tax collector."

As we were walking down the stairs to the dining room, I couldn't help remembering everything my brother told me about Captain Glauser-Röist. I was about to tell Farag, but thought better of it. That kind of information shouldn't be circulated, at least not by me. I preferred to be the final destination for information, not a way station.

When I emerged from my thoughts, seated across the table from the professor, I realized that his turquoise blue eyes were studying me; but I was unable to meet his gaze. During lunch I evaded their burning look, while I desperately tried to keep my voice completely normal. I admit, even though I fought with all my might, that that night I found him... very handsome. I don't know if it was the way his hair fell over his forehead or the way he gestured or how he smiled. As we headed back to the office where the charming Glauser-Röist was waiting for us (Farag was bringing him back some lunch), I felt weak in the knees. I wanted to flee, go back home, run away and never see him again. I closed my eyes in a desperate attempt to take refuge in God, but I couldn't.

"Are you okay, *Basileia?*"

"I want to end this odious adventure once and for all and get back to Rome!" I exclaimed with all my soul.

"Ah!" His voice sounded sad. "That was the last answer I expected!"

When we returned to the office, Glauser-Röist was speedily typing instructions into the computer.

"How's it going, Kaspar?"

"I'm onto something," he muttered without looking away from the screen. "Look at those sheets. You're going to love them."

I picked up a pile of papers lying on the tray of the printer and read the titles: "The Tumulus of Marathon," "The Original Route of the Marathon," "Fidipides' Race," "The City of Pikermiy," and, to my surprise, two pages in Greek, *"Timbos Maratonesono"* and *"Maratonas."*

"What does all this mean?" I asked, alarmed.

"It means you're going to have to run the marathon in Greece, Doctor."

"Run forty-two kilometers?" My voice couldn't have been any shriller.

"Actually, no," the Rock said, furrowing his brow and pursing his lips. "Just thirty-nine. The race they run today doesn't match the one Fidipides ran in 490 B.C. to announce the Athenian victory over the Persians on the plains of Marathon. As the International Olympic Committee explains on its Web page, the modern trajectory of forty-two kilometers was established in 1908, at the Olympic Games in London. It's the distance between Windsor Castle and the stadium in White City, at the western part of the city, where the Olympic Games were held. Between the town of Marathon and the city of Athens, there were only thirty-nine kilometers."

"I don't want to argue," Farag said, falling back into the Arab accent he'd almost lost over the last couple weeks, "but didn't Fidipides die as soon as he delivered the good news?"

"Yes, but not on account of the race, Professor—on account of his battle wounds. Fidipides had already run 166 kilometers several times, carrying messages back and forth between Athens and Sparta."

"Well… How do the 192 Athenians figure into this?"

"In Marathon there are two gigantic tombs, or tumuli," the Rock explained as he consulted the nine pages feeding out of the printer. "Those tombs contain the bodies of those who died in the famous battle: 6,400 Persians on one side and 192 Athenians on the other. That's the figure Herodotus mentions. According to that passage, we should start at sunset, at the tumuli of the Athenians, and arrive in Athens before dawn. I'm still not clear about the destination in Athens: the tax collector."

"Maybe the solution to the test in Jerusalem is the clue for the test in Athens."

"Yes, Doctor. That's why Dante combines both circles in Canto XVII."

"Are they going to mark us with the cross?"

"Don't worry. They will."

"So we're running off to Greece!" laughed Farag.

"As soon as we settle the matter of the tax collector."

"I'm scared," I moaned, taking a seat, reading the papers in my hands. Knowing the captain, I wasn't going to get to say good-bye to my brother.

"Have you searched for the term *tax collector* in Greek, Kaspar?"

"No. The keyboard won't let me. I need to download some updates for my browser so I can write the searches in other alphabets."

He worked for a while as he gulped down the lunch we'd brought him. Meanwhile, Farag and I read the pages on the marathon. I, who'd never done the slightest physical exercise, who led the most sedentary life in the world and who'd never felt drawn to any type of sport, was studying very carefully the details of the historic race I'd have to run very soon. But I didn't know how to run! I told myself, anguished. Stupid Staurofilakes! Why did they think you could run thirty-nine kilometers in one night? In the dark! Did they think I was Abebe Bikil?* I'd probably die alone on some solitary hilltop in the cold light of the moon, with wild animals as my only companions. And for what? To get another lovely tattoo on my body?

Finally the captain announced he was ready to copy the Greek text from the Internet search engines that recognized it. I took his place at the computer. It was hard, because the Latin letters on the keyboard didn't match the Greek letters that popped up on the screen. But I quickly got the hang of it, and could manage prettily easily. I didn't have the slightest idea what I was doing, because as soon as I typed in

---

*Ethiopian athlete, famous for running barefoot. He won the marathon at the Olympic games in Rome (1960) and in Tokyo (1964).

καπνικαιρειας *(kapnicareias)*, the captain sat back down and took over the reins of the computer. Since he still needed my help to know what the pages on the monitor said, we looked like we were playing musical chairs.

Classical and Byzantine Greek are significantly different from modern Greek. There were many words or entire constructions I didn't understand, and I had to ask Farag for help. Between the two of us, we managed to translate what was on the screen. Almost at midnight, a Greek search engine named Hellas gave us a vital clue. A brief note at the foot of the (virtual) page indicated that it had only found a few references, but also that it had twelve similar pages we could also consult. Naturally, we accepted. One of the brief descriptions was of a very lovely Byzantine church, in the heart of Athens, called Kapnikarea. The page explained that Kapnikarea Church was known as the Church of the Princess because it was attributed to Empress Irene, who ruled in Byzantium between A.D. 797 and 802. Its real founder was a rich man who collected taxes on fine furniture. He named the church after his profession: *kapnikarea,* tax collector.

So there it was: We knew the source and the destination. All we had to do was travel to Greece, to beautiful Athens, cradle of human thought. Glauser-Röist was on the phone all night giving instructions, getting information, and, with the help of the Holy Synod of the Church of Greece, organizing the next several days of our lives. The next day we were leaving the region considered Roman Catholic and plunging into the Eastern Christian world. If everything went as we hoped, after Athens, the city where we would run the race against sloth, we would visit greedy Constantinople, gluttonous Alexandria, and lustful Antioch.

*T*he flight from Tel Aviv to Athens's Hellinikon Airport in the small Alitalia Westwind lasted nearly three hours. We worked hard during the flight to prepare for the fourth cornice of Purgatory, located midway up the summit.

Exonerated by the third angel of a new *P,* free of the weight of the sin of wrath, Dante feels nimble and asks his guide a lot of questions. As in the previous circle, very little actually referred to the test. Half of Canto XVII and all of Canto XVIII were spent explaining serious questions about love. Virgil explains that the three large circles they had passed through purge sins—pride, envy, and wrath—that wish one's fellow man ill. They are tied to a type of happiness achieved at the expense of other people's humiliation and pain. On the other hand, in the three smaller circles that remained, the sins—greed, gluttony, and lust—only harm oneself.

> *"O my sweet father, what offense is purged*
> *here on this terrace? Though our steps have stopped,*
> *don't you stop speaking to me." So he said:*

> *"That love of good which failed to satisfy*
> *the call of duty, here is fortified:*
> *the oar once sluggish now is plied with zeal."*

As they wander around the cornice, they get caught up in another long discussion about the nature of love and its positive and negative effects on mankind. This only lasts for forty-five tercets, after Virgil settles the argument by mentioning humans' free will. After that, a mob of lazy penitents appears:

> *And I, having been privileged to reap*
> *Such clear, plain answers to my questioning,*
> *Let my thoughts wander vaguely, sleepily;*

> *but this somnolent mood did not last long,*
> *for suddenly we heard a rush of souls*
> *coming around the mount behind our backs.*

> *[. . .]And then they were upon us—that entire,*
> *Enormous mass of spirits on the run;*
> *Two out in front were shouting as they wept:*

"Mary in haste ran to the hills," cried one, *
the other: "Caesar, Ilerda to subdue,
thrust at Marseilles, and then rushed down to Spain."

"Faster! faster, we have no time to waste,
for time is love," cried others from behind,
"strive to do good, that grace may bloom again."

As before, Virgil asks the souls where to find the opening to the next
cornice. One of them, who runs by without stopping, encourages Virgil
and Dante to follow them, for they will show them the path. But the
poets stay where they are, surprised at how the spirits, who were lazy in
life, were now lost in the distance, running as fast as the wind. Exhausted
from that day's hike, Dante falls into a deep slumber thinking about
what he has seen. That dream serves as a transition between the cantos
and the circles and ends the fourth cornice of Purgatory.

We arrived at the Hellinikon airport at noon; the official car from
His Beatitude the archbishop of Athens, Christodoulous Paraskeviades,
awaited us. We were driven to our hotel, the Grande Bretagne, right on
Plateia Syntagmatos, next to the Greek parliament building. The trip
from the airport was long and the entrance to the city surprising. Athens
was like an old town that had grown very large and had no desire to reveal its nature as a historic capital of Europe, until you reached the
depths of its heart. Only when you saw the Parthenon greeting travelers
from atop the Acropolis did you realize that it was the city of the god-
dess Athena, the city of Pericles, Socrates, Plato, and Fidias; the city
beloved by the Roman emperor Hadrian and by the English poet Lord
Byron. Even the air seemed different, charged with unimaginable secrets—of history, beauty, culture—that cloaked the withered, musty
neighborhoods that now comprised Athens.

A porter in green livery and cap kindly opened the car doors and
unloaded our luggage. The hotel was very old; the enormous reception
area was decorated with multicolored marble and silver lamps. The

---

* Mary runs to visit her cousin Elizabeth when she learns she is pregnant.

manager himself met us, as if we were heads of state. He accompanied us deferentially to a meeting room on the first floor. At the door was a large group of high-ranking Orthodox prelates wearing long beards and impressive medallions. Comfortably seated in a corner, His Beatitude Christodoulos awaited us.

The archbishop's pleasant look and vigor surprised me. He couldn't have been more than sixty years old, and was very well preserved. His beard was still pretty dark, and his gaze was friendly. He stood up as soon as he saw us, and walked over, wearing a wide smile.

"I am delighted to welcome you to Greece!" he said in very correct Italian. "I wish you to know our deepest gratitude for what you are doing for Christian churches."

Setting protocol aside, Archbishop Christodoulos introduced the rest of the clergy. Among them was a good part of the Synod of the Greek Church (I couldn't differentiate between the various Orthodox ranks by their vestments and medals): His Eminence, the metropolitan of Staoi and Meteroa, Seraphim (it isn't customary to include last names when one occupies a high religious post); the metropolitan of Kaisariani, Vyron, and Ymittos, Daniel; the metropolitan of Mesogaia and Lavreotiki, Agatjhonikos; Their Eminences, the metropolitans of Megara and Salamis, of Chalkis, of Thessaloitis and Fanariofarsala, of Mitilene, Erossos, and Plomrion, of ... In all, a long list of venerable metropolitans, archimandrites, and bishops with majestic names. If the meeting we'd had in Jerusalem seemed over the top, the product of the patriarch's curiosity, the meeting in that room in the Grande Bretagne was even more amazing. Without ever intending to, we'd become heroes.

Those priests had enormous expectations for us. Despite our protests, Captain Glauser-Röist finally felt obliged to explain the risky adventures we'd lived through, omitting the details relating to the Staurofilakes. We didn't trust anyone. It wasn't crazy to think that in that agreeable assemblage there could be an infiltrator. He also didn't explain what the test in Athens—set for that very night—consisted of, even though they asked repeatedly. On the plane, we discussed the need to keep it secret, so that the meddling of some curious person wouldn't spoil our plan. Naturally, we would tell His Beatitude Christodoulos as well as some members of the synod close to him. No one else would know that at sunset that day, three strange runners, more librarians than athletes—two of them, at least—would leave their sweat on the ground of Attica to earn the right to keep risking their lives.

We were invited to a magnificent lunch in the hotel banquet room. I was like a kid when it came to the *taramosalata* and the *mousaka*, the *souvlakia* with *tzatziki*—small pieces of roasted pork seasoned with lemon, herbs, and olive oil, accompanied by the famous sauce made with yogurt, pepper, garlic, and mint—and the original *kleftico*. Especially delicious were the incomparable Greek breads made with raisins, spices, greens, olives, or cheeses. For dessert, a little *freska frouta*. Who could ask for anything more? Mediterranean cuisine is the best in the world. Farag proved that by eating enough for three or four people.

When we were free of protocol and the bearded clergy had left, we set to work as quickly as possible, for we still had a lot to do. His Beatitude Christodoulos wanted to stay all afternoon, watching us prepare for the test and organize the race. The presence of such a prestigious person turned out to be quite the opposite of an obstacle. As soon as members of the synod and the bishops from the archdiocese left, His Beatitude revealed a jovial, youthful, athletic spirit. He had more energy than Farag, the captain, and me put together.

His Beatitude told us that the first Olympic Games of the modern era took place in Greece in April 1896. They hadn't been celebrated for more than fifteen hundred years. The winner of the marathon race was a twenty-three-year-old Greek shepherd almost a meter sixty centimeters tall named Spyros Louis. Spyros, who became a national hero back then, ran the distance between Marathon and the Olympic stadium in Athens in two hours fifty-eight minutes and fifty seconds.

"Was he a professional runner?" I asked, engrossed. I had the deep conviction, not just a doubt or insecurity, that I wouldn't pass this test. I knew I'd never run thirty-nine kilometers. It was empirically impossible.

"Oh no!" His Beatitude answered with a wide, proud smile. "Spyros participated in the race by chance. At the time, he was a soldier in the Greek army. His colonel convinced him to enter at the last minute. He ran well, but he hadn't had any training or preparation. He started his running career in the most important Greek race in history. After all, we weren't going to let a foreigner win the race!"

Spyros didn't receive any gold medal for his feat. In those first Olympics, they didn't give the medals to champions. But he got a monthly pension of one hundred drachmas for the rest of his life. He also asked for and received a cart and horse to work his fields.

"Do you know the best part?" His Beatitude added with pride. "Forty years later, he was the Greek delegation's standard-bearer at the opening ceremony of the Olympic Games in Berlin in 1936. He placed a crown of laurels, the symbol of peace, in Adolf Hitler's hands."

"But Spyros wasn't an athlete, right?"

"No, Sister, he wasn't."

"If he wasn't an athlete and it took nearly three hours to run the thirty-nine kilometers, how long will it take us?" I asked, looking at the captain.

"It's not that simple, Doctor."

The Rock opened a billfold-size notebook full of notes and flipped past several pages until he found what he was looking for. "Today is May 29. According to the information the archdiocese gave me, the sun will set in Athens at 8:56 p.m. So we will have nine hours and six minutes to complete the test."

"Oh, that's much better!" exclaimed Farag. He seemed so relieved we all turned to look at him in surprise. "What's wrong? I didn't think I could pass this test!" He, like me, had kept his fear a secret until that very moment.

"I'm sure I won't make it," I said.

"Oh, come on, Ottavia! We have more than nine hours!"

"So?" I jumped up. "I can't run for nine hours. I don't think I could run for nine minutes."

The Rock flipped some more pages in his little notebook. "The men's record for the marathon is under two hours and seven minutes. The women's record is just over two hours and twenty minutes."

"I can't," I repeated obstinately. "Do you know how much I have run in the last few years? Not one bit! Not even to catch the bus!"

"I am going to give you some instructions to follow tonight," continued the Rock, turning a deaf ear to my complaints. "First, don't overdo it. Don't throw yourself into the race as if you really had to win a marathon. Run gently, don't hurry, economize your movements. Take short, even strides, don't wave your arms, breath normally. When you go uphill, do it effortlessly, efficiently, take small steps. When you go downhill, descend quickly, but control your pace. Keep the same rhythm throughout the entire race. Don't lift your knees too much, and try not to lean forward, try to keep your body at a straight angle to the ground."

"What are you saying?" I grunted.

"I am talking about getting to Kapnikarea, remember, Doctor? Or would you rather return to Rome tomorrow morning?"

"Do you know what Spyros Louis did when he got to kilometer thirty?" His Beatitude Christodoulous wasn't used to our bickering. "When he felt very tired, he stopped, asked for a big glass of red wine, and drank it down in one gulp. Then he started a spectacular comeback and flew for the last nine kilometers of the race."

Farag let out hearty laugh. "Well, now we know what to do when we are tired. Drink a nice glass of wine!"

"I don't think the judges would allow that these days," I replied, a bit miffed with Glauser-Röist.

"Why not? Runners can drink anything as long as they don't test positive for doping."

"We will drink sports drinks," announced the Rock. "Doctor Salina, more so than Farag and I, needs to drink more often to recover ions and mineral salts. If you don't, you will suffer really bad leg cramps."

I kept my mouth shut. I preferred Saint Lucia's hot red floor a thousand times over that blessed endurance test I was preparing for.

The captain opened a leather case that lay on the desk and took out three tiny, mysterious boxes. At that moment some far-off clock struck seven.

"Put on these pulse meters," the captain ordered, showing Farag and me the strange clocks. "How old are you, Professor?"

"That's a good one! Why do you ask?"

"You program the pulse meters so they can monitor your heartbeat during the race. If you go over your limit, you could collapse—or, even worse, have a heart attack."

"I don't plan on exceeding my limit," I announced, disgruntled.

"Tell me your age, Professor, please," the Rock asked again, picking up one of the pulse meters.

"I'm thirty-eight."

"Fine, we subtract 38 from a maximum of 220 beats."

"Then what?" asked His Beatitude Christodoulous.

"The recommended beats for a man are calculated by subtracting his age from the maximum cardiac frequency, which is 220. So, the professor will have a theoretical cardiac frequency of 182 beats. If he goes over that number during the race, he could put himself in danger. The pulse meter will beep if he does, okay, Professor?"

"Sure," Farag said, strapping the contraption to his wrist.

"Please tell me your age, Doctor."

I was waiting for that terrible moment. I didn't care if His Beatitude Christodoulous and the Rock knew, but it bothered me that Farag would know I was a year older than he. Either way, I had no way out.

"I'm thirty-nine."

"Perfect." The Rock didn't even blink. "Women have a greater cardiac frequency than men. They can handle a greater effort. So, in your case we will subtract thirty-nine from 226. Your theoretical maximum is 187 beats, Doctor. But since you live a very sedentary life, we will program it at 60 percent—that is 112. Remember, if the pulse meter starts beeping, you need to drop your pace immediately and slow down, got it?"

"Sure."

"These calculations are approximate. Each person is different. Limits can vary according to a person's preparation and constitution. Don't just go by the pulse meter; at the slightest warning signal from your bodies, stop and rest. Now, let's move on to possible injuries."

"Can't we skip that part?" I asked, bored. I certainly wasn't going to injure myself—and I wasn't going to make my pulse meter beep, either. I was going to hold myself to a slow pace, the slowest I could go and still make it to Athens.

"No, Doctor, we can't skip that part. It's important. Before starting we have to do some exercises and stretches to warm up. The lack of muscle mass in sedentary people is the main cause of ankle and knee injuries. In any case, we are really fortunate that the entire course is on asphalt highways."

"Oh?" I interrupted him. "I thought it went through the country-side."

"I bet my pulse meter you pictured yourself dead on some hill, sur-rounded by forests and wild animals!" commented Farag, trying not to laugh.

"Well, yes. I'm not ashamed to admit it."

"The entire course is on highways, Doctor. We can't get lost. Several years ago the Greek government painted a blue commemorative line along the thirty-nine kilometers. For greater safety, you pass through several towns and a city, as you will soon see. We don't ever leave civili-zation."

That was good news; getting lost in the woods was definitely out.

"If at any time you notice a sharp muscular pinch that leaves you breathless, stop. The test is over for you. Most likely you have a fibular tear. If you keep going, the damage could be irreversible. If it feels like a normal pain, even if it's intense, rub the aching muscle. If it's hard as a rock, stop to rest. It could be the beginning of a contracture. Massage it in the direction of the muscle, and when you can, end with some light stretches. If the tension subsides, continue; but if it doesn't, please stop. The race is over for you. Now," he got to his feet, decisively, "please change clothes, and let's go. We'll eat on the way. It's getting late."

Some bizarre sports clothes were waiting for me in my room. It was your standard running suit, but when I put it on, I looked so ridiculous I felt like crawling into a hole, though I must say that when I put on the white running shoes, it looked better. It was even better when I tucked a nice silk handkerchief into the collar of my sweat suit. In the end the outfit wasn't so pathetic, and it did turn out to be comfortable. For several months, I hadn't had a chance to go to the hair salon. My hair had grown so much I had to hold it back with an elastic band. Although it was a bit extravagant, at least it kept the long strands of hair out of my face. I put on my long wool coat (more to cover up than because of the cold) and went down to the lobby, where my companions, the porter in the green livery, and a driver from the archbishopric were waiting for me.

The road to Marathon was full of advice and many last-minute suggestions. I understood that Captain Glauser-Röist didn't have the slightest intention of waiting for Farag or me, and that suited me just fine. His idea was that at least one of us should get to Kapnikarea before dawn. That was essential so at least one of us could continue the tests and get the next clue. Farag or I might not get our tattoos, but we could collaborate with the Rock on the next circles.

The Greek highways were actually more like country roads, not wide and well paved like those in Italy. The traffic wasn't heavy. Traveling in the archdiocese's car was like going back in time ten or fifteen years. Overall, Greece continued to be a marvelous country.

Night was falling when we finally drove into the town of Marathon. Nestled in a valley, with its flat terrain and wide-open spaces, Marathon was the ideal place for an ancient battle. In all other respects, it was no different from other industrial towns in modern-day Europe. Marathon received a throng of tourists, especially athletes and people who wanted to try out the famous race.

The car pulled up to the sidewalk in a strange spot outside of town, next to a knoll covered with green vegetation and some flowers. We got out of the car without stopping to look at the tumulus where one of the most important yet forgotten milestones in history had taken place. If the Persians had won the battle of Marathon, if they had imposed their culture, their religion, their politics on the Greeks, the world as we know it would more than likely not exist. Everything would be different—not better or worse, just different. That battle erected the barrier that allowed our culture to flourish. According to Herodotus, under that tumulus were 192 Athenians who died to make that possible.

The driver said good-bye and sped away, leaving us there on the side of the road. I left my coat in the car because the weather was actually wonderful.

"When do we start, Kaspar?" asked Farag, who was wearing a strange T-shirt with long, white sleeves and light blue running shorts. We each carried a small cloth backpack with the supplies we needed for the test.

"It's eight-thirty and it's just about to get dark. Let's walk over to the hill." The captain looked the best in his terrific red running suit, his physique that of a lifelong athlete.

The tumulus was much bigger than it had looked at first glance. Even the Rock looked as small as an ant when we got to the edge where the grass began. The spot was so solitary we were startled by a voice calling to us in heavily accented modern Greek from the other side of the hill.

"Who is that?" the Rock grumbled.

"Let's go see," I proposed, circling the tumulus.

Seated on a stone bench, enjoying the nice weather and the last rays of evening sun, a group of elderly men, with black hats and sticks fashioned into canes, studied us, seemingly very amused. We didn't understand a word they were saying, and they didn't seem to care. Accustomed to tourists, they must have had a lot of fun at the expense of people who traveled there like us, decked out in running clothes, ready to emulate Spyros Louis. The joking smiles on their leathery, wrinkled faces said it all.

"Could they be Staurofilakes?" Farag asked, staring at them.

"I refuse to think that," I sighed, but the idea had occurred to me. We were getting paranoid.

"Do you two have everything you need?" asked the captain, looking at his watch.

"What's the rush? We have ten minutes left."

"Let's do some exercises, start with some stretches."

A few minutes after our exercise class started, the public streetlights came on. The sunlight was so dim now you could barely see a thing. The old men made jokes we couldn't understand. From time to time one of our stretching positions made them burst out laughing, which dangerously inflamed my mood.

"Calm down, Ottavia. They're just some old peasants. That's all."

"When we find the current Cato, I'm going to tell him a thing or two about his spies."

The old men split their sides laughing. I turned my back on them, furious.

"Professor, Doctor. It's time. Remember—the blue line starts in the middle of town, at the spot where the race started in 1896. Stick with me until then, okay? Ready?"

"No!" I declared. "I don't think I'll ever be ready for this."

The Rock gave me a scornful look, and Farag quickly interceded. "We're ready, Kaspar. Say the word."

We stood there for a few silent seconds, not moving, while the Rock stared at his watch. Suddenly he turned, gave us a nod, and started running. He began at a smooth pace that Farag and I imitated. The heat didn't do me any good. With each stride, I gave a prayer for my knees; they seemed to receive the impact equivalent to a couple of tons. Resigned, I told myself that, no matter what, I had to be a good sport.

A few minutes later, we came to the Olympic monument, where the infamous blue line started. The monument was a simple white stone wall with a heavy, burning torch in front. There, the race started in earnest. My watch read 9:15, local time. We followed the line into the city, and I couldn't help feeling a little embarrassed at what people must have thought when they saw us. But the residents of Marathon didn't seem the least bit interested in us. They were used to seeing all kinds of things.

At the starting point, when we were running on the same highway we'd driven on, the captain picked up his pace and pulled away. I, on the other hand, slowed down until I nearly stopped. Faithful to my plan, I adopted a light pace I planned to keep up all night. Farag turned to look at me.

"Something the matter, *Basileia?* Why are you stopping?"

So he's calling me *Basileia* again, eh? Since Jerusalem, he'd only done that a couple of times—I'd kept track—but never in front of other people. So now it was clandestine, private, only for my ears. Just then my pulse meter beeped. I had gone over the recommended pulses. My run-ning pace didn't warrant it, my heart did.

"Are you okay?" babbled Farag, looking worried.

"I'm perfectly fine. I did my own calculations." I stopped my charm-ing contraption's beeping. "At this pace, it'll take me six or seven hours to get to Athens."

"Are you sure?" he stammered, examining me.

"No, not completely; but once many years ago, I did a sixteen-kilometer run and it took me four hours. That's a simple rule of three."

"But the terrain is different here. Don't forget the mountains sur-rounding Marathon. Besides, the distance to Athens is more than twice sixteen kilometers."

I redid my calculations and didn't feel as sure as before. I vaguely recalled I was half dead when I finished that run, so the outlook wasn't very good. I wished with all my heart that Farag would take off running and get far away from me. But apparently he had no intention of leaving me alone that night.

For the past week, I had desperately forced myself to concentrate on what we were doing and forget those crazy, unsettling feelings that wouldn't leave me alone. Visiting Jerusalem and seeing Pierantonio had helped a lot. However, I noticed that those feelings that I was constantly trying to hold back made me feel terribly bitter and sapped my strength. What started out in Ravenna as a joyful emotion was now affecting the way I reacted to the world. One can fight back an illness or one's destiny, but how was I supposed to fight back the feeling that was pushing me toward that fascinating man? There I was, my obedience to God growing more fragile with each stride I took on the race to Marathon.

Although the blue line was drawn on the asphalt highway, we prudently traveled on the wide tree-covered sidewalk. Soon the side-walk ended and we had to run on the highway's shoulder. Fortunately, the number of cars passing us decreased. We were running on the right side of the road, in the same direction as the cars driving up behind us, which we shouldn't have done. But the only real danger, if you can call it that, was the dark. Here and there, lights were still on at a bar or on a highway near a town or at a little house on the outskirts, but soon they also began to dwindle. Maybe it was a good idea that Farag didn't leave me.

When we came to the next city, Pandeleimonas, we were engaged in an interesting conversation about the Byzantine emperors and the general lack of knowledge that existed in the West about the Roman Empire, which lasted in fact until the fifteenth century. My admiration and respect for Farag's erudition was growing. After a long, gentle ascent, we ran through Nea Makri and Zoumberi immersed in our chat. Time and kilometers were passing without our noticing. I'd never felt so happy; never had my mind been so open and alert, ready to leap at the least intellectual challenge. By the time we got to the sleepy town of Agios Andreas, three hours had gone by. Farag started to tell me about his work at the museum. The night was so magical, so special, so beautiful, that I didn't even feel the merciless cold of the dark Greek countryside. The poor light of the waning moon was no help. Still, I wasn't worried or scared; I traveled along totally absorbed in Farag's words. As he shined his flashlight on the ground in front of us, he talked passionately about the Gnostic texts written in Coptic found in the ancient Nag Hammadi, in Upper Egypt. He had worked on them for several years, locating the second-century Greek sources they were based on and comparing them, fragment by fragment, to other known writings by Coptic Gnostic writers.

We shared a great passion for our work, as well as a deep love for antiquity and its secrets. We felt called to unveil them, to describe what had been lost over the centuries out of abandonment or profit. He didn't share certain nuances of my Catholic focus, and I didn't agree with those postulates he professed on and on about a picturesque Gnostic origin of Christianity. True, nearly everything about the first three centuries of our religion is unknown, and those great gaps have been imaginatively filled with false documents or manipulated testimonies. Even the Gospel had been touched up during those first centuries. They'd been molded to the dominant currents in the nascent church, causing Jesus to commit terrible or absurd contradictions—contradictions that had often gone unnoticed. I couldn't accept that everything needed to be brought to light, that the Vatican's doors had to be open to any researcher who, like him, didn't have the faith necessary to give the right sense to what he discovered. Farag called me a reactionary, a retrograde. He didn't accuse me of usurping humanity's patrimony, but he came close. Still he didn't do it with acrimony. We laughed and laughed, we attacked each other from our respective ideological fortresses with a mixture of tenderness and affection that softened any steel bullet we might have fired at one another. The hours passed by unnoticed.

Mati, Limanaki, Rafina... We had just about reached Pikermi, the exact middle of the marathon. There was no more traffic on the narrow highway, and no sign of Captain Glauser-Röist. I was starting to feel a great fatigue in my legs and a light pain in my back and my glutes, and my feet were burning, but I refused to acknowledge it. During a forced stop, I discovered a couple of huge spots on my feet that had been rubbed raw and had become blisters sometime during the night.

We kept going: one hour, two hours. We didn't realize we were running slower and slower. We had turned the night into a long stroll where time didn't matter. We passed through Pikermi. We left Spata, Palini, Stavros, Paraskevi behind... The clock kept up its impassive march. We didn't realize we weren't going to reach Athens before dawn. We were giddy, drunk on words. We didn't care about anything but our dialogue.

After Paraskevi the road curved slowly to the left, a curve that embraced a leafy forest of very tall pines and was precisely ten kilometers from Athens. Just then Farag's pulse meter went off.

"Tired?" I asked him, worried. I could only see the outline of his face.

He didn't answer.

"Farag?" I insisted. The little machine kept emitting its insufferable alarm. In the silence, it sounded like a fire alarm.

"I have to tell you something...," he murmured mysteriously.

"Well, stop that racket and tell me."

"I can't..."

"What do you mean, you can't? Just push the little orange button."

"I mean..." He was stuttering. "What I mean is..."

I grabbed his wrist and stopped the alarm. Suddenly I realized something had changed. A hushed voice inside me warned me we were treading on dangerous ground. I didn't want to know what he was going to say. I remained mute like a dead woman.

"What I have to say..."

His pulse meter went off again. This time he turned it off himself. "I can't tell you because there are so many hurdles, so many obstacles..." I held my breath. "Help me, Ottavia."

His voice didn't register. I tried to stop him, but I choked up. Now *my* hateful pulse meter went off. We were a symphony of beeps.

"You know what I'm trying to tell you, right?"

My lips refused to open. I unhooked the pulse meter around my wrist and took it off. Otherwise it would have never stopped going off. Farag couldn't stop laughing as he imitated me.

"Good idea," he said. "I... You see, *Basileia*, this is very hard for me. In past relationships, I never had... Things went differently. But with you... God! This is complicated! Why can't it be simple? You know what I'm trying to tell you, *Basileia!* Help me!"

"I can't, Farag," I replied, my matter-of-factness surprising even me.

"Okay, okay..."

He didn't say anything else, and neither did I. Silence fell over us. We ran this way until we came to Holargos, a small town whose tall, modern buildings announced the approach of Athens.

I don't think I've ever lived through a more bitter, difficult moment. God's presence kept me from accepting the declaration Farag tried to make, but my incredibly strong feelings for such a marvelous man were tearing me up inside. The worst part wasn't admitting I loved him. The worst part was that he loved me too. It would have been so easy! But I wasn't free.

"Ottavia! It's five fifteen!" His shout startled me.

For a moment I didn't understand what he was saying. 5:15? So? Suddenly a light went on in my brain. 5:15! We couldn't reach Athens before 6:00! We were at least four kilometers away!

"My God! What're we going to do?"

"Run!"

He took me by the hand and pulled me like a madman. I stopped after just a few meters.

"I can't, Farag!" I moaned, flopping down on the highway. "I'm too tired."

"Listen to me, Ottavia. Get on your feet and run!" His tone of voice was commanding, not one bit compassionate or affectionate.

"My right foot really hurts. I must have injured a muscle. I can't go on, Farag. You go. Run. I'll get there later."

He bent over and got down on my level. He grabbed me by the shoulders, shook me, and looked me straight in the eye.

"If you don't get on your feet right now and start running to Athens, I'm going to tell you what I couldn't say before. And if I do that"— he leaned gently toward me, so his lips were just a few millimeters from mine—"I'll tell you in such a way you'll never be a nun again for the rest of your life. You choose. If you make it to Athens with me, I won't persist."

I felt a horrible desire to cry, to hide my head against his chest and blot out the scary things he'd just said. He knew I loved him, so he gave me a choice between his love and my vocation. If I ran, I would lose him forever. If I stayed there, sprawled on the blacktop highway, he would kiss me and make me forget I had given my life to God. I felt the deepest anguish, the blackest pain. I'd have given anything not to have to make this decision, and wished I'd never met Farag. I took in so deep a breath that my lungs felt as though they were about to explode. I freed my shoulders from his hands with a light jerk, and making a superhuman effort—which took everything I had, and not because of the physical fatigue or the blisters on my feet—I collected myself, straightened my clothes with a decisive look on my face, and turned to him. He was still crouched down, an infinitely sad look on his face.

"Shall we go?"

He looked at me for a few seconds, without moving, without changing the look on his face. Then he stood up, a thin smile on his lips, and started to run.

"Let's go."

I don't remember much of the towns we passed, except their names

(Halandri and Papagou). I do know I kept an eye on my watch, trying not to feel the pain in my legs and the pain in my heart. Somewhere along the way, the cold dawn froze the tears that were streaming down my face. We entered Athens on Kifissias Road, at 5:50. If we kept running at that pace, we'd never finish the test. But that didn't stop us, and neither did the sharp pain in my side which cut short my breath. I was drenched in sweat, and I thought I'd faint. It felt like I had knives jabbing my feet, but I kept running. If I didn't, I'd have to face something I couldn't deal with. More than running, I was fleeing—fleeing Farag. I'm sure he knew it. He stayed next to me when he could have run far ahead of me. But he never abandoned me. True to my habit of feeling guilty about everything, I felt responsible for his failure. That beautiful, unforgettable night was ending in nightmare.

I don't know how long Vassilis Sofias Avenue is, exactly, but it seemed like an eternity. Cars were driving along as we ran in desperation, dodging telephone poles, streetlights, trashcans, trees, bulletin boards, and iron benches. The beautiful capital of the ancient world awoke to a new day that signaled the beginning of the end for us. Vassilis Sofias just wouldn't end. My watch read 6:00 a.m. It was too late. I looked right and left, but I couldn't see the sun anywhere. It was still as dark as an hour before. What was going on?

The blue line that had guided our steps all night was lost on Vassilis Konstantinou, the cross street that split off from Sofias and continued directly to the Olympic stadium. We ran down the avenue that ended at Plateia Syntagmatos, the enormous esplanade of the Greek Parliament, on the same corner as our hotel. We flew by it without stopping. Kapnikarea was located in the middle of Ermou Street. It was 6:03.

My lungs and heart exploded; the pain in my side was killing me. All that kept me going was my following the faithful nocturnal darkness in the sky, that black covering that wasn't lit up by a single ray of sunshine. There was still hope. But just as I entered the crosswalk on Ermou Street, the muscles in my right leg decided for themselves that my running was over and I had to stop. A sharp jab stopped me cold. I put my hand on the painful spot and moaned. Farag whipped around. Without uttering a single word, he understood what was happening. He came back, put his left arm under my shoulders, and helped me up. With our next ragged breath, we started running again, this time together. I took a step with my good leg, then leaned all my weight on him when I had to use the bad one. We swung from side to side like a ship in a storm, but we didn't stop. My watch read 6:05. Just three hundred meters to go. At the end of Ermou, a small Byzantine church, half buried in the ground, appeared like a strange, unimaginable apparition, out of the center of a narrow traffic circle.

Two hundred meters. I could hear Farag's labored breathing. My good leg started to resent our last-ditch effort. One hundred fifty meters. 6:07. We moved slower and slower. We were spent. A hundred and twenty meters. With a rough push, Farag hoisted me up again and grabbed me tighter, holding steady my hand draped around his neck. One hundred meters. 6:08.

"Ottavia, you have to put up with the pain," he jabbered, out of air. Seas of sweat ran down his face and neck. "Please keep going."

Kapnikarea offered us a view of its left-side stone walls. We were so close! We could see the small cupolas covered with red tiles, crowned by small crosses. I couldn't breathe or run. It was torture.

"Ottavia, the sun!"

I didn't even look up. The soft blue tinting of the dark sky said it all. Those three words were the spur I needed to find a granule of strength. A chill went through me, and at the same time, I felt such hatred for the sun for failing me. I breathed deep and hurled myself toward the church. Sometimes in life, blind stubbornness, cussedness, or pride takes over and forces us to throw ourselves unchecked toward that single goal that overshadows everything else. That imprudent response must have a lot to do with survival instinct, because we acted as if our life depended on it.

Sure, I was in pain and my body was like a limp rag. But the thought of the rising sun was stuck in my mind, and I simply couldn't act prudently. More important than my physical problems was my duty to cross Kapnikarea's threshold.

So, I threw myself into running as I hadn't run all that night. Farag was right next to me. We ran down the stairs to the church and came to the charming portico that sheltered the door. Above it an impressive Byzantine mosaic of the Virgin and Child twinkled in the dim light from the grounded streetlights. Overhead a heaven of golden mosaics outlined a Constantine chrismon.

"Shall we knock?" I asked weakly, putting my hands on my waist and bending over so I could breathe.

"What do *you* think?" Farag exclaimed. I heard the first of his furious seven blows against the weathered wood. With the last of his blows, the hinges creaked softly and the door opened.

A young Orthodox clergyman, with a long, shaggy black beard, appeared. His brow furrowed, a stern look on his face, he said something in modern Greek that we didn't understand. Seeing our baffled faces, he repeated it in English.

"The church doesn't open until eight."

"We know, Father, but we need to enter. We must purify our souls bending down before God as humble supplicants."

I gave Farag an admiring look. How did he remember to use the words from the prayer in Jerusalem? The young clergyman examined us from head to toe. Our bedraggled condition seemed to move him.

"In that case, come in. Kapnikarea is all yours."

I wasn't fooled. That young man in the soutane was a Staurofilax. Farag read my thoughts.

"By chance, Father...," I asked wiping the sweat off my face with my sleeve, "have you seen our friend around here, a runner like us, very tall, with blond hair?"

The curate seemed to think it over. He was such a good actor you wouldn't know he was a Staurofilax. But he didn't fool me.

"No," he answered after thinking it over a while. "I don't recall anyone matching that description. But come in please. Don't stand there in the street."

From that moment, we were at his mercy.

The church was charming, one of those rare wonders which both time and civilization respect. Hundreds of thin, yellow tapers burned at the back and to the right of the church, allowing light to glimmer onto the iconostasis.

"I'll leave you alone to pray," he said, distractedly, as he turned to throw the latch and seal the door. We were prisoners. "Please call if you need anything."

What could we possibly need? He barely finished speaking those kind words when a hard blow to the back of my head made me stagger and collapse on the floor. That's all I remember. I was just sorry I didn't get to see Kapnikarea better.

I opened my eyes under the glacial glare of several white neon tubes and tried to move my head. I sensed someone at my side. An excruciating pain stopped me. A woman's voice mumbled some incomprehensible words, and I lost consciousness again. Some time later I awoke again, and several people dressed in white were leaning over my bed, examining me meticulously, raising my limp eyelids, taking my pulse, and gently moving my neck. In the fog, I realized a very thin tube ran from my arm to a plastic bag filled with a transparent liquid, hanging from a metal pole. I fell back to sleep. After several more hours, I regained consciousness and had a better grasp of reality. My dosage of drugs must have been high, because I felt no pain, although I did feel nauseous.

Seated on some green plastic chairs pushed back to the wall, two strangers observed me, mortified. When they saw my eyelids flutter, they jumped to their feet and approached the head of my bed.

"Sister Salina?" one of them asked in Italian. When I fixed my gaze on him, I saw he was dressed in a soutane and wore a cleric's collar. "I'm Father Cardini, Ferrucci Cardini, from the Vatican embassy. My companion is His Eminence from the archimandrite, secretary of the Permanent Synod of the Church of Greece. How do you feel?"

"Like someone hit me on the head with a mallet, Father. How are my friends, Professor Boswell and Captain Glauser-Röist?"

"Don't worry, they're fine. They're in the next rooms. We just saw them, and they too are regaining consciousness."

"Where am I?"

"The *nosokomio* George Gennimatas."

"The what?"

"The Athens general hospital, Sister. Some sailors found you and your companions late yesterday afternoon on a pier at the port and took you to the nearest hospital. When the emergency room personnel saw your Vatican diplomatic credentials, they contacted us."

A tall, dark-haired doctor with a huge Turkish moustache ripped back the plastic curtain and approached my bed. As he took my pulse and examined my eyes and tongue, he directed his questions to His Eminence from the archimandrite, Theologos Apostolidis, who then spoke to me in English.

"Dr. Kalogeropoulous wishes to know how you're feeling."

"Fine. I'm fine," I answered, trying to get up. I no longer had the drip bag hooked to my arm.

The Greek doctor said something else. Then Father Cardini and the archimandrite Apostolidis turned their faces to the wall. The doctor pulled back the blanket that covered me. All that clothed me was a horrible, short, light salmon-colored gown that left my legs exposed. I wasn't surprised to see my feet bandaged, but I was surprised to find bandages on my thighs.

"What happened?" I asked. Father Cardini repeated my question in Greek. The doctor gave a long-winded answer.

"Dr. Kalogeropoulos says you and your companions have some very strange wounds. He says they were packed with an herbal chlorophyll substance they can't identify. He asks if you know how you got the wounds. They discovered some other older wounds like them on your arms."

"Tell him I don't know anything. I'd like to see them, Father."

At my request, the doctor very carefully pulled back the bandages. Then, with the two chastised priests turned to the wall and me in an untied hospital gown, he left the room. The situation was so tense I didn't dare say a word. Fortunately Dr. Kalogeropoulos returned with a mirror. By flexing my legs, I could see the tattoos. There they were: a decussate cross on the upper part of my right thigh and a Greek cross on my left thigh. Jerusalem and Athens engraved on my body forever. I should have felt proud; but, my curiosity satisfied, all I wanted to see Farag. When I saw my face in the mirror, I was astonished. Not only did

I have sunken eyes and pale skin; wrapped around my head was a volu-
minous amount of bandage resembled a Muslim turban. Seeing my surprise, Dr. Kalogeropoulos fired off another string of words.

"The doctor says," Father Cardini related, "that your friends were
also hit with a blunt object and have significant contusions on their
skulls. Tests show you also consumed alkaloids. He wants to know what
substances you ingested."

"Does this doctor think we're drug addicts or something?"

Father Cardini wasn't joking.

"Tell the doctor we didn't take anything and we don't know anything, Father. He can ask all he likes, but we can't say anything more.
Now, if you don't mind, I'd like to see my companions."

That said, I sat on the edge of the bed and lowered my legs to the
floor. The bandages on my feet made lovely slippers. When he saw me
get out of bed, the doctor tried to restrain me, but I resisted with all my
might. I needed to see my friends.

"Father Cardini, please, will you be so kind as to tell the doctor that
I want my clothes and inform him that I'm going to take this bandage
off my head?"

The Catholic priest translated my words, which was then followed
by some rapid, agitated dialogue.

"That's not possible, Sister. Dr. Kalogeropoulos says you have not
recovered yet. You could suffer a relapse."

"Tell Dr. Kalogeropoulos that I am perfectly fine. Father, do you
know how important our work is?"

"I have an idea, Sister."

"Then tell him to give me my clothes. Now!"

That produced another exchange of irritated words. The doctor
stormed out of my room. Soon a young nurse entered the room and left
a plastic bag at the foot of my bed, without saying a word. Then she
came over and started to free my head from the gauze turban. I felt a
huge relief when she took it off, as if those strips of gauze had been
holding my head prisoner. I ran my fingers through my hair to aerate it
and felt a large bump on the top of my head.

I hadn't finished getting dressed when I heard some knocks on the metal door frame. I hurried to change, and pulled back the curtain when I was ready. Farag and the captain, decked out in matching short blue robes that covered their short hospital gowns, looked at me in surprise from under their own respective turbans.

"How come you're dressed and we're still in these getups?" asked Farag.

"You two don't know how to push your weight around," I replied, laughing. I was so happy to see him again. My heart was racing. "Are you guys okay?"

"We're perfectly fine, but these people insist on treating us like little boys."

"Do you want to see this, Doctor?" Glauser-Röist asked, holding out the familiar folded, thick paper from the Staurofilakes. I took it with a smile and opened it. This time there was only one word: Αποστολειον (*Apostoleion*).

"We start again, right?" I asked.

"As soon as we get out of here," murmured the Rock, casting a grim look around the room.

"Well, then, that will be tomorrow," warned Farag, putting his hands in the pockets of his robe. "It's eleven o'clock at night. I don't think they'll discharge us at this hour."

"Eleven o'clock?" I exclaimed. We had been unconscious all day.

"Let's sign the voluntary release form or whatever they call it in this country," the captain fumed, and headed for the nurses' station.

I took advantage of his absence to look freely at Farag. There were dark circles under his eyes too. His beard was starting to grow down his neck, which made him look like an odd, blond desert nomad. Thinking back to the night before, I felt as though I had a secret only he and I shared. Still, Farag didn't seem to remember a thing; the look on his face was of sympathetic indifference. I was perplexed and worried. Had I dreamed it all?

I didn't get him to talk to me all night, not even when we left the hospital and got into the car sent by the Vatican embassy. (His Emi-

nence Theologos Apostolidis bade us farewell amicably at the door of
the George Gennimatas Hospital and left in his own car.) Farag only
spoke to the captain or Father Cardini, and when his eyes met mine, they
skipped past me, as if I were invisible. If he was trying to make me suffer, he was doing a good job, but I wasn't going to let that destroy me. I
shrouded myself in silence until we got to the hotel. Back in my room, I
couldn't sit comfortably, on account of my tattoos. I prayed stretched
out on the bed until I surrendered to sleep at around three in the morning. Anguished, I begged God to help me, to return to me the certainty
of my religious vocation, the peaceful stability of my former life. I
wanted to take refuge in his love until I found the peace I needed. I slept
well, but my last thought then and my first thought when I woke up were
of Farag.

He didn't look at me once during breakfast or during the trip to the
airport or as we were getting into the Westwind and taking our seats
(very gingerly) in the passenger cabin. The plane was starting to feel
cozy, like home base. It was our only stable point of reference. We took
off from Hellinikon Airport at around ten in the morning. Once in the
air, Paola, our favorite stewardess came around, offering food, drinks,
and even entertainment. After fearing for the life of the poor girl as she
stumbled down the aisle, Captain Glauser-Röist told us smugly that he
had run the distance between Marathon and Kapnikarea in only four
hours and that his pulse meter hadn't gone off once. Farag laughed and
congratulated him with a handshake and some affectionate punches in
the arm. I sank into complete misery recalling the beeping of Farag's
and my pulse meters in those precious moments we spent together on
the silent highway from Marathon.

The flight between Athens and Istanbul was so short that we barely
had time to prepare for Purgatory's fifth circle. In Constantinople we
would aim to purge ourselves of the sin of avarice. We would do it, according to Dante, spread-eagle on the ground:

> When I came out and stood on the Fifth Round,
> I saw spirits stretched out upon the dust,
> Lying face downward, all of them in tears.

Adhaesit pavimento anima mea,*
I heard, accompanied with heavy sighs
That almost made the words inaudible.

"That's all we have to go on?" Farag asked. "It's so very little, and Istanbul is so big."

"We also have the *Apostoleion*," Glauser-Röist reminded him, calmly crossing his legs as if he weren't in any pain from the tattoos or those nasty blisters the Marathon highway had left us as a souvenir. "The Vatican enunciator in Ankara and the patriarch of Constantinople have been working on that since last night. When we get to the hotel, I'll get in touch with Monsignor Lewis and Father Kallistos, secretary to the patriarch. The latter informed me that the *Apostoleion* was the famous Orthodox church of the Holy Apostles. It served as the royal pantheon to the Byzantine emperors until the eleventh century, and it was the largest church after the church of Saint Sofia, but nothing remains of it today. Mehemet II, the Turkish conqueror who brought down the Byzantine Empire, ordered its destruction in the fifteenth century."

"There's nothing left of it?" I was shocked. "What do they suggest we do? Excavate the city in search of its archeological remains?"

"I don't know, Doctor. We'll have to investigate. Emulating the emperors, Mehemet II had his own mausoleum built there, the mosque of Faith Camii, which is still in use. Nothing remains of the *Apostoleion*, not even a stone. We'll have to wait for documents from the enunciator and the patriarchate to learn more."

"What did you ask them to investigate?"

"Everything. Absolutely everything, Doctor: the complete history of the church in great detail; also the history of the Faith Camii; the plans, maps, and drawings of its construction, names of its architects, objects, works of art, all the books that talk about them, the ritual of burying the emperors, and more. As you can see, I haven't left out a single detail. I am sure that the enunciator and the patriarchate are working on the matter. The apostolic nuncio, Monsignor Lewis, told me we

*Psalm 118, 25: "My soul is stuck to the ground."

would have the help of the Italian embassy's cultural attaché, an expert on Byzantine architecture. The patriarchate is especially anxious to collaborate because it has suffered the Staurofilakes' villainy. What little remains of the fragment of the True Cross that Constantine received directly from Saint Helen disappeared a month ago from the patriarchal Church of Saint George. The Patriarchate of Constantinople, so powerful long ago, is so poor today that it can't use any of its resources to protect its relics. There are barely any Orthodox faithful left in Istanbul. The process of Islamization has been so intense and nationalism has turned so violent that nearly 100 percent of the population is Turkish and Muslim."

Just then, the commander of the Westwind announced we would be landing in the Atatürk International Airport in Istanbul in less than a half hour.

"We must hurry," Glauser-Röist urged, opening the book again. "Where were we?"

"We had just started," Farag said, opening his copy of the *Divine Comedy.* "Dante was listening to the spirits of greed recite the first verse of Psalm 118: 'My soul is stuck to the ground.'"

"Fine, let's continue. Virgil asks them to point out the entrance to the next cornice."

"Have they already taken the mark off Dante's forehead?" I interrupted. I gently touched the decussate cross on my right thigh.

"Dante doesn't always explicitly say that the angels are going to erase the scars of the deadly sins in every circle, but at some point, he always indicates this after each new ascent, a moment in which he feels freer. From time to time he realizes they've removed a *P.* Do you need more details, Doctor?"

"No, thank you. Please continue."

"The avarice souls answer the poets:

"'If you have been exempt from lying prone,
And wish to find the quickest way to go,
Be sure to keep your right side to the edge.'"

"That is to say," I interrupted again, "they should turn to the right, leaving the precipice to their right side as well." The captain nodded.

True to form, Dante gets involved in a lengthy conversation with one of the spirits, Pope Adrian V, whom history records as a very greedy person. I suddenly realized that the poet placed a large number of holy pontiffs among the souls in *Purgatory*. I wondered if there was an equal number in the *Inferno*. Clearly, the *Divine Comedy* wasn't a work that glorified the Catholic Church. Just the opposite.

I listened to the captain read the first tercets of Canto XX, in which Dante describes the difficulties he and his teacher face as they walk along that cornice, with so many weeping souls stuck to the ground:

> *"My master moved ahead close to the cliff,*
> *Wherever there was space—as one who walks*
> *along the ramparts hugs the battlements:*

> *"The mass of souls whose eyes were, drop by drop,*
> *Shedding the sin which occupies our world*
> *Left little room along the terrace edge."*

We skipped over the part of the canto where several souls walk along singing about the punishment for greed: King Midas, the rich Roman Craso, and others. Suddenly an apocalyptic tremor shakes the ground in the fifth circle. Dante is frightened, but Virgil calms him down. *"You need not fear while I am still your guide."* Canto XXI starts with the explanation of such an event: A spirit had fulfilled his punishment and was purified, thus his stay in Purgatory was over. On this happy occasion, it was the soul of the Naples poet, Publius Papinius Statius. His penance complete, he'd just detached from the ground. Estacio, who didn't know to whom he was talking, explained that he became a poet out of a deep admiration for Virgil. This confession, of course, causes Dante to laugh. Estacio is offended, not knowing that the Florentine is amused because the person Estacio so admired is there in front of him.

Clearing up the confusion, Estacio falls to his knees before Virgil and begins a long string of admiring verses.

Our plane's descent was so rough my ears popped immediately. Paola came around to remind us to buckle our seatbelts and to offer one of her tasty treats one last time before we landed. I accepted a glass of the horrible bottled juice she carried on a tray, and I drank it to keep the air pressure from destroying my eardrums.

We didn't even have to enter the Istanbul airport. A car with a small Vatican flag on one of its headlights collected us at the Westwind's stairs. Escorted by two Turkish police cars, our automobile left the wide runway behind and drove through a side door in the security gate. Running his hand over the car's elegant leather upholstery, Farag admired how far we'd come since Syracuse.

I had visited Istanbul for a few days during the investigation for which I won my first Getty Prize in 1992, and I recalled a much prettier, more intimate city. I was caught off guard by those horrible blocks of apartments, like concrete anthills. Something terrible had happened to the city that was once, for more than five hundred years, the capital of the Turkish Empire. The car ambled down back streets to the Horn of Gold headed for the Fhanar neighborhood. That's where we would meet the patriarch of Constantinople. Before, there had been little wooden cabinas with beautiful shutters painted the colors of the rainbow. Now, groups of Russians were crowded together to sell trinkets, and young Turks sporting shaggy Islamic beards instead of the traditional Ottoman mustache ate garbanzo beans and pistachios from paper cones. I was shocked at the number of women wearing the turban, the traditional black veil pinned under their chins.

Constantinople, where imperial Rome survived until the fifteenth century, was the most prosperous capital in ancient history. From Blaquerna Palace, on the shores of the Marmara Sea, the Byzantine emperors governed a territory that stretched from Spain to the Near East, passing through northern Africa and the Balkans. They say that in Constantinople you could hear all the languages of the globe. Recent excavations showed that in Justinian and Theodora's time there were more than

160 bathhouses lining the streets. As I traveled down its streets that day, all I saw was an impoverished, backward city.

If Vatican City was the center of the Catholic world, splendid in its beauty, magnificence, and riches, then the center of the Orthodox world was that humble Patriarchate of Constantinople, located in a poor neighborhood in an extremely nationalistic suburb of Istanbul. Growing traditionalist aggressions had forced the patriarchate to build a protective stucco wall around itself that barely fulfilled its function. Who would have thought that, after fifteen hundred years of glory and power, such an important Christian throne would end in such a deplorable state?

The Turkish police parked at the entrance to the Fhanar and waited. The embassy's car crossed the central plaza and braked at the front steps of one of the humble buildings that made up the ancient patriarchate. The elderly Father Kallistos, secretary to the patriarch, came out to greet us and to accompany us to Bartolemeos I's offices, where he said many people had been waiting for us since dawn.

The office of His Most Divine Holiness was a meeting room. Sunlight streamed in through a pair of huge windows that looked out on the patriarchal Church of Saint George. The ancient symbols of power, the imperial eagle and crown, were everywhere: woven into the designs of the rugs and tapestries on the floors and walls, carved into the beautiful engravings in the tables and chairs, depicted in the paintings and art work that covered every surface. His Most Divine Holiness was a rather tall man of around sixty who hid behind an extremely long, snow-white beard. He was dressed as a simple Orthodox pope, with a habit and black cap dating from the time of the Medicis. He wore enormous glasses—they seemed to slide down his nose at will—yet he emanated such dignity that I felt I was in the company of a long-gone Byzantine emperor.

Next to the patriarch was the Vatican nuncio, Monsignor John Lawrence Lewis, dressed as a clergyman. He rushed over to welcome us and to start the introductions. Monsignor Lewis bore a surprising resemblance to the Duke of Edinburgh, Queen Elizabeth's husband. He was just as tall and thin, equally ceremonial, and on top of it all, just as big-eared. I stared at him, trying not to laugh. A female voice wrenched me from my reflections.

"Ottavia, dear, don't you remember me?"

I didn't recognize the woman who approached me just as Monsignor Lewis was introducing us to the patriarch. She was one of those women who, having crossed the threshold of middle age, becomes scandalously flashy with excessive makeup and jewelry. Her light brown hair cascaded onto her shoulders, and she was wearing an elegant light-blue suit jacket and a miniskirt.

"No, I'm sorry." I was sure I'd never seen her before. "Do I know you?"

"Ottavia, it's me, Doria!"

"Doria?" I stammered. A vague memory, the hazy faces of the Sciarra sisters started to emerge. "Doria Sciarra? Concetta's sister?"

"Ottavia!" she exclaimed, happy I'd finally recognized her, throwing her arms around me and giving me a big hug (careful not to mess up her makeup). "Isn't this great, Ottavia? How long has it been? Ten, fifteen years?"

"Twenty," I said with disgust.

How short they seemed at that moment! Doria Sciarra was the one person in the world I couldn't stand, that vain little girl who sowed discord everywhere she went and ruined everything without the slightest thought. I knew she was not fond of me either, so I didn't understand why she was making all that fuss. I could foresee that she was about to cloud my mood for the rest of the day.

"Why! Isn't this marvelous?" she said, dreamily. She was as phony as a Barbie doll. "Who would have guessed? Life takes such amazing turns!" She emitted some childish, singsong giggles.

That girl who was once as big as a house and as brunette as burnt wheat now flaunted a borderline anorexic body and a golden mane of hair. I remembered my family saying that "we have some problems with the Sciarra family," that they were invading our markets and waging a dirty war.

"I am so sorry about your father and brother, Ottavia. Concetta told me a few weeks ago. How's your mother?"

I was on the verge of answering her rudely, but I contained myself. "I'm sure you can imagine…"

"It's terrible. You don't know how I suffered two years ago when my father died. It was frightening."

"What're you doing here, Doria?" I cut her off in what must have been a curt tone of voice, because she looked at me surprised.

"Monsignor Lewis asked me to help out. I'm the cultural attaché to the Italian embassy here in Turkey. I accompanied the monsignor from Ankara to lend a hand."

What next! Doria was "the expert on Byzantine archeology" the nuncio offered us? She undoubtedly was well-informed of our mission. Great.

"Old friends reunited, right?" the monsignor said, appearing suddenly at our side. "What a stroke of luck to have your friend, Doria, help us out with this project, Sister Salina; even the Turks ask for her advice!"

"Not as much as they should, Monsignor," Doria said in a mellifluous voice of reproach. "Byzantine architecture is more a nuisance to them than a marvel worthy of conservation."

Monsignor Lewis turned a deaf ear to Doria's troublesome words. He took me by the arm and whisked me over to His Most Divine Holiness Bartolomeos I, who extended his pastoral ring for me to kiss. I genuflected lightly and brought my lips to the jewel, asking myself how long I would have to tolerate the presence of "my old friend." It got worse when I turned to look for my companions and was struck by the image of Doria talking to Farag, eating him up with her eyes. He was so stupid that he didn't even pick up on that harpy's carnivorous attitude, and simply smiled at her innuendos. A bitter, bilious poison filled my stomach and heart.

Seated around a big rectangular table with the patriarch's coat of arms (a gilded Greek cross in a purple circle) engraved in its center, we held a meeting that lasted well past the dinner hour. His Holiness Bartolemeos, in a halting tone that he unconsciously marked with his right hand, explained that the Church of the Holy Apostles was erected by Emperor Constantine in the fourth century with the idea of converting it into a family mausoleum. The emperor died in Nicomedia in 337 and his body was brought to Constantinople years later and inhumed in the *Apostoleion*. His son and successor, Constancio, brought the relics of Saint Luke the Evangelist, Saint Andrew the Apostle, and Saint Timothy to the church.

Doria cut the patriarch short to say that two centuries later, during Justinian and Theodora's reign, the temple was completely rebuilt by the famous architects Isidoro de Mileto and Antemio de Talles. After that learned interruption, Doria had nothing more to add.

The patriarch went on to explain that until the eleventh century, many emperors, patriarchs, and bishops were buried there. The faithful flocked there to venerate the important remains of martyrs, saints, and priests. After the *Apostoleion* was destroyed, those relics traveled from one site to another over the centuries, until they ended up in the nearby patriarchal church.

"Except of course," His Holiness said very slowly, "the ones the crusaders stole in the thirteenth century: relics, gold and silver goblets with precious stones, icons, imperial crosses, vestments trimmed with jewels. Today most of them are in Rome and in Saint Mark's Church in Venice. The historian Nicetas Chroniates confirms that the Latins also profaned the emperors' tombs."

"After similar misfortunes and an earthquake in 1328," added Doria, looking as if she'd been personally offended by his comments about Latins, "the *Apostoleion* had to be rebuilt. At the end of the thirteenth century, Emperor Andronicus II Paleologo ordered its restoration, but he never returned to see it. Plundered of its relics and objects of worth, it was abandoned and forgotten until the fall of Constantinople in the middle of the fifteenth century. In 1461 Mehemet II ordered its demolition, and in its place he built his own mausoleum, the Mosque of the Conqueror, or Fatih Camii."

At the other side of the table, the captain was growing more impatient by the second. Farag, however, seemed enchanted with the Doria's exposition, nodding when she was speaking and smiling like a fool when she looked at him.

"Could you comment on what the church looked like?" asked the Rock, stabbing straight into the heart of the matter.

Doria opened a notebook in front of her and passed around some large illustrations.

"The basilica was laid out in the shape of a Greek cross. It had five enormous blue cupolas—one at each end of the four arms, and another gigantic one in the center. Directly under that was the altar made entirely of silver and covered by a pyramid-shape marble ciborium. Columns lined the interior walls, forming a gallery on the upper floor called *cute-chumena*, accessible only by a spiral staircase."

"If there is nothing left of the church, how do you know all that?" The Rock at times was marvelously suspicious. I felt indebted to him for questioning Doria's knowledge. At that point, the first of the illustrations reached me. It was a virtual reconstruction of the *Apostoleion*, in black and white, showing its five cupolas and numerous windows the length and width of the walls.

"Why, Captain!" Doria protested in a delightfully witty timbre. "Do you want me to list my sources?"

"Yes, I do," grumbled Glauser-Roist.

"Well, to start with, today there are two churches that were constructed in imitation of the *Apostoleion*: Saint Mark's in Venice, and Saint-Front, in Perigeus, France. We also have descriptions by Eusebio, Philostorgio, Procopio, and Teodoro Anagnostes. And there is a long poem from the tenth century called *Description of the Apostles' Building*, composed by one Constantine of Rhodes in honor of Emperor Constantine VII Porphyrogenite."

"Of course," I cut her off, "this emperor wrote a magnificent treatise on the norms of court behavior. That manual was adopted by the European courts at the end of the Middle Ages. Have you read it, Doria?"

"No," she said softly, "I haven't had the opportunity."

"Well, read it when you get the chance. It's very interesting."

I suspected her illustrious knowledge on Byzantium was limited to architecture. Her cultural knowledge wasn't as broad as she wanted us to believe.

"Of course, Ottavia. Returning to the matter at hand," she said, ignoring me completely from then on, "I should tell you, Captain, I have many sources at my disposal, although it would be tedious to list them all. If you wish, I would be delighted to pass my notes along to you."

The Rock rejected her offer with a brusque monosyllable and sank down in his seat.

"Tell us about the location, Doria, please," Farag requested, smiling, as he leaned over the table, his hands crossed, like a fawning scholar.

"My location?" said the twerp with a smile, not taking her eyes off him.

Farag grinned very easily at her joke. "No, no, of course not! The *Apostoleion*'s location."

"Ah!" she said with a flirtatious smile. "Of course."

I felt like getting up and killing her, but I controlled myself.

"Based on what we know, Constantine the Great ordered his mausoleum built on the highest hill in Constantinople. The primitive Church of the Holy Apostles was erected around this circular building. Over the centuries, the church was expanded until it reached the same dimensions as Saint Sofia. After that, it fell into a decline. Mehemet II left nothing when he razed his mosque."

"Can we visit Fatih Camii?" the Rock asked.

"Naturally," responded the patriarch. "But you mustn't disturb the Muslim faithful. You would be expelled without a second thought."

"Can women also enter?" I asked. I wasn't well versed on Islamic customs.

"Yes," Doria answered quickly, with charming smile, "but only in certain areas. I'll be accompanying you, Ottavia."

I looked at the captain out of the corner of my eye; he responded with a slight shrug that meant, We can't avoid it. If she wants to come, so be it.

The second illustration reached me just then. In a sumptuous Byzantine illumination, you could clearly see the golds and reds of the cupolas and the walls, just as they must have been at the church's moment of greatest splendor. Inside, as tall as the columns and the walls, Mary and the twelve apostles contemplated the ascension of Jesus to the heavens. I couldn't help an admiring exclamation.

"What a charming miniature!"

"Well, it's yours, Ottavia," replied Doria, sarcastically. "It belongs to a Byzantine codex from 1162. You'll find it in the Vatican Library."

It wasn't worth answering her. If she wanted me to feel responsible for the historic ravages made by the Catholic Church, she could always try.

"Let's recap," answered Glauser-Röist, thrusting forward in his chair as he smoothed his elegant but wrinkled jacket. "Here's a city known as the richest, most splendid in the ancient world, with untold riches and treasures. In this city we must purge ourselves of greed, who knows how. We must do it in a church that was dedicated to the apostles but which no longer exists. Do I have it right?"

"You're exactly right, Kaspar," Farag said, rubbing his beard.

"When do you wish to visit Fatih Camii?" inquired Monsignor Lewis.

"Immediately," the Rock answered. "Unless the doctor and Professor Boswell need to know anything else."

We both gently shook our heads.

"Fine. Then let's go."

"But, Captain!" said Doria in her phony singsong voice. "It's lunchtime! Professor Boswell, wouldn't you agree we should have something to eat before we go?"

I was seriously thinking about killing her.

"Please, Doria, call me Farag."

My insides churned, tearing me into microscopic, venomous fragments. What exactly was going on here?

Dragging my soul behind me, I walked alongside Father Kallistos to the patriarchate's dining room, where a couple of old Greek women, their heads covered in Turkish style, served us a meal I barely tasted. Doria was sitting to my right, between Farag and me. I had to put up with her absurd prattle. I think that's what took away my appetite; but so as not to call attention to my distress, I ate some fish and a bit of stuffed vegetables with spicy pasta that reminded me of the tasty Sicilian *caponatina*. For dessert, the patriarch devoured three or four small milk puddings as white as his skin. Everyone followed his example, except me. I preferred a soft junket of goat's milk to calm my unsettled indigestion.

During coffee, Doria pried herself away from Farag and started up a conversation with me. While the men discussed the Staurofilakes' strange behavior and their incredible history and organization, my "friend" dove into a subject I would've rather avoided: our distant childhood memories. Her insatiable curiosity about the members of my family surprised me. She seemed to know a lot about them, but she always lacked some detail to complete the puzzle. At last, bored with her obsessive questions, I rudely took a big leap in the conversation.

"How is it, Doria, that you live in Turkey yet stay so up on what we Salinas are doing in Palermo?"

"Concetta talks a lot about you all on the phone."

"Why is that, with all the tension between our families right now?"

"Well, Ottavia," she said sweetly, "we Sciarra girls don't hold a grudge. Our father's death pained us a lot, but we've forgiven you all for it."

"Forgive me, Doria, but you're saying foolish things. What are you talking about? Why do you need to forgive us for your father's death?"

"Concetta always says your mother was wrong to hide your family's business from you, Pierantonio, and Lucia. You know nothing about it, do you, Ottavia?"

Her candid look and that sibylline smile showed she was ready to tell all. I gulped down some coffee in order to steady my nerves. I don't know what got into me, but when I finished, I shot back one of my mother's habitual sentences: *"Passu longu e vucca curta,* Doria."*

"Come now!" she said, surprised. "You know perfectly well what I'm talking about!"

---

* "Long step and short mouth." Motto of the *Omerta*, the code of honor of the Sicilian Mafia. With this phrase the mafiosi reminded each other of the famous "Law of Silence."

I looked at her in astonishment. "I asked you to stop!"

"Oh, come on, Ottavia, don't act like a little girl! You can't ignore that your father was a *campieri!*"

I couldn't believe my ears. "My father wasn't a *campieri!** You're insulting the Salinas' memory and good name!"

"Well," she sighed. "There's nothing sadder than a blind man who will not see. Anyway, Pierantonio knows the truth."

"Doria, you've always been a bit odd, but with this, I can say you've finally gone nuts. I'm not going to allow you to insult my family."

"The Salinas of Palermo?" she asked, surprised. "Who own Cinisi, the most important construction business in Sicily? Who are the only shareholders of Chiementin and have exclusive control over the million-dollar cement business? Who own the stone quarries in Biliemi that provide the stone for all public buildings? Who own every share of the Bank of Sicily that launders dirty drug and prostitution money? Who own nearly all the productive lands on the island? Who control the fleet of trucks, the distribution networks, and the 'security' of the businessmen and vendors? Are you referring to the Salinas of Palermo?"

"We are businessmen!"

"Sure, dear! Well, so are the Sciarra of Catania! The problem is that in Sicily there are 184 mafia clans organized into just two families: the Sciarras and the Salinas. 'The double S,' the antimafia authorities call us. My father, Bernardo Sciarra, was the don of the island for twenty years, until your father, a loyal *campieri* who never caused any trouble, slowly took over and killed off the most prominent capos."

"You're crazy, Doria. I beg you, for the love of God, stop."

"Don't you want to know how your father killed the great Bernardo Sciarra and how he got control of the capos and *campieris* faithful to my family?"

"Shut up, Doria!"

"Well, you see, Ottavia, he used exactly the same method we used to terminate your father and your brother Giuseppe: a supposed traffic accident."

---

* In the terminology of the Cosa Nostra, a rural mafioso.

I was dumbfounded.

"My brother has four children. How could you do something like that?"

"You still don't get it, dear. We're the Mafia, the Cosa Nostra! Our great-grandfathers were mafiosi. We kill, control governments, plant bombs, shoot off Luparas,* and respect the *Omerta*. No one can bypass the rules and ignore the vendetta. And you want to know the funniest part?"

As I listened to her, I clenched my jaws so tight they ached. I tried to breathe and hold back my tears, while contracting the muscles in my face until there was a grimace of pain on it. That seemed to delight her; she smiled like a happy child on her birthday. My entire life was crumbling. I closed my eyes, they were hurting so bad, and the knot in my throat was choking me. Doria was malignant, she was perversity incarnate, but maybe I deserved all that. Maybe I had closed myself up in the dreamworld of the church so I didn't have to accept reality. I shut myself away so nothing could hurt me. And in the end, it had done me no good.

"The funniest part is that your father never could stomach being a don. He was a *campieri;* he liked being a *campieri.* Behind him was someone who *did* have the strength and ambition to start a turf war. Do you know who I'm talking about, Ottavia, dear? No? I'm talking about your mother, my friend, your mother—Filippa Zafferano, who now is the acting don of Sicily!"

She broke out in happy cackle, throwing up her hands to show how funny that was. I looked at her without blinking, without erasing the sad look on my face, without doing anything except swallow my tears and purse my lips.

"Filippa, your mother, feels strong and safe in Villa Salina. Tell her to stay inside and not come out, because there are many dangers." As much as I didn't want to believe her, I realized it was a clear threat.

That said, she turned back to Farag, who was talking with His Most

---

* Sawed-off double-barrel shotguns that use bird shot as ammunition.

Divine Holiness. My entire body was paralyzed, almost lifeless. My head, on the other hand, was a whirlwind of thought. Now I understood why they sent Pierantonio, Lucia, and me away to boarding school when we were so young. Now I understood why my mother never allowed the three of us to take part in certain family matters. Now I understood why she had always encouraged us to stay as far away from home as possible and to devote ourselves so completely to the church. It all fit so perfectly. The puzzle of my life was now in place; the picture complete. My mother had selected us to be her counterweight, her spiritual and earthly guarantee. Pierantonio, Lucia, and I were her jewels, her works of art, her justification. To my mother's old-fashioned way of thought, that absurd, compensatory view of the world fit perfectly. It wasn't so bad that the Salinas were Mafia if the three of us were near God, praying for the rest, occupying positions of responsibility or prestige within the church, as a way to expunge our name. Yes, it all made perfect sense. Suddenly, the great respect and admiration I'd always felt for her transformed into immense pain in the face of the enormity of her sins. I wanted to call her and talk to her, ask her to explain why she had acted so, why she had lied to Pierantonio, Lucia, and me all our lives. Why she used my father as an instrument of her greed. Why she let her other six children—now just five, with Giuseppe dead—kill, extort, and rob. Why she allowed her grandchildren, whom she said she loved, to grow up in that environment. Even now, she wanted to head an organization that went against the laws of God and mankind. Nonetheless, I knew I couldn't ask her for those explanations. If I did, she would probably quickly figure out how I'd learned the truth, and the war between the Salinas and the Sciarras would leave too many dead in Sicily's gutters. The time for deceit had passed. I had to acknowledge that I wasn't as innocent as she would have liked. Neither was Pierantonio; after all, his dirty dealings inside the church simply followed a family tradition. Good Lucia wasn't much better, always on the fringe, so detached and naïve. The three of us blissfully lived a lie in which our family was like a fairy tale, a perfect family with its closets filled with corpses.

I was so absorbed in my thoughts I didn't hear Captain Glauser-Röist calling me, but I got to my feet like a robot. Farag and Doria's infatuation didn't matter. Nothing could be more painful than what I was feeling. I didn't care if they stayed together for the rest of their lives. My mind was going from the past to the present, from the present to the past, tying up loose ends and merging lost threads into one. Everything in my life took on a new color.

Suddenly I felt very alone, as if the entire world had emptied of people, as if my ties with life had unraveled. My brothers and sisters had lied to me, too. They all had kept quiet and played the game my mother decreed. They weren't the siblings I thought they were. We didn't form that indivisible group we were so proud of. In fact, Giuseppe and Filippa's real children were those five living in Sicily; they were the ones who were part of the family business. We three who lived apart were deceived, detached from the daily reality of the household. Giuseppe—may he rest in peace—Giaconda, Cesare, Pierluigi, Salvatore, and Agueda must have always felt we were marginalized or perhaps that we were privileged. The trust among the nine siblings had always been a sham: Three were destined for the *church;* the other six shared the fortune and disgrace, the truth and fiction. They lied because their mother ordered them to. And Father? What was Father's role in all that? At that moment, I understood that my father was only a *campieri,* a simple *campieri* who liked his hateful work and gave in to the orders of his wife, the great Filippa Zafferano. Everything fell into place. It was so simple.

"Dr. Salina? Are you feeling alright?"

Family images were erased from my mind, and out of the fog emerged the Rock's face. We were in the vestibule of the patriarchate and I had no idea how I'd gotten there. I'd seen the captain every day for the last three months, but he suddenly looked like a total stranger, like Doria before she told me her name. I knew I knew her, but her face gave me no clue to her identity. Parts of my brain had short-circuited and weren't functioning. I was feeling completely lost.

"Dr. Salina, please." He shook me by my arms. "What's going on with you?"

"I need to call home."

"You need to do what? Everyone's in the car, waiting for you."

"I need to call home," I repeated mechanically, as I noticed how my eyes were flooding with tears. "Please, please..."

Glauser-Röist observed me for a couple of tense seconds. He must have concluded that things would go faster if he let me call than wait for my distress to pass or argue with me. He turned me loose suddenly, went over to Father Kallistos and the patriarch, on the other side of the glass doors, and explained that we needed to call Italy. They exchanged a few words; then the captain returned to my side, somewhat annoyed.

"You can call from the phone in that office over there. Be careful what you say. The lines are bugged by the Turkish government."

I didn't care. All I wanted was to hear my mother's voice to end once and for all that hateful feeling of abandonment and solitude that was at that moment twisting my soul. Something told me that if I talked to her, even for just a minute, I would be able to come to my senses and get my feet back on the ground. I closed the door, picked up the phone, dialed home to Sicily, and waited for the phone on the other end to ring.

Matteo answered—the most serious and laconic of my nephews, one of Giuseppe and Rosalia's children. As usual, he didn't show the slightest joy at hearing my voice. I asked him to pass the phone to his grandmother, and he told me to wait; apparently she was busy. I suddenly realized even the children were involved. I'm sure they'd been told thousands of times not to explain what anyone was doing when Uncle Pierantonio, Aunt Lucia, or Aunt Ottavia called. When we were around, they shouldn't ask questions or comment about this or that. Once again I felt the vertigo of the hypocrisy, the solitude, and that strange feeling of abandonment eating me up inside.

"Is that you, Ottavia?" My mother's voice sounded delighted to get my call. "How are you, dear? Where are you?"

"Hi, Mom." It was difficult to wrench my voice out of my body.

"Pierantonio told me you spent a few days with him in Jerusalem!"

"Yes."

"How was he? Okay?"

"Yes, Mom," I said, trying to feign a happy tone of voice.

My mother laughed. "Well, well. How about you? You haven't told me where you are!"

"Right, Mom. I'm in Istanbul, in Turkey. Listen, Mom, I've been thinking... I wanted to tell you... You see, Mom, when this is all over, I'll probably quit my job at the Vatican."

I don't know why I said that. I hadn't even been thinking about it. Maybe I just wanted to hurt her, return part of my pain. There was silence on the other end.

"Is that so?" she finally asked, an icy edge to her voice.

How could I explain it to her? It was such an absurd idea, sheer lunacy. However, at that particular moment, leaving the Vatican represented freedom to me.

"I'm tired, Mom. I think a retreat to one of the houses my order owns in the country would do me good. There's one in Connaught, Ireland, where I could take over the archives of several libraries in the area. I need peace, Mom—peace, silence, and a lot of prayer."

It took her several seconds to react. When she did, she took a very disparaging tone. "Come on, Ottavia, that's nonsense! You aren't going to quit your job at the Vatican. Are you trying to upset me? Now, when I have so many other problems? Your father's and brother's deaths are still very fresh. Why do you tell me these things? Well, that's enough. Let's not talk about this any more. You're not leaving the Vatican."

"What if I did, Mom? I think the decision is mine."

It was my decision, no doubt, but it also was an issue for my mother.

"Enough! Are you determined to upset me? What's the matter, Ottavia?"

"Nothing really, Mom."

"Then come on, get to work. Don't think about this foolishness any more. Call me another day, okay, dear? You know how much I love hearing from you."

When I got in the car, my feet were firmly anchored to the ground again. I knew I wouldn't forget the matter for a second, because my mind was functioning in obsessive spurts. But at least I could face my current situation without losing my mind. As much as it pained me, as much as I rejected the idea, it was inevitable: I would never be the same. A painful fracture had occurred in my life; a fissure split me into two irreconcilable parts and distanced me from my roots forever.

*T*he car we took to the Fatih Camii wasn't from the Vatican enunciator. To be discreet, Monsignor Lewis and the captain thought it best to take an unmarked car from the patriarchate. Only Doria came along to drive us; she sped down the Horn of Gold and Atatürk Boulevard. The Mosque of the Conqueror loomed suddenly at the far end of the Boxdogan Kemeri (the Aqueduct of the Brave)—enormous, solid, and austere, with very high minarets covered with balconies and a large central cupola encircled by a large number of semicupolas. Bordered by madrassas, it looked down on the faithful coming and going across the esplanade in front.

Doria and I didn't say a word to each other during the entire trip. She parked in front of an apartment building at the far end of the plaza, from where we walked to the entrance like any prowling tourists. Farag lagged farther and farther behind until he was at my side, abandoning Doria to the captain. I didn't have the strength to deal with him, so I walked faster and caught up with the Rock. Because of his standoffishness, he was the only one sure to leave me in peace. I didn't feel like talking to anyone.

We crossed the threshold and found ourselves in a large, covered patio with trees and a central shrine that looked like a newspaper kiosk but was actually a fountain used for ablutions. The atrium columns were colossal, and it struck me that, despite being a Muslim building, the entire complex had a distinct neoclassical look. This initial impression disappeared completely when we took off our shoes and went inside. Doria and I also covered ourselves up in long black veils given to us by the old doorman whose charge it was to oversee the morality of the infidel tourists. I held my breath before such splendor. Mehemet II had constructed a mausoleum truly worthy of the conqueror of Constantinople. Covering the floor were gorgeous red rugs that compared favorably to Saint Peter's in the Vatican. Brightly colored stained-glass windows were wisely placed in the cupola's domes and in the niches of the three cupolas. A powerful, horizontal light filtered in through those windows and filled the space. The arches and domes stood out, accented by their showy red and white voussoirs. On each pendentive, large or small, was an eye-catching blue medallion containing luminous inscriptions from the Koran. A web of cables held up a multitude of gold and silver lamps.

The women's galleries were located on the first floor. I was afraid the doorman would force us to stay there while Farag and the captain looked around. Fortunately, he didn't. Doria and I moved around the mosque as we pleased. Apparently, foreign female tourists enjoy privileges Muslim women don't.

For more than an hour we wandered high and low, inspecting absolutely everything. We started with the *qibla*, the temple wall that faced Mecca. At its center, carved into the stone, was the *mihrab*, the most sacred spot in the building, a recess that pointed in the exact direction of Mecca. It was much more difficult to examine the *maxura*, which was near the *qiba*, the imam's pulpit. After that, we split up and Farag studied the numerous hanging lamps with immense patience. I examined each and every one of the columns on the three floors, including the women's gallery. The captain, clutching his utility backpack as if it were made of gold, analyzed the motifs woven into the huge rugs and benches and every piece of wood, as well as the plain sarcophagus that held the remains of Mehemet II. Doria looked over the stained-glass windows and doors. The only thing we didn't do was pry the flagstones from the floor.

By the time we finished our inspection, the conqueror's mosque was practically empty of worshippers except for a few old men dozing next to the pillars. But that silence was none other than the calm before the storm. The muezzin's call to prayer over the loudspeakers startled us, and we looked at each other, disconcerted. The captain motioned for us to join him at the door and leave at once. We barely had time to regroup. Surging in waves, out of nowhere, hundreds of the faithful entered the temple, arranging themselves in orderly, parallel rows for the midday prayer.

"It's the *adhan*, the call to prayer," Doria said. Of course, the human tide had somehow pushed her against Farag.

"*La ilah illa Allah wa Muhammad rasul Allah*," the muezzin's amplified voice shouted over and over. "There is no other God but Allah and Mohammed is his prophet."

"Let's get out of here," the Rock said, using his body as a battering ram to make way through the current.

With great difficulty, we managed to get to the open-air patio, the *sahn*, just in time—for right before we could retrieve our shoes, the mosque was completely full.

"Tomorrow's another day," Farag said cheerfully, looking around with a smile.

"Let's go," Doria said. "I'll take you to the hotel so you can rest. I'll call Monsignor Lewis and have them bring your luggage from the airport."

"Is it still on the plane?" I asked, surprised. I immediately regretted having directed a comment to her, even a simple question.

"I had them leave our bags on the plane," Glauser-Röist explained, "in case we solved the test today."

"I'm afraid that won't be possible, Kaspar."

"If you like," Doria continued, flashing her brightest smile as she took the veil off her hair, "tonight I'll take you to dinner at one of the best places in Istanbul. It's a very fun place where you can see a real belly dance."

"Before we leave, we should examine this patio," I cut her off, ill-humored.

What a strange lot we were that day... The only link between us was the Rock, who had no idea what was really going on.

"But right now they're praying!" Doria protested. "We may upset the worshippers. Better wait until tomorrow."

Glauser-Röist looked at her. "No, the doctor is right. Let's examine this place. If we do so discreetly, we won't bother anyone."

"Someone should keep an eye on the doorman," proposed Farag. "He hasn't taken his eyes off us."

"He could be the Staurofilax watching over the test," I said ironically.

Stupid Doria whipped around to look at him. "Really?" she nearly shouted. "A Staurofilax!"

"Doria, please!" I scolded her. "This isn't a game! Stop looking at him!"

The elderly doorman, with a thin beard, his head covered by a white cap that looked like an eggshell, frowned and glared at us.

"Doria, go over there," the Rock ordered. "Talk to him, put your veil back on, and distract him as much as you can."

With a wicked smile on my lips, I handed Doria my turban and stayed with Farag and the captain.

"Let's split up," Glauser-Röist said as soon as Doria was far enough away. "Let's each examine a third of the patio. Doctor, don't go near the fountain of ablutions. You could set off a revolution. We'll take that part."

They left me alone and headed for the *sabial*. The section I was assigned to, at the extreme left of the enclosure, had nothing of interest. The ground was stone and the trees had slender trunks. There was nothing unusual about the walls separating the enclosure from the street. Poking around lazily under the portico, I amused myself by watching Doria throw herself into conversation with the doorman. The old man looked at her as if she were an idiot—which she was—or the devil incarnate, and looked ready to throw her out with loud, reverberating shouts. I'd love to know what foolishness she was saying to the poor man to make him contort his face in such an annoyed manner.

I didn't have time to figure it out. Farag grabbed me by the arm and forced me to turn toward him. With an enchanting smile, he cut his eyes in the captain's direction.

"We found it," he whispered, still smiling. "Let's hurry."

Walking calmly, we headed for the side of the *sabial* where Glauser-Röist was standing.

"What did you find?" I asked, smiling, as we approached.

"A Constantine chrismon."

"In a Moslem fountain for ablutions? That's impossible."

Before the five daily prayers proscribed by the Koran, Muslims must go through a complex ritual of ablutions, washing their face, ears, hair, hands, arms up to their elbows, ankles, and feet. All mosques have a fountain at the entrance where the faithful must pass through before entering the *haram,* or prayer room.

"It's perfectly hidden," Farag explained to me. "It's like a jigsaw puzzle whose pieces have been scattered on the bottom of the fountain."

"On the bottom of the fountain?"

"There're twelve water spigots, and the water falls into a stone drain whose bottom contains the pieces of our chrismon. That means the clue is in the *sabial.* The captain is still investigating. We have to hurry. Doria can't keep the doorman busy forever. Look quickly and move away as soon as you can."

I followed Farag's instructions to the letter, exchanging a knowing look with the captain as soon as I got close enough. Their assessment was right. At the center of the fountain was a stone cylinder from which twelve copper spigots jutted up. Under them was a drain a little less than a meter wide, surrounded by a small parapet. At the bottom, nearly obfuscated by the dirty water, one could see the stone ashlars with worn down reliefs on which one could perfectly make out the disconnected parts of a Constantine chrismon.

Even though I'd been warned about being near the *sabial,* I turned one of the spigots without thinking. Although I didn't cause any cosmic cataclysm, it gave me an idea. I took off my shoes before Farag's and the captain's horrified eyes, and climbed into the drain to see if what we had to do was step on the stones. Obviously, nothing happened. But since the stones were very slippery, as I was getting out, I slipped and bumped against the spigot's head. The curious thing was that the spigot turned upside down but didn't break. There I found a spring that proved we were onto something. When Farag and the captain saw the spring, they followed my lead and got into the drain, shoes and all, turning all the spigots like crazy. No more than a minute could have passed from the time I got in the water until we had twisted all twelve faucets and the ground opened up under our feet.

The twelve stones at the bottom of the fountain gave way under our weight, dropping us into a void. As we were sinking, we saw the light grow faint and then disappear. At any other moment of my life (like when we fell from the crypt of Saint Mary in Cosmedin into the Cloaca Maxima) I would have screamed like a crazy woman, my arms flailing, trying to grab on to anything I could. But here, in the fifth circle of Purgatory, I knew anything was possible, and I wasn't the least bit afraid. I plunged with a great splash into a deep pool of water that received me gently. The only thing that startled me was how freezing cold the water was. I held the air in my lungs, and when I stopped sinking, I kicked my feet to push myself to the surface. Besides smelling awful, that place was as dark and ominous as the inside of a wolf's mouth. Next to me, I heard splashes.

"Farag? Captain?" My voice echoed back to me many times over.

"Ottavia!" shouted Farag, from my right. "Ottavia! Where are you?"

I heard another splash next to me. "Captain?"

"Damn it! Damn all those Staurofilakes!" Glauser-Röist roared. "My clothes are soaking wet!"

I couldn't help laughing as I tread water. "That's just great! What are we to do, Captain? Your clothes are wet! What a catastrophe!"

"What a terrible shame!" panted Farag.

"Laugh all you want! I'm fed up with these guys!"

"Ah, well, I'm not," I said.

At that moment, the Rock turned on his flashlight.

"Where are we?" Farag asked. When the light went on, we saw that we were in a stone tank filled with murky water.

The good thing about living through adventures like this one and being submerged in water used to wash hundreds of sweaty feet is that the problems of daily life, the really painful ones, fade and disappear. Immediate concerns use up all of our physical and psychological resources. In this case our immediate concern was to keep from vomiting, trying not to think too much about the infections such filth could cause to the wounds on our feet and in our tattoos.

"It's a kind of Sargasso Sea. Instead of algae, there are fungi," I said.

Farag burst out laughing.

"Doctor, please! Stop saying such disgusting things!" the Rock thundered. "Let's look for a way out, quickly!"

"Then shine the flashlight on the walls. Let's see if we can make anything out."

The cistern's stone walls were covered with large blotches of black moss, separated by thick lines of filth that showed the different heights the water had risen to over the last five hundred or a thousand years. Apart from the humidity and the layer of vegetation, we didn't see anything to help us scale the walls. On the other hand, the distance to the *sabial's* drain was so great it was impossible to reach it. If there were a way out, it had to be below us.

"We've purged more than greed," Farag murmured. "We'll purge our pride with this humility bath."

"We're not done yet, Professor," pronounced the Rock.

"We have only one flashlight," I said, starting to notice the fatigue in my legs. "So if we're going to dive, we have to do it together."

"No, Doctor, we have three flashlights. Hold on a moment, and I'll give you yours."

He searched in his wet backpack and took it out with great difficulty. Then he handed another one to Farag. In all that light, that place wasn't so disgusting as it was sinister. I didn't want to think about it too much, because the whole episode made me gag. I wasn't about to add more filth to the water.

"Ready?" the Rock asked. Without hesitating, he took a breath, puffed out his cheeks, and sank into that soup.

"Let's go, Ottavia," Farag urged me, looking at me with smiling eyes, the same goofy way he'd been looking at Doria all day. If he was trying to bring us closer together, he was tangling with the most stubborn person in the world. Not saying a word or turning around to acknowledge what he said, I filled my lungs with the infected air in the cistern and submerged myself in pursuit of the captain. The water was so muddy that Glauser-Röist's light was barely visible a few meters below. Farag followed me, lighting up the inner walls of the tank. There was nothing to see except for the large branches of white moss that seemed to wave as we passed by.

I was the first to run out of air, so I had to ascend. I breathed such large mouthfuls of air after I broke the surface that I didn't even notice the smell. After a while, each of us flipped over and started the ascent; but throughout our successive immersions, we descended much faster because we had grown familiar with where we were swimming. Although the water got colder and colder, the sensation of gently glid-ing, head first, in complete silence was wonderful, absolutely wonderful. Then Farag accidentally bumped into me and his legs pressed against mine for a few seconds. He looked amused when he shined his flashlight on us, but I remained as serious as possible, though against my will I clung to the way that slight contact had made the water feel a little warmer.

Finally, approximately fifteen meters deep, just about spent, with a terrible pressure in our ears, we discovered the enormous round mouth of a conduit. We surfaced to rest for a few minutes and breath, and then we dove quickly toward the mouth and swam into it. For a second I was worried that that conduit might not end before I ran out of air. Plus, I was trapped with the captain in front and Farag behind me. I prayed for help and focused on the Lord's Prayer to keep myself from nervously consuming what little oxygen I had left. Just when I thought my time had come, the conduit ended. Far above our heads, I made out a trans-parent surface through which light was visible. Feeling that my heart was about to explode, I threw myself upward, controlling the instinct to breathe. Finally, like a buoy leaping into the air, I flung more than half my body out of the water and gasped.

I was panting like a locomotive. It took me a while to gain control over my body, which was depleted by the cold. We found ourselves at the same level as in the cistern, but the landscape was completely different. There was a wide platform sloped toward the water like a stone beach that took up half the grotto. It was lit up by dozens of torches hanging on the walls. Without a doubt, the most extraordinary thing was the gigantic chrismon chiseled into the rock, outlined by torches that could be detected at the bottom.

"My God!" Farag said, deeply moved.

"It's like a cathedral dedicated to the Monogram of God," the captain observed.

"Look at the torches," I whispered. "They were clearly expecting us."

The silence of the place, broken only by the far-off crackle of a fire, overwhelmed us. We felt we were in a sacred enclosure, and started to swim very slowly toward the shore. Even barefoot, I was glad to have the ground under my feet again as I walked out of the water. I was so cold that the air in the grotto seemed warm. As I wrung out my skirt (I couldn't have picked a worst day to wear a skirt), I cast a distracted eye around the place. My heart stopped when I caught Farag watching me closely from a short distance away. His eyes glowed as if they were shooting fire. I tensed and turned my back but his image remained engraved on my retinas.

"Look!" the Rock exclaimed. "The entrance to a cave under the chrismon! After you, Doctor!"

"Why do I always have to lead the way?" I protested with a certain apprehension.

"Because you're such a brave woman," he added with a smile, to urge me on.

"I don't see it that way, Captain."

But I complied and set off down the path. Well past that entrance, the Staurofilakes' real test must be waiting for us. Walking carefully in bare feet, I wondered how Dante Alighieri would have solved the problem of the cistern. A serious, circumspect man like him would have been very angry after the tenth dunking in that disgusting water.

The distance to the cavern wasn't very far, about two or three hundred meters, but I remained ultra alert as I walked, for I felt that the Staurofilakes weren't ones to be trusted.

Finally we saw a light at the end of the walkway. When we reached the light, we saw an enormous circular space, a type of Roman circle, covered by a stone cupola high overhead. In the exact center of that space, a solitary sarcophagus of porphyry—blood red and big enough to hold an entire family—rested on four beautiful, life-size, white lions. Despite their frightful appearance, they seemed to be asking us to step up and examine them.

"What a place!" Farag declared. A deafening noise muted his words and made us suddenly turn 180 degrees, frightened. An iron gate had fallen from above, sealing off the cave.

"We're in a fix now," I exclaimed, indignant. "These people never let up."

"Stop complaining, Doctor. Focus on the task at hand."

Without realizing it, I looked at Farag, seeking his complicity. Suddenly the veil that had hidden my feelings lifted, and emotions rushed through me like an electric charge. Professor Boswell's hair was plastered to his face, his beard was wet, and his sunken eyes were ringed by a black halo that worried me. In spite of that, he looked very handsome. I felt as if I had loved him all my life, as if I'd always been at his side, hand in hand, glued to his body, fused to him. An inexplicable tremor shook me all over. How can certain mental images make the earth move? I'd never experienced anything like that. This can't go on, I told myself. I worried that I'd gone too far, confused ambition with vocation. Could I have called surrender and love what was just a job and a way of life? In the end, it would almost be better. Then that error would justify to my conscience what I was feeling for that handsome, intelligent man. At the same time it would excuse my hypothetical abandonment of my religious life... But what was I thinking? Hadn't I seen him fooling around all day with Doria Sciarra? I cast him a scornful look and turned my back just as he started to smile. He must have thought I'd gone crazy or that all this was an illusion. With a sharp pain in my heart, feeling like I was roasting over a slow fire, I walked toward the sarcophagus, with the Rock right behind me.

Lined around the circular marble floor were twelve strange, tubular cavities, all at the same height. If we weren't dealing with a Christian sect, I would've sworn they were sinister *bothroi*, openings in the wall where libations for the dead were poured and where victims were beheaded. They were not particularly large, and looked like the burrows of small, noxious animals, evenly spread out. On an arch over each cavity were strange engravings, which at first I didn't pay attention to. Hanging from iron holders, torches glittered between them.

The impressive lions that held up the large sarcophagus were chiseled in white marble. When I approached the bier, my astonishment increased. Not only were its sides wondrously engraved with incredible scenes, but all its adornments and inlays were pure gold. Even the two ring-shaped handles (as thick as my fist) that must have been used to move it were artfully decorated. The lions' claws, eyes, and teeth and the moldings on the cover were also made of gold, as were the laurel leaf design that framed the porphyry carvings. Without a doubt, this was a sarcophagus worthy of a king. Close up, the top, or *lauda*, above my head confirmed my suspicions. I examined the scene drawn on one of its sides; it was divided into two levels. On the lower level was a depiction of a crowd raising their hands imploring a central figure, who was dressed in Byzantine imperial clothes. This figure distributed handfuls of coins and was flanked by what looked like important court dignitaries and high-ranking functionaries.

I walked around to the feet of a bier and saw a medallion carved with the same imperial figure, on horseback, escorted by two much smaller figures wearing crowns, palms, and shields. Incredulous, I noticed a nimbus of saints encircling the emperor's head; and on their shields was the monogram of Constantine. Not accepting the crazy idea forming in my head, I kept circling to get to the other side. The scene was of a Christ Pantocrator seated on his throne. Before that throne, the monarch performed *proskinesis*, the traditional act of tribute to the Byzantine emperors in which one knelt down and touched his forehead to the ground, his hands extended in prayer. Again the figure had a halo encircling his head, and his features were the same as in the two previous scenes. It was clear that they all represented the same emperor, and that the remains of that emperor were in that stone vessel.

"Wow, this is incredible!" Farag said behind me. He let out a long, admiring whistle. "Do you know who this grouchy old winged Hercules is, Ottavia?"

"What are you talking about, Farag?" I replied, annoyed, turning to face him. Above one of the *bothroi*, the Hercules Farag spoke of blew blasts of air out his mouth as he held a young maiden in his arms.

"It's Boreas! Don't you recognize him? The personification of the cold north wind. See how he blows through the conch and how snow covers his hair."

"How can you be so sure?" I chided him. I got my answer when I read the sign underneath the figure: *Βορεας.* "Okay, don't tell me, I get it."

"Over there is Noto, I'm sure," he said, as he hurried over to check it out. "Noto, the warm, rainy wind of the south."

"So, each one of those twelve cavities has a wind above it," the Rock commented.

Actually, they were the twelve children of dreadful Eolo, worshiped in antiquity as gods, the most powerful manifestations of nature. To the Greeks, the winds were the divinities that changed the seasons and bestowed life. They formed clouds and caused storms, moved the seas and brought the rain. They also controlled the rays of the sun that warmed the earth or burned it. The Greeks believed that human beings would die if the wind didn't enter their bodies as breath. Life, for them, was thus completely dependent on these gods.

Going clockwise, in the first spot was the harsh, old North wind, exactly how Farag had described him. Next was Helespontio, symbolized by a storm; then Afeliotes, a full field of fruits and grain; on to beneficent Euro, "the good wind" of the east, "the one that flows well," who appeared as a completely bald, mature man; then Euronoto; next, Noto, the southern wind, represented as a young man, his wings dripping with dew; after that was Libanoto; then Libs, a smooth-skinned adolescent boy with puffed-out cheeks who carried an *aphlaston;** then young Zephyr, the west wind, who, along with his lover, Cloris the nymph, scattered flowers over his black *bothros;* then Argestes, depicted as a star; then Trascias, crowned with clouds; and, finally, the horrible Aparctias, with his heavily bearded face and furrowed brow.

---

* Curved stern of a ship.

Between the last two was the sealed-up mouth of the cavern we had come through.

The four cardinal winds, Boreas, Euro, Noto, and Zephyr, were represented by the largest, most complete figures; the others, by smaller, less-detailed ones. The beautiful Byzantine images were comparable to the reliefs that depicted pride on the floor of the Cloaca Maxima. It had to be the same artist. What a shame his name hadn't been recorded for history, for his work ranked with the best. Maybe he'd worked only for the brotherhood, which added to the value to his work.

"What about the sarcophagus?" Glauser-Röist asked suddenly.

"Impressive, isn't it?" I murmured. "Its dimensions are extraordinary. Notice, Captain, that the *lauda* is as high as its head."

"So, who's buried inside?"

"I'm not sure. I need to examine the high-relief on its lid."

Farag walked over to the large porphyry mass. I walked to the head to study one last engraving before I dared to verbalize my delirious hypothesis. All my doubts fell away when I recognized the familiar profile delicately carved in the *lauraton* of the red rock. The same face surrounded by a crown of laurels, the same raised eyes with a neck like a bull appeared on the *solidus*, the gold piece known among historians as the medieval dollar, the powerful currency created in the fourth century by Emperor Constantine the Great.

"It can't be…," Farag shouted, hopping around. "Ottavia, you're not going to believe what's in here!"

I looked around, trying to see where Farag's voice was coming from. When I heard his next shout, I looked straight up at him. On all fours on top of the sarcophagus's *lauda*, Professor Boswell, wide-eyed, wore a stupefied grin.

"Ottavia, you're not going to believe me!" he kept shouting. "I swear you're not going to believe me, but it's true, Ottavia!"

"Stop the foolishness, Professor!" The captain's voice vibrated to my right. "Will you please explain?"

Farag ignored him and turned to me with a crazy look on his face. "*Basileia*, I assure you, it's incredible! Know what it says up here? Know what it says?"

My heart went off like a shot when he called me *Basileia* again. "Tell me," I said, swallowing hard. "I can't guess, but I have a sneaking suspicion."

"No, no, you don't! Impossible! Not in a million years could you guess the name of the dead man inside here!"

"How much do you want to bet?" I said, mockingly.

"Whatever you want!" he exclaimed, very convinced. "Don't bet too much, because you're going to lose!"

"Emperor Constantine the Great," I said, "son of Empress Helen, who discovered the True Cross."

His face reflected a huge surprise. He was in shock for a few seconds, then he stammered. "How did you guess?"

"From the scenes recorded in the porphyry. One of them shows the emperor's face."

According to Farag, on the *lauda*, in addition to the emperor's chrismon, was a simple inscription that said *Konstantinos enesti*—that is, "Constantine is here." It was the greatest discovery in many centuries. At some point between 1000 and 1400, Constantine's tomb was lost forever under the dust from the sandals of the crusaders, the Persians, or the Arabs. We now were next to the sarcophagus of the first Christian emperor, founder of Constantinople. This proved, once and for all, that the Staurofilakes had always been willing to preserve anything that had anything to do with the True Cross. As soon as this charming allegory of purgatory was solved and after I ended my many years of work in the Classified Archives, I would lock myself away in the house in Connaught and write a series of articles on the True Cross, Staurofilakes, Dante Alighieri, Saint Helen, and Constantine the Great. I would tell the world the location of the emperor's important remains.

"I don't think Emperor Constantine is inside there," the Rock unexpectedly declared.

Farag and I looked at him, astonished.

"How could that be possible?" the captain continued. "Such an important person would not have ended his days as part of the initiation tests of a cult of thieves."

"Come on, Kaspar, don't be such a skeptic!" Farag replied, climbing down. "These things happen. In Egypt, for example, in new archaeological deposits, the most unlikely things are discovered every day. Hey! What's going on?" he exclaimed. The sarcophagus's *lauda* had started to slowly shift and was about to throw him to the ground, pushing him down the sarcophagus's neck.

"Jump, Farag! Get off!"

"What have you done, Professor?" the Rock shouted.

"Nothing, Kaspar, I swear," declared Boswell, jumping wide, then pirouetting on to the marble slabs. "I just put my feet in the gold hoops to climb down more easily."

"Well, clearly that was the way to open the sarcophagus," I murmured, while the porphyry plate stopped sliding with a loud screech.

Using one of the lion heads as a stirrup and dragging himself to the edge of the tomb, Glauser-Röist pushed himself up to look in.

"What do you see, Captain?" I was dying to know.

"A dead man."

Farag raised his eyes to heaven with a look of resignation and followed the Rock, climbing up on the other lion.

"You've got to see this, Ottavia," he said, smiling broadly.

I didn't think twice. I pulled on the captain's jacket to get him to climb down, and with all my strength I climbed to witness for myself what was inside. Like those Russian nesting dolls, the gigantic sarcophagus held several coffins, and the last one actually held the emperor's body. They all had glass covers, so the remains of Constantine could be clearly viewed. Of course, it seemed rash to announce that *this* was Constantine the Great. While his skull was like anyone else's, his imperial adornments revealed his lineage. That regular old skull wore a breathtaking gold *stemma** covered with jewels. Even more astonishing, he was adorned with gorgeous *catatheistae*† that hung under his *toufa*.‡ The rest of the skeleton was covered by an impressive *skaramangion*,§ held in place on his right shoulder by a clasp, intricately embroidered in gold and silver,

* Imperial crown.
† Ornaments that hung from the imperial crown.
‡ Imperial diadem that bore a comb of peacock feathers.
§ Tunic that formed part of the imperial Byzantine vestments.

trimmed with amethysts, rubies, and emeralds, and edged with pearls. Around his neck he wore a *loros** and around his waist was tied an *akakia,*† a must for any Byzantine emperor.

"It *is* Constantine," affirmed Farag with a weak voice.

"I guess so…"

"When we publish all this, *Basileia,* we're going to be very famous."

I quickly turned my head toward him. "What do you mean, *we?*" I was infuriated. Suddenly I understood that we both had a right to scientifically exploit the discovery. I would have to share the glory with Farag and Glauser-Röist. "Do you want to publish it, too, Captain?" I asked.

"Of course, Doctor. Did you think you have exclusive rights to all this?"

Farag chuckled and dropped to the ground. "Don't take it so hard, Kaspar. Dr. Salina has a hard head but a heart of gold."

I was about to give him the answer he deserved, when, suddenly, the faint noise that had begun just a few minutes before became incredibly loud. The noise sounded like furiously turning windmills. Suddenly a strong blast of air coming from the *bothros* blew my skirt up and pushed me against the sarcophagus.

"What's happening?"

"I'm afraid the party's starting, Doctor."

"Hold on tight, Ottavia."

Before Farag had finished speaking, the gust of wind became a strong wind, and then a hurricane. The torches went out and we were in the dark.

"The winds!" Farag shouted, clutching the sarcophagus with all his might.

Captain Glauser-Röist, who was caught out in the open, turned on his flashlight and covered his eyes with his arm. He tried to make his way to us, some two or three meters away. The currents were so strong that they kept him in check. There was no way he was reaching us quickly.

Farag and I grasped the sarcophagus with our hands, in order to

---

* Jeweled shawl that was only worn by the emperors and people of imperial rank.
† Silk bag filled with dust that comprised part of the imperial attributes.

keep the demented cyclone from dragging us to the ground. I realized it wouldn't be long till I lost my grip. My fingers were aching from squeezing the stone so tight. I had very little strength left, and my hope of surviving this test began to wane.

The overbearing gales forced the moisture from my eyes into long rivers of tears that ran down my cheeks. I've never felt so uncomfortable, my eyes stung with dryness, my face soaking wet. But that wasn't the worse part: Boreas, Aparctias, and Hellespont, gods of wind, gradually cooled the chamber's air until it seemed like it was freezing. Although Trascias and Argestes weren't as cold, drops of water began to fly from their passageways, creating the effect of a horizontal rainstorm. The room was so cold that the moisture turned into hail. We were pelted by the granules of ice. It felt like we were being shot at with a BB gun. The pain was so intense I let go of the sarcophagus and fell to the ground. Dante's words became dazzlingly clear.

My eyes were burning due to the harsh, dry air that emanated from Afeliotes and Euro. But while Trascias and Argeste were spitting hail, Euronoto, Noto, and Libanoto began to rattle with activity. A sudden exhale of violently hot air now filled the room, which melted the small amount of accumulated ice and burned my skin. At that point, I desperately missed my pants, which would have protected my legs from the furious hail and the burning air. I again tried to cover my face with my arms, but the hot air burned up much of the room's oxygen, making it difficult to breathe. All I could think of was reaching Farag. I couldn't move. I couldn't look for him. It was impossible to peel myself off the ground, much less move an arm or a leg. I called out to him, shouting with all the energy I could muster. The roar from the wind in the chamber was deafening; I couldn't hear my own voice. It was definitely the end. How would we ever get out of there? It was impossible.

But then I felt something at my feet. I looked down and noticed something rubbing against my ankle. I then realized the rubbing was a hand which began to make its way up my leg. I had no doubt it was Farag. The captain would never have been so bold as to even touch me. Plus, the last time I had seen him he was ahead of me, not behind. As disconcerting as the hand on my leg was, it helped me not lose my head. I then felt an arm loop around my waist and after a second, a body next to mine. I must admit that even though I was dying because of the burning winds and the painful hail, that long instant it took Farag to reach my face was one of the most disturbing in my life. And the strangest thing was that those new feelings that should have made me feel guilty were actually turning me into a free and happy person. I wasn't even worried about explaining those feelings to God as if I knew He would approve of them.

As soon as Farag's face was at my head, he stuck his lips to my ear and began pronouncing incoherent sounds I couldn't understand. He repeated them again and again until, with some imagination, I made out that his fragments formed the words "Zephyr" and "Dante." I thought about Zephyr, the west wind, who, along with his lover, the maiden Cloris, casts flowers.

Zephyr, the wind, was always praised in great poems of antiquity as a light, soft, spring breeze. It sounded corny, but I'd read it somewhere— in Pliny, maybe: Zephyr, the wind of sunset, out of the west as the day is ending, as the winter is ending. Ending... Maybe that was what Farag was trying to say. The end of that nightmare, the way out. Zephyr was the exit. But how to get there? I couldn't move a muscle. Where was Zephyr's *bothros?* My mind reeled with panic. Until I suddenly remembered:

> *If you have been exempt from lying prone,*
> *And wish to find the quickest way to go,*
> *Be sure to keep your right side to the edge.*

Dante's tercet! That was what Farag was trying to tell me. Remember Dante's words. I racked my brain to remember what we'd read in the airplane that morning:

> *My master moved ahead close to the cliff.*
> *Wherever there was space—as one who walks*
> *along the ramparts hugs the battlements.*

We had to get to the wall. The wall! If we stuck to our right until we reached Zephyr, the soft, temperate wind, we'd find relief. It was the only way.

Using all my strength, I took Farag's hand and squeezed it so he knew I understood. Helping each other, we slowly made our way forward, like sloths. It took a long time for us to make our way to the far wall, and we needed each other to move. We could never have made our way alone. Avoiding the typhoon-force winds coming from the *bothros*, we zigzagged in search of open air pockets that allowed us momentary relief, which then enabled us to increase the pace of our crawl. Fleetingly, I thought we weren't going to make it, that our effort was all in vain. But then we finally reached the stone wall, and I knew we had a chance to make it out.

Now we had to worry about Glauser-Röist. If we could get to our feet, as Dante instructed, and stick to our right, and the wall, we might be able to find the light of his flashlight.

Getting up off the ground was not simple. Like children learning to walk who grab onto furniture to stand, we had to dig our fingers into every solid chink in the walls around us. And yet, we had been right. As soon as we managed to keep our maneuvering to the far wall, the wind's force lessened, and we could breathe easier. It wasn't what you'd describe as calm—far from it—but the openings of the *bothros* were situated in such a way that the various air streams blasting through neutralized one another, creating partially calm spaces throughout the chamber.

If moving and breathing were hard, opening our eyes was almost impossible. They dried out in seconds and stung as if pins were being pushed into them. Yet we still could not find Glauser-Röist. With a colossal amount of effort, I finally spotted him at the far end of the grotto, between Trascias and Aparctias, stuck to the wall like a shadow, his head tilted back, his eyes tightly shut.

Calling to him was useless; he'd never hear us. We had to make our way to him. Since we stood between Euronoto and Noto, we crawled north, toward Boreas, following Dante's instructions to always keep to our right. Unfortunately, the captain must not have remembered

Dante's clues. Instead of heading toward Zephyr in the same direction we were, he was making his way toward us, crouching when he passed in front of each violent *bothros*. It was the best he could do to keep the whirlwind from hurling him through the air and against Constantine's sarcophagus.

I was exhausted. If it hadn't been for Farag's hand, I probably would never have gotten out of there. Fatigue held me down on the ground every time we had to drop to crawl in front of a *bothros*. My fatigue grew with each advancing moment.

Finally, we met up with the captain at Hellespont. With a nod, the three of us joined our hands in a tight, emotional squeeze. It was more eloquent than any word we could have said to each other. The real trouble started when Farag expressed that he wanted to keep heading toward Zephyr. Incredibly, Glauser-Röist flatly refused to retrace his steps and stubbornly blocked our way. I saw Farag shout something in the captain's ear. The captain kept shaking his head no and pointing in the opposite direction. Farag tried over and over, but the Rock kept refusing and pushed Farag toward me, backtracking the way we had just come.

There was no way to convince him. No matter how hard we shouted, gestured, and tried to move to our right, the captain forced us to do as he indicated. I didn't let myself think about what terrible things would happen to us if we didn't follow Dante's instructions. Farag and I saw desperation in each other's faces. The captain was mistaken, but how could we get him to understand that we were acting in accordance with the clue?

It took about half an hour to cross the five winds, in the opposite direction from where we were headed, toward Zephyr. I envied the captain's physical strength and Farag's natural resilience. When all this was over, I thought to myself, I was determined to get into shape. I couldn't hide behind the stereotypic excuse that women were weaker than men; I was totally to blame for my sedentary life.

At last we came to the dead space between Libs and Zephyr. I sighed with relief, and broke into a smile. I was in front at that point, so it fell to me to approach. If our analysis was correct, we would soon find calm. I moved my right hand very slowly toward the *bothros*. My heart exploded with joy when I verified that, although Zephyr was a little more violent than the poets had claimed, his airy vehemence wasn't anything like that of his eleven brothers. The wind from Zephyr didn't burn or freeze or spit frost or hail. My extended hand undulated in its soft breeze as though I were sticking my arm out the window of a moving car. We'd found the exit!

Zephyr took me in and saved my life. I fell to the ground like a sack of sand when I ventured into the narrow *bothros*. I breathed its tame, delicate air unobstructed; it was perfume to my lungs. I would have lain there a long time, perfectly still, but I had to keep going so Farag and the captain could enter behind me. I knew they were in when I heard Farag shouting furiously at Glauser-Röist.

"Will you please tell me why the hell you made us trek through three-fourths of the grotto!" he roared, indignant. "We were almost at Zephyr when we found you! Don't you remember Dante said to keep going right?"

"Quiet down!" Glauser-Röist snapped back. "That is what I did!"

"Are you crazy? Can't you tell we went clockwise! Don't you know right from left?"

"Please!" I exclaimed. "We're out and we're okay. Please stop shouting."

"Listen, Professor," the Rock roared. "What did Dante say? He said you always had to keep your right on the outside."

"To the right, Kaspar! The right, not the left! You still don't get it!"

"Your right on the outside, Professor! You're the one who doesn't get it!"

I frowned. Our right on the outside? Dante and Virgil advanced around the cornice of a mountain. Their right was, obviously, next to the precipice, to the void. But we were stuck to a wall, so our right was the center of the grotto; our free side was its interior, not the outside as in Dante's case. Either way, we would have reached Zephyr, though it would have been shorter if we had gone the other way.

"We would never have gotten here the other way, Doctor!"

"What are you saying?" I asked.

"I see you both have forgotten Trascias and Argestes. They were the last winds we'd have had to cross before getting to Zephyr! We would never have made it!"

There was silence in that arched corridor; neither Farag nor I could contradict him. The captain had saved us from retracing our steps. We could never have made it past Trascias and Argestes and the hail that stormed into the chamber. The heat from the other *bothros* acted as a balance to ice, creating a controlled environment and providing us with a safe path toward Zephyr.

"Do you understand or must I explain it again?"

He was right. He was completely right, and I said so. Farag didn't hesitate to ask the Rock's forgiveness in every language he knew. He began with Coptic, followed by Greek, Latin, Arabic, Turkish, Hebrew, French, English, and Italian. We laughed at ourselves, and the tension dripped off the moment.

"Stop with all the nonsense, and let's get down this hole."

"Why do I always have to go first?" I grumbled again, tired of honoring their ridiculous chivalry.

"Doctor, please..."

"Ottavia..."

He didn't have to say another word, of course.

On all fours, holding my flashlight between two buttons of my blouse, I began the trek, sorry again that I had worn a skirt that day. It brought back bad memories of that time in the tunnel in the catacombs of Santa Lucia. Farag was then also behind me. I promised myself, if we got out of there, I'd throw all my skirts in the trash.

The truth is, crawling was hard. I couldn't do it to save my soul. So I was so glad when the soft aroma of resin reached my nose. The familiar white powder began to fill the passageway.

"I believe we're in luck."

"What did you say, *Basileia?*"

"That we'll get some sleep. Don't you smell resin?"

"No."

"It doesn't matter. I'll say my farewells. See you when we wake up."

"*Basileia...*"

A slight stupor made its way through me. "Yes?"

"What I said to you during the marathon was a lie."

"What did you say to me during marathon?"

There was white smoke, that blessed white smoke, in the air. Like a good sleeping pill, it would give me some much needed hours of rest. I stretched myself out on the ground. The Staurofilakes could do what they wanted to my body. I didn't care. I just wanted to sleep.

"If you got on your feet and ran to Athens, I'd never pester you again."

I smiled. He was the most romantic man in the world. I wanted to look at him. No, I thought again, better to sleep. Besides, the Rock was listening to everything.

"It was a lie?" My smile opened my eyes, now half-closed by the sleep.

"A complete lie. I had to warn you. Was that so bad?"

"It was fine. I agree with you."

"Okay, then, just wanted to be clear," he murmured. "Kaspar, are you asleep?"

No," he muttered. "Your conversation is very intriguing tonight."

My God, I thought, and found myself instantly asleep.

CHAPTER

6

*T*he shouts of children playing woke me. The midday sun fell on me like a shower of light. I blinked, coughed, and sat up, groaning. I was sprawled facedown on a carpet of weeds. The smell was unbearable. It was the smell of trash that had accumulated over years, and fermented in the Eastern heat. The children kept shouting and spoke in Turkish. Their voices grew faint.

I managed to sit up and open my eyes. I found myself in a patio where bits of the Byzantine masonry were mixed in with piles of trash. Clouds of blue flies as big as elephants flew overhead. To my left, I saw a very sinister looking car repair shop, which emitted noises from a chain saw and a blowtorch. I was dirty. Dirty and barefoot.

Farag and the captain were still lying facedown in the grass in front of me. I smiled when I looked at Farag, and my stomach did a somersault.

"So it was a lie?" I mused, walking over to him and looking at him with a smile on my face.

I brushed a lock of hair off his forehead and amused myself by looking at the small lines etched on his skin. They were the traces of the time he'd spent without me, some thirty-odd years he'd lived far from me. He had lived, dreamed, worked, breathed, laughed, and even loved without suspecting that I was waiting for him. It continued to strike me miraculous that someone like Farag would latch on to someone like me, when I didn't even have a hint of the beauty that he seemed to have too much of. Of course, looks aren't everything, but they definitely are important. Even though beauty was something I had never even worried about, at that precise moment I wished I were beautiful and attractive so that Farag would have been completely blown away by me when he woke up.

I sighed and laughed under my breath. I wasn't asking for a miracle. I had to resign myself. I looked around and didn't see anyone. So I leaned over very slowly and gave him a kiss on those lines on his forehead. He was sound asleep.

"Doctor... Are you all right, Dr. Salina? How's Professor Boswell?"

My heart raced, and my face burned. I sat up as if I had a spring attached to my back.

"Captain? Are you okay?" I asked, recoiling from Farag, who was still sleeping.

"Where are we?"

"That's what I'd like to know."

"We have to wake the professor. He speaks Turkish."

He leaned on his hands and started to raise his body, but a rictus of pain paralyzed him mid-stride.

"Where the hell did they mark us this time?" he grumbled.

The tattoo! I raised my hand to the top of my shoulder, to my cervical vertebrae. That's when I felt the familiar jab of pain.

"I think we've got the first of the three crosses that go on our spines."

"Well, it hurts!"

Why hadn't I noticed? The pain suddenly became intense. "Yes, yes it hurts," I agreed. "I think it hurts more than the previous ones."

"It will pass. We have to wake the professor."

He didn't think twice and started shaking him mercilessly. Farag groaned.

"Ottavia?" he asked without opening his eyes.

"Sorry, Professor," growled the Rock. "It's Captain Glauser-Röist. Not Dr. Salina."

Farag smiled. "Not quite the same. Ottavia?"

"Here I am," I said, taking his hand. He opened his eyes and looked at me.

"Sorry to bother you two," the captain said, ill-tempered, "but we have to get back to the Patriarchate."

"Have you checked your clothes yet, Captain?" I asked, still gazing at Farag and still smiling. "The clue for the test in Alexandria is important."

Glauser-Röist quickly turned out all the pockets in his pants and jacket. "Here it is!" he exclaimed, lifting up the familiar folded piece of paper.

"Let's see," said Farag. He sat up, still holding my hand. "Have they marked us on our backs?" he asked quickly, very surprised.

"On our cervical vertebrae," I confirmed.

"Hey! This one really hurts!"

The captain read from the clue and held it out to Farag. "If you don't let go of the doctor's hand, it'll be very hard for you to take it."

Farag laughed and quickly caressed my fingers before letting them go. "I hope you don't mind, Kaspar."

"It's not my concern, Professor," the Rock affirmed, very serious. "Dr. Salina is a big girl. She knows what she's doing. I suppose she'll straighten things out with the church soon enough."

"Don't worry, Captain," I clarified. "I haven't forgotten for a minute that I'm a nun. This is a private matter, but since I know well what you are thinking, allow me to tell you that I am fully conscious of the problems this will cause."

The poor man was so obtuse about certain things, and I thought it was better to appease him.

Farag examined the paper and his jaw dropped. "I know what this is!" he blurted out, very agitated.

"Of course you know, Professor. The next test is in Alexandria."

"No. No!" He shook his head frenetically. "I've never seen this place in my life, but I know I could find it."

"What are you two talking about?" I asked, snatching the paper from Farag's hands. This time the message wasn't written on that rough paper, but was rather crudely drawn in charcoal. One could make out the image of a bearded snake wearing the pharaonic crowns of High and Low Egypt. It also had a medallion with the head of Medusa. From the creature's rings, tied up like a sailor's knot, emerged the thyrsus of Dionysus, the Greek god of vegetation and wine, and the staff of Hermes, the messenger god. "What's this?"

"I don't know," answered Farag, "but we won't have any trouble finding it. We have a computerized catalogue of the city's archeological finds in the museum." He looked over my shoulder and pointed to the drawing. "I would have sworn I could recognize nearly any Alexandrian work with my eyes closed. Even though this image looks familiar, I can't remember where I've seen it. See the mixture of styles? Hermes's staff and the pharaohs' crowns? The bearded serpent is a Roman symbol. Such a bizarre combination is typical of Alexandria."

"Professor, would you mind going over to that garage and asking where we are?" the Rock interrupted us again. "And ask if they have a phone. My cell phone was ruined in the cistern."

Farag smiled. "Don't worry, Kaspar. I'll take care of it."

"Here's the Patriarchate's number," Glauser-Röist added, handing Farag his daybook, open to the number. "Tell Father Kallistos where we are and ask him to come get us."

I wasn't one bit happy that Farag walked so decisively toward that junk pit and disappeared, but he wasn't gone five minutes. When he returned, he had a broad smile on his face.

"I spoke with the Patriarchate, Captain," he shouted as he walked back. "They'll be here right away. We are on the remains of what was the Great Palace of Justinian and Theodora."

"The Great Palace of Justinian...this place?" I said, looking around skeptically.

"That's right, *Basileia*. We're in the Zeyrek neighborhood, in the old part of the city. This patio is all that's left of the imperial palace of Justinian and Theodora." He walked over and took my hand.

"I don't understand, Farag," I murmured, distressed. "How could they let things get this bad?"

"Byzantine remains don't have the same value to the Turks as they have for us, *Basileia*. They don't understand any religion but their own, with all the cultural and social implications that come along with that. They preserve their mosques, but do not feel the need to preserve the sacred places of foreign religions. This is a poor country. It can't be concerned with a past that does nothing for their best interest."

"But it's culture, history!" I was furious. "It's who we are!"

"Here, people survive as best as they can," he replied. "The old churches are converted into houses, the old palaces into garages. When those fall down, they look for other churches and palaces where they can set up their homes or businesses. It's a different mentality. Simply put, why preserve it, if you can reuse? We should be grateful they preserved Saint Sofia."

"As soon as the Patriarchate's car gets here, we'll go directly to the airport," Glauser-Röist announced laconically.

I was alarmed. "From here? Without changing our clothes or taking a shower?"

"We'll do that in Alexandria. It's just a three-hour trip, and we can freshen up on the Westwind. Would you rather explain what we did down there?"

Naturally, I didn't want to do that, so I didn't put up any more objections.

"I hope it's not too difficult to get me back into Egypt…," murmured Farag, worried. When he left his country, he had been accused of stealing a manuscript from the Monastery of Saint Catherine of Sinai and was forced to cross the border into Israel with a fake passport from the Vatican.

"Don't worry, Professor," the Rock calmed him down. "The Iyasus Codex has been returned officially to the monastery we *borrowed* it from."

"Borrowed!" I exclaimed sarcastically. "There's a slight euphemism."

"Call it what you like, Doctor. The important thing is that the codex is back in the Saint Catherine Library, and the Catholic Church and the Orthodox churches have given the abbot appropriate apologies and explanations, and Archbishop Damianos has rescinded his accusation. So, Professor, you are completely free to return to your home and your work."

Farag couldn't believe his ears. He began to get angry, very slowly, like a caldron that heats up and builds pressure. The captain stayed calm, but my legs were trembling. Although Farag had an affable personality, I knew he had a short fuse.

"Since when is the codex in Saint Catherine?" he muttered, his teeth clenched.

"Since last week. A copy of the manuscript was made, and we had to return it to its original state. I reminded them of the condition we found it in, unbound and its pages loose. Then, through the Coptic-Catholic patriarch of your church and the patriarch of Jerusalem, His Beatitude Michel Sabbah, the conversations with Archbishop Damianos ensued. His patriarch, Stephano II Ghattas, also talked with the director of the Greco-Roman Museum of Alexandria. As of yesterday, you have special access indefinitely. I thought you would like to know that."

Farag's face deflated, and incredulous, he looked at me and looked at Glauser-Röist several times before he could say a word. "I can go home...," he stuttered. "I can go back to the Museum..."

"Not to the Museum, at least not yet. But you can go home this afternoon. Does that sound good?"

Why was he so emotional about the possibility of returning to Alexandria and getting back his job in the Greco-Roman Museum? Didn't he tell me that being Coptic in Egypt was like being a pariah? Didn't the Islamic war kill his little brother, his sister-in-law, and his five-week-old nephew on the steps of the church just the year before? He had told me all this the first time we had lunch.

"Oh my God," he exclaimed, lifting his arms to the sky like a runner who reaches the finish line. "Tonight, I'll be home."

As he was expounding on how much I was going to like Alexandria and how happy his father would be to see him and meet me, the car from the Patriarchate drove down one of the side streets and picked us up on the opposite end of the dump. It took me an eternity to reach the other side because the ground was covered with sharp refuse which would have cut my feet. After I sat down in the car with a big sigh of relief, I discovered the drive wasn't going to be the peaceful respite I had hoped. Sitting beside me in the backseat of the Patriarch's chauffer-driven car was our expert in Byzantine architecture, Doria Sciarra.

The captain sat next to the driver. I made sure Farag got in through the other door, so that he sat on the other side of Doria, trapping her between us. I acted delighted to see her, as if the day before hadn't had the slightest impact on me. I was amused when she wrinkled her nose at our smell. She was hurt because we had left her behind to entertain the doorman at the Fatih Camii. When she went back to the patio and didn't find us anywhere, she walked to the car and waited until nightfall. Worried and alone, she returned to the Patriarchate. She wanted us to tell her everything, but we ducked her questions with insipid answers, telling her superficial things like how hard the test had been and the terrible pain and torture we'd endured. Frustrated, she lost interest. Neither of us could tell her about one of the greatest discoveries in history, our finding the burial chamber of Constantine the Great.

Farag was as charming toward her as he had been the day before. But he didn't play her game and didn't respond once to her silly insinuations. I was perfectly calm and at peace with myself: at peace about Farag and about how Doria had wanted to hurt me and only managed to do so fleetingly. She still wanted to make a fool out of me, and I didn't let her. I smiled, chatted, and joked as if the day before had been a day like any other, not the day my world had come crashing down around my head, only to be raised again by the tenderness of Farag's hand. Now he was all that mattered to me; Doria was nothing.

When the Patriarchate's car left us at the vast hangar where the Westwind was parked, I said good-bye to my old friend with a couple of kisses on her cheeks despite her discreet attempt to avoid them. I'll never know if she ducked my kisses because she felt guilty or because of how I smelled, but the fact remained I kissed her forcibly and repeatedly thanked her "for everything." Farag and the captain shook her hand. She sped away in the Patriarchate's car, never to be seen again.

"What did Doria tell you yesterday that changed your mood after lunch?" Farag asked me as we climbed the stairs.

"I'll tell you later," I hedged. "Why is it that you didn't come up to me if you had noticed how upset I was?"

"I couldn't," he explained as he greeted Paola and the rest of the crew. "I had cornered myself in my own trap."

"What trap?" I asked surprised. Glauser-Röist had finished talking to the pilot as we took our usual seats. I thought I should wash up a bit before plopping onto the white upholstery, but I was very curious about what Farag was saying, and I didn't want Glauser-Röist to interrupt him before he finished.

"Well…The thing with Doria, you know." In his eyes shone a mocking smile I didn't understand.

"No, I don't know. What trap are you talking about?"

"Ottavia, don't be so serious!" he joked. "In the end everything turned out fine."

"I hope it's not what I'm thinking, Farag," I warned seriously.

"I'm afraid so, *Basileia*. I had to get your attention somehow. Are you happy?"

"Happy! What do you mean am I happy? You put me through hell!"

Farag exploded in a fit of laughter, more a little boy than a grown man.

"That was the whole point, *Basilea!* In Athens I thought I had lost it all! You have no idea how it was for me to see you get up and say to me 'Shall we go?' At that moment I looked at you and understood that to persuade a woman as stubborn as you, I'd have to use a nuclear bomb. And Doria worked out fine, didn't she? The bad part was that after bombing you, you wouldn't even look at me, and if you did it was with utter…" The Rock had joined us. "I'll tell you later."

"That won't be necessary." I responded as I got up and pulled my toiletries out of my bag. "You're a cheater."

"Of course I am!" he explained, delighted. "And many other things, too."

The Rock fell into his chair, and I heard him sigh.

"I'm going to freshen myself up a bit," I said without looking back.

"Remember, you have to be sitting here when we take off."

"Don't worry."

The flight to Alexandria took three hours. During the trip we ate, talked, laughed. Farag and I almost mutinied when the captain took the *Divine Comedy* out of his backpack and suggested we prepare for the next circle of Purgatory. In spite of feeling fresh and rested after almost twelve hours of sleep, I was mentally exhausted. If it had been possible, I would have asked for a vacation and followed Farag to the ends of the earth, some place where nothing and no one reminded me of the life I was leaving behind. A changed woman after that, I would have been more willing to finish the tests we still had to take to get to the blessed earthly paradise. I felt uprooted. My home was now that airplane; my family was Farag and Captain Glauser-Röist; my work was hunting down those centuries-old relic thieves. Thinking about Sicily was painful; it made me sad, and I knew I'd never go back to the apartment in the Piazza delle Vaschette. What would I do when all this was over? Thank heavens I had that unscrupulous trickster, Farag Boswell, I thought, looking at him. I was sure he loved me and would be at my side until I put my life back together.

Around five in the afternoon, the pilot announced that we were about to land at Al Nouzha Airport. It was a sunny, 80-degree day.

"We're home!" Farag exclaimed, thrilled.

There was no way to keep him in his seat as we landed. Poor Paola pleaded with him a hundred times. But he wanted to see his city, wanted to get there before the plane did. I wouldn't have let anyone stop him for anything in the world.

Not even in my wildest dreams had I imagined that Alexandria would become a special place because of the love I had for this man. Of course, I'd read about Lawrence Durrell and Konstantinos Kavafis. Like everyone else, I knew some facts about the city, founded by Alexander the Great in 332 B.C. I listened to Farag talk about its famous library, which housed more that half a million volumes on the entirety of human knowledge at that time, and about its lighthouse, one of the World's Seven Wonders and how it guided the hundreds of merchants who entered its port, the largest in classical antiquity. I knew that for centuries it had been not only the capital of Egypt and the most important part on the Mediterranean, but more important, the literary and scientific capital of the world. Its palaces, mansions, and temples were admired for their elegance and wealth. It was where Eratosthenes measured the Earth's circumference, where Euclid systematized geometry, and where Galen wrote his tomes on medicine. It was also in Alexandria that Mark Anthony and Cleopatra fell in love. Farag Boswell himself was an example of what Alexandria had been until not too long ago. A descendant of Englishmen, Jews, Coptics, and Italians, he was a mixture of cultures and characteristics which conferred on him, at least for me, a unique and wonderful status.

"Are we going to have a welcome committee, Captain?" I asked the Rock, who had spent a long time talking on the phone in the plane.

"Of course, Doctor. A car from the Greco-Orthodox Patriarchate of Alexandria will pick us up. We will meet with the patriarch, Petros VII, at his headquarters, along with His Beatitude Stephanos II Ghattas and His Holiness Shenouda III, leader of the Copto-Orthodox Church. Our old friend, Archbishop Damianos, abbot of Saint Catherine of Sinai, will also be there."

"Looks like it's going to be a party...," I grumbled. "You know, Captain? I never would have believed there were so many holinesses and beatitudes. At this moment my head is a jumble of holy pontiffs."

"And how about the ones you're not going to meet, Doctor," he answered ironically, crossing his legs. "For Orthodox Christians all the apostles were equal. Each has the same authority when they govern their flock."

"I know, but it's still hard for me to equate them to the pope. As a Catholic, I've been educated to believe there is only one legitimate successor to Peter."

"Long ago I learned that everything is relative," he explained in one of his rare fits of openness. "Everything is relative, everything is temporary, and everything is mutable. Perhaps that's why I search for stability."

"You?" I was surprised.

"What's wrong, Doctor? Can't you believe that someone like me is human? I'm not as bad as Pierantonio told you."

I was silent because I know he'd caught me.

"There's always an explanation for what we do and who we are," he continued. "And, if you don't believe me, just take a look at yourself."

"You know about my family, too?" I whispered, lowering my head. I realized I didn't want to discuss that with anybody, least of all Glauser-Röist.

"Naturally!" He let loose one of his rare outbursts of laughter. "I knew when I met you in Monsignor Tournier's office. Just like I knew you were the sister of Pierantonio Salina, guardian of the Holy Land. That's my job, remember? I know everything, and I see everything. Somebody has to do the dirty work, and that, unfortunately, falls to me. I don't like it, I don't like it one bit, but I'm used to it. You're not the only one who's going to give their life a new twist. Someday I, too, will leave the Vatican and live calmly in a little wooden house next to Lake Leman, devoting myself to what I really like: tending the soil, trying out new growing techniques and production systems. Did you know I studied agricultural engineering at the University of Zurich before I became a soldier and Swiss Guard? That was my true vocation, but my family had other plans for me. You can't always escape what your family inculcates in you from the day you were born."

I didn't say anything for several minutes, looking out the window and thinking about the captain's words. "Why do we think we live our own lives," I said, finally, "when our lives are living us?"

"That's true," he replied, brushing the dirt off his slacks. "But we always have the opportunity to change. You're already doing it, and I will, too, I assure you. It's never too late. I'm going to confess something to you, Doctor. And I hope you can keep a secret: This it is my last job for the Vatican."

I looked at him and smiled. His sharing this information with me had just sealed our friendship.

We drove down the streets of Alexandria in a black Italian limousine, a car belonging to Patriarch Petros VII. Farag sat silently in the front seat.

The vehicle traveled down wide, modern avenues, clogged with traffic, which passed by golden sand beaches stretching on and on. The Alexandria I saw had little in common with what I'd imagined. Where were the palaces and the temples? Mark Anthony and Cleopatra? The elderly poet Kavafis, who walked around Alexandria at dusk leaning on his cane? If it weren't for the people in Arabic dress strolling down the sidewalks, this could have been New York.

Once we left the beaches behind and entered the heart of the city, the chaotic traffic increased to an unspeakable degree. On a narrow, one-way street, our car got stuck between a line of cars behind us and an even longer line in front of us. Farag and the driver exchanged some sentences in Arabic, then the driver opened the door, got out, and began to shout. I suppose the idea was to get the cars going in the opposite direction to back up and let us pass. Instead, it started a violent argument among drivers. Of course, there wasn't a single policeman to be seen.

After a while, Farag also got out of the car, spoke with our driver, and came back. Instead of getting back in his seat, he opened the trunk and took out his suitcase and mine.

"Let's go, Ottavia," he said sticking his face in the window. "My father lives just two streets over."

"Just a minute!" the captain said, looking glum. "Get back in the car, Professor! They're expecting us!"

"They're expecting *you*, Kaspar," Farag said, opening my door. "All these meetings with the patriarchs are useless! When it's over, call me on my cell phone. Monsignor Kolta, His Beatitude Stephanos's vicar, has my number as well as my father's number. Let's go, *Basileia!*"

"Professor Boswell!" the Rock exclaimed. "You can't take Dr. Salina!"

"Ah, no? Remind me of that tonight. We'll be expecting you for dinner at nine. Don't be late."

We darted off like fugitives, leaving behind the car and Captain Glauser-Röist, who had to apologize repeatedly to important religious authorities for our absence. Octogenarian Patriarch Stephanos II Ghattas had specifically asked for Farag, whom he'd known since he was a little boy. Needless to say, he did not believe a word of the captain's lame excuses.

As soon as we got out of the car, we ran, loaded down with our lug-

gage, down a side street that ended at Avenue Tareek El Gueish. Farag
took the two suitcases and I took his and my hand luggage. I couldn't
help laughing as we escaped at full speed. I felt happy, free like a fifteen-
year-old girl who was bucking authority.

"He lives in the lower floor, and I live on the upper."

"So, we're going to *your* house?" I was worried.

"Naturally, *Basileia!* I said it was my father's house not to scandalize
Glauser-Röist."

"But now I'm the one who's scandalized!" I could barely speak because I couldn't breathe.

"Don't worry, *Basileia*. First we'll go to my father's house, then we'll
go up to mine to shower, doctor our tattoos, put on a clean set of
clothes, and fix dinner."

"You're doing this on purpose, aren't you, Farag?" I reprimanded
him, stopping in the middle of the street. "You want to scare me."

"Scare you!" he was surprised. "What you are afraid of?" He leaned
over. I was afraid he'd kiss me right there. Fortunately, we were in an
Arab country. "Don't worry, *Basileia...*" I smiled when I heard him stut-
ter. "I understand.... I assure you, even if it costs me my life, you have
nothing to fear...nothing. I can't guarantee one hundred percent, of
course, but I'll do everything I can. Agreed?"

He was so handsome, standing in the middle of the street, staring at
me with those dark blue eyes. I was afraid I was acting against my true
desires. Desires? What desires? All this was so new to me. I should have
had these feelings twenty years ago. I was taking such a giant step backward, I was afraid I'd make a fool of myself.

"Let's go to your father's house right away," I exclaimed.

"I hope you clear up your affairs with the church soon, like Glauser-
Röist says. It's going to be very hard to be around you, knowing I can't
touch you."

I was about to tell him that I was as untouchable as I decided to be,
but quickly refrained from doing so. If, by magic, I were suddenly free
of my religious status at that very moment, I still wouldn't be ready to
break my second vow without having officially separated from my commitment to God and my order.

"Let's go, Farag," I said with a smile. I'd have given anything to kiss him.

"Why did I have to fall in love with a nun?" he shouted in the middle of the street. Fortunately, he said so in ancient Greek. "With all the pretty women in Alexandria!" Now that he was back home he was a changed man. Different from the one I had first met in Rome.

"Let's go, Farag," I repeated patiently, a smile still on my face, knowing that I had a few terrible weeks ahead of me.

The Boswell family home was on a street with a wide panorama of old buildings that had elegant, English-style facades. It was dark and cool; traffic wasn't allowed. That did not prevent covered carts and bicycles from traveling down it, dodging strolling wayfarers. Despite its European air, the doors and windows of the houses were decorated with harmonious arabesques in intricate patterns of leaves and flowers. It was a pretty street, and the people on it seemed pleasant.

Visibly moved, Farag took a key out of his pocket and opened the iron gate. A slight scent of mint wafted out of an opening in the wall. The doorway was wide and shady, typical of a warm country like Egypt.

"Don't make a sound, *Basileia*," Farag whispered to me. "I want to surprise my father."

We climbed the stairs quietly and stopped in front of a large wooden door with panels of polished glass. The doorbell was set in the doorframe, at eye-level.

"I have a key," he explained to me, pressing the button, "but I want to see the expression on his face."

As its ring echoed in my ears, furious barks approached from inside.

"That's Tara!" Farag whispered, smiling really big. "It was my mother's idea. She loved *Gone with the Wind*," he added as an excuse, guessing my thoughts.

When the wooden door opened slowly, I noticed a tall, thin man, about seventy, with white hair and intense, dark blue eyes, filtered by charming bifocals. He was as handsome as his son. He had the same Jewish features, the same dark skin, the same expression... I understood how Farag's mother left everything for a man like this and felt a complicity with her because I was acting similarly.

Their embrace was long and emotional. The dog, an unfortunate mix of Yorkshire and Scottish terriers, barked desperately, jumping into the air like a rabbit. Butros Boswell kissed his son's hair over and over, as if each and every day Farag had spent far away had been torture for him. Also he murmured joyful words in Arabic. His eyes even filled with tears. When they finally let go of each other, they came toward me.

"Papa, let me introduce Doctor Ottavia Salina."

"Farag has spoken of you so often these last several months, Doctor," he said in perfect Italian as he shook my hand. "Come in, please."

Followed by Tara, who wagged her tail frenetically, obviously delighted with Farag's caresses, we entered the foyer of their spacious house. There were books everywhere, even piled on the sideboard in the entrance. Old family photographs abounded in the hall and around all the rooms. The decoration was a motley mixture of English, Viennese, Italian, Arab, and French furniture: a Lalique vase here, a silver repoussé teapot over there, a turn-of-the-century English *trumeau*, a wood box inlaid with mother-of-pearl, an Arabic set of glasses, wooden chairs ornamented with curved scrolling placed around an old, round pedestal table, holding a chessboard with ivory figurines... But what caught my attention most were the pictures hanging on the walls in the hall. When he saw my interest, Butros Boswell came over and explained, not without some pride, who all those people were.

"This is my grandfather, Kenneth Boswell, the discoverer of Oxirrinco. Here he is in this old, black-and-white photograph standing next to his colleagues, Bernard Grenfell and Arthur Hunt, in 1895, during the first excavations. And this...," he said and pointed to the next picture. A very beautiful woman looked out at us, dressed in an elegant cocktail dress and very long black gloves that came almost to her shoulders. "This was his wife, Esther Hopasha, my grandmother, and one of the most beautiful Jewish women in Alexandria."

Pictures of Ariel Boswell, their son, and his wife, Miriam, an Egyptian Coptic with dark skin and henna-dyed hair, also hung on the walls in the hall. The place of honor was held by the photo of a young woman, not especially beautiful, but with laughing, flashing eyes that broadcast out an infinite love of life.

"This was my wife, Doctor Salina, Farag's mother, Rita Luchese." His face became gloomy. "She died five years ago."

"Papa," Farag huffed, carrying Tara in his arms. "We have to take the luggage upstairs to my apartment."

"Will you have supper here tonight?" Butros wanted to know.

"We'll have supper upstairs, with Captain Glauser-Röist. I plan to order something from the Mercure."

"Fine," Butros replied. "Then I'll see you later, son. Don't leave Alexandria without saying good-bye."

"You're also invited, Papa!" Farag exclaimed, tossing Tara into the air. The dog, who must have weighed quite a bit, landed gracefully on the ground. Without hesitating, she came straight to me. She had an intelligent look in her huge eyes; her fur was a cinnamon color except where her neck and chest were white. I petted her head with some apprehension. Unexpectedly, she got up and braced her front legs against my stomach.

"I hope she's not bothering you, Doctor," Butros observed, smiling. "It's her way of saying she likes you."

"Your father is charming," I said to Farag when we were almost to the landing of his house, on the third floor.

"I know," he replied, unlocking and pushing the door open.

"Who lives on the middle floor?"

"Right now, no one," Farag explained, entering the dark interior and setting the suitcases on the ground. "My brother, Juhanna, used to live there with his wife, Zoe, and their son."

"It's hard to believe what you told me. What happened to them is just horrible."

"I'd rather not think about it," he said, taking the bags and closing the door behind me. "We have other things to do."

Yes, we certainly did. That didn't include turning on the lights, or opening the blinds or taking a tour of the house. I had never imagined it would be so hard, so terribly hard to stick to my second vow. I knew there was a limit, but I...I never knew how simple it would be to cross that line. I didn't, though. At the last minute, fighting against my tormented instincts, I remembered I had to fulfill a promise. It was absurd, it was madness, it was the most ridiculous thing in the world, I knew. For some reason, I had to be faithful to the commitment I still had to God, my order, and the church. It was dreadful to pull away from Farag's lips, Farag's body, Farag's tenderness and passion. It was like shattering into a thousand pieces.

"You promised… You promised you would help me," I said as I pushed him away.

"I can't, Ottavia."

"Farag, please," I begged. "Help me! I love so you much!"

He stood there, still as a statue for several seconds. Then he leaned over and kissed me.

"I love you, *Basileia,*" he said pulling away. "I'll wait."

"I promise I'll call Rome tonight," I said, putting my hand to his heavily-bearded cheek. "I'll speak with Sister Sarolli, the assistant director of my order, and explain the situation to her."

"Please do it," he whispered, kissing me again. "Please."

"I promise," I repeated. "This very night."

I showered and changed the bandage on the tattoo on the cervical vertebrae (this time, a branched cross) and put on clean clothes. Obeying my orders, Farag opened doors and windows, wiped the dust off the furniture, and got his house ready for visitors. Then we switched places. He'd already phoned the restaurant at the nearby Hotel Mercure and ordered supper. He went into the bathroom—inviting me to accompany him, of course. He left me free in that unfamiliar place to snoop around. Hypocritically, I asked him if there was anything he didn't want me to pry into.

"Make yourself at home, *Basileia.* Look anywhere you like," he said, then disappeared.

That's exactly what I did it. If he thought I wasn't curious about his life, he was very wrong. In that half hour, I turned everything upside down. Farag's house, with its smooth, white walls and light terrazzo floors, had only two bedrooms but, typical of old houses, they were huge. One of the rooms, a very austere one with a large bed in the center, was his; the other, at the other end of the house, had two smaller beds and seemed to be used just to store books—hundreds of books—as well as history, archaeology, and paleography magazines. The living room had a long sofa in it and several cream-colored armchairs. On one side was a large dining room table made of dark wood. The rest of the furniture was also dark wood: beds, closets, shelves, tables, chest of drawers, cabinets ... He must really like cushions a lot, because, in colors ranging from copper to white, they were everywhere. Another thing of interest was the photographs, as abundant as in the house downstairs: Farag with his father, his mother, his brother, his sister-in-law, his nephew. I discovered several of him as a small boy, with classmates, others with college classmates and friends, and several others with the same two friends. But the photographs of trips around the world were, invariably, with very attractive girls, different ones in every country. The photographs taken in Rome, for example, showed a very young Farag with a blonde with a long, pointed nose; those in Paris, next to a brunette with a funny smile; those in London, with an Asian woman with short, black hair; those in Amsterdam, with a statuesque model with perfect teeth. I realized I had fallen in love with Casanova, or worse, with a cad of the highest order.

I collapsed, desolate, onto the sofa, hugging one of the cushions as I watched the dusk sky through the windows. I doubted seriously if I'd make that call to Sister Sarolli. There was still time to retreat to the house in Connaught. Just then, the little tune on Farag's cell phone went off. The phone was on one of the small bookshelves in the hall, next to the bathroom door.

"Ottavia!" Casanova shouted. "Answer it! It must be the captain!"

I didn't answer him. I just pressed the green button on the phone and said hello to the Rock, who seemed displeased.

"Is the meeting over, Captain? How did it go?"

"Same as always."

"Then get out of there and come over here. Dinner is nearly ready."

"Where are you going to sleep tonight, Doctor?" he asked me point-blank.

"Well," I vacillated. "I hadn't given it much thought. Where are you going to sleep?"

"Does the professor have enough rooms for all three of us?"

"Yes. There are two bedrooms and three beds."

"Here, at the Patriarchate, there's room, too. They want to know what we are going to do."

"Do we need computers or anything else to prepare for the test?"

"Doesn't the professor have a computer?" Glauser-Röist asked, very surprised, not understanding what I had insinuated.

"Yes, he has one in his office, but I don't know if it's connected to the Internet."

"Yes, it is!" shouted Casanova, who was following our conversation closely. "I'm connected to the Internet, and I have access to the muse-um's database!"

"He says he does, Captain," I repeated.

"You decide, Doctor," I heard doubt in his voice. He must have felt uneasy.

"Come on over, Captain. We'll be more comfortable here. What's the address, Farag?" I asked through the door.

"33 Moharrem Bey, top floor!"

"You heard him, Captain."

"I'll be there in half an hour." He hung up without saying good-bye.

Fortunately the restaurant delivery boy got here before the Rock did. We arranged the table quickly to make the captain think we'd fixed it ourselves.

"Wouldn't you rather call Sister Sarolli before Kaspar gets here?" Farag asked me as we carried the cups and glasses from the kitchen. I couldn't think what to say, so I kept quiet. But he insisted, "Ottavia, aren't you going to call Sister Sarolli?"

"I don't know, Farag! I'm not sure!" I exploded.

"What are you saying?" he was surprised. "Did I miss something?"

If I explained my reason, I was sure he'd laugh at me. I felt foolish for being so absurdly jealous of his romantic history, but I wasn't sure if it was really jealousy I was feeling. Sleeping with Farag was something more than a comparatively small offense. I'd never had anyone in my past. He, on the other hand, had an assortment of ex-lovers. No matter how many times I turned it over in my mind and weighed the consequences, I came out the loser.

He must have seen something in my face. He set the dishes on the table and came over and put his arms around my shoulders.

"What's wrong, *Basileia?* Are we starting to have secrets?"

"That's what this is about!" I wailed, pointing an accusatory finger at the group of travel photos. "Have you been married? Because if you have…" I left my threat hanging in the air.

"I haven't been married, ever," he babbled. "What are you getting at?"

I continued to point accusatively at the photographs but he still didn't understand my hopelessness and incredulity.

"My God, Farag! You really don't get it? You've had too many women in your life!"

"Oh, okay," he sighed. "I didn't realize you were referring to that! Well, what do you think, Ottavia? Did you really expect me to be a virgin for thirty-nine years?" He was kind to add a year to equal my age.

"Why not? I have!"

If I expected excuses or for him to argue that I was a nun, I was left high and dry. All he did was flop down on the sofa, laughing loudly like a lunatic. When I saw there wasn't going to be any attack—his face was drenched with tears—I took my wounded pride and headed for the room where my suitcase was. But I didn't make it. Taking big strides, Professor Boswell caught up with me in the hall and pinned me against the wall.

"Don't be silly, *Basileia,*" he said between hiccups, trying to hold back his laughter. "I will tell you once and hope you are clear: Make that call to Italy, say farewell to Sister Sarolli and the Blessed Virgin Mary. Erase all the women I may have had in my life from your mind. I didn't feel for any of them what I feel for you, and this is the first time I am sure of how I feel. I love you like I've never loved anyone else." He leaned down and kissed me. "While you're talking with Sister Sarolli, I'll take down all those photographs and get rid of them, okay?"

"Okay."

"Well, okay." He nodded, rubbing his nose against mine. "You have five seconds. Pick up that damn phone."

"Now you're talking like Glauser-Röist."

"I think I'm starting to understand him."

I walked to my room under Farag's inquisitive look. I preferred to talk alone, calmly, instead of having him stuck to me like a shadow, hanging on every word. As I listened to the ringing at my order's main house in Rome, I also heard the doorbell. The captain had arrived, and Butros came up right after that.

My conversation with Giulia Sarolli was one of the most difficult conversations I've had in my entire life. She used the same scornful tone she used to tell me I'd been exiled to Ireland, far from my community and my family. No matter how much I insisted, she didn't explain the steps I had to take to leave the order. She obfuscated, repeating over and over that the legal part of the matter wasn't important. All that mattered was the spirit, the donation I'd made of my life.

"That donation, Sister Salina," she said, "is a donation of love, a love that tries to overcome our ego and opens us up to the rest of the world. That's why community life exists. The ideal we sisters aspire to is to say as St. Paul did, 'I have the freedom to do this and that, but I also have the freedom not to do what I want but rather what the rest of the world expects of me.' Do you understand?"

"I understand, Sister Sarolli, but I've thought it over, and I am sure I couldn't be happy if I stay in religious life."

"But that life is all about following Christ!" Giulia Sarolli couldn't understand how I could renounce such a lofty goal. She talked as if any other option wasn't worth considering. "You were called by God, how can you turn a deaf ear to the voice of Our Lord?"

"That's not what this is about, Sister. I understand that it's hard to grasp, but things aren't always that easy."

"You haven't fallen in love with a man, have you?" she asked in a grave voice after a few seconds of silence.

"I'm afraid so."

The silence persisted for a few more seconds.

"You took vows," she stressed, accusatorily.

"I haven't broken them, Sister. That's why I want you to explain exactly what I need to do to go back into the secular life."

But I didn't have any luck this time either. Sarolli didn't understand or didn't want to understand that when some things come to an end, there's no turning back. She kept trying to convince me to reconsider a while longer before making such a serious decision. I knew our conversation would be long, but I didn't realize how long.

"You need to trust that God will continue to call you," she repeated.

"Listen, please, Sister," I said, feeling irritated and tired. "I'm sure God is still calling me, but I am calling you from Egypt, and you aren't answering me. Please, tell me, once and for all, what I have to do to leave the order!"

"Next December, when you speak with the mother superior of your community for your annual review, tell her you don't want to renew your vows at the next Fourth Sunday of Easter and that's it."

"What are you saying?" I was alarmed. "That I have to wait till the annual review? Sister Sarolli, I already know that. I am asking you what I should do to leave the order *now*."

I heard her sigh over the phone line. "You need dispensation from the bishop," she groaned. "As I recall, it hasn't even been a month since you renewed your vows."

"No, Sister Sarolli, I didn't renew my vows."

"What do you mean?" she said alarmed.

"The Fourth Sunday of Easter was May 14. That day I had to go to Sicily, for my father and brother's funeral; they died in an accident...a car wreck."

"And you didn't renew your vows the following Sunday either? You didn't sign the paper when you came back?"

I heard her open and close some drawers and take out some papers. Then she covered the mouthpiece with her hand. I heard her say something to someone who must have been close by. I was starting to fret over what that long international call would cost Farag. After a while, she finally seemed convinced of the truth of my words. In a resigned voice, she gave me the news.

"Legally, Sister, you don't have to do a thing. Contrition before God is another matter. That is personal, and you will take that up with Him in solitude. You must send a letter to the general director of your community and to the mother superior of your community, Sister Margherita. Those letters will be placed in your file, and at that point, we will terminate your membership in this order."

"That simple? I'm out? It's done?" I couldn't believe what I was hearing.

"It will be, as soon as we receive those letters. If there's nothing more, Sister...," her voice wavered as she spoke that last word.

"And my salary? Will I receive it all, directly from the Vatican?"

"Don't worry about that. We will arrange all that when we get those letters. However, remember that your contract with the Vatican is contingent upon your status as a nun. I'm afraid you will have to settle that matter with the prefect of the Classified Archives, His Reverend Father Guglielmo Ramondino. It's fairly likely you'll have to find another job."

"I realize that. Thank you for everything, Sister Sarolli. I will send those letters as soon as possible."

I hung up the phone and a dizziness swept over me. I had a precipice in front of me. Turning back was no longer a possibility, and the truth was, I didn't even want to. I sighed and glanced at Farag's room. When my mother found out, she'd probably have a heart attack. No, she'd have at least two or three. I couldn't even imagine my brothers' and sisters' reactions. Pierantonio might understand. I just wanted to be with Farag for the rest of my life, but the practical Salina side of me weighed every possibility. In spite of everything, returning to Palermo was an option. There I would always find shelter. I would also have to look for another job, but that didn't worry me. With my professional history, my awards, and my publications that wouldn't be too hard. That work would also determine where I would live. I sighed again. Some way or another, I would go forward and find a way to cross this precipice.

The door to the room opened very slowly and Farag's chin appeared through the crack.

"How did it go? We heard you hang up."

"You aren't going to believe it," I replied arching my eyebrows. "I'm free."

Farag's jaw dropped. I got to my feet and went toward him.

"Let's go eat. I'll tell you about it in detail."

"But...but...you're no longer a nun?" he babbled.

"Technically, no," I explained, pushing him toward the door. "Morally, yes,...at least until I send my resignation in writing. But let's go eat, please. The food must be getting cold, and I feel guilty leaving your father and the captain alone."

"She's not a nun anymore!" he shouted as we entered the dining room. Butros smiled, ducking his head, revealing a deep happiness. The Rock, his eyes hooded, stared at me for a long time.

The meal was very pleasant. My new life couldn't have begun any better. I had no doubt why the Staurofílakes chose Alexandria for purging the sin of gluttony. It would have been hard to find dishes more succulent with better condiments than those typical Alexandrian dishes. Before the *baba ghanouj* (a puree of eggplant, tahini,* and lemon juice), and then *hummus bi tahine* (a chickpea puree with the same seasonings), we sampled an assortment of the tastiest salads accompanied by a lot of cheese and *fuul* (some enormous brown string beans). As Butros explained, the Alexandrians inherited Roman and Byzantine cuisines, but they also added the best of the Arabic cuisine. Every stew contained olive oil, honey, bay leaf, yogurt, garlic, thyme, black pepper, sesame, cinnamon, and other spices.

I tried them all. Glauser-Röist drank a couple of bottles of Stella Egyptian beer. Farag's father did him one better.

"Did you know beer was invented in ancient Egypt?" he said. "There's nothing like a nice glass of beer before bed. It helps you get to sleep and is a natural relaxant."

Despite that, Farag and I just drank mineral water and cold *karkade,*

---

* A white sauce or paste made with sesame.

a dark red soft drink made with hibiscus flowers, which gave it a somewhat sour taste. Egyptians drink it all day, along with *shai nana*, very strong black tea they brew with mint.

The worst part was the desserts. I say the worst part, because there was no limit to the variety served. The Alexandrians, true to the Byzantine tradition, were like the Greeks, great lovers of sweets. Farag, an upstanding Alexandrian, had ordered enough cakes, puff pastries, and cookies to feed a starving army rather than the four people already satiated by a great meal: *om ali,** *konafa,*† *baklaoua,*‡ and *ashura,*§ a typical dessert that Muslims consumed especially on the tenth of the month of Moharram. Farag and his father devoured it every chance they got. Glauser-Röist and I exchanged discreet looks of surprise at the outrageous capacity of the Boswell family to consume sweets without restraint.

"Doesn't look like you're worried about diabetes, Farag," I joked.

"Not diabetes or obesity, or arterial hypertension," he said with difficulty, gobbling down a great big piece of *konafa*. "This is just what I needed—a good meal!"

"Alexandria boasts the terrible distinction…," the Rock recited somberly. Farag's father froze, his eyes wide and in the middle of chewing. The Rock continued, "…of being known for perversely practicing the sin of gluttony."

"What did you say, Captain Glauser-Röist?" he asked, incredulous, after swallowing his *baklaoua* with the help of a quick gulp of beer.

"Calm down, Papa." Farag smiled. "Kaspar isn't crazy. He just made a joke."

But it wasn't a joke. I couldn't get out of my head Cato's message about the city and its guilt.

"I understand that," the Rock said, quickly changing the subject, "in Arabic countries, Internet access is restricted. Is that true in Egypt, too?"

---

* A mixture made with milk, nuts, raisins, and coconut.
† Puff pastry made with honey.
‡ Puff pastry made with sugar, pistachios, and coconut.
§ Cookies of ground wheat, milk, dried fruit, raisins, and rose water.

Butros folded his napkin meticulously and set it on the table before he answered. (Farag kept eating *konafa*.) "That's a serious matter, Captain," he said, his forehead furrowed in worry. "Here in Egypt we don't have to put up with the restrictions that exist in Saudi Arabia and Iran, where they censor and restrict citizens' access to a thousand pages of the Internet. Saudi Arabia, for example, has a center for technology on the outskirts of Riad where they control all the pages seen by its citizens. They block hundreds of new addresses daily which, according to the government, go against their religion, morals, and the royal Saudi family. It's even worse in Iraq and Syria, where the Internet is completely forbidden."

"Why are you upset, Papa? You barely know how to turn on a computer, and in Egypt we don't have those problems."

Butros looked at his son as if he didn't know him. "A government shouldn't spy on its own people, son, or act like a jailer or censor opinions and freedoms. And it especially shouldn't censor religion. The hell described in books isn't in the next life, Farag. It's here, on this side. So many men say they interpret God's word, but they are lying, like the governments that restrict their citizens' freedoms. Think about what our city was like before and what it's like now. Remember your brother Juhanna and Zoe and little Simon.

"I won't forget them, Papa."

"Search for a country where you can be free, my son," Butros spoke to Farag as if the captain and I weren't there. "Find that country and leave Alexandria."

"What are you saying, Papa?" Farag's knuckles were white as they pressed against the wood.

"Leave Alexandria, Farag. If you stay here, I would never be at peace. Get out of here. Leave your work at the museum and close up the house. Don't worry about me," he rushed to say, looking at me and smiling with evil amusement. "As soon as you two find that place, you'll sell this house and buy another one there."

"Would you leave Alexandria, Butros?" I asked, smiling.

"The deaths of my son, Juhanna, and my grandson sealed my break with this city." His friendly expression barely hid the deep pain he felt.

"Alexandria was glorious for thousands of years. Today, for those who aren't Muslim, it's just dangerous. There aren't any Jews, Greeks, or Europeans left. They all fled and only come here as tourists. Why should we stay?" Again he looked at his son with bitterness. "Promise me you'll leave, Farag."

"I've thought about it, Papa," Farag admitted, looking at me out of the corner of his eye. "I'm so happy to be back that it's really hard for me to make that promise."

"Do you know that if Farag stayed in Alexandria, he could die at the hands of the *Al-Gama'a al-Islamiyya*, Ottavia?"

I remained silent. Maybe Butros was obsessed, but his words affected me. I communicated that to Farag with my eyes.

"Okay, Papa. You have my word. I won't stay in Alexandria."

After that, no one said a word. I'd never imagined I would live with so much fear. I thought sadly about the people in Sicily, threatened by families like Doria's and mine. Why is the world such a terrible place? Why does God let such terrible things happen? I'd lived in a glass bubble, and now I finally had to face reality.

"What do you say we work for a while?" proposed the Rock, laying his napkin on the table.

I shook my head like someone waking from a dream. I looked around surprised. "Work?"

"Yes, Doctor, work. It's...," he said as he looked at his watch, "eleven at night. We can still get in a couple of hours. What do you say, Professor?"

"Fine...fine...Kaspar!" he stammered. "I don't think we'll have a problem gaining access to the museum's database. I hope they didn't erase my access code."

Between the four of us we cleared the table and quickly straightened up the kitchen. Then, as if he would never see us again, Butros said good-bye to his son and to me with hard, loving hugs and affectionately shook the captain's hand.

"Be very careful," he begged us as he went down the first flight of stairs.

"Don't worry, Papa."

Farag sat down at the computer, while the Rock cleared a pile of magazines off another chair and pulled it up to the machine. I didn't want to be reminded of the Staurofilakes, so I leafed through the books on the bookshelves.

"Okay, here we are," I heard Farag say. "Enter your username: Kenneth," he revealed in a loud voice. "Enter your access code: Oxirrinco. Great, it accepted them. We're in," he announced.

"Can it search images?"

"Not really. But I can search for specific texts and access the related images. I'll look for 'bearded snake.'"

"What language do you do search in?" I asked without turning around.

"In Arabic and English," he explained. "Usually English. It's easier with this keyboard in the Roman alphabet. I have another keyboard in Arabic next to that bookcase over there, but I rarely use it."

"Can I see it?"

"Sure."

While they jumped into the hunt for bearded snakes, I picked up the Arabic keyboard. I'd never seen anything so strange; it really amused me. It was the same as ours, of course, but with Arabic characters on the keys instead of the Roman alphabet.

"Do you really know how to write with this?"

"Yes. It isn't complicated. The hardest part is changing the configuration of the computer and the programs. That's why I always work in English."

"What does it say there, Professor?" the Rock inquired, his eyes glued to the monitor.

"Where? Let's see… Oh yeah, that's the museum's collection of images of bearded snakes."

"Perfect. Let's go."

They became engrossed in studying photographs of reptiles and snakes engraved or painted on art objects belonging to the Greco-Roman Museum. After quite a while, they came to the conclusion that none of those images had anything to do with the Staurofilakes' drawing, so they started all over again.

"Maybe it isn't here," Farag ventured, a bit unsure. "We only encompass six hundred years of history, starting from 300 B.C. It could be before that."

"The style of the drawing is Greco-Roman, Farag," I pointed out as I leafed through a magazine on Egyptian archeology, "so it has to fall in that time span."

"Yes, but there's nothing here, and that's really odd."

They decided to consult the general catalogues of Alexandrian art, published by the museum for the city government and available in the database. There they had more luck. They found a bearded serpent wearing the pharonic crowns of Upper and Lower Egypt that closely resembled our drawing.

"Where was that work found, Professor?" The Rock asked, bent over the copy coming out of the printer.

"Oh, in...the catacombs of Kom el-Shoqafa."

"Kom el-Shoqafa...? I think that I just saw something about that around here." I retraced my steps to three wobbly stacks of back issues of *National Geographic*. I remember the article about Shoqafa because it sounded like *konafa*, the huge puff pastry with honey that Farag gobbled down.

"Don't bother, *Basileia*. I don't think Kom el-Shoqafa has anything to do with the test."

"Why not, Professor?" the Rock asked coldly.

"Because I worked there, Kaspar. I was the director of excavations in 1998. I know the place quite well. If I'd seen that image from the Staurofilakes' drawing, I'd have remembered it."

"But it looked familiar to you," I said, as I hunted for the magazine.

"Because of the mixture of styles, *Basileia*."

Despite the late hour, they dove back into the catalogue of Alexandrian art from the last fourteen hundred years. They never seemed to get tired. Just as I came across the copy of *National Geographic* I was looking for, they'd come across a second important piece of information: a medallion with Medusa's head on it. Judging from the captain's exclamation—he'd just matched the crumpled, charcoal drawing with one on the screen—I knew they'd made a significant find.

"It's identical, Professor," he said. "See for yourself."

"A Medusa from the late Hellenistic period? It is quite common, Kaspar!"

Yes, but this is exactly the same! Where is that relief?"

"Let me see... Hmmm..., in the catacombs of Kom el-Shoqafa," he said very surprised. "How strange! I don't remember it..."

"You don't remember the god of wine's thyrsus, either?" I asked, holding up the magazine, opened to the page with an enlarged reproduction. "Because it's identical to the one on that disgusting animal's rings and it's in Kom el-Shoqafa."

The captain shot out of his seat and grabbed the magazine out of my hand.

"It's the same one, I have no doubt," he pronounced.

"It's Kom el-Shoqafa," I confirmed.

"But that can't be!" Farag objected indignantly. "The Staurofilakes' test can't be there. That funeral enclosure was totally unknown until 1900, when the ground sank suddenly out from under a poor donkey that happened to be walking down the street. Nobody knew the place existed, and there was no other entrance! It was lost and forgotten for more than fifteen centuries."

"Like the mausoleum of Constantine, Farag," I reminded him. He stared at me from across the monitor. He was sprawled back in his chair, gnawing on the end of a pen, an angry grimace on his face. He knew I was right, but he refused to admit he was wrong.

"What does Kom el-Shoqafa mean?" I asked.

"It's the name it was given when it was discovered in 1900. It means 'pile of rubble.'"

"That's original!" I replied, smiling.

"Kom el-Shoqafa was a three-story, underground cemetery. The first floor was dedicated exclusively to funeral banquets. It was called that because thousands of fragments of drinking vessels and plates were found there."

"Look, Professor," the Rock pointed out, returning to his seat, still holding the *National Geographic,* "say what you will, but even the bit about the feasts and the dishes seems to be related to the test of gluttony."

"True," I said.

"I know those catacombs like the back of my hand. It can't be the place we're looking for. Bear in mind, they were excavated down to the rocky subsoil and have been explored completely. This overlap with certain details in the drawing is not significant. There are hundreds of sculptures, drawings, and reliefs throughout. On the second floor, for example, there are large drawings of the dead who are buried in the niches and sarcophagi. It's impressive."

"What about the third floor?" I asked, trying to suppress a yawn.

"It was also used for burials. The problem is, right now it's partially flooded by underground waters. Anyway, I assure you it has been studied thoroughly and contains no surprises."

The captain stood up and looked at his watch. "When are those catacombs open to visitors?"

"If I remember right, they open at nine thirty in the morning."

"Okay, let's get some rest. Let's be there at nine thirty sharp."

Farag looked at me, distressed. "Do you want to write those letters to your order now, Ottavia?"

I was really tired, no doubt on account of all the new emotions I'd been presented that first of June and the rest of my life. I looked at him sadly and shook my head.

"Tomorrow, Farag. Tomorrow we'll write them, when we are on board the plane to Antioch."

What I didn't know was that we'd never get on the Westwind again.

At nine thirty on the dot, just as Glauser-Röist said, we were at the entrance to the catacombs of Kom el-Shoqafa. A bus full of Japanese tourists had pulled up in front of that strange, round house with a low ceiling. We were in Karmouz, an extremely poor neighborhood where numerous donkey carts drove down narrow streets. It wasn't so strange that one of those poor animals had discovered such an outstanding archaeological monument. Flies flew over our heads in dense, noisy clouds and settled on our bare arms and faces with repulsive insistence. The Japanese didn't seem to mind one bit the corporal visits of those insects, but they were getting on my nerves. I observed enviously as the donkeys shooed them away with effective switches of their tails.

Fifteen minutes after opening time, an elderly civil servant who must have been well past the age to be enjoying a well-deserved retirement, parsimoniously approached the door and opened it as if he didn't see the fifty or sixty people waiting there. He sat in a little wicker chair behind a table that held several ticket books, muttered a gruff *Ahlan wasahlan,** and gestured that we should approach in a single file. The guide for the Japanese group tried to cut in line, but the captain, who was half a meter taller than him, put his hand on the guide's shoulder and stopped him cold with some well-chosen words in English.

Farag, being Egyptian, only had to pay fifty piasters. The civil servant didn't recognize him, even though he'd worked there just two years before. Farag didn't reveal his identity either. Glauser-Röist and I, being foreigners, paid twelve Egyptian pounds apiece.

Just inside the door, we came across a hole in the floor with a long spiral staircase excavated in the rock that left a dangerous hollow space in its center. We started our descent, treading carefully on the steps.

"At the end of the second century," Farag explained, "when Kom el-Shoqafa was a very active cemetery, bodies were slid on cords through this opening."

The first staircase ended at a sort of vestibule with a perfectly leveled limestone floor. There you could just make out, in the very bad light, two benches dug out of the wall and inlaid with seashells. This vestibule opened onto a great rotunda in whose center were six carved columns with capitals in the shape of papyrus. As Farag had said, everywhere around us there were strange reliefs in which the mixture of Egyptian, Greek, and Roman motifs bore an amazing similarity to the strange women in the *Mona Lisa* paintings by Duchamp, Warhol, or Botero. There were so many funeral banquet rooms that they formed a labyrinth of galleries. I could imagine a typical day in that place, around the first century of our era, when all those rooms would have been full of families and friends, seated on cushions placed on the stone seats, celebrating

---

* An Arabic greeting.

feasts in honor of their dead by torchlight. It's amazing how different the pagan mentality was from the Christian one.

"In the beginning," Farag went on to say, "these catacombs must have belonged to a single family. With time, some corporation must have acquired it and turned it into a place of massive burial. That would explain why there are so many funeral chambers and so many banquet rooms."

On one side was an enormous crevice opened by a cave-in.

"On the other side is what's called Caracalla Hall. In it we found human bones mixed with horses' bones." He ran his palm along the edge of the breach as if he were the owner of it all. "In 215 Emperor Caracalla was in Alexandria and for no apparent reason, he decreed a draft of strong, young men. After reviewing the new troops, he commanded that men and horses be assassinated." [*]

From the rotunda, a new spiral staircase descended to the second level. If we thought the light on the previous level was bad, on this level we couldn't make out anything except the scary silhouettes of life-size statues of the dead. The Rock automatically dug out his flashlight and switched it on. We were completely alone; the throng of Japanese tourists had stayed above. In this vestibule, two enormous pillars, crowned by capitals decorated with papyruses and lotuses, flanked a frieze in which two hawks escorted a winged sun. Carved in the wall, two figures, a man and a woman also life-size, observed us with empty eyes. The body of the man was identical to the figures in ancient Egypt: hieratic, with two left feet; but his head was in Hellenistic Greek style, with a very beautiful, extremely expressive face. The woman, on the other hand, wore an affected Roman hairdo on another passive Egyptian body.

"We believe they were the occupants of those two niches," Farag explained, pointing down a long corridor.

The size of the chambers was impressive; their luxury and strange decoration surprised us. On one side of a door was the god Anubis, with the head of a jackal; on the other side was the crocodile-god, Sobek, also the god of the Nile, both adorned with loricas of the Roman Le-

---

[*] Historia Augusta, *Antonino Caracalla*, by Elio Esparciano (13,6,2–4).

gion, short swords, lances, and shields. We found the medallion with Medusa's head inside a chamber that contained three gigantic sarcophagi, along with Dionysus's staff carved into one side. Around this chamber was a passageway full of niches; each one, according to Farag, had enough space to hold up to three mummies.

"They aren't still inside there, are they?" I asked apprehensively.

"No, *Basileia*. Almost all the niches were stripped of their contents before 1900. As you know, in Europe, mummy dust was considered an excellent medicine for all types of illnesses, until well into the fourteenth century. Worth its weight in gold."

"Then you can't be sure there wasn't another entrance in addition to the main one," the Rock commented.

"It has never been found," Farag replied, annoyed.

"A fortuitous cave-in," the Rock persisted, "revealed the Caracalla Hall. Why couldn't there have been another undiscovered chamber?"

"Here's something!" I said, looking at a nook in the wall. I'd found our famous bearded serpent.

"Good, now all we need is Hermes's *kerykeion*,"* Farag said, coming over.

"The caduceus, right?" the captain asked. "It reminds me more of doctors and pharmacies than messengers."

"Because Asclepio, the Greek god of medicine, carried a similar staff but his had only one serpent. In a mix-up, doctors adopted the symbol of Hermes."

"We're going to have to go down to the third level," I said, heading for the spiral staircase, "I'm afraid we're not going to find anything else here."

"The third level is closed, *Basileia*. The galleries are flooded. When I worked here it was already very difficult to study that last floor."

"So what we are waiting for?" the Rock declared, following me.

The stairs going down to the deepest part of the catacombs of Kom el-Shoqafa were, indeed, closed off by a small chain with a metal sign

---

*Staff crowned with two wings and two intertwined serpents. It was the symbol for Hermes, messenger for the gods.

saying *no entry* in Arabic and English. The captain, brave explorer that he was, never let convention stop him. He ripped the chain out of the wall and started down the stairway with Farag Boswell's grumbling as background music. Above our heads, an advance team of Japanese tourists was excited about reaching the second level.

Right then, poised on the last step of the staircase, I noticed I'd stepped in a pool of lukewarm liquid.

"He who warns is not a traitor," Farag joked.

The vestibule on that floor was a lot bigger than both of the upper vestibules and the water came up to our waists. I was starting to think maybe Farag was right.

"Do you gentlemen know what this reminds me of?" I asked in a joking tone.

"Surely it's the same thing I'm thinking," Farag shot back. "It's as if we're back in the cistern in Constantinople, right?"

"Actually that wasn't it," I answered. "I was thinking we never read the text of Dante's sixth circle."

"You two may not have read it," Glauser-Röist rushed to answer contemptuously, "but I certainly did."

Casanova and I gave each other a guilty look.

"So, tell us about it, Kaspar, so we know what's going on."

"The test in the sixth circle is much simpler than the previous ones," the Rock began, as we entered the galleries. There was an intense stench of decomposition, and the water was as cloudy as the cistern in Constantinople. Fortunately, this time, its off-white color was due to the limestone, not the sweat of hundreds of fervent feet. "Dante utilizes the cone shape of Purgatory Mountain to reduce the size of the cornices and the magnitude of the punishments."

"May God be listening to you!" I exclaimed, hopeful.

The reliefs on this level were as strange as those on the first and second levels. The Alexandrians of the Golden Age did not have religious problems or limiting beliefs. They left their remains in catacombs under Osiris's watchful eye, yet decorated with reliefs of Dionysus. That well-developed eclecticism was the basis of Alexandria's prosperous society. Sadly, all that ended when primitive Christianity, which violently rejected other religions, became the official religion of the Byzantine Empire.

"The sixth circle includes Cantos XXII, XXIII, and XXIV," the Rock continued. "The souls of the gluttonous go around the cornice incessantly. On opposite ends of this cornice are two apple trees whose treetops are in the shape of an upside down cone."

"That closely resembles the Egyptian papyrus plant," Farag pointed out.

"Certainly, Professor. You could take that as a veiled reference to Alexandria. In any case, from those treetops hang abundant, mouth-watering fruits the penitents can't reach. Plus, an exquisite liquor drips from them and they can't drink it either. So they go around and around the cornice, their eyes sunken and their faces pale due to their hunger and thirst."

"Dante must run into tons of old friends and acquaintances, as usual, right?" I asked. At the same time I thought I spotted the figure of the caduceus on the back wall of a chamber. "Let's go that way. I think I saw something."

"But how does he complete the test?" Farag insisted.

"An angel in red, flickering like fire," the Rock concluded, "shows them the way up to the seventh and last cornice, and then erases the mark of gluttony from Dante's forehead."

"That's it?" I asked, fighting against the water to advance more quickly to the wall where I clearly saw a large caduceus of Hermes.

"That's it. Things are getting simpler and simpler, Doctor."

"I'd give anything, Captain, for that to be true."

"So would I."

"The *kerykeion!*" Farag blurted out, putting his hands on the image the way a devout Jew puts his hand on the Wailing Wall. "I swear this wasn't here two years ago."

"Come, come, Professor...," the Rock rebuked him. "Don't be so proud. Admit you might have forgotten it."

"No, Kaspar, no! There are too many chambers to remember them all, it's true, but a symbol like that would have caught my attention."

"They must have put it there for us," I said ironically.

"Doesn't it seem odd that we found the reproductions of the Medusa, the serpent, and thyrsus on the second floor and the one of the caduceus on the third floor, far from the rest?"

The Rock and I thought that over.

"Just a moment! What did I tell you?" said Farag, showing us the palms of his hands. They were covered in mud.

"The wall is crumbling," the Rock added perplexedly, poking his hand in and drawing out a handful of doughy mortar.

"It's a false partition! I knew it!" Farag said. He started to tear it down with such fury that he was soon covered in mud up to his eyebrows, like a little boy. By the time he was out of breath and sweaty, he had opened a big hole in the wall. I wiped my wet hand over his face several times to clean him off a little. He looked so happy.

"We're so smart, *Basileia!*" he repeated, wiping plaster off his chin.

"Come see this," the Rock's voice said from the other side of the partition.

Glauser-Röist's powerful flashlight lit up a spectacular sight. Below where we were standing was an enormous hypostyle room with numerous Byzantine columns forming long, vaulted tunnels. It was half submerged in a calm, black lake that gleamed in the captain's beam like a moonlit ocean.

"Don't just stand there," the Rock said. "Get in this oil deposit with me."

Luckily, it was just water collected in a dark tank. The off-white spot of water seeping smoothly from the catacombs stood out against the water in the tank. We squeezed around what was left of the mortar wall and climbed down four big steps.

"There is a door at the back of the room," the captain said. "Let's go over there."

With the water up to our necks, we advanced silently down one of those corridors. You could have sailed a fishing boat down it without any problem. Clearly we'd come to the city's old cistern. The Alexandrians stored drinkable water so they could survive the annual drought when the water level in the Nile dropped all the way to the delta, dragging along red soil from the south, the famous plague of blood that Yahweh sent to free the Jewish people from slavery in Egypt.

When we walked over to the sturdy, ashlar stone wall where the door was, we came across the first of four other steps that, when we climbed them, took us out of the water. We weren't surprised to find Constantine's chrismon etched in the wooden door; it would have actually surprised us *not* to find it. With complete confidence, the captain grasped the iron handle and pushed. We froze. We found ourselves before a funeral banquet room identical to many on the first floor of Kom el-Shoqafa.

"What in the world is this?" Glauser-Röist roared when he saw the stone benches covered by soft damask cushions and a table in the center filled with exquisite food.

Farag and I went to one side and entered. Several torches lit up the chamber. The walls and floors were covered by precious tapestries and carpets. Although you couldn't see another door anywhere, somebody had left very quickly, since the food was steaming on the plates, having just been served up. The alabaster glasses overflowed with wine, water, and *karkade.*

"I don't like this!" the Rock kept bellowing, very upset.

When I heard him, fear took hold of me. Suddenly, without knowing why, I detected something sinister in that chamber so delicately laid out, filled with aromas from the exquisite meat, greens, and vegetable dishes.

"Dear God!" babbled Farag behind me. "No!"

I turned as fast as lightning, alarmed by the anguished tone in his voice. He had bared his chest and was holding on to each side of his shirt. His torso was covered with some strange black, wriggling lines, thick and long like fingers.

"My God," I screamed. "Leeches!"

In a frenzy, Glauser-Röist set the flashlight on the table and grabbed at the buttons on his shirt. His chest, like Farag's, was covered by fifteen or twenty disgusting worms, which, due to the warm blood they were ingesting, seemed to grow fatter before our eyes.

"Ottavia! Take off your clothes!"

I could have made a joke, but it wasn't the time for it. I unbuttoned my blouse with trembling hands, on the verge of a nervous breakdown, while Farag and the captain took off their pants. They both had pretty hairy legs, but that didn't seem to bother the leeches; they'd stuck to their skin in untold numbers. My body was also covered with those repugnant creatures. Gagging in disgust with my stomach churning, I grabbed at one of the nine or ten on my belly—it was soft and warm like gelatin and wrinkly to the touch—and tugged at it.

"Don't do that, Doctor!" Glauser-Röist shouted. I didn't feel any pain, but no matter how much I stretched it, I couldn't get it loose. Its round mouth was cupped to my skin and was simply not letting go.

"You can only remove them with fire."

"What are you saying?" I asked, tears of disgust and desperation streaming down my cheeks. "We're going to burn ourselves!"

The Rock had already climbed on to one of the benches, stretching up as high as he could and grabbing a torch. I saw him come toward me in a decisive gesture with a fanatical look in his eyes that made me shrink back in fear. I experienced an indescribable urge to retch as I backed against the wall and felt the sticky, elastic mass of worms plastered to my back. I couldn't control myself and vomited. Before I had time to recover, Glauser-Röist brought the flame next to my body and the animals started to fall like ripe fruit. I, too, was burned and the pain was so intense I couldn't hold back, my screams of pain changing to alarm when the Rock applied the torch a second time.

Meanwhile, the leeches on Farag's and the captain's bodies grew more engorged. They grew round and puffed at the head. I don't know how much blood those creatures could swallow, considering the number stuck to us, but we must have lost liters and liters.

"Put the torch down, Captain!" shouted Farag suddenly, appearing from behind the Rock with an alabaster cup in his hand. "I'm going to try something!"

He dipped his fingers into the cup holding a liquid that smelled like vinegar. He smeared one of the leeches on my thigh with the liquid. The leech writhed like a demon under the blessed water and fell right off my skin.

"On the table there's wine, vinegar, and salt! Mix them together and brush it on like I did to Ottavia!"

Repeating the process, Farag moistened the creatures; they dropped off me and fell lifeless to the ground. I thanked God for that solution because the parts of my body where the Rock had applied the torch hurt so much it was like someone had stuck knives into me. But if the burns hurt, why didn't the leeches' bites hurt? I couldn't feel a thing and hardly noticed that they were still sucking my blood. The only thing that got to me was the sight of our bodies covered in those disgusting black creatures.

Instead of applying the mixture to himself, Glauser-Röist walked over to Farag and detached the worms on his back, one by one. Some worms were now as fat as rats. But there were too many. The ground was covered with them. The worms moved heavily due to the enormous amount of blood they had sucked out of us; however, it didn't seem that their numbers had decreased. When one of them detached from our skins, it left a star-shaped mark (similar to the Mercedes-Benz logo) from which blood continued to flow abundantly. That is, on top of sucking blood, they also had bit us with three sharp sets of teeth.

"The torch would be better, Professor," the Rock observed. "I believe a leech's bite bleeds for a long time. The fire will stop that. And don't forget the sixth circle of Dante: The angel who pointed out the exit was red and fiery."

"No, Kaspar. Believe me. I know these creatures. I've seen leeches since I was a little boy. There are a lot in Alexandria, on the beaches and the banks of Lake Mareotis.* There's no way to stop the hemorrhaging. Their saliva has a very strong antiseptic and potent anticoagulant. The wound bleeds for about twelve hours." Farag's brow was furrowed, and he concentrated as he spoke, grabbing one worm after another. "We would have to cause very deep burns to stop the bleeding. Besides, how could we cauterize an entire body?...All we can do is get those creatures off as quickly as we can. They can swallow up to ten times their weight."

---

* Lake in northern Egypt, in the western part of the Nile delta. Alexandria is situated on the strip of land between the lake and the Mediterranean.

I was so thirsty. Suddenly my mouth was dry and I couldn't quit looking at the water and the *karkade* on the table. The captain, who still had fifty or sixty leeches attached to him, walked unsteadily over to the glasses; picked them up with a trembling hand, gave one to Farag and another to me. Then he drank that water like a thirsty camel, unable to control himself. I would have given anything to be able to drink more, but the dehydration and terrible weakness that immobilized me didn't let me. Farag got the last of the worms off my body and began to help Glauser-Röist, who was as white as paper, teetering around like a drunkard. I felt dizzy so I leaned against the soft tapestry on the wall and noticed suddenly that it was drenched and getting stained. Uncountable little threads of blood were flowing from my star-shaped wounds. It was an unstoppable flow that formed pools inside my shoes and around them on the ground.

"Drink, Ottavia!" I heard Farag say. "Drink, my love, drink!"

His voice was nearly inaudible, but I felt the edge of a cup on my lips. My ears were buzzing. I remember my eyes were half-closed just before I fell to the ground, unconscious. The captain, covered with worms, was lying next to one of the benches. Farag, pale and dissipated, his cheeks and eyes sunken, his blurry image was the last thing I remembered.

We were extremely weak for over a week. The men who cared for us forced us to drink plenty of water and eat some gruel that tasted like pureed greens. Still it took us a long time to recover from our savage blood loss. My bouts of unconsciousness were prolonged, and I remember long, delirious, strange hallucinations in which the most absurd things seemed logical and possible. When the men gave me something to eat or drink, I opened my eyes slightly and saw sunlight filtering through a cane roof. I wasn't sure if that image was real or part of my delirium, but whatever it was, I wasn't myself.

The second or third day—I couldn't be sure—I realized we were on a boat. The sway of the waves and water lapping against the hull near my head started to filter into my nightmares. I remember looking around for Farag and finding him next to me, unconscious, but I didn't have the strength to sit up and go over to him. In my dreams I saw him glowing and heard him say in a sad voice: "At least you have the consolation of believing that in a little while you'll start a new life. I'll sleep forever." I stretched my arms toward him to grab hold and beg him not to abandon me, not to go away, to come back to me. Smiling nostalgically, he said, "For a long time I've been afraid of death, but I didn't allow myself the weakness of believing in God to save me from that fear. Then I discovered that when I went to bed at night and slept, I died somewhat. It's the same process, didn't you know that? Do you remember Greek mythology? The twin brothers, Hypnos, sleep, and Thanatos, death, brothers of the Night… Remember?" His image changed into the hazy profile I saw before I passed out in the funereal banquet hall in Kom el-Shoqafa.

We must have been very close to not ever waking up. After a while, the water, beer, and gruel that now included pieces of fish began to make our weak bodies healthy. The boat docked alongside the beach at night. Men carried us on their shoulders, took us from the boat's cabin, and transported us over land, placing us in the cart of a *shai nana* vendor. I inhaled the strong odor of black tea and mint and saw a crescent moon in an endless, starry sky.

I began to regain consciousness. We were in a boat again, but this one was larger, which meant that it didn't rock as much. With superhuman effort, I sat up. I had to see Farag and find out what was going on. Surrounded by ropes, old sails, and mountains of nets that smelled of rotten fish, he and the captain were stretched out next to me, fast asleep, covered up to their necks in a fine, yellow linen fabric that protected them from the flies. My effort to sit up was too much for my feeble body to bear; I fell back onto the straw mattress, weaker than before. One of our caretakers shouted something from the deck in a language that sounded like Arabic but wasn't. Before falling back to sleep, I thought I heard something like "Nubiya" or "Nubia" but I couldn't be sure.

I was never awake at the same time as Farag or the Rock. Soon, I came to the conclusion that the food they fed us contained something more than fish, vegetables, and wheat. That type of sleep wasn't normal and our bodies were stabilized by then so there was no reason for us to still be submerged in such a deep slumber. Yet I was afraid to stop eating, so I kept swallowing the gruel and drinking the beer brought to us. The men who helped us wore immaculate white loincloths that stood out against their dark skin. Under the spell of the drugs, I relived the Transfiguration of Jesus on Mount Tabor, when his clothes acquired a resplendent whiteness and an intense glow as he heard the voice from the sky say, "This is my beloved son in whom well I am pleased. Listen to him."

The men wore thin, white scarves on their heads, tied with a cord at the neck, and the ends hung down their backs. They talked very little among themselves, and when they did, they spoke in a strange language I didn't understand. A couple of times, I tried asking them for something to see if I could articulate a word, but they always answered by negatively waving their hands in the air, and with a smile saying *"Guiiz, guiiz!"* over and over again. They were always friendly and treated me with concern; they gave me food and drink with a tenderness worthy of the best mother. Yet they weren't Staurofilakes because their bodies were free of tattoos. The day I noticed that detail, I had to calm myself down by telling myself that if they were bandits or terrorists they'd have killed us by now. This was just part of the brotherhood's twisted plans. If they weren't Staurofilakes, how would we have fallen into their hands at Kom el-Shoqafa?

We changed boats five times, always at night; then we trekked a long way on land, in the back of an old truck hauling wood. We stuck close to the riverbank, but I could tell that past the riverbank, just beyond a dark chain of palm trees, lay the vast, empty, cold desert. I recall thinking that we were getting back on the Nile heading south and that those periodic nocturnal boat changes meant we were going around the dangerous waterfalls that tore up the riverbed, which probably meant we were in Sudan, at the very least. But what about the test at Antioch? If we were heading south, we were a long way from our next destination.

Finally, they stopped drugging us. I became lucid when I felt Farag's lips on mine.

"*Basileia...*"

"I'm awake, my love," I whispered.

The turquoise of his blue eyes shot through me like lightning when I opened mine. He was emaciated but as handsome as ever. However, I don't think I'm exaggerating if I say he smelled worse than one of those dirty fishing nets.

"It's been so long since I last heard your voice, *Basileia,*" he murmured still kissing me. "You were always asleep."

"They drugged us, Farag."

"I know, my love, but they didn't harm us. That's what matters."

"How do you feel?" I asked, pulling back from him and stroking his face. His blond beard was already more than a couple of inches long.

"Perfectly fine. These guys must be rich if they traffic in the drugs used in these tests."

Only then did I realize that the walls of this new, luxurious berth were as thin as paper. Light and noise crept their way in.

"What about the Rock?"

"He's over there," he pointed with his chin toward the front wall, "sound asleep. But it won't be long till he wakes up. Something is about to happen and our captors want us alert."

He was still talking when the linen curtain that covered one side of the cabin folded back, letting one of our caretakers in. Curiously, only then did I see them clearly, as if previously my sight had been clouded by shadows. They were tall and thin, nearly skeletal, and they all had thick short beards that gave them a savage look.

"*Ahlan wasahlan,*" said the one who seemed to be in charge. He crossed his skinny dark arms and agilely dropped to the ground beside us. The others stayed standing.

Farag answered his greeting and they began a prolonged conversation in Arabic.

"Ready for a surprise, Ottavia?" Farag asked, looking at me with disconcerted eyes.

"No," I said sitting down, tucking my legs under the linen. I was dressed in just a short white tunic, and my dignity forbade exposing myself. When it dawned on me that some of those silent men must have been washing the most intimate parts of my body, I felt terribly ashamed.

"Well, it's bad, but I have to tell you," Farag continued without noticing the abrupt change in the color of my face. "This good man is Captain Mulugeta Mariam and the others are members of his crew. This ship the... *Neway?*" He asked, looking at Captain Mulugeta, who nodded imperceptibly, "is one of the many he owns along the Nile to transport merchandise and passengers between Egypt and, as he calls it, Abyssinia. Or, Ethiopia."

I opened my eyes wide at what Farag was saying.

"For hundreds of years his people, the Anuak of Antioch, in the region of Gambela, near Lake Tana, in Abyssnia, have collected sleeping passengers in the Nile Delta and transported them to his village..."

"Who are they delivered to?" I interrupted.

Farag repeated this question in Arabic and Captain Mariam answered laconically, "*Staurofilas.*"

We remained silent, looking horrified.

"Ask him," I stammered, "what they're going to do with us when we get there."

After another exchange of words, finally Farag looked at me. "He says we will have to pass a test that has been part of the Anuak tradition since God gave them the earth and the Nile. If we die, they will burn our bodies on a pyre and scatter our ashes to the wind. If we survive..."

"What?" I was scared.

"*Staurofilas,*" he concluded, gloomily imitating Mariam's way of talking.

I didn't know what to do other than dumbfoundedly shake my head and brush my hands over my filthy hair.

"But... But we were only supposed to discover where the earthly paradise is and capture the thieves," at this point, it was my fear talking. "How are we going to warn the police if they've taken us prisoner?"

"It all makes sense, *Basileia.* Think about it. The Staurofilakes couldn't let us leave the seventh circle scot-free. Or any of the aspirants, for that matter. It's easy to change your mind or betray an ideal at the last minute, when the goal is within arm's reach. Faced with a threat like that, what can they do? After all, it seems obvious, don't you think? We should have suspected that the last cornice would be different from the others. In our case, what are they going to do? Let us pass the test and give us the final clue so that we could reach the earthly paradise on our own? All we'd have to do was, as you say, notify the authorities of the location of the hiding place so an entire army could fall on them. They aren't stupid."

Mulugeta Mariam looked at us without understanding a word but he didn't seem at all impressed. As if he had lived that situation hundreds of times, he remained calm. Finally, faced with our prolonged silence, he rattled off a long string of words that Farag listened to attentively.

"The captain says it won't be long till we reach his village of Antioch. That's why they woke us up. We left the Nile several days ago and entered one of its tributaries, the Atbara. According to this nice gentleman, it belongs to the Anuak, like the Nile does."

"But how did we get to Ethiopia?" I shrieked. "Aren't there any borders between countries? Aren't there any customs police?"

"They cross borders at night and are expert at sailing the boats typical to the Nile, which can silently pass next to the police posts without awakening suspicions. I suppose they also use bribes and the like. In these parts, that's standard procedure," he murmured biting his lower lip.

I could hardly breathe. "So, where are we going exactly?" I still struggled to talk. I felt as though I was lost in an unexplored part of a vast planet.

"I've never heard of the Anuak or their town named Antioch. But I do know where Lake Tana is. It is the birthplace of the Blue Nile.* It isn't exactly a civilized area or easy to get to. Forget that the world is about to enter the twenty-first century. Go back a couple thousand years, and you'll be close to what's here."

---

*The Nile is formed by the confluence in Khartoum, capital of Sudan, of the White Nile and the Blue Nile. The White Nile starts in central Africa and contributes only 22 percent of the volume, while the Blue Nile starts in Lake Tana, in the Ethiopian plateau, and contributes the remaining 78 percent.

"What are you talking about, Professor?" grunted the Rock, throwing back the covers like a little boy. "What do you think you are saying?" he repeated, outraged.

Mulugeta, Farag, and I looked at the poor man as he tried to wake up shaking his head hard against the warm air and the flies in the cabin.

"That we're in Ethiopia, Kaspar," he said, extending a hand to help him stand, which the captain rejected. "According to Captain Mariam, we crossed the Sudanese border several days ago. We are about to arrive in Antioch, the city of the next test."

"Damn it!" he grunted, rubbing his palms over his face, trying to come out of his stupor. His face begged for a good razor. "Aren't we going to Antioch?"

"Well, we thought we were," I replied, as perplexed as he was. "But it turns out it's an Ethiopian village named Antioch that we're going to, not to ancient Antioch, in Turkey."

"That's what we don't know," Farag sighed, more resigned than we were to this unexpected turn of events, "whether they are the same. They are two correct forms of the name. And there are several cities named Antioch in the world. I didn't know that one of them is in Abyssinia."

"It did seem strange to me," I said, running my hand through my disgusting hair, "that they would take us from Turkey to Egypt, and then back to Turkey. It would have been a very strange twist for a medieval pilgrim who made the trip on foot or horse."

"There's your explanation, *Basileia*," Farag declared, shaking Captain Mariam's hand, as he went back to leading the trip. "Now, how about we get out of here, breathe some fresh air, and wash up in the river?"

"It sounds like an excellent idea to me," I agreed, getting to my feet. "I smell awful!"

Mariam assured us we'd be in no danger if we dove into the blue waters of the Atbara. So we threw ourselves off the roof. I felt all my muscles and my poor, stunned brain renew themselves. The water was fresh and seemed clean, but the Rock said not to drink even a sip, because malaria, cholera, and typhus were diseases endemic to most African countries. Nobody would have thought that, looking at the smooth, transparent current. Just in case, we obeyed him to the letter. The sky was such an incredibly perfect blue, and the two shores, separated by a good distance, seemed to be covered all the way up to the edge by a thick green. Many tall, leafy trees jutted out, and plenty of birds flocked from one treetop to another. You could hear their quacks and trills and the echo of our splashes and voices in the river. Everything was so beautiful that I swore I could hear, woven in the wind, a huge choir of voices singing in time to the air and the river's current, in tune with the harmony of the sky and water.

Although I did not take off the white dalmatic to jump into the water, it floated around me, and I'd have given anything to take it off. Farag and the Rock took theirs off. The men on the boat, who were hoisting the boat's triangular sails on a double mast, could see me as God brought me into the world, but I didn't really care. It probably wasn't the first time they'd seen a naked woman, and they didn't seem very interested, either. "How you've changed, Ottavia!" I said to myself, as I swam like a mermaid from one side to the other. I, a nun who had spent all my life studying or working underground in the basement of the Vatican's Classified Archives, among parchments, old papyruses, and codices, now floated and dove into the waters of a river in the middle of untamed nature. Best of all: A few meters away was the head of the man I loved with all my soul and who devoured me with his eyes, not daring to touch me.

For my happiness to be complete, all I lacked was a little soap and some shampoo. I had to make do with a little bar of glycerin soap the Rock took out of his priceless, life-saving backpack that even the Staurofilakes had to respect. After our dunking, we climbed onboard; and our clothes were waiting for us washed and folded inside the squalid stateroom. Dressed and clean, I felt like a queen when the men handed me a huge plate of delicious fish right out of the river, hot off the fire.

That afternoon we sat on deck with Captain Mulugeta Mariam, who informed us we would arrive at Antioch that very night. He was a man of few words, but what he did say made me nervous.

"He asks us to pray a lot before beginning the test," Farag translated, "because his town suffers whenever a saint must be incinerated."

"What saint?" the Rock asked, who hadn't caught on.

"Kaspar, we are the saints. The aspiring Staurofilakes."

"Try and see if you can extract any information from them on those relic thieves."

"I tried," Farag protested. "This man believes he's fulfilling a sacred mission. He would kill himself before he'd betray the Staurofilakes."

"*Staurofilas,*" Captain Mariam pronounced with reverence. Then he looked at us and asked Farag something, who burst out laughing.

"He wants to know some things about you, Kaspar."

"Me?" the Rock was surprised.

Mulugeta continued speaking. I couldn't guess his age, not even with that gray spot in his beard. His face seemed young, and his black skin shone like polished metal, in the sunlight. There was something old in the look in his eyes and in his extremely thin body.

"He says you are twice a saint."

I couldn't help bursting out laughing.

"He is crazy!" said the Rock, with a bellow.

"And he wants to know what you did before you became a saint."

Farag and I tried, without success, to contain our laughter.

"Tell him I am a soldier, and I am far from being a saint!" he roared.

Mulugeta protested furiously when Farag struggled to translate Glauser-Röist's words. When he heard what Mulugeta said, Farag suddenly froze.

"Take off your shirt, Kaspar."

"Have you gone crazy, too, Professor?" he raged indignantly. Farag's change in attitude surprised me. "Why don't you take yours off?"

"Please, Kaspar! Do as I say!"

The Rock, as surprised as I was, started to unbutton his shirt. Farag rested his left hand on the captain's shoulder, and bent way over to look at his back.

"Look at this, Ottavia. Mariam says that Glauser-Röist is twice the saint because the Staurofilakes have marked him with...this." He put his index finger on the captain's dorsal vertebrae.

"What the hell are you talking about, Professor?"

In the exact center of the Rock's back, you could clearly make out a feather-shaped tattoo, instead of the usual cross.

"What did they tattoo on you, Farag?" I asked, lifting up his shirt. In contrast to the Rock, Farag had what we anticipated, a Egyptian ansata cross above his dorsal vertebrae, located under the branched cross they'd tattooed on us in Constantinople. Just like on Abi-Ruj Iyasus's body.

"Abi-Ruj Iyasus was Ethiopian!" I blurted out, excited by my memory of the man whose death had first launched our quest.

"That's right," the Rock said, calmer after covering up. "And we're in Ethiopia."

"I wonder if the earthly paradise could be here...," I mused. "Could Ethiopia be the origin and destination of the mystery?"

"We'll soon find out," Farag commented, pulling back the neck of my blouse. "You have an ansata cross, too. This cross is the symbol *anj* of the hieroglyphic Egyptian language, the symbol that represents life."

His hand caressed my tattoo (unnecessary and delightful, I must add) while I... "Why of course!" he exclaimed suddenly. "The ostrich feather! That's what you have on your back, Kaspar. In Alexandria, Farag and I were marked with an ansata cross that is an Egyptian hieroglyph. You were marked with a different symbol, the ostrich feather, the feather of Maat, that stands for justice."

"Maat...? Justice?" the Rock asked, confused.

"Maat is the eternal law that rules the universe," Farag explained, all worked up. "Precision, truth, order, and rectitude. The main duty of the Egyptian pharaohs was to make sure Maat was fulfilled so disorder and iniquity wouldn't reign. Its hieroglyphic symbol was the ostrich feather. That feather was placed on one of the dishes of Osiris's scales during the judgment of the soul. The dead man's heart was placed on the other. That heart had to be as light as the feather of Maat to earn the right to immortality."

"They tattooed all that on my back?" the Rock articulated, stupefied.

"No, Kaspar. Just the hieroglyph representing the feather of Maat,"

Farag calmed him down. He frowned adding, "Captain Mariam is convinced that's why you are twice a saint. Or, more saintly than we are,
since we don't have that feather."

"All this is very strange," I said, with concern. Farag was laughing.

"Stranger than anything else that's happened to us up to now? Come
on, *Basileia!*"

There was no feather of Maat on Abi-Ruj Iyasus's body. I knew that
the captain—military career, policeman, the black hand of the Vatican—was the only one of us who presented a real danger to the Staurofilakes. Wasn't he uneasy that he alone had been marked with a hieroglyph
symbolizing *justice?*

I couldn't shake that surprise, not even as we read through the *Divine
Comedy* to prepare for the last circle of Purgatory. The boat, the *Neway,*
slowly approached the port of Antioch, a simple platform made of
poles on the right bank of the Atbara.

Like us, Dante, Virgil, and Estacio, the poet from Naples who had
joined them in their ascent to earthly paradise, were nearing their final
destination. Night was falling so they had to hurry to reach the seventh
circle, the one with lustful souls:

We had, by now, arrived at the last round
and, having made our usual right turn,
our minds became absorbed by something else:

there, from the inner bank, flames flashed out straight,
while, from the ledge, a blast of air shot up,
bending them back, leaving a narrow path

along the edge where we were forced to walk
in single file; I was terrified—
there was the fire, and here I could fall off!

Virgil repeatedly begs his pupil to watch where he steps; the slightest mistake could prove fatal. Dante paid no attention; hearing some

voices singing a hymn that begged for purity, he turns around to dis-cover a large group of souls advancing amid the flames. One of them asks Dante why the sunlight doesn't pass through him:

"I'm not the only one—all of us here
Are thirsty for your words, much thirstier
Than Ethiopes or Indians for a cool drink."

"This is too much!" Farag exclaimed, when he heard the last verse.

"That's true," I agreed.

"Why didn't we see that before? Why didn't we pick up on that when we read the entire *Purgatory* in Rome?"

"When you read it for the first time, Professor, could you have even imagined what the seven tests consisted of?" the Rock asked. "Don't pose that question now. What if it had been India instead of Ethiopia? Dante said what he could, he took a chance because he knew he had a good story. He was ambitious, but he wasn't crazy and didn't want to take any chances."

"And yet, they killed him," I replied with sarcasm.

"Yes, but he didn't want that to happen, so he concealed the facts."

In the distance, where the shores of the Atbara converge, I could just make out the village of Antioch and its dock. A weak ray of twilight sun warmed my right shoulder. My stomach lurched when I saw the thick columns of smoke rising to the sky from the village. If only the *Neway* had turned around, but it was too late now.

The soul of that lustful man, who turned out to be the poet Guido Guinicelli (a member of the secret society of the Fidei d'Amore like Dante), asks our hero why he blocked the sunlight. Another group of spirits approaches from the opposite direction walking down the burn-ing path. When he hears what both groups say, as they kiss each other and rejoice at running into each other, Dante deduces that some are lust-ful heterosexuals and others are lustful homosexuals. Uncharacteristi-cally, he consoles them—perhaps because he feels kindly toward that sin or because the majority of them are literati like him. He reminds them they don't have very far to go to reach God's peace and forgiveness and a heaven full of love.

The day is practically over when Canto XXVII begins; the three travelers come to a point where the entire road is in flames. A joyful angel of God appears and encourages them to cross the flames. Horrified, Dante covers his face with his arms, feeling like someone stuck in a grave. Seeing him so frightened, Virgil calms him down:

> *Both of my friendly guides turned toward me then,*
> *and Virgil said to me: "O my dear son,*
> *there may be pain here, but there is no death.*

> *"Believe me when I say that if you spent*
> *A thousand years within the fire's heart,*
> *It would not singe a single hair of yours."*

"That'll work for us, too, right?" I interrupt, hopeful.

"Don't jump to any conclusions, *Basileia.*"

The Rock, staying calm, kept reading how Dante, terrified, froze before the flames, not daring to take a step.

> *"And, entering the flames ahead of me,*
> *he asked of Statius, who, for some time now*
> *had walked between us two, that he come last.*

> *"Once in the fire, I would have gladly jumped*
> *into the depths of boiling glass to find*
> *relief from that intensity of heat.*

> *"My loving father tried to comfort me,*
> *Talking of Beatrice as we moved:*
> *'Already I can see her eyes, it seems!' "*

A voice singing from afar "Blessed are the pure of heart" turns out to be the last guardian angel, who appears as a blinding light amid the flames. He erases the last *P* on Dante's forehead. They figure out how to get out of the fire and find themselves before gleaming earthly paradise. Content and happy, they begin their ascent. As they are climbing, night falls, and they have to stretch out on the stairs because they were warned at the beginning that one can't climb Purgatory Mountain at night. Lying there on those steps, Dante sees a sky full of stars, "larger and clearer than I'm used to." Contemplating them, he falls deeply asleep.

The *Neway* had veered off toward Antioch's dock where hundreds of townspeople dressed in white from head to toe—tunics, veils, scarves, and loincloths—shouted in welcome and jumped or waved their arms in the air. Apparently, the return of Mulugeta Mariam and his sailors was reason for great joy. The village was made up of thirty or forty adobe houses crowded around the dock. Their walls were painted lively colors with thatched roofs all sporting black tubes, a type of chimney that spanned a ditch. The thick smoke I'd seen when we were still at a great distance came from somewhere behind the village, somewhere between it and the forest. From up close, it seemed really huge, like the arms of titans as they struggled to touch the sky.

We were about to dock, but Glauser-Röist didn't seem ready to put down the book.

"Captain, we've arrived," I told him.

"Do you know exactly what you're going to face in this town, Doctor?" he challenged me.

The shouts of the men, women, and children of Antioch could be heard on the other side of the boat's hull.

"No, not exactly."

"All right, then, let's keep reading. We must not get off this boat without knowing all the details."

But there weren't any more details.

To conclude, Dante Alighieri describes, with a beautiful melancholy in his words, how he wakes up at dawn and sees Virgil and Estacio already up, waiting for him to finish climbing the steps to the earthly paradise. His teacher tells him:

"That precious fruit which all men eagerly
go searching for on many boughs
will give, today, peace to your hungry soul."

Dante rushes ahead, impatient. When he finally gets to the last step and sees the earthly paradise's sun, the bushes, and the flowers, his beloved teacher bids him farewell forever:

"You now have seen, my son, the temporal
and the eternal fire, you've reached the place
where my discernment now has reached its end.

"I led you here with skill and intellect;
From here on, let your pleasure be your guide:
The narrow ways, the steep are far below.

"Expect no longer words or signs from me.
Now is your will upright, wholesome and free,
And not to heed its pleasure would be wrong:

"I crown and mitre you lord of yourself!"

"That's it," the Rock announced, closing the book. He seemed less like the Rock than normal, as if he'd said good-bye to an old friend forever. Over the last several months, Dante Alighieri had been an integral part of our lives. That last, fleeting verse left us alone, without a guide.

"I believe this is the end of the line...," Farag whispered. "It feels like Dante has abandoned us. I feel like an orphan."

"Well, he made it to the earthly paradise. He reached his goal—the glory and the crown of laurels. We," I said, smelling the strong smell of smoke, "must still pass the last test."

"You're right, Doctor. Let's go." Glauser-Röist jumped to his feet. I saw him secretly caress the cover of his well-thumbed copy of the *Divine Comedy* before he dropped it in his backpack.

The village of Antioch received us with loud cheers. The minute they saw us on the dock, their shouts of joy and clapping grew deafening.

"What if this is a town of cannibals cheering for the arrival of supper?"

"Farag, don't make me nervous!"

Captain Mulugeta Mariam, like a master of ceremonies, walked down the narrow path opened by the multitude amid exclamations, kisses, shoves, and hugs, just like a Hollywood star. Behind him walked Captain Glauser-Röist, whom the Anuak children watched from below with fearful smiles and admiration in their eyes. He was so blond and so tall; they'd never seen such an impressive male specimen in their short lives. The women paid more attention to me, dying of curiosity. There mustn't have been many female saints who came down the Atbara to attempt the last test of Purgatory; and I could tell from the looks in their eyes that they were proud to see a woman who had succeeded. Farag's dark blue eyes caused havoc. A young girl, not more than fourteen or fifteen, egged on by her friends huddled around her, dying of laughter, rushed up and tugged on his beard. Casanova let out a burst of laughter, absolutely enchanted.

"See what happens when you don't shave?" I said to him in low voice.

"I'll never shave again!"

I poked him in the ribs, which only delighted him more.

The leader of the village, Berehanu Bekela, a gigantic man with enormous pendulous ears and gigantic teeth, welcomed us with full honors. He and several others wore many ceremonial white handkerchiefs around their necks which formed a thick, warm stole, very inappropriate for that temperature. Then, on a straight path from the dock, they took us to the center of a dirt esplanade. Houses were grouped around it, brightly illuminated by torches tied to long wood poles, stuck in the ground. Once we got there, Berehanu shouted some incomprehensible words and people exploded in wild cheers that kept up until the leader raised his hands in the air.

In seconds, the esplanade was filled with stools, rugs, and cushions. Everyone took his place, ready to attack the mountains of food carried out of the houses on wood trays. They quit paying attention to us to concentrate on the mounds of meat on great green leaves that served as platters.

With their own hands, Berehanu Bekela and his family served us our food that looked like a pile of raw meat. They watched expectantly to see what we would do.

"*Injera, injera!*" a darling girl of about three said seated at my side.

Mulugeta spoke with Farag who watched the captain and me with a serious look on his face.

"We have to eat this even if we die of disgust. If we don't, we'll deeply insult the leader and the entire town."

"Don't say such foolish things!" I exploded. "I don't plan to eat raw meat!"

"Don't argue, *Basileia.* Eat!"

"How I am going to eat those pieces of who-knows-what?" I argued apprehensively, picking up something that looked like a black, plastic tube.

"Eat!" Glauser-Röist muttered gritting his teeth, putting a handful of that stuff in his mouth.

The celebration grew larger and larger as the bottled beer flowed among the townspeople like the Atbara River. The little girl kept staring at me; her large black eyes gave me the courage to open my trembling lips and insert, very slowly, a pinch of raw meat. Managing not to gag, I chewed as well as I could, then swallowed what I later learned was a piece of antelope kidney, almost whole. Next I bolted down a piece of stomach with a milder flavor than the kidney. To finish, I gulped down a small slice of still hot liver that stained my chin and the corners of my lips with blood. Ethiopians seemed to love those delicacies. I gulped down a bottle of beer and would have drunk another if Farag hadn't grabbed my wrist.

The celebration went on for a long time. When the meal was over, a group of young girls, among them the girl who had tugged on Farag's beard, entered the circle and began a very strange dance in which they never stopped shaking their shoulders. It was incredible. I never thought a body could move like that, at such speed, as if they were disjointed. The music had a simple beat marked by a single drum. Soon others joined in, and then another and another, until the cadence became hypnotic. Between that and the beer, my head was no longer on my shoulders. The girl who apparently had decided to adopt me rose from the ground and sat down between my crossed legs as if I were a comfortable chair and she, a small queen. I liked watching her carefully tie and arrange her veil so it covered her head, hanging all the way down to her waist. Again and again, I had to put the veil back in place but that white linen never stayed still on her curly, black hair. When the dancers disappeared, she leaned back on my stomach and got comfortable as if I actually was a throne. Just then, the thought of my niece Isabella struck my mind. I would have loved to hold her in my arms as I was holding that little girl. In an Ethiopan village, lost in the middle of nowhere, under the light of the moon and the burning torches, my mind flew to Palermo. I realized that sooner or later I would have to go back home to try to make things better. Although I knew I would never succeed in doing so, my conscience told me I should give them one last chance before I left forever. That tribal attachment, so similar to that of the Anuak people, that my mother had inculcated in me, stopped me from cutting all ties with them even though I knew now how disappointing my family really was.

As soon as the drums went silent and the dancers left the scene, Berehanu Bekela walked with measured steps to the center of the plaza, deep in silence. Even the children stopped fidgeting; they ran to their mothers and stood there, quiet and still. The occasion was solemn and my pulse began to race. Something told me the real party was just about to begin.

Berehanu delivered a long discourse that Farag explained in a whisper. He spoke of the very ancient relationship between the Anuak and the Staurofilakes. The simultaneous translation by Mulugeta and Farag left much to be desired, but our interpreters were doing their best, so the Rock and I had to make do with half phrases and half words.

"The *Staurofilas*," Berehanu said, "came to Atbara hundreds of years ago in great boats . . . the Anuak the word of God. Those men of . . . the faith and showed us how to move rocks, to farm . . . to make beer and build boats and houses."

"The *Staurofilas* made us Christians," the leader continued, "and taught us what we know. All they asked in exchange . . . their secret and bring the saints from Egypt to Antioch. We Anuak have . . . that Mulu-alem Bekela gave in honor of our town. Today, three saints . . . over the waters of the Atbara, the river that God gave to . . . we are responsible for . . . and the *Staurofilas* expect us to fulfill our duty."

Suddenly the people broke out into a deafening ovation. A small squad of fifteen or twenty young men got to their feet and set off, disappearing into the darkness.

"Men, go prepare the road for the saints," Farag translated after the fact.

Everyone started to dance in time to the drums. In the middle of the party, hands grabbed Farag, the Rock, and me and took us to different houses to prepare us for the upcoming ceremony. The women who took care of me took off my sandals, pants, blouse, and underwear, leaving me completely naked. They sprinkled water on my body with a bundle of branches and then dried me off with linen. They took away my clothes, so I had to make do with a shirt, white of course, that fortunately hung down to my knees. They refused to return my shoes. When they led me from the house, I minced along as if I were walking on pins and needles. I didn't feel any better when I saw Farag and the Rock dressed the same way. I was surprised, however, to see my reaction when I saw Farag. The fact is, I still wasn't used to the unexpected behavior of my hormones. My eyes were stuck on his brown skin, glowing under the light of the torches, on his hands, his long and soft fingers, his body, tall and lean. When our gazes finally met, my stomach felt as tight as a knot, and I wondered what was actually in that raw meat.

Between applause and beats of their drums, they led us down dark alleys and in the direction of large dense clouds of smoke, which gave off a disconcerting purple glow. The night sky was full of stars. Farag took my hand and squeezed it gently to calm me down. With all the preparations and drumming, a tremor had taken hold of my spirit. I felt like Jesus en route to Calvary with the Cross on his shoulders. Could the so-called True Cross be that very cross, the one the Staurofilakes were retrieving piece by piece? Surely not. We were here because of it, even if it was fake. I felt my legs trembling, my body sweating, and my teeth chattering.

Finally we came to a new esplanade; the people of Antioch were standing around it, in silence. Several immense bonfires consumed the last logs of wood with great sparks as the young men spread a thick wheel of glowing embers on the ground with the help of some long, sharp lances. Striking the coals with those lances, they broke apart the biggest pieces and smoothed out the surface, roughly about twenty centimeters thick by about four or five meters long from the interior to the exterior. They left a narrow walkway uncovered, wide enough so we could go down the center. When Mulugeta Mariam said something to Farag, he translated it right away so I'd know exactly what he was saying. At that moment Mulugeta was the joyful angel of God who comes to Dante in the seventh circle and tells him he must enter the fiery walkway.

I squeezed Farag's hand tightly and leaned my cheek on his shoulder; I was so frightened I could barely breathe.

"Cheer up, my love," he whispered bravely to me burying his nose in my hair and kissing me softly.

"I'm scared, Farag," I said, closing my eyes.

"Listen, we'll get out of this as we got out of all the other tests. Don't be afraid, my dear Ottavia!" But I was inconsolable. I couldn't stop the chattering of my teeth. "Remember—there's always a solution, *Basileia.*"

As I stared into that immense ring of fire, a solution seemed more a fantasy than a certainty. I admit I had violated, to a greater or lesser degree, the other six deadly sins at some time in my life. But I would not die for the sin of lust. Up to that very day, I was completely innocent of that sin. Besides, if I died in the fire, I'd never get the chance to sin against God's sixth commandment: to commit with Farag those famous impure acts I'd heard so much about.

"I don't want to die," I said, pressed against him.

Glauser-Röist had silently come up behind us. "'*O my dear son,*'" he recited, "'*there may be pain here, but there is no death. Believe me when I say that if you spent a thousand years within the fire's heart, it would not singe a single hair of yours.*'"

"Oh, come on, Captain," I shrieked with acrimony.

Mulugeta Mariam insisted. We couldn't stand there all night; we had to walk down that path.

I walked like a condemned man headed for the gallows, held up by Farag's strong arm. Two meters from the tapestry of embers, the heat was so unbearable I felt it scorch my skin. As soon as we stepped on the path that led to the center, I felt, literally, that I was being incinerated and that my blood was boiling. It was unbearable. Farag's and the captain's beards were fluttering gently, stirred by the hot air. That red lake emitted a muffled crackle.

Finally we arrived at the center, and as soon as we got there, the group of young men who had made all the preparations covered our path with another pile of embers. Corralled like animals, Farag, the captain, and I looked stunned at the circle of Anuaks, a few meters from the ring of coals. They seemed to be impassible ghosts, pitiless judges, lit up by the fire's glow. No one moved, no one breathed, and neither did we as the burning air filled our lungs.

Suddenly a strange song rose from the crowd, a primitive cadence that I could not make out clearly due to the crackle of the wood. It was a single musical phrase, always the same, repeated tirelessly like a slow, meditative litany. Farag's arms around my shoulders tensed like steel cables and the Rock shifted uneasily on his naked feet. Mulugeta Mariam's shout brought us back to reality.

Farag said, "We have to cross the fire. If we don't, they'll kill us."

"What!" I exclaimed, horrified. "Kill us? They didn't tell us that! How can we walk across *that!*" The top layer of embers was turning black.

"Think, please," begged the Rock. "If our only choice were to start running, I'd do it right now, even though I might wind up dead, with

third-degree burns all over my body. But before I commit suicide, I want
to know for sure that there's no other option, that there's nothing in our
brains that can help us."

I twisted around to see Farag's face. He also leaned over to look at
me. Gazing at each other, our brains shared in a split second all the
knowledge we'd accumulated over our lives. But we couldn't come up
with a single reference to walking on fire.

"I'm sorry, Kaspar." Farag was sweating copiously, but the surrounding heat caused the sweat to immediately evaporate. We didn't need the
Anuak's help to die. If we stayed there, we would die on our own, of
dehydration.

"We only have Dante's text," I mused, distressed, "but I don't recall
anything that can help us."

A sharp projectile cut the air. One of the lances they'd used to spread
the coals stuck in the ground neatly between my feet. I thought my heart
would never beat again. They were throwing lances at us.

"Leave her alone!" cried Farag, literally becoming a wild man.

The monotonous chant grew louder and clearer. It sounded like they
were chanting in Greek, but I thought that was just a hallucination.

"Maybe the answer is in Dante," the Rock said pensively.

"But when Dante enters the fire, Captain, he only says that if he
could, he would have thrown himself into a pool of boiling glass to cool
down."

"True…"

We heard another lance cut the air. The captain stopped mid-
sentence. A new lance stuck in the ground, this time in the space formed
by our three pairs of defenseless feet. Farag went crazy, shouting a string
of insults in Arabic that I'm glad I didn't understand.

"They don't want to kill us! If they did, they would have done it by
now. They just want to get us to start!"

The musical chant grew louder. You could clearly hear the Anuaks'
voices now: *"Macarioi hoi kazaroi ti kardia."*

"'Good fortune to the pure of heart,'" I exclaimed. "They're singing
in Greek!"

"That's what the angel was singing when Dante, Virgil, and Estacio were inside the fire, right, Kaspar?" asked Farag. Since the Rock had gone mute with the second lance, he just nodded. Farag was revved up now. "The solution has to be in Dante's tercets! Help us, Kaspar! What does Dante say about the fire?"

"Well…," the Rock stammered. "He doesn't say anything, damn it! Nothing!" he exploded, disheartened. "Just that the wind parts the fire!"

"Wind?" Farag frowned, trying to remember. "*There, from the inner bank,*" he recalled, "*flames flashed out straight, while, from the ledge, a blast of air shot up, bending them back, leaving a narrow path.*"

A strange mental image formed in my head: a foot that fell swiftly from above, cutting the air.

"*A blast of air shot up…*" Farag murmured, pensive. Just then, another lance cut through the red glow of the coals and stuck deep in front of the right toes of the double saint.

"Damn them!" he bellowed.

"Listen to me!" cried Farag, very excited. "I've got it, I know what to do!"

"*Macarioi hoi kazaroi ti kardia,*" the people of Antioch repeated over and over, loud and grave.

"If we step very hard, really hard, we will create a pocket of air on the bottoms of our feet, and we will cut the combustion off for a couple of seconds! The blast of air that shoots up will drive back the flames and moved them away from us. That's what Dante was telling us!"

The Rock stood motionless, trying to get what Farag said through his hard head. I understood immediately—it was a simple game of applied physics: If our feet fell from above with a lot of force and struck against the coals, for a very brief period of time the air accumulated on the bottom of our feet and retained by the shoes of fire that formed around the skin would impede burns. To accomplish this you had to step very, very hard and fast, just like Farag said. You couldn't get distracted and lose your rhythm. If you did, nothing could stop your skin from being calcinated. The embers would devour the flesh in a heartbeat. It was very risky, but it was the very thing that fit Dante's instructions. It was the only idea we had, and besides, we were running out of time. Mulugeta Mariam announced that fact, shouting from where he stood next to Berehanu Bekela.

"Be very careful not to fall," the Rock added, when he finally understood what Farag was saying. "'*And I feared the fire or the fall*,' says Dante. Don't forget. If the pain or anything else makes you lose heart or lose your footing, you will be burned."

"I'll go first!" Farag said, leaning over and giving me a kiss on the lips that also quashed my protests. "Don't say anything, *Basileia*," he whispered in my ear so the Rock couldn't hear. Then he added, "I love you, I love you, I love you, I love you, I love you…"

He didn't stop saying that until he made me laugh. Then, he pulled away from me and went into the fire, shouting, "Watch, *Basileia*, and don't repeat my mistakes!"

Farag stepped rhythmically and decisively on the fire. I couldn't watch. I hid my face in the Rock's chest. He held me tight. I cried as I'd never cried before, racked with such sobs, such pain and grief, I couldn't hear Captain Glauser-Röist when he shouted.

"He's out, Doctor! He did it! Dr. Salina!" He shook me like a rag doll. "Look, Dr. Salina, look! He's out!"

I raised my head, not understanding what the captain was saying. I saw Farag waving his arms from the other side.

"He's alive, my God!" I screamed. "Thank you, Lord, thank you! You're alive, Farag!"

"Ottavia!" He shouted, and suddenly toppled over onto the ground senseless.

"He's burned! He's burned!"

"Come on, Doctor! Now, it's our turn!"

"What are you saying?" I babbled, but before I realized what was happening, the Rock had grabbed me by the hand and was pulling me to the fire. My survival instinct rebelled and I braked, digging my feet firmly in the ground.

"Right this second! Now, step! Step hard!" Glauser-Röist told me, undaunted by my abrupt stop. Proximity to the coals must have made me react because I raised my foot and slammed it down with all my might.

My life stopped. The world ceased its eternal gyration and Nature fell silent. I entered a type of silent white tunnel which proved that Einstein was right—time and space *are* relative. I looked at my feet and saw one of them sunk slightly into some white, cold stones. The other ascended in slow motion to take the next step. Time had expanded and stretched, allowing me to study that strange pathway without haste. My second foot fell like a bomb on the stones, making them jump in the air. My first foot had already started its indolent ascent. I could see how my toes extended, how the bottom of my foot expanded to offer more resistance to the rocky bed. Now it was descending very slowly so when it hit, it caused another gigantic earthquake. I laughed. I laughed because I was flying. A second before it hit the surface, the other foot lifted off the ground, leaving me suspended in the air.

I couldn't erase the joy off my face the entire time that incredible experience lasted. It was only ten steps, but the longest ten steps of my life, and the most surprising. Suddenly the white tunnel ended and I entered reality, falling abruptly to the ground, propelled by the hot air. The drums were sounding, the shouts were deafening, dirt was stuck to my hands and feet, and I was all scratched up. I didn't see Farag or Glauser-Röist anywhere although I sensed they were close by. Someone was covering Farag up with a large white linen cloth and carrying him off into the night. I too became a roll of linen. Hundreds of hands held me in the air in the middle of a deafening uproar. Then they laid me on a cushioned surface and unrolled me. I was dazed, completely soaked in my own sweat, exhausted as never before. I was so terribly cold; I shivered, as if I were freezing. Two women offered me a large glass of water, and I realized they weren't Anuaks from Antioch. They were blond with translucent skin; and one of them even had green eyes.

After I drank what was in the glass, which didn't taste anything like water, I fell asleep.

CHAPTER

7

I detached myself from my slumber,
floating out of the deep lethargy I'd
sunk into after we stomped over the
wheel of fire. I felt relaxed, comfortable even, with an incredible sense of well-being.
A delightful scent of lavender told me I wasn't in
Antioch. Half-asleep, I smiled at how good that
familiar fragrance made me feel.

I heard women's voices, whispering softly,
not wanting to disturb my sleep. My eyes still
closed, I paid attention to the sounds around me.
To my great surprise, I realized that for the first
time in a lifetime of study, I had the immense
honor of hearing Byzantine Greek spoken.

"We should wake her up," whispered one of
the voices.

"Not yet, Zauditu," answered another.
"Please leave without making any noise."

"But Tafari told me the other two are already
eating."

"Fine, let them eat. This woman can sleep as
long as she wants."

I suddenly opened my eyes. I was stretched
out on my side, facing the wall, and the first thing

I saw was a pleasant fresco of flautists and dancers painted on the smooth wall across from me. The colors were brilliant and intense, with magnificent details in gold surrounded by an array of browns and mauve. Was I still dreaming? I suddenly understood: I lay there in the earthly paradise.

"See?" said the voice of the woman who wanted to let me sleep. "You and your chatter. You woke her up!"

I hadn't moved a muscle, my back was still to them. How did they know I was listening? One of them leaned over me.

"*Hygieia,** Ottavia."

I turned my head very slowly and found myself looking into a middle-aged female's face, with white skin and gray hair gathered up in a bun. I recognized her by her green eyes: she was one of the women who had given me something to drink in Antioch. Her mouth wore a beautiful smile that formed lines around her eyes and lips.

"How are you?"

I was just about to open my mouth when it dawned on me I'd never spoken Byzantine Greek. I quickly translated from a language I knew only on paper to an oral language I had never tried speaking. When I tried to say something, I realized how badly I sounded.

"Very well, thank you," I said haltingly, interrupting myself with each syllable. "Where am I?"

The woman stood up and stepped away from me, making room for me to sit up. The sheets were made of very fine silk, softer and more delicate than satin or taffeta. I slid in them when I moved.

"In Stauros, the capital of *Paradeisos.*† And this room," she said looking around, "is one of the guest rooms in Cato's *basileion.*‡

"So," I concluded, "I'm in the Staurofílakes' earthly paradise."

The woman smiled and the other younger woman hiding behind her did the same. Both were dressed in flowing white tunics held up by clasps at the shoulders and girded by a belt at the waist. The white of

---

* Greek greeting that means "Greetings!"
† Paradise, in Greek.
‡ Palace, in Greek.

those garments had no equal. The white clothes the Anuak wore would have looked gray and dirty in comparison. Everything struck me as beautiful; an exquisite beauty I couldn't stay indifferent to. The alabaster glasses placed on one of the magnificent wooden tables glinted with the light of innumerable candles. Vibrantly colored rugs covered the floors, and there were extraordinarily large and fragrant flowers everywhere I looked. The most disconcerting thing was the room's walls—they were completely covered by Roman-style murals, complete with scenes depicting daily life in the Byzantine Empire of the thirteenth or fourteenth century A.D.

"My name is Haide," the green-eyed woman said. "Stay in bed a while longer if you like and take it all in. You seem to thoroughly enjoy the items that surround us."

"I love it," I exclaimed. So much luxury, good taste, and Byzantine art gathered in one room. It was the perfect time to study firsthand what I could only guess at in examining adulterated reproductions in books. I added, "I'd really like to see my companions." I'd always been so proud of my vocabulary in that language; now it proved woefully lacking. I said "compatriots" (*simpatriotes*) instead of "companions." But they seemed to understand.

"*Didaskalos** Boswell and *Protospatharios*† Glauser-Röist are eating with Cato and the twenty-four *shastas.*"

"*Shastas?*" I repeated, surprised. *Shasta* was a word in Sanskrit meaning "wise" or "venerable."

"The *shastas* are . . . ," Haide hesitated before finding the right way to explain such a complex concept to a neophyte like me, "Cato's assistants, although that isn't exactly their role. Be patient in your apprenticeship, young Ottavia. There's no need to hurry. In *Paradeisos* there is always time."

As she said this, Zauditu opened barely visible doors in the wall and removed from a closet covered in murals a tunic identical to theirs. She laid it out on an ornately carved wooden chair. Then she opened a drawer

---

* Professor, in Greek.
† Byzantine military rank, equivalent to captain.

tucked under the top of one of the tables, took out a case and set it carefully on my knees, which were still covered by sheets. To my surprise, in the enameled case was an incredible collection of gold brooches and precious stones, valuable as much for the Byzantine engraving and design as for their raw materials. The goldsmith who worked those wonders had to be a first-class artisan.

"Choose one or two, if you like," said Zauditu timidly.

How do I choose between such beautiful objects, especially when I was not accustomed to wearing any type of jewelry?

"No, no. Thank you," I apologized with a smile.

"Don't you like them?" she said surprised.

"Oh, yes, of course I do. But I'm not used to wearing such expensive things."

I was on the verge of telling her I was a nun who had taken a vow of poverty, before I remembered that aspect of my life was now a thing of the past.

Distressed, Zauditu walked over to Haide, but the young lady's attention was elsewhere. She talked calmly with someone standing on the other side of the door. Zauditu picked up the box and set it on the nearest table. I then heard the soft sound of a lyre playing a festive melody.

"That's Tafari, the best *liroktipos** of Stauros," said Zauditu with pride.

Haide returned, with languid grace and rhythmic steps. Later I discovered that this fluid way of walking was the way all the inhabitants of *Paradeisos* moved, in Stauros, as well as in Crucis, Edem, and Lignum.

"I hope you like the music," Haide commented.

"Very much," I replied. Then I realized I had no idea what day it was. With all the turmoil, I had lost complete track of time.

"Today is the eighteenth of June," Haide responded. "Our Lord's day."

Sunday, the eighteenth of June. It had taken us three months to get here and we'd been missing more than fifteen days.

---

*One who plays the lyre.

"She doesn't want any clasps," Zauditu interrupted, very worried. "How will she hold up her *himation?*"*

"You don't want any clasps?" Haide was astonished. "But that's not possible, Ottavia."

"They're... They're too much... I never wear such things; I'm not accustomed to such things."

"Could you please tell me how you plan to fasten your *himation?*"

"Don't you have anything simpler? Pins, needles." I had no idea how to say "safety pins."

The two women looked at each other, confused.

"The *himation* can only be worn with clasps," Haide declared. "It can be held up differently if you prefer, with one or two of them, but you can't just hold it up with simple pins. They wouldn't hold up under your movements or the weight of the fabric itself, and they'll end up tearing it."

"But those clasps are too ostentatious!"

"Is that what bothers you?" asked Zauditu, growing more and more surprised.

"Well, Ottavia, don't worry about that," Haide said. "Let's talk later. Now choose some clasps and sandals, and we'll go to the dining room. I sent word with Ras, and they'll be expecting you. I believe *Didaskalos* Boswell is eager to see you."

And I was eager to see him. I jumped out of the bed, and indiscriminately chose a pair of clasps. One had a lion's head with two incredible rubies for eyes and the other one was a cameo depicting a waterfall. I started to take the long nightgown I'd been sleeping in off over my head.

"My hair!" I exclaimed in Italian.

"What did you say?" Zauditu asked.

"My hair, my hair!" I repeated, letting the garment fall over my body, looking for a mirror. I ran over to a full-length silver mirror hanging on a wall, next to the door. My blood froze when I saw my head completely shaved. Incredulous, I raised my hands to my scalp and tried

*Tunic, in Greek.

to remember what my head felt like with hair. As my fingertips probed my head, I felt a sharp pain. I twisted my neck slightly downward and there it was: On the very top of my head, in the very center, I had a tattoo like Abi-Ruj Iyasus, a capital sigma.

Still in shock, unable to react to Haide's words of consolation, I took the shirt off again and stood there naked. Another six capital Greek letters were distributed over my body: on the right arm, a tau; on my left arm, an epsilon; on my heart, between my breasts, an alpha; on my abdomen, a rho; on my right thigh, an omicron; and on my left thigh, another sigma like the one on my head. Adding up all the crosses I'd gotten for completing the series of tests, along with the great chrismon de Constantine on my navel, I looked like a mental patient with a penchant for body art.

Suddenly, Haide appeared by my side in the mirror, also naked; a moment later, Zauditu was there, too. They had the same marks, although they'd long since healed.

"I will get over it...more or less..." I stammered, on the brink of tears.

"Your body didn't suffer," Haide calmly explained. "We were always sure you were deep asleep before cutting your skin. Look at us. Are we so horrible?"

"I believe they are very beautiful symbols," Zauditu observed, smiling. "I love the tattoos on Tafari's body, and he likes mine a lot, too. See this?" she added, pointing to the letter alpha between her breasts. "See how delicately they made it. Its edges are perfect, smooth and rounded."

"Think how those letters," continued Haide, "form the word, *Stauros*. It will be with you wherever you go. It is an important word, and, therefore, they are important letters. Remember what it took to get them and feel proud."

They helped me get dressed, but I couldn't stop thinking about my hair and my body, now covered with tattoos. What would Farag say?

"Perhaps it will calm you to know that the *didaskalos* and the *protospatharios* look just like you," Zauditu said. "It does not seem to bother them."

"They're men!" I protested while Haide tied the sash around my waist. They exchanged a knowing look and tried to hide a look of patient resignation.

"It may take you some time, Ottavia, but you will learn that focusing on those differences is trivial. Now, let's go. They are expecting you."

I said nothing and followed them out of the room, surprised at how modern the Staurofilakes were. On the other side of the door was a wide corridor furnished with tapestries, armchairs, and tables; it opened onto a patio full of flowers. A large fountain shot water into the air. Although I tried to look for the sky, I could only make out strange black shadows so far above me that I couldn't estimate their height. Then I realized the light of the real sun didn't reach where I stood. There was no sun anywhere, and what light there was, was in no way natural.

We walked down many other corridors similar to the first, with more and more patios and ornamental gardens with jets of water forming incredible effects. The sound was relaxing, like the gentle sound of a noise made by a running creek. I was starting to get nervous. If I concentrated on everything around me, a thousand signs pointed to something very unsettling.

"Where is *Paradeisos* exactly?" I asked my silent guides. They walked in front of me without hurrying, looking into the patios from time to time, arranging the tablecloth on a table or smoothing the waves in their hair. A lilting laugh was my answer.

"What a question!" added Zauditu, delighted.

"Where do you think it is?" Haide felt obliged to add, with the same tone of voice she would use in talking to a small child.

"In Ethiopia?"

"That's what you think?" she answered as if the solution were so obvious. The question was superfluous.

My guides stopped before two impressive doors and opened them gradually without the slightest strain. Behind them was an enormous room, as beautifully decorated as everything else I had seen. At its center was a colossal circular table.

Farag Boswell, the baldest *didaskalos* I'd ever seen, leaped to his feet when he saw me. The rest of those at the meal also stood. His arms open wide, he started to run toward me, tripping on the hem of his tunic. I got a lump in my throat when I saw him walking toward me, and for a second, forgot everything around me. They had shaved his head, true, but his blond beard was as long as ever. I pressed against him feeling like I couldn't catch my breath. I felt his warm body pressing into mine and took in his scent—not the light sandalwood smell of his *himation*, but the familiar smell of the skin on his neck. We were in the strangest place in the world, but in Farag's arms, I began to feel safe again.

"Are you okay? Are you okay?" he repeated, anguished, holding on tight as he kissed me.

I was laughing and crying at the same time, torn by my emotions. Grabbing his hands, I pulled back to get a better look at him. What a strange sight he made. Bald with a beard, his white tunic flowing all the way to his feet. Even Butros would have had trouble recognizing him.

"Professor," said an ancient voice that echoed through the room. "Please bring Dr. Salina over."

Crossing the room under the gaze of cordial onlookers, Farag and I came to a hunched-over old man. Except for his advanced age, neither his clothes nor his position at the table gave away that he was Cato CCLVII himself. When I figured out who he was, I was filled with respect and fear; at the same time shock and curiosity drew me to examine him in detail as we drew closer. Cato CCLVII was an elderly man of medium complexion and build. He rested the weight of his overwhelming old age on a delicate cane. A slight tremor due to weak knees and muscles shook his body head to toe, but it didn't diminish his solemn dignity one bit. I'd seen parchments and papyrus less wrinkled than his skin; it looked about to split into a thousand pieces where the wrinkles overlapped and crossed. The sharp expression on his face and his radiant gray visage seemed infinitely wise. I was so impressed I was tempted to kneel and kiss his ring, as though I was at the Vatican and stood before the pope himself.

"*Hygieia*, Dr. Salina," he said in a weak, trembling voice. He spoke perfect English. "I am delighted to finally meet you. You can't imagine the interest with which I have followed these tests."

How old could this man be? He seemed to carry on his brow the weight of eternity, as if he had been born back when water covered the entirety of the planet. Very slowly, he extended his trembling hand to me, palm up, his fingers lightly bent, waiting for me to give him mine. When I did, he raised it to his lips with a gallant gesture that won me over.

Only then did I see the Rock—as serious and circumspect as ever— standing behind Cato. Despite his serious expression, he looked much better than Farag and I. Since he always wore his nearly white hair very short, I didn't even notice, at first, that they had shaved his head.

"Please, Doctor, have a seat next to the professor," said Cato CCLVII. "I really want to talk with you all, and there's nothing better than a good meal to enjoy the conversation."

Cato was the first to sit down; twenty-four *shastas* did the same. One servant after another entered through several doors hidden by fresco paintings, with trays and carts full of food.

"First, allow me to introduce you to the *shastas* of *Paradeisos*, men and women who strive every day to make this the kind of place we aspire to be. Starting on the right from the door is young Gete, translator of the Sumerian language; next Ahmose, the best builder of chairs in Stauros; next to her, Shakeb, one of the professors at the school of Opposites; next Mirsgana, the water master; Hosni, *kabidarios...*"*

He continued the introductions until he finished all twenty-four: Neferu, Katebet, Asrat, Hagos, Tamirat... All were dressed exactly the same; they smiled the same way when they were mentioned, greeting us with a nod. What got my attention most was that despite those strange names, a third of them were as blond as Glauser-Röist and some were even redheaded, some brunette, still others were dark-skinned. Their features were as varied as all the races and peoples in the world. Meanwhile the servants parsimoniously set out a huge amount of dishes with no meat in sight. Almost all the dishes held ridiculous quantities, as if the food were more for decoration—the presentation was magnificent—than nourishment.

---

*Engraver of precious stones.

The greeting ceremony concluded, Cato started the banquet. Everyone had hundreds of questions about how we passed the tests and what we thought about them. Yet, I wasn't as interested in satisfying their curiosity as much as their satisfying ours. The Rock was like a cauldron ready to burst; I even thought I saw smoke coming out of his ears. Finally, when the murmuring had gotten rather loud and questions fell on us like rain, the captain exploded.

"I'm sorry to remind you that the professor, the doctor, and I aren't aspiring Staurofilakes. We're here to stop you."

The silence in the room was impressive. Only Cato had the presence of mind to save the situation. "Calm down, Kaspar," he said calmly. "If you want to stop us, do it later. Right now, don't spoil such a pleasant meal with such bravado. Has anyone here spoken harshly to you?"

I was petrified. No one had ever spoken that way to the Rock. At least, I'd never seen it. Now, surely, he would turn into a wild beast and hurl the round table into the air. To my surprise, Glauser-Röist looked around the room and calmed down. Farag and I took each other's hand under the table.

"I apologize for my behavior," the captain said unexpectedly, without lowering his eyes. "It's unforgivable. I'm sorry."

The conversation started up again as if nothing had happened. Cato chatted in a low voice with the captain, who didn't seem at all ill at ease, but listened attentively. Despite his age, Cato CCLVII still had an undeniably powerful, charismatic personality.

The *shasta* named Ufa, the horsemaster, came over to Farag and me to allow the Rock and Cato to talk privately.

"Why are you two holding hands under the table?" The *didaskalos* and I were petrified. How did he know that? "Is it true that, during the tests, you fell in love?" he asked in Byzantine Greek with all the naiveté in the world, as if his questions were not an intrusion. Several heads turned to hear our answer.

"Uh, well, yes... In fact...," Farag stuttered.

"Yes or no?" the *shasta* named Teodros insisted. More heads turned.

"I do not believe Ottavia and Farag are accustomed to that type of directness," commented Mirsgana, who was in charge of water.

"Why not?" Ufa asked, surprised.

"They aren't from here, remember? They're from the *outside*," Mirsgana pointed her head upward.

"Why don't you tell us about you and *Paradeisos?*" I proposed, imitating Ufa's naiveté. "For example, where exactly is this place; why have you stolen fragments of the True Cross; and how do you plan to stop us from putting you into police hands?" I sighed. "You know, that sort of thing."

One of the servants, who was filling my wineglass just then, interrupted me. "That's too many questions to answer at one time."

"Weren't you curious, Candace, the day you woke up in Stauros?" Teodros answered.

"That was so long ago!" he answered as he served Farag. I realized that people I'd thought were servants weren't that at all, or, at least not in the usual sense. They were all dressed exactly the way Cato, the *shastas*, and we were; they participated in the conversations with complete ease.

"Candace was born in Norway," Ufa explained to me, "and he arrived here about fifteen or twenty years ago, right, Candace?" He agreed, wiping a dry cloth over the mouth of the jar. "He was *shasta* of foods until last year. Now he has chosen the kitchens of the *basileion*."

"Delighted to meet you, Candace," I hurried to say. Farag did the same.

"Enchanted… Believe me: If you wish to get to know the true *Paradeisos*, start by taking a walk down its streets, without asking questions." Saying this, he moved toward the doors.

"Candace may be right," I said, resuming the conversation and taking the glass in my hands, "but taking a walk down the streets of *Paradeisos* is not going to clear up where this place is exactly, why you stole fragments of the True Cross, and how you plan to stop us from turning you over to the police."

The number of *shastas* listening to our conversation grew; others listened to what the Rock and Cato were saying privately. The table was divided into two.

Waiting for the answers which had taken all the courage in the world for me to ask, I sipped more wine.

"*Paradeisos* is in the safest place in the world," Mirsgana said finally. "We didn't steal the Wood since it has always been ours. Regarding the police, we're not particularly worried." The others nodded. "The seven tests are the entrance into *Paradeisos.* Those who pass them usually possess qualities that make them incapable of doing gratuitous, senseless harm. You three, for example, couldn't either," she added very amused. "No one has never done that, and we have existed for more than sixteen hundred years."

"What about Dante Alighieri?" Farag sprung on her without warning.

"What about him?" Ufa asked.

"You killed him," Farag said.

"Us...?" several shocked voices asked all at once.

"We didn't kill him," Gete, the Sumerian translator, assured us.

"He was one of us. In the history of *Paradeisos,* Dante Alighieri is a key figure."

I couldn't believe what I was hearing. Either they were artful liars or Glauser-Röist's theory had collapsed like a house of cards.

"He spent many years in *Paradeisos,*" added Teodros. "He came and went. In fact, he began writing the *Convivio* and *De vulgari eloquentia* here in the summer of 1304. The idea for the *Commedia,* to which publisher Ludovico Dolce added the '*Divina*' in 1555, arose during a series of conversations with Cato LXXXI and *shastas* in the spring of 1306, shortly before he returned to Italy."

"But he recounted all the stories of the tests and paved the way so people could discover this place," Farag pointed out.

"Naturally," Mirsgana replied, with a bit of a smile. "When we hid in *Paradeisos,* in 1220, during the time of Cato LXXVII, our numbers started to dwindle. The only aspirants to the brotherhood came from associations like Fede Santa, Massenie du Saint Graal, Cathari, Minnesänger, Fidei d'Amore, and, to a lesser extent, from military orders such as the Knights Templar, Hospitalers of Saint John, or the Teutonic Knights. The problem of who would protect the Cross in the years to come was really alarming."

"For that reason," Gete continued, "Dante Alighieri was put in charge of writing the *Commedia.* Do you understand now?"

"It was a way to attract people capable of seeing beyond what's in front of their nose," Ufa explained, "nonconformists who like to look under rocks."

"What about his fears about leaving Ravenna after publishing *Purgatory?* Those years when nothing is known about him?" Farag asked.

"They were political fears," Mirsgana said. "Remember, Dante actively participated in the wars between the Guelfs and the Ghibelline. He was the attorney for the white Guelfs and faced the party of the black Guelfs. He always opposed the military policy of Boniface VIII, of whom he was a great enemy on account of the shameful corruption during his papistry. His life was in danger a number of times."

"You mean the Catholic Church killed him on the Holy Day of the True Cross?" I asked sarcastically.

"Actually, the church didn't kill him either, and we aren't certain he died exactly on the Holy Day of the True Cross. We're certain he passed away either the night of the thirteenth or the fourteenth of September," explained Teodros. "We would like for it to have really been the fourteenth because it would be a nice coincidence, an almost miraculous one, but there's no way to prove that. You are very mistaken about his being murdered. His friend Guido Novello sent him as ambassador to Venice. Upon his return, traveling through the lagoons of the Adriatic coast, he fell ill with malaria. We had nothing to do with it."

"Well, it's still suspicious," observed Farag with distrust.

There was an overwhelming silence in our group's conversation.

"Do you know what beauty is?" asked Shakeb, professor of the school of Opposites, who had been silent up to then. Farag and I looked at him in confusion. He had a round face and large, expressive black eyes. On his chubby hands he wore several rings that cast spectacular sparks of light. "See how the flame on that candle flickers, the shortest one, the gold one above Cato's head?"

The torch he mentioned was barely a luminous spot in the distance.

How could we make out the shortest candle and, on top of that, its flickering flame?

"Can you detect the scent of cabbage jam coming from the kitchen?" he continued. "How about the pungent aroma of marjoram they put in it and the acrid aroma of rhubarb leaves they cover the jam with in clay bowls?"

Frankly, we were confounded. What was he talking about? How could we possibly smell that? Without moving my head or lowering my gaze, I tried, without success, to guess the ingredients in the exquisite dish right under my nose, but I could only remember—and that was because I'd just taken a bite—that its flavors were very concentrated, much more intense than normal.

"I don't know what you're getting at," Farag said to Shakeb.

"Could you tell me, *didaskalos,* how many instruments are playing the music accompanying our meal?"

Music…?What music, I thought. Then I realized a beautiful melody was coming from behind our seats. I hadn't heard it because I wasn't paying attention and because it was played so softly. It would have been completely impossible to distinguish each musical instrument.

"Or how that drop of sweat sounds," he continued unperturbed, "that's sliding down Ottavia's back at this very moment?"

I was frightened. What was he saying? I kept my mouth shut when I noticed that, on account of nervous tension and excitement, a very small drop of sweat did rush down my spine.

"What's going on?" I exclaimed, totally disconcerted.

"Ottavia, tell me," the man with the rings was implacable, "at what rate is your heart beating? I can tell you: like this…" He tapped the table with two fingers, perfectly in time with the palpitations I felt at the center of my chest. "And how does the wine you're drinking smell? Have you noticed its spices, the slightly buttery texture it leaves in your mouth, and its dense, dry woody flavor?"

I was from Sicily, the greatest wine-growing region of Italy. My family has vineyards and we drink wine at meals, but I'd never noticed anything like what he was describing.

"If you can't perceive what is around you or feel what's happening to you," he concluded with an amiable but clear and firm tone, "if you don't enjoy the beauty because you can't even detect it, and if you know less than the youngest children in my school, don't pretend to be in possession of the truth or allow yourself to fear those who have welcomed you warmly."

"Come on, Shakeb," Mirsgana said, coming to our defense. "That is all well and good, but that's enough. They just got here. We need to be patient."

Shakeb changed his expression quickly, showing some repentance.

"Forgive me," he asked. "Mirsgana is right. But accusing us of murdering Dante was impertinent on your part."

These people certainly spoke their minds.

Farag, on the other hand, was tense and clearly deep in thought. As he followed Shakeb's logic, I was sure I could hear the gears in his brain turning at top speed.

"Forgive me, Shakeb, for what I'm about to say," he said in a monotone voice. "Although I accept the possibility that you can see that flame from afar or smell the aromas of the cabbage jam coming from the kitchen, I refuse to accept that you can hear Ottavia's heart beating or a drop of sweat sliding down her back. It's not that I doubt you, but..."

"Well," Ufa interrupted him, taking up Shakeb's reply, "in fact we all heard that drop and right now we can hear the beats of your heart, just like we can hear in your voice how nervous you are or how the food in your stomach is digesting."

I couldn't have been more incredulous; my unease increased at the thought that something in all that was true.

"No, that's impossible," I stammered.

"Want proof?" Gete offered amiably.

"Of course," Farag replied curtly.

"I'll give it to you," declared Ahmose, the builder of chairs, who had not joined in till then. "Candace," she whispered, as if she were speaking in the servant's ear. I looked around, but Candace wasn't in the room. "Candace, would you please bring some of that elderberry flower pastry you just took out of the oven?" She waited a few seconds, then smiled with satisfaction. Candace answered: "Right away, Ahmose."

"Ha!" Farag blurted out. Farag had to swallow his disdain when, almost immediately, Candace came through one of the doors bringing a plate of a white pudding that had to be what Ahmose had requested.

"Here's the elderberry flower pastry, Ahmose," he said. "I fixed it thinking about you. I have already put aside a piece for you to bring home."

"Thanks, Candace," she replied with a happy smile. There was no doubt they lived together.

"I don't understand." My distrustful *didaskalos* continued to be suspicious. "I really don't understand."

"You do not understand…but you're starting to accept it," said Ufa, raising his wineglass joyfully in the air. "Let's toast to all the wonderful things you are going to learn in *Paradeisos!*"

Everyone in our group raised their glasses and toasted enthusiastically. Those in the Rock and Cato's group didn't moved a muscle, fascinated by whatever it was they were listening to.

Shakeb was right. The wine smelled of spices; its flavor was dense and dry like wood. A minute after we toasted, its smooth buttery texture lingered on my taste buds.

*T*hat afternoon we strolled through Stauros accompanied by Ufa, Mirsgana, Gete, and Khutenptah, the *shasta* of agriculture, who became quick friends with Captain Glauser-Röist. She came along to show us the greenhouses and their overall agricultural production system. The Rock, ever the agricultural engineer, was extremely interested in this aspect of life in *Paradeisos.*

When we left Cato's *basileion* after lunch, we walked back through numerous rooms and patios. Our guides, who spoke English, cleared up the mystery of the absence of the sun.

"Look up," Mirsgana said.

Overhead there was no sky. Stauros was located in a gigantic underground cave whose colossal dimensions were delineated by walls and a ceiling you couldn't see. If hundreds of excavating machines, like those that dug the English Channel, had worked nonstop for a century, they couldn't have dug a space like the one Stauros occupied at the heart of the Earth. Its size was equal to that of Rome and New York combined. But Stauros was just the capital of *Paradeisos*. Three other cities were built in grottos just as large. A complex system of corridors and amazing galleries connected the four urban centers.

"*Paradeisos* is a marvelous whim of Nature," Ufa explained, who'd insisted on taking us to the stables where he trained horses, "the result of terrible volcanic eruptions in the Pleistocene era. Hot water flowed through here and dissolved the limestone, leaving just lava rock. Our brothers found this place in the thirteenth century. Can you believe that, after seven centuries, we still haven't explored the entire area?"

"Tell us how the light works here, without the sun," Farag requested, taking my hand as he walked by my side. The city streets were paved with rocks. Down them traveled riders on horseback and horse-drawn carts that seemed to be the only means of transportation. On the sidewalks, bright mosaic tiles depicted natural landscapes or scenes depicting musicians, craftsmen, and other snapshots of daily life, all in pure Byzantine style. Several Staurofilakes swept the grounds and gathered trash with strange mechanical shovels.

"Stauros has more than three hundred streets," Mirsgana said, waving to a woman who watched from a first-floor window. The houses were made of the same volcanic rock, but the cornices and decorative touches, the drawings and colors of the facades, conferred upon them a delicate, extravagant, or distinguished air, depending on the owner's taste. "In the city there are seven lakes, all navigable, baptized by the first settlers with the names of the seven cardinal and theological virtues that counter the seven deadly sins."

"The lakes, especially Temperance and Patience, are full of blind fish and albino crustaceans," Khutenptah pointed out, who looked very familiar to me. My memory is excellent; I was sure I'd seen her before, outside *Paradeisos*. She was very attractive; her black hair and eyes and classic features (including a delicate nose) were triggering a memory within me.

"We also have," Mirsgana continued, "a delightful river, the *Kolos*,* that springs from below just outside of Lignum, and flows through our four cities, forming Lake Charity in Stauros. The *Kolos* provides the energy to light up *Paradeisos*. Forty years ago we bought old turbines whose hydraulic wheels generate electricity when water flows across them. I'm not well-versed on this subject," she apologized, "so that's all I can tell you. I only know we have power. Up above," she said pointing to the immense vault, "even though you can't see them, are copper cables that run from Stauros to different locations."

"But Cato's *basileion* was illuminated with candles," I countered.

"Our machines aren't powerful enough to light all the houses, which is not our intent. Illuminating the city's open spaces is sufficient. Have you needed more light at any time? During centuries of darkness, the craftsmen of *Paradeisos* developed candles with very intense light. What's more, our vision is wonderful, as you may have noticed."

"Why?" Farag asked quickly. "Why is your vision so good?"

"That," said Gete, "you'll understand when we visit our schools."

"You have schools to improve vision?" the Rock asked admiringly.

"In our education system, the senses and everything related to them are fundamental. If not, how could children study Nature, experiment, draw their own conclusions, and verify them? It would be like asking a blind man to draw a map. The Staurofilakes who arrived seven centuries ago had to pass very difficult hardships that inspired them to develop very useful techniques to improve quality of life and instill survival."

"The first settlers discovered that fish lost their eyesight and the crustaceans their color because they didn't need them in the dark waters of *Paradeisos*," Khutenptah explained with a slight smile. "They also noticed some species of bird nested in the cliffs that didn't use their eyes to fly because they had developed their own system of sight, like bats. They studied thoroughly the fauna of this place and reached interesting conclusions. Through a series of very simple exercises and a lot of practice, human beings adapted. This is what the children in our schools are taught as well as newcomers in *Paradeisos*, like you."

*Truncated, in Greek.

"But is that possible?" I persisted. "Can you sharpen your vision or your hearing with exercises?"

"Of course. It's a slow process, but very effective. How do you think Leonardo da Vinci studied and described the smallest detail of birds' flight and then used that knowledge to design his flying machines? He had sight similar to ours, and he obtained it through a visual training system which he devised."

On the surface, we made machines that supplemented our sensorial deficiencies (microscopes, telescopes, loudspeakers, computers…); while down in *Paradeisos*, they had worked for centuries to perfect their faculties, sharpening them and developing them to imitate Nature. Like the *teoto* in *Purgatory*, this sensory achievement opened the doors to a new way of understanding life, the world, beauty, and everything that surrounded them. Up above we were rich in technology; down here they were rich in spirit. The mystery of the inexplicable theft of the *Ligna Crucis* was cleared up: Thieves carried out perfect robberies, without clues, violence, or traces of any kind. What kind of monitoring system could stop the Staurofilakes, with their highly developed senses, from taking what they wanted from the most heavily guarded place in the world?

We crossed streets, where carriages and carts traveled calmly, and plazas and gardens where people amused themselves by juggling balls and maces, an activity that was part of the training curriculum, in this case to become ambidextrous. We came to the banks of the *Kolos*. It must have been more than sixty or seventy meters wide, its irregular rocky shores had been reinforced with railings carved with flowers and palms. I rested my hand on the guardrail as I watched boats sail by and I felt like I had put my hand on a patch of grease, but it wasn't so. My hand was clean, and what seemed like a greasy surface was actually a spectacularly polished one. It was then that I remembered that stone in Santa Lucia that slid so smoothly down the tunnel as if it had been greased.

Canoes and pirogues slid through the quiet waters of *Kolos* with one, two, up to three people grasping the oars. More eye-catching boats transported merchandise. They looked like big, heavy doughnuts whose belly had up to three rows of short, wide oars, like Greek and Roman boats. Those ships, explained Ufa, were the principal means of transporting people and goods between Stauros, Lignum, Edem, and Crucis. Stauros was the capital and the biggest city, with almost fifty thousand inhabitants; the smallest, Crucis, had twenty thousand.

"How can you still use rowers?" I asked scandalized. "Who are those poor men, condemned to the galley, spending their life sweating, poorly fed, and ill in the bowels of a dark boat?"

"Why not?" The four were surprised.

"It's inhumane!" the Rock roared, as scandalized as Farag and I.

"Inhumane? It is a very sought after position!" Gete said, watching the boats longingly. "I was only allowed three months."

"Rowing is a very fun job," Mirsgana hurried to explain, when she saw our look of astonishment. "The young people, boys and girls, all want to get a place on a transport ship. It's in very high demand. So everyone can be a rower, only three-month licenses are granted, as Gete said."

"You'll have to try it," Gete added, with a nostalgic look. "The speed and different styles of the oars that propel the boat, the synchronized movements, the group effort, the camaraderie... You grasp the oar very firmly, lean forward, flex your legs, then push off backward. It is a great sequence that really strengthens your shoulders, back, and legs. What's more, you get to know a lot of new people and the bonds of friendship between the four cities are strengthened."

I thought it might be a good idea to remain silent for the rest of the visit. The looks I exchanged with Farag and Captain Glauser-Röist showed they were thinking the same thing. Everyone seemed happy to do hard, even unpleasant tasks. Maybe they weren't so hard or unpleasant after all. Could it be that other very different reasons—social opinion, economic status—were what made them unpleasant?

We walked down the boulevard that bordered the river, watching people swimming happily at its banks. Apparently, like the entire grotto that formed *Paradeisos,* those dark waters maintained a constant temperature of twenty-four or twenty-five degrees centigrade. Given what I had learned about the rowers, I didn't need to ask how those swimmers reached and surpassed many of the canoes that glided along, most propelled by two or three people. There was so much to learn, so many interesting things in *Paradeisos.* I was sure neither Farag, nor the Rock, nor

I could ever expose these people. The Staurofilakes were right when they said we would be incapable of doing senseless, gratuitous harm to them, like all those who had passed that way before. How could we allow hordes of uniformed police to enter this place and end such a culture? We hadn't considered that various churches would fight among themselves to appropriate what had been and what would be the brotherhood's property or turn this place into a center of religious curiosity or pilgrimages. The Staurofilakes and their world would disappear forever, after sixteen hundred years of isolation. They would become a massive attraction for journalists, anthropologists, and historians. If they had stolen the True Cross, all they had to do was give it back. We would never denounce them. I was sure the captain and Farag felt the same way.

We strolled along peacefully. Stauros had numerous theaters, concert halls, exhibition halls, amusement centers, museums (of natural history, archaeology, plastic arts), libraries... Over the next several days, I was astonished to find original manuscripts by Archimedes, Pythagoras, Aristotle, Plato, Tacitus, Cicero, Virgil... in addition to first editions of *Astronomica* by Manilio, *Medicine* by Celsius, *Natural History* by Pliny, and other surprising incunabulars. Nearly two hundred thousand volumes were housed in what the Staurofilakes called "Rooms of the Life." The strangest part was that the vast majority of people in *Paradeisos* could read the texts in their original language because studying languages, dead or alive, was one of their favorite pastimes.

"Art and culture increase harmony, tolerance, and understanding between people," Gete said. "Only now are you starting to understand that up above."

In Ufa's stables—the largest of the five stables on the outskirts of Stauros—horses, mares, and colts stood in the wide corral. In the harness room were hundreds of halters and bridles of all types and countless saddles (all made of finely tooled leather) with strange, colorful cinches and wooden stirrups. Ufa served us dry fruits and *posca* made of water, vinegar, and eggs, which the Staurofilakes drank all day long.

They told us horseback riding was a favorite sport in *Paradeisos.* Jumping—at a trot or a gallop—was considered a high art. They also had races or contests of ability on horseback throughout the galleries.

*Iysoporta** was very a popular game among the children. But Ufa's job, and his passion, was taming the horses.

"The horse is a very intelligent animal," he told us with conviction, softly petting the hindquarters of a colt that had docilely approached us. "All you have to do is teach him to understand signals with your legs, hands, and voice so he connects with his rider's mind. Here we don't need spurs or whips."

As the afternoon was slipping away, he went on with a long explanation on the need to keep insufficiently trained horses from competing in jumping. As long as he had been a *shasta*, he had wanted to introduce the art of horse taming in the schools. It was the best way to know the natural movements of the animal before starting to ride or guide a horse.

Fortunately Mirsgana interrupted him discreetly and reminded him that Khutenptah had come along to show us the cultivation system. Ufa offered us the best horses in his stables, but since I didn't know how to ride, he gave Farag and me a small buggy with which we were able to follow the others to a part of Stauros that had hectares and hectares of parcelated land. On our way there, Farag and I were finally able to be alone for a while, but we didn't waste our time commenting on the strange things we were seeing. We deeply needed one another, and I remember we spent the whole trip laughing and joking. In fact, we discovered that horse-drawn carriages are much safer than cars since one can easily take one's eyes off the road without there being any danger.

Khutenptah showed us her domain with the same pride as Ufa did his stables. It was a treat to watch her walk, enthralled, between the rows of vegetables, forage plants, grains, and all types of flowers. Glauser-Röist followed her with his eyes, engrossed in what she was saying.

"The volcanic rock," she said, "provides excellent oxygenation to the roots and a clean substrate, free of parasites, bacteria, and fungi. In Stauros we have dedicated more than three hundred furlongs† to agriculture. The other cities have more because they use some of the galler-

---

* A very popular game in Byzantium. Two teams on horseback, separated by a dividing line, had to capture a stone, marked on one side, as soon as it was thrown into the air. That stone decided which team chased the other.
† In Byzantium, the furlong equaled one eighth of a Roman mile, that is, 185 meters.

ies. Since *Paradeisos* lacks cultivatable ground, the first settlers had to go aboveground to buy food or procure it through the Anuak, running the risk of being discovered. So they studied in-depth the system the Babylonians used to create their wonderful hanging gardens and discovered you don't need soil...."

I started to pay attention to what Khutenptah was saying. Farag and I had been caught up in our own conversation, apart from the rest. I hadn't realized we were walking on rock, not dirt. All the products that flourished in *Paradeisos* were grown in large, long clay pots that contained only rocks.

"With the city's organic crops," Khutenptah explained, "we manufacture the nutrients for the plants and feed those nutrients to the plants in the water."

"Up above that's known as hydroponic cultivation," Glauser-Röist said, examining carefully the green leaves on a bush and stepping back finally with a satisfied look. "They all look magnificent," he pronounced, "but what about light? You need sunlight for photosynthesis."

"Electric light also works. We also provide it by adding certain minerals and sugar resins to the nutrients."

"That's impossible," the Rock objected, stroking the roots of an apple tree.

"Well, *Protospatharios*," she said very calmly, "if that's so, then you are hallucinating and you're touching air."

He drew his hand back quickly. He flashed one of his rare smiles, it was wide and luminous. Just then I recalled how I knew Khutenptah. No, I'd never seen her before, but in Glauser-Röist's house in Lungotevere dei Tebaldi, in Rome, were two photographs of a girl who was identical to her. That's why the Rock was so dazzled. Khutenptah must remind him of the other girl. The pair found themselves in a complicated conversation about sugar resins used in agriculture. In the same way that Farag and I had so rudely stood apart, they walked off from Ufa, Mirsgana, and Gete.

We returned to Stauros very late in the afternoon. People were strolling home after a long day of work. The parks were full of shouting children, silent onlookers, groups of teenagers, and jugglers throwing objects in the air and catching them. Juggling helped them be ambidex-

trous and being ambidextrous made them fantastic jugglers. I don't
know if they knew it or if they intuited it, but using both hands for any
activity increased the simultaneous development of the two hemispheres
of the brain, thus increasing artistic and intellectual capabilities.

Finally Ufa, Mirsgana, Khutenptah, and Gete led us to the last stop
on our tour before we returned to the *basileion* for dinner. Despite our
pleas, they wouldn't reveal our destination. Finally the Rock, Farag, and
I decided it would be more enjoyable to be obedient disciples and follow
along without question.

The streets abounded with chaotic vitality. Stauros was an unhur-
ried, relaxed city, but it vibrated with the pulse of a perfect ecosystem.
These Staurofilakes we had long pursued looked at us expectantly since
they knew who we were. They smiled and called out friendly greetings
from their windows, carriages, and mosaic sidewalks. The world in reverse, I recall thinking. Or was it? I squeezed Farag's hand tightly. So
many things had changed. I had changed too and I needed something
strong and safe to hold on to.

Our carriage turned a corner and came suddenly to an immense
plaza. At the plaza's back behind a garden, you could see an extraordinary building six or seven stories high. Its facade was covered with
stained-glass windows; its many towers were topped in pointed pinna-
cles. I knew we had come to the end of our journey, the end of a long
journey we had started so impetuously many months before.

"The Temple of the Cross," Ufa announced solemnly, waiting for
our reaction.

It was the most emotional and grandiose moment of my life. None
of us could take our eyes off that temple, stunned by having reached the
last stage of our journey. I was even sure the captain harbored no intention of reclaiming the reliquary in the name of factions we no longer
cared about. Reaching the heart of earthly paradise, after all that effort,
anguish, and fear, with just Virgil and Dante as guides, was too important a moment to squander a single ounce of emotion.

We entered the temple seized by the grandiosity of the place. It was
brightly illuminated by millions of tapers, which cast a gold and silver
light on the mosaics and domes of the cupola. It wasn't a conventional

church; it was exceptional for its decorations, a mixture of Byzantine and Coptic styles, a harmonious mix of austere simplicity and ornate excess.

"Here," Ufa said, holding out some white scarves. "Cover your heads with these. Here, one shows maximum respect."

Similar to Ottoman women's *turban*, one placed those long veils on the hair, letting the ends hang loose on the shoulders. It was an ancient form of religious respect we'd abandoned in the West a long time ago. Men also wore white *turbans* in the temple. Everyone inside, children included, were respectfully covered with white veils.

As I made my way down that immense nave, I caught sight of it. Directly across from the entrance was a hollow in the wall where a beautiful wooden cross hung. There were people seated on benches in front of it or on rugs on the ground, Muslim-style. Many were praying aloud or silently; some seemed to be rehearsing allegorical plays; and children, separated by age group, genuflected as they'd been taught. It was a pretty strange way to address religion and, more than religion, the religious space. The Staurofilakes had already surprised us so much we were no longer shocked. Still, there before us was the True Cross, completely reconstructed as an unmistakable sign the Staurofilakes were who they were and would always be.

"It is made of pine," Mirsgana told us in an affable voice, aware of the emotion that paralyzed us. "The vertical wood measures nearly five meters, the horizontal cross piece, two and a half meters. It weighs about seventy-five kilos."

"Why do you venerate the Cross so much and not the Crucified Man?" I suddenly thought to ask.

"We do venerate Jesus," said Khutenptah, in a pleasant tone of voice. "But the Cross is the symbol of our beginnings and the symbol of the world we have taken great pains to construct. From the Wood of that Cross our flesh is made."

"Forgive me, Khutenptah," mused Farag. "I don't understand."

"Do you really think this is the Cross Christ died on?" Ufa asked.

"Well, no… Actually, no," he stuttered. His certainty wasn't so much about doubting that the Cross was a fake. He just didn't want to offend the Staurofilakes' faith and beliefs.

"Well, it is," affirmed Khutenptah, very certain. "This is the True Cross, the authentic Holy Wood. Your faith is weak, *didaskalos,* you should pray more."

"This Cross," Mirsgana said, pointing to it, "was discovered by Saint Helen in 326. The Brotherhood of the Staurofilakes was formed in 341 to protect it."

"That is the truth," said Ufa very satisfied. "September 1, 341."

"So why did you decide to steal the *Ligna Crucis* now?" asked the Rock, vexed. "Why now?"

"We didn't steal them, *Protospatharios,*" Khutenptah responded. "They were ours. The safety of the True Cross was entrusted to us. Many Staurofilakes died to protect it. It gives our existence meaning. When we went into hiding in *Paradeisos,* we had the largest piece. The rest was parceled out to churches and temples in various-sized fragments, sometimes just splinters."

"Seven centuries have passed," declared Gete. "It was time to return the Cross to its past integrity."

"Why not return the pieces?" I asked. "If you did, you wouldn't be in such danger. Many churches were founded on the faithful worshipers' devotion to the churches' fragment of the True Cross," I exclaimed.

"Is that so, Ottavia?" inquired Mirsgana, skeptical. "No one pays attention to the *Ligna Crucis.* In Notre Dame in Paris, in Saint Peter's in the Vatican, or in Saint Croce Church in Gerusalemmne, for example, they have relegated their relics to their museums of curios, what they call treasuries or collections. You have to pay to see them. Hundreds of Christian voices are raised to declare those objects fake, and the faithful aren't very interested in them either. Faith in the holy relics has declined a lot in the past few years. We only wanted to complete the piece of Holy Wood we have, a third of the *stipes,* the vertical wood. When we realized how easy it would be to get all the rest, we didn't think twice about recovering them all."

"It's ours," the young Sumerian translator repeated obstinately. "This Cross is ours. We didn't steal it."

"How did you organize a...recovery on such a grand scale from down here?" Farag asked. "The *Ligna Crucis* were very widely distributed. After the first rob...recoveries, they were very well guarded."

"You met the sacristan at Saint Lucia," Ufa said, "Father Bonuomo of Santa Maria in Cosmedin, the monks in Saint Constantine Acanzzo, Father Stephanos of the basilica of the Holy Sepulchre, the popes of Kapnikarea, and the ticket vendor at the catacombs of Kom el-Shoqafa?"

The three of us looked at each other. Our suspicions had been right.

"They are all Staurofilakes," the horse trainer continued. "Many of us choose to live outside *Paradeisos* to carry out certain missions or for personal reasons. To be here below isn't mandatory, but it's considered the greatest glory and the highest honor for a Staurofilax who gives his or her life to the Cross."

"There are many Staurofilakes all over the world," Gete commented, amused. "More than you can imagine. They come and go, spend time with us, then return to their homes. Like Dante Alighieri did, for example."

"There's always one or two of us near every fragment or splinter of the True Cross," concluded the water master. "So the truth is, the operation was really quite easy."

Ufa, Khutenptah, Mirsgana, and Gete looked at each other, satisfied. Then, remembering where they were, they devoutly knelt before the True Cross—impressive for its grand scale and the careful way it was displayed. They took time to carry out a series of complicated reverences and prostrations, murmuring ancient litanies from Byzantine rituals.

Meanwhile, God's presence tugged hard on my heart. I was in a church, and no matter what, some places are sacred; they elevate your spirit and bring you closer to God. I knelt down and started a simple prayer of thanks that we had come here and that the three of us were safe and sound. I begged God to bless my love for Farag, promising him I would never abandon my faith. I didn't know what would become of us or what the Staurofilakes had in store for us, but while I was in *Paradeisos*, I would come every day to pray in that magnificent temple in whose apse hung the True Cross of Jesus Christ by invisible threads. I knew it wasn't authentic; it wasn't the Cross Jesus died on. In those days, crucifixion was a common punishment. When he died on Golgotha, the crosses were used over and over until they became unusable and worm-eaten. Then they were used as firewood for the soldiers. The cross before me wasn't the True Cross of Christ, but it was the cross St. Helen found in 326 under the temple of Venus on a hill in Jerusalem. Its pieces had received the adoration and love of millions of people over the centuries. It gave rise to the Staurofilakes. And after all, it was the cross that had brought Farag and me together.

Back at Cato's *basileion* for dinner, the lights in *Paradeisos* were dimmed, creating an artificial nightfall that wasn't any less beautiful. Everyone re-turned peacefully to their homes. Our companions said good-bye in front of the large door into the *basileion*, which always remained unlocked.

Glauser-Röist and Khutenptah arranged to meet the next morning in the cultivation area. Ufa left a horse so the captain could ride there. The Rock seemed very impressed by the sugar resins—and by Khutenptah—and wanted to study the matter in depth. At least that's what he said. Gete offered to show Farag and me sites in *Paradeisos* we hadn't seen the first day. So we only said good-bye to Ufa and Mirsgana, although we promised to visit them again.

Dinner was more peaceful than lunch. In a different room, smaller and cozier than the vast hall, the ancient Cato CCLVII acted as host; his only companions were the *shasta* Ahmose, who was his daughter as well as a builder of chairs, and Darius, the administrative *shasta* and canon-arca* for the Temple of the Cross. Candace was again the server who attended our table. A melody that reminded me of popular medieval canzonets played in the background.

As an intense and complicated conversation unfolded, I managed to put into practice what I had learned at noon about tastes and smells. I realized that to detect so many details and enjoy them, one had to eat and drink very slowly, the way the Staurofilakes did. What was easy for them turned out to be a superhuman effort for me, because I was used

---

* In Byzantine and orthodox monasteries, the canonarca was the monk in charge of directing the psalmody in the church and calling the monks to prayer by striking a log.

to chewing quickly and swallowing all at once. I really enjoyed a new drink they offered me called *eukras*, a delicious pepper-and-anis concoction they would have at night.

Cato CCLVII wanted to know our plans and questioned us in-depth. Farag and I were very clear that we wanted to return to the surface, but surprisingly the Rock vacillated.

"I'd like to stay here a while longer," he said, tentatively. "There are many things to learn here."

"But, Captain," I said alarmed, "we can't go back without you. Don't you remember? Half the churches in the world are waiting for our news."

"Kaspar, you have to return with us," Farag insisted, very serious. "You work for the Vatican. You have to show your face."

"Are you going to expose us?" Cato sweetly asked.

That was a very serious question. How could we keep the Stauro-filakes' secret if Monsignor Tournier and Cardinal Sodano riddled us with questions when we returned? We couldn't spring from the earth as if nothing had happened and say we had been playing cards since we disappeared in Alexandria seventeen days before.

"Of course not, Cato," Farag hurried to say. "But you have to help us come up with a convincing story."

Cato, Ahmose, and Darius laughed, as if that were the easiest thing in the world.

"I'll take care of that, Professor," the Rock said abruptly. "Remember, that's my specialty. The Vatican itself taught me all I know."

"Come back with us, Captain," I begged, staring into his gray eyes.

But the mention of his work in the Vatican seemed to convince him to stay in *Paradeisos* even more. His resolve became more apparent.

"Not right now, Doctor," he declared, shaking his head. "I have no desire to keep cleaning up the church's messes. I never, ever liked doing it and now it's time to change. Life is giving me a second chance. I'd be a fool not to take advantage of it. I'm not going back. I'll stay, at least for a while."

"So what are we going to say? How do we explain your disappearance?" I asked, anguished.

"Tell them I died," he replied without hesitating.

"You're crazy, Kaspar!" Farag exclaimed, very angry. Cato, Ahmose, and Darius listened closely to our conversation without interrupting.

"I'll give you the perfect alibi that will spare you the church's interrogations and still allow me to return in a few months without arousing suspicion."

"We can help, *Protospatharios*," Ahmose said. "We have many centuries of experience doing this very thing."

"Is your resolve to stay for a while firm, Kaspar?" Cato asked, savoring a spoonful of ground wheat with cinnamon, syrup, and dried plums.

"It's firm, Cato," Glauser-Röist answered. "I'm not saying I'm convinced about your ideas or your beliefs, but I thank you for letting me rest awhile here in *Paradeisos*. I need to think about what kind of life I want to lead."

"You should have never done something that disgusted you so."

"You don't understand, Cato," protested the Rock, with a look of determination. "Up above, people don't always do the work they like. Just the opposite. My faith in God is strong and has kept me going during the years I worked for the church, a church that has forgotten all about the gospel. To keep from losing its privileges, it lies, cheats, and interprets the word of Jesus to its advantage. No, I have no desire to return."

"You can stay with us as long as you like, Kaspar Glauser-Röist," declared Cato, solemnly. "And you, Ottavia and Farag, you can leave when you like. Give us a few days to organize your departure. Then you can return to the surface. But do know that you're always welcome in *Paradeisos*. This is your home, when all is said and done. In case it hasn't dawned on you, you are Staurofilakes, and the marks on your bodies attest to that. We will give you contacts on the outside so you can communicate with us. Now, with your permission, I will retire to pray and sleep. My many years don't allow me to stay up late," he explained, smiling.

"Don't be afraid," Darius said, observing our faces. "I know you are worried and that's logical. The Christian churches can make your life difficult. But with God's help, it will all turn out all right."

Just then, Candace appeared with a tray holding glasses of wine. Ahmose smiled. "I knew you would bring us a glass of the best wine in *Paradeisos!*" she exclaimed.

Darius quickly stretched out his hand. He was about fifty years old, with thinning, gray hair and ears so small you could barely see them.

"Let's toast," he said when everyone held an alabaster wineglass. "Let's toast to the *protospatharios,* may he be happy with us, and to Ottavia Salina and Farag Boswell, may they be happy though they are far from us."

We all smiled and raised our glasses.

*H*aide and Zauditu had prepared my room and put the finishing touches on the flowers and my clothes. Everything was delightful; the light from the little candles gave a magical glow to the room.

"Would you like anything else, Ottavia?" Haide asked me.

"No, no thank you," I answered, trying to hide my nervousness. As we were leaving the dining room, Farag asked if he could come to my room as soon as we were alone. I didn't have to speak; my smile was my answer. Everything was settled and I only wanted to be with him. Many times, as I looked at him, the craziest thought occurred to me: If I had more than one life, I still wouldn't have enough time by his side. I wasn't sure how, but suddenly certain things became clear to me, and spending the night with Farag was one of them. I knew if I didn't, I'd reproach myself for the fear I felt and I'd never feel secure with this new phase of life. I was absolutely in love with him, absolutely blind with love. Maybe that's why I didn't see anything wrong about what I was planning to do. Thirty-nine years of abstinence were enough. God would understand.

"I think the *didaskalos* is impatient to come in," Haide said. "He's pacing back and forth in his room like a caged lion."

Farag's room was on the other side of the corridor.

I smiled. What else could I do? I couldn't speak. I only wanted them to leave, and Farag to come in. They finally headed for the door.

"Good night, Ottavia," she whispered and disappeared.

I slowly walked up to the mirror and looked at myself. I didn't look my best right then. My head resembled a cue ball and my eyebrows floated like islands in a hairless sea. But there was a glow in my eyes and a silly smile on my lips that I couldn't erase. I was happy. *Paradeisos* was an incomparable place—behind in the material realm but advanced in many other ways. They didn't know haste, anguish, the daily struggle to survive a world full of dangers. Life unfolded calmly. They knew how to appreciate what they had. I wanted to take back with me their marvelous capacity to enjoy everything, no matter how insignificant. I planned to start that very night.

I was afraid. My heart was pounding in my chest, and I realized it was because of what I was missing. Without knowing it, my whole life had been preparation for that moment. I'd untied all those knots, lived through such incredible things, left behind the tight armor I'd put on my spiritual body so long ago. Now I had the great fortune of finding the most wonderful man in the world. Why was I so frightened? Farag had set me free and had waited with infinite sweetness until I broke out of my former life. His kiss was a firm promise. If I could lose myself in his lips, why couldn't I lose myself in his body?

I heard three discreet knocks on the door.

"Come in," I said, delighted and nervous. "You don't have to be so cautious. If they want to hear us, they'll hear us."

"You're right," he agreed, very bewildered, as he entered my room. "I always forget they can read our thoughts."

"Let 'em!" I replied, going to him and throwing my arms around his neck. Farag was as nervous as I was. I could see it in his eyes; they blinked nonstop and his voice trembled.

He kissed me very slowly.

"Are you completely sure you want me to stay?" he asked me.

"Of course I want you to stay." I kissed him again. "I want you to stay with me all night. Every night."

I lost all notion of time, and I lost my heart too. It was fused to his heart forever. I stopped being me; I stopped being the Ottavia Salina who had existed up until that moment. I made it to bed although I don't remember how because the taste of his mouth was so intense that I re-member thinking it was the taste of life itself, concentrated on the lips of Farag Boswell.

The night passed. United with Farag's body, fused skin to skin, I became a river of sensations. Like the tides, I went from the gentlest tenderness to furious lunacy. What I was doing wasn't the terrible act religions had inexplicably condemned over the centuries. Were they crazy? What was wrong with discovering that absolute happiness was possible in this world? His strong, slender body was all I desired. I felt transformed into something new. At first, insecurity shackled me, but then, my heart about to break into pieces, I realized that Farag and I weren't alone in that bed. False taboos and the ridiculous hypocrisies I'd been schooled in had climbed into bed with me, imprisoning me. It was a fleeting thought but important. Naked, I got on my knees on the sheets and looked at Farag. Weary and happy, he looked at me with curiosity.

"Do you know what I need to tell you, Farag?"

"No," he replied, letting out a muffled laugh. "But I'm ready for anything."

"Making love is the most wonderful thing in the world," I said, convinced.

He laughed again softly. "I'm happy you discovered it," he whispered, taking my hands and pulling me to him. Sitting on his legs, I stroked his chest. "Do you know that I can't imagine life without you? I know that sounds silly, but it's the truth."

"Well, then, rest easy because now we're a perfect match."

"Do you have any idea how much I love you?" I whispered and bent down to kiss him again.

"What about you? Do you have any idea how much I love you?"

"No, that hasn't sunk in. Tell me again."

He sat up and grabbed me by the waist, kissing me again and again. The night grew short, and the new day came without our having slept a wink.

Thankfully, in the two weeks we spent in *Paradeisos*, we caught up on all the sleep we'd lost over the last three months.

*O*n the thirteenth day of our stay in *Paradeisos*, returning from a visit to Edem and Crucis (we'd been to Lignum a couple of times), we were summoned to Cato's *basileion* to receive final instructions before our departure. A committee of *shastas* had taken care of the necessary preparations.

We were led down some corridors we'd never walked through before and came to an enormous rectangular room with very high ceilings. The *shastas* were waiting for us, sitting in two rows on either side of the room. Cato CCLVII sat in front of some fresco paintings of Staurofilax Dionisios de Dara, dressed as an important Muslim dignitary, at the door of Nikephoros Panteugenos's humble home holding the relic of the True Cross. He was leaning on his slender cane as always, with a look of satisfaction on his face.

"Come in, come in," he said when he saw us hesitate at the door. "We have finished organizing the last details. Kaspar, sit down here with me, please. Ottavia and Farag, you take those seats in the center."

The Rock hurried over and sat next to Cato, gathering the *himation* like a true Staurofilax. It was gratifying to see how that former captain of the Swiss Guard had fit into daily life in *Paradeisos*. He was assimilating it all so quickly; he would soon pass for one of them. I commented to Farag that Khutenptah's influence was part of that change. Stubborn as a mule, he insisted that the captain was simply erasing the past and inventing a future for himself, setting off on a new life. Whatever it was, the Rock was starting to look more like a Staurofilax. Besides occupying himself with Khutenptah, the gardens, and organizing our departure, he also began the training curriculum offered in *Paradeisos*.

"You will leave here tomorrow morning, at first hour," Cato began. I saw Mirsgana to my right in the second row and gently waved to her. She waved back. "That way you will discover the exact location of *Paradeisos*," he added with a smile. "A group of Anuaks will be waiting for you and will take you to Antioch. There you will set sail again with Captain Mulugeta Mariam and retrace your steps on the route you took to get here. Mariam will follow the Nile to the delta and will leave you in a safe place near Alexandria. After that, you mustn't mention this place anymore except to each other and never in anyone else's presence. It's your turn, Teodros."

Teodros, seated in the front row on the left, stood up. "The last contact the new Staurofilakes had with the Christian churches was in the patriarchate of Alexandria, the first of June, this year, exactly one month ago. After that, in the outside world they've had no word of Kaspar, Ottavia, and Farag. According to reports we have received, the catacombs of Kom el-Shoqafa have been examined in depth by the Egyptian police, who obviously haven't found anything. The churches are about to send in another team of investigators who will use the information you three obtained to pick up where you left off. It will be a futile effort, of course," Teodros added, very confident. "What those three did," he said pointing first to the Rock and then to the two of us, "forces us to suspend the tests for aspirants until we can resume them in full confidence of complete secrecy."

"Why don't we change them or just do away with them?" asked someone behind us.

"We have to respect tradition," Cato said, raising his head then resting it back on his palm.

"So for the next ten or fifteen years, there will be no more tests," Teodros continued. "Timely messages have already been sent so the brothers on the outside can erase all traces and be warned of possible interrogations. The doors to *Paradeisos* are being sealed. That just leaves the subterfuge that Ottavia and Farag will use to return to the outside, which Shakeb will now explain."

Young Shakeb, sitting two seats down from Mirsgana, stood up as Teodros sat down, gathering the hem of his *himation* with an elegant gesture.

"Ottavia, Farag…," he said, looking directly at us. Despite his round face, he was handsome with lively, expressive dark eyes. "When you return to Alexandria, a month and a half will have passed since you disappeared. You'll have to tell the authorities where you've been and what you've done all that time and of course what happened to Captain Glauser-Röist."

The expectation in the room was palpable. Everyone wanted to know what lie we would have to tell to defend ourselves against the inquisition we were certain to face.

"In the catacombs of Kom el-Shoqafa, the brothers in Alexandria have started to dig a false tunnel that ends at a remote corner of Mareotis Lake, near the ancient Cesarium. You will say that you were captured on the third level of Kom el-Shoqafa, that you were hit over the head, and that you lost consciousness, but that first you got a good look at the entrance to paradise. We will provide you with a very simple map that will help you locate it. You will say you awoke in a place called Farafrah, an oasis in the Egyptian desert, which is very difficult to reach, and that the captain didn't wake up. The men who captured you said that he died while they were tattooing those crosses and letters on your bodies, but that they didn't let you see the body. That leaves the door open for his possible return within a few months. Your description of the population of the place will match that of the village of Antioch. That way you won't make any mistakes. Since the oasis of Farafrah doesn't remotely resemble this town, you will send them on a merry chase. Don't mention any names, only the name of the Bedouin who brought you your meals three times a day in the cell where they locked you up: Bahari. This name is so common in Egypt it will throw them completely offtrack. As a description of Bahari, you can describe Chief Berehanu Bekela—just be sure to make his skin lighter." He took a breath and continued. "The evil Staurofilakes held you in the cell all this time." The comment was met with laughter. "They repeatedly threatened to kill you until finally today, the first of July, they knocked you unconscious and dumped you near the mouth of the tunnel to Lake Mareotis with a written warning that you mustn't say a word about what happened. You, of course, have no desire to continue the investigation. When the interrogations stop, you will look for a discreet place to live. You will go as far away from Rome—or better yet from Italy—as possible and disappear. We will keep a close watch so nothing happens to you."

"We'll have to find work...," I said.

Cato interrupted me, raising his hand. "With respect to this matter, we Staurofilakes want to give you a farewell gift." The Rock flashed us a mysterious smile. "Before, I said you had to learn to respect traditions. Of course, you must also renounce traditions or change them. During the tests of the seven deadly sins, as usually happens to those who reach the end, you, Ottavia and Farag, altered your life in a definitive and irreversible way. Jobs, countries, religious commitments, beliefs, philosophy... You changed everything to get here. Now there's almost nothing left for you back there, but you are ready to go back and build the life you desire. Farag can get his job back in the Greco-Roman Museum in Alexandria, but Ottavia, you can't set one foot in the Vatican Hypogeum. Nevertheless, you can count on your academic dossier which will open many doors for you. But still, what if we give you something that will let you decide your future with absolute freedom?"

I felt Farag's hand squeeze mine. The muscles in my neck tensed out of anxiety. The Rock smiled so hard you could see both rows of his teeth.

"The expiation of the sin of avarice in Constantinople is going to change location. We will ask the brothers of that city to, over the next several years, organize the test of the winds in another part of the city without changing its content. That way you can 'discover' the mausoleum and the remains of Emperor Constantine the Great. This is our farewell gift to you."

Farag and I were stunned for a few seconds. Baffled, we turned our heads very slowly to look at each other. I was the first to jump: I gave a leap of joy so big I dragged the *didaskalos* with me. It was a miracle I didn't yank his arm out of its socket. I had given up on Constantine the moment I met the Staurofilakes and had forgotten all about him. Too many interesting things were happening to waste my time thinking about Constantine. So, when Cato gave us the discovery of the mausoleum with the emperor's remains, our options suddenly opened up. Our future had been given to us on a gold platter.

We hugged and kissed each other; then hugged and kissed the Rock. We left that important assemblage and went to the great dining hall of the *basileion* where Candace and his acolytes had prepared an authentic feast for the senses.

Music played until the wee hours of the morning; the dancing lasted way beyond a prudent hour. Along with the *shastas* and the servers, we tumbled into the streets of Stauros, ready to swim in the warm waters of the *Kolos*. Cato had retired hours earlier. The first hour came when our partying reached its apogee. Then the Rock and Khutenptah told us we had to leave. The Anuak had already arrived, and we couldn't wait any longer.

We said good-bye to hundreds of people we didn't know, we kissed right and left, not knowing who we were kissing. Finally, Khutenptah and the Rock, with help from Ufa, Mirsgana, Gete, Ahmose, and Haide, dragged us from the arms of the Staurofilakes and led us away from earthly paradise.

Everything was ready. A carriage with our few belongings waited at the entrance to the *basileion.* Ufa climbed into the driver's seat. Farag and I got in the back, still clutching Captain Glauser-Röist's hands.

"Take care of yourself, Kaspar," I said, calling him by his first name for the first time, about to burst into tears. "I've enjoyed knowing and working with you."

"Don't lie, Doctor," he muttered, hiding a smile. "We had a lot of problems at first, remember?"

Suddenly, something came into my head I had to ask him. I couldn't leave without knowing.

"Kaspar," I said, nervously, "did Michelangelo design the uniforms the Swiss Guards wear? Do you know anything about that?"

It was important. We're talking about an old, unsatisfied question I had never found the answer to. The Rock let out a belly laugh.

"Michelangelo didn't design them, Doctor. Neither did Rafael, as some have said. This is one of the best-kept secrets in the Vatican, so don't go around telling everyone what I'm about to tell you."

Finally, the answer.

"Those flashy uniforms were designed by an unknown Vatican seamstress in 1914. The pope, Benedict XV, wanted his soldiers to wear something unique, so he asked the seamstress to dream up a new formal uniform. As you can see, the woman was inspired by the paintings of Raphael that show brightly colored clothing with gored sleeves, very fashionable in sixteenth-century France."

I was speechless for a few seconds, shocked by the deception, and looked at the captain as if he'd just stabbed me with a dagger.

"Then…" I wavered. "Michaelangelo didn't design them?"

Glauser-Röist laughed again. "No, Doctor, Michaelangelo didn't design them. A woman designed them in 1914."

Maybe I'd drunk too much and slept too little, but I was angry and I frowned. "Well, I wish you hadn't told me." I exclaimed, furious.

"Why are you so mad?" Glauser-Röist asked surprised. "Just a moment ago you were telling me you'd enjoyed knowing me and working with me!"

"Do you know what she calls you in private, Kaspar?" Judas-Farag blurted out. I stomped on his foot so hard it would have made an elephant tremble. "She calls you 'The Rock.'"

"Traitor!" I exclaimed, looking at him sullenly.

"Don't worry, Doctor," Glauser-Röist laughed. "I always called you... No, I'd better not tell you."

"Captain Glauser-Röist!" I began, but at that very moment, Ufa raised the reins and let them fall on the horses' hindquarters. I had to grab on to Farag to keep from falling. "Tell me!" I shouted as we drove away.

"Bye, Kaspar!" Farag shouted, waving one arm in the air as he pushed me into my seat with the other.

"Good-bye!"

"Captain Glauser-Röist, tell me!" I kept shouting futilely as the carriage drove away from the *basileion*. Finally, defeated and humiliated, I sat next to Farag.

"We'll have to come back someday so you can find out," he said to console me.

"Yes, and so I can kill him," I agreed. "I always said he was a very disagreeable man."

EPILOGUE

*F*ive years have passed since we left *Paradeisos*. During those five years—as I foresaw—we were interrogated by police forces from the countries we traveled through, by those in charge of security at various Christian churches, and especially by the Rock's replacement, one Gottfried Spitteler, also a captain in the Swiss Guard. He didn't buy a single word of our story and quickly became our shadow. We spent a few months in Rome, to put an end to the investigation and so I could wrap up my affairs with the Vatican and my order. Afterward, we traveled to Palermo to stay with my family for a few days. But things didn't go so well with my family, so we left earlier than planned. Although, on the surface, I loved my family as before, the abyss that opened between us was no longer reconcilable. I decided the only thing I could do was put distance between them by moving a safe distance away, no matter how much pain it caused me. We returned to Rome and then caught a plane for Egypt. Despite his reticence, Butros received us with open arms, and a few days later, Farag returned to his job at the Greco-Roman Museum in Alexandria. We wanted to attract as little attention as possible, adopting a low-key way of life, just as the Staurofilakes recommended.

Months passed. Meanwhile, I dedicated myself to studying. I appropriated Farag's office and contacted old friends and acquaintances in the academic world who immediately started to send me job offers. I only accepted those investigations, publications, and studies I could do from home, from Alexandria, which didn't force me to leave Farag. I also learned Arabic and Coptic. My new passion was the Egyptian hieroglyphic language.

We were happy in Alexandria from the start. But during the first months, the constant presence of the charming Gottfried Spitteler, who followed us from Rome and rented a house in the Saba Facna neighborhood right next to our house, became a real nightmare. After a while, we discovered that the trick was not to pay any attention to him; we ignored him as if he were invisible. It will soon be a year since he completely vanished from our lives. He must have gone back to Rome, to the Swiss Guard's barracks, convinced at last—or not—that the story about the Oasis of Farafrah was true.

One day, soon after we settled down on Moharrem Bey Street, we received a strange visit. An animal dealer brought us a beautiful cat. According to the note that came with it, it was "a gift from the Rock." I still don't understand why Glauser-Röist sent us this cat with enormous pointy ears and dark brown, spotted fur. The dealer told Farag and me, as the animal with enormous, wary eyes studied us, that it was a very valuable Abyssinian cat. Since then, this tireless creature roams around the house as if he owns the place. He has conquered the *didaskalos'* heart (but not mine) with his games and demand for affections. We named him Rock in Glauser-Röist's honor. Sometimes between Tara, Butros's dog, and Rock, Farag's cat, I feel like I'm living in a zoo.

Recently we have started to prepare for our trip to Turkey. It's been five years since we left *Paradeisos*, and we still haven't collected our "present." Now it's time to do so. We are planning a way to "accidentally" come upon Constantine's mausoleum without having to pass through the fountain of ablutions at Fatih Camii. This project has monopolized all our attention until this morning. The same merchant who brought us Rock, the cat, has brought us—finally—an envelope with a long letter from Captain Glauser-Röist. Farag was at the museum, so I put on my shoes and jacket and went to the museum to read it with him.

From what we could deduce from his missive, the Rock was up to date on all we had done. He even knew we hadn't gone to Constantinople. He urged us not to wait any longer "since things have completely calmed down." He told us he's been living with Khutenptah for five years now, and that sadly, the elderly Cato has died. Cato CCLVII left this world fifteen days ago now, and the new Cato, number two hundred fifty-eight on the list, has been selected and will be officially installed in a month in the Temple of the Cross in Stauros. The Rock extends a thousand million pleas for us to come to *Paradeisos* on that day. According to him, Cato CCLVIII would be more than delighted and more than happy to have us there. That day, he added, needs to be the most complete in the life of Cato CCLVIII, and it won't be complete if we don't attend the ceremony.

I looked up from the paper—the same thick, rough paper the Staurofilakes used for the clues during the tests—and looked questioningly at Farag.

"Well, of course we're interested, whoever it may be." I observed, very puzzled. "But who do you think will be the new Cato? Ufa, Teodros, Candace…?"

"Look at the signature," Farag stuttered, his eyes wide, an amused smile on his lips.

The letter from Captain Glauser-Röist, written in Captain Glauser-Röist's hand, with the name Captain Glauser-Röist on the envelope was signed Cato CCLVIII.

ACKNOWLEDGMENTS

To create worlds, characters, and stories using words as only tools is an activity that can only take place in solitude and, in my case, in silence and at night. During the day, however, I need all those people who accompany me in the beautiful and incredible process of writing a novel. Therefore, it would be quite selfish of me to publicly ignore their collaboration and make readers believe that I am the only one behind the book they now hold in their hands. First and foremost, I would like to thank Patricia Campos for her constant support and for reading—*every single day*—the few pages I wrote, and for rereading the text as many times as was necessary, never complaining, and always offering me wonderful insights, comments, and suggestions. Second, I would like to thank José Manuel Baeza for his precious help on the Greek and Latin translations, and for being the best researcher in the world: he is capable of finding the oddest information from the oddest of all books. Third, I would like to thank Luis Peñalver, the most conscientious and meticulous copyeditor an author can have. I will not tell here how far he is willing to go, but all those who appear on this page have countless anecdotes that have made us laugh out loud. Fourth, I would like to thank a group of people who read the book in installments, and who served as an experimental laboratory, of constant support (if they were unable to figure out certain things, neither would the reader): Lorena Sancho, Lola Guilas, and Olga García (from Plaza y Janés). Thank you also to Cristina Mora for going over the English translation of the book.

It would be impossible for me to finish writing this page without mentioning my favorite editor, Carmen Fernández de Blas. People say that the two most personal things an author can have is her agent and her editor, and that's true. Carmen has been my editor since I published my first novel, and I have always considered her to be *my* editor, even though the comings and goings of the publishing world have led her to take care of, cherish, and protect other authors, just as she once took care of, cherished, and protected me during her stupendous time at Plaza y Janés. I plan on calling her "my editor" for years and years to come. Amen.